Dear Reader,

As a native of Scotland, I have always been drawn to the rugged beauty of the Isle of Skye, and the great history found in this land of churning seas, gentle countryside, ancient castles and local village pubs.

In *The Lost Dreams* I am thrilled to return to Strathaird Castle and the MacLeod clan. It is here, in this ancient fortress, that American Bradley Ward, caught between inherited responsibilities and new possibilities, must jump from being CEO of a multinational company and learn to become "Lord of the Manor." Strathaird is also where Charlotte MacLeod must finally face the demons of her past, in order to reclaim her passions and her strength to face the future.

Some of you may already have met the MacLeod family in my previous novel *The Stolen Years*, which introduced readers to twins Gavin and Angus MacLeod, and to Flora, the woman they both loved. I, too, loved these characters. In fact, they became so dear to me that I had to discover what happened to the next generation of this captivating extended family. I hope you, too, will enjoy sharing their struggles, their secrets, their passions, fears and hopes, and most of all, the lost dreams they had never thought to find.

Happy reading!

Fiona Hood-Stewart

FIONA HOOD-STEWART

THE LOST DREAMS

MIRA

ISBN 1-55166-670-7

THE LOST DREAMS

Copyright © 2003 by Fiona Hood-Stewart.

Visit us at www.mirabooks.com

Printed in U.S.A.

To John with love

ACKNOWLEDGMENTS

As always, my love and thanks to my sons, Sergio and Diego, for their patience and support. Many thanks to Andrew, Jojo and Francesca Grima for their help in researching the jewelry described in the text. To my sister, Althea Dundas-Beeker for her input on the management of a Scottish estate, and to my editor Miranda Stecyk, and Dianne Moggy.

Into my life you came
When least expected.
Out of the dark
You stole my guarded heart.
Led me by the hand
To new tomorrows,
Showed me love,
Then taught me to impart.

Gone are the tears of yesterday,
The sorrows.
Shed, the lingering shadows,
Gone the pain.
Now, in their stead
The flame of your love lingers,
Wonder, light and joy
Their newfound name.

Dream a little dream
And let it wander.
Dare to listen
Deep inside your soul.
Breathe love's tender joys
And heartfelt treasures—
Can't lose the dream
When now, at last, it's known.

F.H.S.

1

Did he feel anything? Charlotte Drummond wondered, gazing at the thin, waxlike body lying perfectly still under pressed white sheets. Was it possible that, despite medical evidence to the contrary, the seemingly lifeless man before her somehow sensed her presence?

She shuddered, took a deep breath, and quickly shifted her gaze to the sterile hospital wall, then reached out blindly to pull the gray plastic chair back from the side of the metal bed and sat down wearily. The trip to Glasgow and the hospital was both physically and mentally wearing. Now, as she prepared to wait out the self-imposed hourly visit she undertook once every two weeks, as she had for the past year, she forced herself to get a grip on her emotions. She gazed at him once again in a more detached manner, studying the vestiges of those strong, handsome features that once had set the world on fire. Although the devastating smile that had flashed across movie screens and into the hearts of millions around the globe was gone now, obscured by the respirator tubes that kept him alive, his good looks were still evident.

Then another image flashed. Not so pleasant, but just

as memorable. Instinctively she tensed and her fingers moved to her cheek, where more than once she'd felt the impact of his hand, sending her reeling. She trembled involuntarily, knuckles gripping the metal bed rail, hoping he would never wake, afraid that he would.

She rose nervously, moved quickly away, toward the long, paned window, and stared at the midday traffic trundling slowly under a thin summer drizzle in the street below, wishing she could somehow outrun the obsessive thoughts that always haunted her visits here. Memories she'd never escape, she realized, passing a hand over her eyes. She would never forget the sleepless nights and the obsessive fear that over the years had brought her to her knees. It was only when she'd finally hit rock bottom that she realized anything, even death, would be better than the life she was living, that to survive, she must climb out of the abyss by whatever means, and at whatever cost. It had taken several months, but finally she'd built up enough courage to make the break. Then came that last, harrowing quarrel, her rage and humiliation when he'd laughed at her threat to end the marriage once and for all. A vision of his face, white with fury, as he'd slammed the door, and her surge of satisfaction that at last she'd stood up to him. Then the call, several hours later, that had shattered her newfound confidence; she'd rushed through the streets of London to the emergency room at St. Thomas' hospital, praying, begging for the news not to be true.

The rest of that awful day was a blur of images: the bleak, desperate faces of the director and the producer, the doctor's blunt explanation of just how the fall from the high-rise building, a stunt he normally would never have attempted, had left him in a coma. For how long?

she'd asked, recalling the suffocating desperation. But nobody knew.

Worse had been the remorse. Shame for the unexpected rush of freedom, the relief of knowing that he couldn't hurt her mentally or physically ever again, accompanied by the deep-rooted fear that she was the one to blame.

Charlotte's head drooped. She closed her eyes and thrust trembling fingers into her long titian hair. *Oh God.* Was it her fault he'd left the house in such a towering rage that day? Was this his way of punishing her? For punish her he had, holding her prisoner, silently forcing her on this fortnightly pilgrimage of penance, keeping himself and her guilt alive for as long as he remained tied to the machines that linked him to life.

Perhaps, even in his comatose state, he sensed the guilty secret that she harbored, the unvoiced wish that they'd simply pull the plug.

No. That was impossible. Even considering such a thing was wicked. While there was still an ounce of hope, she had no right. Just as she couldn't possibly divorce him now, however much Mummy and Moira insisted she should. After all, whatever he'd done in the past, he was still her husband and she must stand by him. It was the only decent thing to do.

But what if he did suddenly wake up? It had been known to happen. She doubled over again, willing the wave of nausea to pass, schooling her mind, driving out demons, replacing them with problems of the moment, ones she could do something concrete about.

Raising her aching head, she fixed her gaze carefully beyond the body and the bed to the wall behind, and forced herself to think of something else.

Anything else.

Bradley Ward. She considered his impending visit and felt better. Wonderful, decent Brad, her dear friend and cousin. Well, she reflected ruefully, only a distant cousin, but still, family all the same. But he was also the man who was forcing her to leave Strathaird, that rugged dauntless fortress she adored, the place she called home. In winter, the untamed North Sea plundered the craggy rocks below its grim facade, in summer, laughing frothy crests lapped gently. It was home. Her beloved ancestral home. The one place that had never let her down. Within the sanctuary of its massive stone walls that for centuries had withstood enemy onslaughts, raiding Vikings and plundering rival clans, within the cozy embrasure of the worn chintz window seat of her bedroom or curled under the old mohair rug in the deep leather armchair next to the library fire, watching the rain slash the sturdy diamond-shaped windowpanes, she felt safe from the world.

And now Strathaird would be hers no longer.

Not that Brad had wanted the property—he'd done everything possible to get the estate's entail voided in favor of her mother and herself, but the rule of law apparently trumped a generation of occupancy and dedication to the land.

And broke her heart.

Charlotte swallowed the lump in her throat. Even though she was grateful the estate would be in Brad's capable hands, she didn't think she could bear to witness the changes his tenure would inevitably bring.

And now he'd be coming with a bride.

His engagement had been a complete surprise, one she was still trying to fathom and accept. She should have known that one day it would happen. Not that she objected, of course—far from it; she planned to pull his leg royally at the wedding, then be the first to toast his good fortune. It just felt odd to think of her Brad tied permanently to another woman, when he'd always been there for her. Now, she supposed reluctantly, she'd have to learn to share his strength with someone else.

All at once, Brad's image materialized before her. Not as he was now, but as he'd been that night in Chester Square all those years ago, when he'd taken her in his arms and she'd felt his lips on hers. It had been years since she'd given it any thought, ages since she'd remembered. So why now? she wondered, eyes still carefully pinned above the bed, tracing shadows on the wall, trying to make some sense of these irrational thoughts. It was so silly. For over a decade, they'd had nothing more than a close friendly relationship. Still, she sighed involuntarily. The fact remained that after Brad married Sylvia, things would never be quite the same again.

The loud beeping of a monitor brought her crashing back to earth. She blinked uneasily at the panel of lights to the right of the bed, knowing the nurses would be in soon to check the apparatus. She flexed her fingers nervously and got up, feeling frustrated and cramped, and paced the room, agitated as a caged cheetah. If only there was some way to tear herself away, reach beyond this restless, dark-edged world that hovered constantly. But that was wishful thinking. Like it or not, she was stuck in a deadly impasse, unable to relinquish the past and powerless to claim the future.

She tried desperately to breathe, to regain composure, and realized with shock that she was trembling. Every instinct rebelled. She refused to regress. But as she cast a final fleeting glance at the motionless figure in the hospital bed, she felt the familiar ache rising in her throat; fear gripped her and panic hit.

The chair toppled as she fled from her husband's side.

Scrambling on the linoleum floor, she grabed her purse with a new sense of urgency, flung open the door and hurtled into the corridor, unable to stand it a moment longer.

A peacock blue sea sparkled, gulls soared and a warm west wind, herding clouds like woolly sheep, announced rain. But that would only come later, Penelope MacLeod realized, peering out the window of her daughter's new home. The brine-filled breeze caressed her hair as she shook the duster vigorously and watched, mind adrift, as specks of dust sank into the rose bed. That, too, needed a good weeding, she thought, straightening her back, stiff from hours of sweeping, scrubbing and polishing. Her lips curved and she looked about her, amused. If she'd realized just how much elbow grease it was going to take to get Rose Cottage into some semblance of livability, she might not have offered her services to Charlotte quite so readily. Yet, as she gazed across the fields stretching out toward Strathaird Castle and the familiar knot caught once more in her throat, she knew that Charlotte had done the right thing by moving out. It was time to move on, and easier to deal with the logistics of the transfer before Brad arrived.

She sighed, gazed at the stark walls and turrets of what had always been their home, and thought about past and future. So much had happened in the past few years, so many revelations, so many unexpected twists and turns of fate that had changed life forever. Who would have imagined that Charlotte would move from that fast-paced life she'd led within the ambit of the movie business and the house in Notting Hill, back to Skye and now to the tiny thatch cottage left her by Granny Flora? More amazing was that her daughter seemed perfectly content to live away from the hubbub that not long ago had been her lifeline, with her young daughter Genny.

How one's children change, Penelope reflected, thinking back to the restless, long-legged filly Charlotte used to remind her of. Then, turning her back to the window, she tucked a stray strand of soft blond hair behind her ear and took a good look at her handiwork. The cottage sparkled and she felt pride in the job. Charlotte would come home tonight to a tidy new home, where Penelope hoped very much that she'd be happy. Perhaps this was another sign her daughter was finally beginning to move on from the guilt and self-doubt she'd lived with these last many years.

The first sign of progress had been Charlotte's sudden determination to open a gallery in the village to exhibit the jewelry designs she created. It had come as a welcome surprise, a signal that she was learning to trust in herself again. Penelope sighed and looked about her again. At least the cottage was a world away from London and all the craziness that had been her daughter's life before her husband's accident. A far leap from the castle half a mile down the dirt road, too, she realized with a sigh and a smile.

But right now, the cottage was where Charlotte wanted and needed to be.

She picked up the duster, eyes flitting over the sienna-colored walls Charlotte had painted with loving care, a warm backdrop to the many picture frames, lamps and two voluminous sofas discovered on a rainy afternoon binge in the attic at Strathaird. The sofas had cleaned up rather nicely, she reckoned, tilting her head and casting a critical eye over them. Covered with Charlotte's extravagant throws and cushions, they looked comfy and welcoming.

The raid on the attic had yielded a number of other treasures. An ancient Indian chest with brass fittings and ivory inlays, a relic of the Raj that must have belonged to Great-Uncle Dougal MacLeod, who'd married the daughter of a local maharajah, now served as a coffee table, decked with heavy beeswax candles, a splattering of art books and a couple of artsy ashtrays. Penelope shook her head in admiration, amazed at her daughter's ability to create an atmosphere straight out of *House & Garden* with old attic remnants and personal flair. Where had her child inherited her vivid imagination? she wondered. Neither David, her late husband, nor she were particularly artistic. Yet Charlotte oozed originality and creative talent.

Penelope glanced doubtfully at the tiger skin—probably another of Great-Uncle Dougal's trophies—staring up at her from the grate with wide questioning eyes. She frowned, wondering whether Genny would be upset by its presence in the house. It pained her to see how sensitive her granddaughter was, how small things touched her in unanticipated ways. She hesitated. Perhaps if they gave the animal a name they could all become friends, and Genny wouldn't mind. Rudyard Kipling came to mind. That was it! They'd name the tiger Arun, and her possible distaste would be allayed.

Smiling, she moved to the mantelpiece and carefully straightened great-great-grandfather Hamish MacLeod's freesia-filled silver christening mug, making sure it was dead in the center of the Chippendale mirror frame above. She glanced at the photos Charlotte had placed on either side. Her gaze hardened as it fell upon John Drummond's handsome, devil-may-care face staring up with confident arrogance, the photo shot days before the stunt that had caused his accident. Why couldn't he have just died? she asked herself bitterly, not for the first time. The thought was wrong, of course, but she didn't give a damn. The man had nearly ruined her daughter's life. Could she be blamed for wishing him dead and Charlotte free? Even now, as he lay passive in his hospital bed, he continued to wield power. Charlotte was neither a wife nor a widow. God knows she'd tried to persuade her to carry on with the divorce proceedings she'd finally had the courage to face up to on that fatal day of the accident. But it was useless. Despite all the abuse she'd suffered from him—or perhaps partly because of it—Charlotte refused to be swayed.

Penelope sighed and shifted her gaze quickly to a picture of Genny and Charlotte, arms entwined aboard a yacht in Ibiza, then paused at the photo placed to the far right, featuring Brad, her husband, David, and her beloved son, Colin. Tears welled and she swallowed. Would she ever come to terms with her son's sudden disappearance in the avalanche, or David's heart attack so soon afterwards? In the space of a year she'd been deprived of the two men she most loved. And now Brad was the new Lord MacLeod and would be here in a couple of days to take Strathaird's reins, and life as they knew it would change forever. Still, she was thankful it was him and not a stranger, as might well have been the case.

Penelope turned firmly away from the mantelpiece, determined not to let herself plunge once more into depression. Life went on. David and Colin would always be dearest to her heart, but now she must face the future alone. And there was her nephew to help. Brad would need all her assistance as he assumed his new role. It was not an easy position to be landed with at any time, much less so when you weren't born and bred to it and were a foreigner, to boot.

The thought of him cringing at his new title cheered her up considerably and she laughed out loud. Poor boy. He was so cosmopolitan, yet at times he could be so wonderfully American too, the mere thought of an aristocratic title not at all in keeping with his views!

Well, he'd just have to get used to it. But she couldn't help wondering if he was truly prepared to shoulder this new set of responsibilities when his grandfather had already saddled him with so much.

The problem, she realized, a tiny smile hovering at the edge of her full mouth, was that Brad was too nice. Anyone else would have been thrilled to inherit Strathaird Castle for all the wrong reasons. Considered it their right.

But not Brad.

Instead, he'd gone to great lengths to try to have the entail on the estate reverted to Charlotte and herself.

She picked up an empty mug from the bookshelf and stared again at the photograph. What a handsome, fine, strong man he'd grown up to be. And how thrilled she was that he'd finally met someone with whom to share his life.

Not that Sylvia would have struck her as Brad's type. But then, what did she know about it? She remembered the smart, desperately chic woman she'd met briefly at a luncheon at the Savoy Grill several months earlier and hoped Sylvia would take to the people on the estate and enjoy them as much as she did.

A sudden vision of the sophisticated New Yorker had her gazing blindly at the bowl, hands falling dejectedly to her sides. How could poor Sylvia possibly be expected to learn in a few weeks what came handed down over generations? Again she sighed and shrugged. There was little use worrying. But how would old Mrs. McKinnon fare without her weekly cup of tea, where she brought Penelope up to date with all her latest aches and pains? And how would Tom, the crofter, get to his doctor's appointment on Tuesday afternoons now that his granddaughter was at university in Glasgow?

These and many other seemingly insignificant thoughts preoccupied her, followed by an unexpected memory of Brad and Charlotte years ago, playing tennis at La Renardière, the family home in Limoges. They'd been as thick as thieves then, hardly needing anyone else in their entourage, having so much fun together. But that easy familiarity and bantering had all changed when Charlotte became pregnant and married John Drummond fourteen years ago.

She'd wondered back then if Brad's feelings for her daughter had reached deeper than he'd cared to admit. There had been a look in his eyes, not to mention his unswerving determination to protect Charlotte. She was almost certain, she reflected, giving the nearest cushion on the sofa a pat, that Brad had loved Charlotte at one time. But for years now, nothing but old friendship had reigned. Like all mothers, she desperately wished that her child could have found happiness, instead of all the misery she'd encountered, and was still enduring.

Leaving the mug and duster in the kitchen, Penelope left the shepherd's pie she'd prepared, ready for Charlotte to pop in the oven, and picked up her old Barbour jacket. It was a long drive back from Glasgow and the hospital, and Charlotte would get back late. If only she'd do some much-needed shopping instead of sitting for hours in that dreadful sterile atmosphere, a morgue filled with live corpses. But there was little use trying to persuade Charlotte; once she set her mind to something, neither man nor mountain could move her.

She glanced at her watch. Armand would be back for tea soon. Her late husband's French cousin, a Parisian fashion designer, was not the easiest of guests. Still, she should be thankful he was taking such an interest in Charlotte's jewelry designs, she realized, dashing off a quick note that she placed in front of the pie. He seemed genuinely delighted with the gallery and its creations, and Charlotte had blossomed under his praise. Life was full of surprises, she reflected ruefully. Sometimes help came from the most unexpected sources.

Heading for the door, she picked up the basket she'd left on the front step. Looping it on her arm, she took a doubtful look at the somber sky before venturing briskly down the hill toward Strathaird, hoping it wouldn't rain before she reached home, as she'd forgotten her brolly.

Sylvia Hansen glanced speculatively at Brad, leaning back in the plush leather desk chair, hands entwined behind his neck, eyes glued on the enormous corner-office window. It was well into the evening, and already the lights of Manhattan vividly dotted the night sky. She stifled a yawn but reminded herself once again how damn lucky she was to have him. Bradley Harcourt Ward was gorgeous, successful and ambitious—all the things she considered herself to be.

She smiled briefly. Together they made one hell of a team. She had no doubt at all that soon they would be one of the city's premier power couples. Despite the travails of the past that were hers alone, she was finally about to achieve what would have seemed impossible not so long ago. Yes, she reflected, her expression softening as she watched him, Brad was well worth the wait, even though she'd almost taken the initiative and proposed to him herself in the end. Now she sported an impressive diamond that had once belonged to his great-grandmother on her finger, and a fabulous winter wedding was scheduled at the St. Regis. Not bad for a girl who grew up on the wrong side of the tracks in Little Rock.

She shuddered inwardly. The past and the shadows sometimes lingered, but she cast them aside and concentrated on what Brad was saying, swallowing a weary sigh when she realized he was back on the subject of Strathaird. During the past weeks, she'd heard more about that wretched Scottish castle he'd inherited by some stroke of ill-fated chance than she cared to recall, and was sorely tempted to leave him sitting here in the office and get their driver to take her home. Surely he must realize it wasn't *that* important? Couldn't he simply hire people to take care of the place? Scotland and his new inheritance could hardly require the kind of involvement he seemed determined to give it. She smoothed her skirt over her knees and crossed her legs, aware of a new inflection in his tone. Wondering if she'd missed something, she frowned. "What exactly are you getting at?" she asked, eyebrows knit.

"Well—" Brad twiddled his Mont Blanc pen thoughtfully "—as I've already mentioned, Strathaird is going to require my personal attention. At the beginning, at least. Which is why I was considering hopping over to Skye by myself first." He glanced briefly at her, across the vast expanse of desk. "You know, there's going to be a heck of a lot to do—or learn, rather. The truth is, Syl, I know as much about running a Scottish estate as training the New York Mets." He raised a hand and grinned. "I take that back. At least I know the rules of baseball and have scored a couple of home runs in my time, but to me this is estate management 101. Arriving there on my own would give me half a chance to start sorting things out before you arrive.'' He smiled, his riveting eyes seeking hers, as though her agreement was important.

Sylvia came awake with a jolt. ''You want to go there alone?''

''Why not? It'd only be a few days—a week at most. It'd give me an opportunity to wet my feet, meet the tenants, become familiar with a number of issues, and let you finish whatever you have to do here, instead of sitting around the castle alone with me busy all day.''

Sylvia nodded doubtfully. The prospect of sitting about in a musty old castle on the Scottish moors was not especially compelling, particularly if Brad was going to spend his days elsewhere. Normally, she'd have used the downtime to get more work done, but he'd already laughingly assured her there wasn't a cell tower within a hundred miles of Strathaird. The thought of surviving without her BlackBerry pager gave her a serious pause. ''All right,'' she mused, ''you have a point. I'm still working through those Australian contracts and need to wrap them up in the next two weeks.'' She glanced up at him, shirtsleeves rolled up, tie still in place, the tan from their trip to St. Barthes still glowing despite a full week's work, and smiled into his piercing blue eyes. ''Okay. You go and I'll stay. After all, one of us had better stay on board the ship.''

''Good girl.'' He grinned, leaned across the desk, past memos and the array of telephones, and took her hand in his. ''You're a great gal, Syl. I know I can always count on you.''

''Thanks.'' She mustered a sassy grin, knowing he

meant it as a compliment, and wondered why his words made her feel like a well-worn trench coat.

"Right." He brought his hand down firmly on the desk. "Well, now that we've settled that satisfactorily, we should consider food. Do you want to go out for dinner or shall we order in?" He raised an inquiring eyebrow.

"We had a reservation at Town, but I canceled about an hour ago. Tell me, when exactly are you planning to leave?" she asked, frowning.

"At the end of the week or so." Brad began tidying his papers. "That is, if all goes well with Seattle and Chicago. I'm glad you see the sense of me heading over there alone," he continued, getting up. "It'll give me time to catch up with the family, too," he remarked, stretching. Moving toward the large panoramic window, he stared broodingly out the window at the streaming traffic fifty-two stories below. "You know, I haven't had a real heart-to-heart talk with Charlotte in a couple of years. Time goes by so fast. We barely even get the chance to talk on the phone anymore." He turned and picked up his jacket.

Sylvia followed suit, slipping the large black Prada purse that contained her life over her shoulder, and frowned. "I met Charlotte in London that time we went to the Chelsea Flower Show," she murmured, glancing at him. "I didn't realize you were close. You and Charlotte call each other regularly?"

"Not lately. But we used to spend hours on the phone. Of course, that was a while back. I tried to help her through some of her problems. She had a bad marriage. So, which is it going to be?" he asked, changing the subject and slipping an arm around her. "Thai, or will you whip us up one of your superb omelettes? If I have any say in the matter, I'll opt for the omelette.''

"Sounds good to me. I'm too tired to go out," she replied, leaning into him.

"Then omelettes it is. I'll even give you a back massage, how's that?" He gave her a brief hug as they moved toward the door.

"What'd I do to deserve that?" She tilted her head up at him as they traversed the quiet hall.

"You're the best," he teased, reaching for the button of the elevator.

"Yeah, right!"

"I swear. You understand everything, you never bitch. What more could a man ask for?" He grinned down at her and pinched her cheek. "Remind me to send an e-mail to Aunt Penn, will you? I just remembered it's Charlie's birthday on Friday. Maybe I could arrive as a surprise," he added as the wide metallic doors slid open on the marble and mirrored elevator.

"But we're going to the Walsh dinner party on Saturday night," Sylvia exclaimed, taken aback. Jake Walsh was one of the Street's legendary arbitrageurs, and she'd spent the last year carefully cultivating a friendship with his young wife, Karen, who was on most of the city's most prominent charity boards. Anyway, the ones she was interested in joining.

"We are?" Brad grimaced. "It's not that important, is it? Can't we reschedule?"

They reached the lobby of the Harcourts building and walked toward the car waiting at the curb. Sylvia swallowed her frustration. "Well," she muttered grudgingly, "it's not *essential*, but I'd hate to miss the chance to check out their penthouse. I hear it's phenomenal."

"Then you go, honey, you'll enjoy it," he answered,

smiling absently as they slid into the back of the vehicle, and Ramon, the driver, glided smoothly into the Manhattan evening traffic.

"That's not the poi—" She bit back the words, afraid she'd sound petty and childish. For some reason, this sudden eagerness to get to Scotland had upset her, and the fact that he wanted to go alone left her strangely empty and anxious. She shrugged, leaned over and poured them each a scotch, knowing it was ridiculous to be so uptight. Brad was straight as an arrow; he traveled all the time by himself and she never gave it a thought. Still, something about this particular trip left her uneasy. It just wasn't her world.

Taking a long sip, she stared out the car window at late stragglers hurrying toward the subway, noticing a dog walker clutching the leashes of six hounds under a streetlight. What kind of person wanted a job as a dog walker? she wondered absently. Then, leaning back in the soft cream leather, she slipped her hand in his, determined to relax the rest of the drive home.

It was dark by the time Charlotte finally reached Rose Cottage and walked through the tiny hall into the kitchen. Pungent summer scents, dried flowers, and herbs hanging from low, waxed beams welcomed her as she tossed her bag on the counter. To her surprise, the house was spic and span. Then she caught sight of the shepherd's pie and lifted the note with a tired smile. How sweet of Mummy to have taken all this trouble when she had so much to cope with before Brad's arrival. And, despite her sadness at leaving Strathaird, she recognized how good it felt to be in a place entirely her own once more. Living at the castle with Mummy and Genny had been fine, but there was something to be said about opening your own front door and knowing you were home.

The phone rang and she picked up.

"Hello, darling." Charlotte's mouth curved as her daughter's voice poured down the line in an excited, thirteen-year-old rush.

"Yes, of course you can sleep over, darling. But don't be a nuisance to Mrs. Morison. Give them my love."

Charlotte hung up, glad Genny had new friends. She'd been so alone and shy when they'd first returned to the island after John's accident. Making the change from London hadn't been easy. The other children had not willingly accepted her, and of course her limp hadn't helped.

She switched on the kettle, absently inserted the pie in the oven, and shoved the recurring guilt over the night when she'd fallen asleep at the wheel. Genny had paid the price, her leg crushed in the twisted metal. The accident had left her with a serious limp that Charlotte prayed would diminish with time. She quickly shifted her thoughts back to the present before remorse engulfed her and reflected on all that had happened in the past few months. Change, it seemed, was the order of the day.

Of course, it was unrealistic to believe that life would go on forever as it always had. Brad and his soon-to-be wife, Sylvia, could hardly be expected to put up with the inconveniences that were a part of Strathaird, she acknowledged, taking a chipped Winnie the Pooh mug off the hook above the sink and opening the tea tin. It was ironic, she reflected, that she, who so desperately longed for change in her personal life, could not bear the thought of seeing Strathaird transformed even a little. Which was why she'd left. She was only half a mile up the road, she realized, but mentally she was gone. Strathaird, with its draughts, the lift that always got stuck and the broken step leading down to the lawn that for some reason never got repaired, was a part of her past. But for all her life, it had represented *home*.

She dangled the mug carelessly, engulfed by sudden nostalgia, then stopped short, remembering the mammoth-size crates filled with gym equipment that had been delivered three days ago, now looming ominously in the Great Hall. Moving out was *definitely* the right thing to do, she realized with a shudder, picturing Sylvia, sleek and blond, mounted on the treadmill.

Selecting a ginger snap from the dented biscuit tin, she set it beside the tea mug. The image of Brad's smooth, sexy, sophisticated fiancée flashed vividly in her mind's eye. A smart, highly organized, modern woman, she reflected, remembering the one time they'd briefly met, two years ago, long before there was any talk of marriage. Pouring boiling water into the mug, she bit dismally into the cookie, feeling suddenly dowdy and drab. The woman probably had a color-coded closet. Her bags full of designer outfits were probably already carefully packed for her stay on Skye—or would Prada and Calvin Klein remain stashed in her pristine Manhattan apartment?

Not that she cared.

Charlotte straightened her drooping shoulders and sipped her tea cautiously. Sylvia could look as good as she liked, and she wished Brad very happy. After all, the woman was obviously the perfect choice for him: neat, orderly, efficient, the ideal companion for a man with all his responsibilities.

The acrid scent of burning food made her swivel toward the oven, the shepherd's pie that she'd forgotten a sharp reminder of just how absentminded and unorganized she could be. Sylvia, she reflected somberly, probably never did silly things like leave the oven on. Then, hoisting a slender hip up onto the counter, she grinned as she imagined Sylvia's apartment; probably somewhere in the upper east sixties, the perfect address, *très* slick, Italian furniture—modern, of course—a very clean, minimalist look, all ecru and beige with touches of chrome. Not a thing out of place.

A crack of laughter broke the silence as she slipped on a pair of charred oven gloves, opened the oven door and pictured Brad and the twins in this hypothetical home. She grimaced at the burned crust, glanced despondently at the oven's too-high setting and pulled herself up guiltily. She had no business criticizing Sylvia, who from all accounts was delightful and who adored Rick and Todd, Brad's half brothers whom he'd taken in eight years ago when their parents died tragically in a plane crash. What right had she to judge someone who, according to general opinion, was the perfect wife for him?

Charlotte gazed down at the pie, burned to a crisp, whose destination was the rubbish bin. She decided to give her mother a thank-you call before she went to bed, although she wouldn't mention the burning bit. Mummy was a brick. It was so decent of her to have finished the cleanup, which she'd been dreading returning to.

Dumping the pie temporarily in the sink, she took her tea to the old wooden table and sat down on one of the rickety wooden chairs with a thud, the day's emotions and the long drive finally catching up with her. She jiggled the stool warily. Perhaps Mummy was right and she should invest in some new furniture on the next trip into Glasgow. But she hated crowds and shops and people and decisions—even minor ones such as choosing chairs or curtains seemed insurmountable right now. And that went for clothes too, an issue her mother brought up constantly. Why she should care what she looked like here on Skye was beyond her. After all, there were only the sheep and now Armand de la Vallière to see her—and Armand, though very fashion-conscious, was gay, so he didn't really count.

Her mind wandered back to Brad wondering how he truly felt about inheriting Strathaird. She swung her foot absently, remembering their talks of old. It had been a while since they'd sat down for a long cozy chat. God knows, in the dark bleak days when she and John leaped from one argument into another, knowing he was a phone call away had been a lifesaver. But since the accident, their conversations had somehow fizzled out. She had felt guilty talking to him for so long and so often without a specific reason. Before John's injury, there had always been a motive. She'd poured out some of her pain. And although she'd rarely taken his advice, it had helped. But since the accident, any talk had been businesslike and to the point. Oh well, Charlotte sighed, it was probably best. They each had their lives to live.

She rose briskly and brushed her hair away from her face, considering whether Brad fully realized all that inheriting Strathaird implied—the people, the everyday worries, the plans and intricacies? Or did he think he could run it like he ran Harcourts, the multimillion-dollar porcelain and upscale decorating enterprise he'd inherited from his grandfather? She refilled her cup, sipped absently. "Hell's bells," she swore crossly when she burned her tongue and the tea spilled, dirtying her T-shirt. This was definitely not her day, she reflected grimly, closing her eyes and taking a deep breath. And why was she so concerned about Brad, when she had more than enough on her own plate? Ridiculous! Brad was a big boy. He knew the place well, had been coming here since he was a child and could very well take care of himself. There was no reason for her to worry. Or was there? It was one thing to pop over for short visits to see his grandparents, flying in on a chopper, then wafting out again. But this was a different kettle of fish altogether, and she doubted whether even the eternally well-prepared Brad had the slightest inkling of all that would be expected of him as laird.

A meow from the windowsill brought her out of her reverie. Hermione sat curled on the outside ledge, preening her whiskers and cleaning her soft tabby fur. Charlotte rose, opened the window and allowed the cat to pad daintily over the sink toward her basket by the stove. As she reached to close the window, a sudden movement caught her eye. She frowned, wondering if a sheep had wandered in from the fields. All at once she shivered, then pulled herself together, deciding she was even more tired than she'd realized. This was Skye, and there was no danger here. She turned and thoughtfully eyed the cat.

"Where have you been?" she inquired, picking her up and stroking gently. "I'm glad to see you know your new way home. How do you like it?" She was reassured by a satisfied purr. "Good," she murmured, letting the animal slip from her arms. "At least one of us is happy."

She was about to leave the kitchen when the sound of a muted cough made her stand stock-still. There was definitely someone out there.

Warily Charlotte slipped into the hall, opened the antique chest on the floor and picked out a cricket bat. Just as stealthily, she opened the front door. As she emerged, a shadow flitted near the gate.

"Stop," she called, rushing forward, wielding the bat

wildly. A figure stumbled through the gate and she hurled herself toward it.

"Dinna' hit me, Miss Charlotte, dinna', please."

The pleading voice of Bobby Hewitt made her drop her arms in sudden relief.

"Bobby! What on earth are you doing here?" she exclaimed, limp with irritation and relief. "You gave me the most awful fright."

"I wasna' doing anything wrong."

"But what are you doing out here? It's past ten o'clock." She glanced at the bowed figure. Poor Bobby was a simple, harmless soul in his mid-forties who'd been trailing her adoringly since she was a child. But he had never snooped around at night. Of course, she realized with a frown, she'd always been ensconced in the castle. Now, on her own at Rose Cottage, things were different.

"Come here," she said, taking him by the arm of his worn jacket and making him stand under the porch light. "Bobby, you can't wander around at night spying on people."

"I wasna'," he remarked, his mouth taking on a stubborn twist. "I was making sure everything was all right. There's strangers about."

"They're called tourists, Bobby." Her face broke into a smile and she shook her head. "So you thought to guard the cottage? Don't worry about me, Bobby, everything's fine. There are no marauders around here. You know that."

"Ye canna' be too careful."

"No, of course not. Still, you mustn't come scaring me like that. I almost went after you with Colin's cricket bat." She swung it over her shoulder. "Now get back to your mother's cottage and no more roaming around here after dark, promise?"

"Aye." He nodded penitently, seeking forgiveness.

Charlotte smiled at him. "If you wait two seconds, I'll get you some of Mrs. McTavish's toffees. You like those, don't you?"

He nodded in eager response, like a small child.

Charlotte sighed, propped the bat against the hall wall and went back to the kitchen where she found a bag of toffees. Perhaps something should be done to help Bobby, although he seemed perfectly content.

"Here you are. Now off you go, straight home, and don't let this happen again."

"Aye. Thanks, Miss Charlotte. I'm sorry I scared ye. I didna' mean any harm."

"I know. Now run along."

She watched as he hurried off, his shoulders slightly stooped, long hair trailing thinly on his shoulders. Poor Bobby. She should have realized he might get up to something like this, but frankly, Bobby Hewitt was the last person on her mind right now.

She locked up and glanced at the heavy gold watch on her wrist. Gosh, it was late. Better give her mother a buzz, then get to bed.

The library fire dwindled, embers stuttered, coals shifted and Armand de la Vallière sighed. It was his favorite room in the castle.

He sat in solitary contemplation, surrounded by leather-bound books, heavy mahogany furniture and the ancient French-damask curtains installed so many years ago by Tante Hortense, a balm to his strained nerves. He peered through the mullioned windows into the inky summer evening, vaguely aware of Penelope's voice echoing through the Great Hall. Concentrating, he leaned forward, staring once more at the packed shelves of books, eyes narrowing. It would be a difficult search, one that would require all his ability. The sheer physical impediment of having to climb up to the highest shelves made it almost impossible to take a good look at the books without attracting suspicion. He stared into the dying flames, obliterating the haunting images that lurked in his memory since childhood, replacing them instead with shining scenes of glitz, glamour and glory. It was a technique he'd perfected over the years, and infallibly it worked.

Now, as fleeting shadows played on the spines of the ancient book covers and the darkened walls, he replaced the packed shelves with visions of splendid jewels. They shimmered in his imagination, and he sighed. The method acted as effectively as any hallucinogen. Slowly his tense muscles relaxed and he breathed easier, entranced, visualizing the catwalk, the agitated buzz, models preparing to strut the runway, hairdressers, makeup artists and seamstresses, all waiting for his final orders. His fingers unclenched as he pictured himself directing operations, adding the finishing touches with a master's skill. Finally he would place each of Charlotte's exquisite pieces at precisely the right angle before sending the model forth, waiting with bated breath for the murmured hush of the crowd.

A frisson of satisfaction left him sighing. Nothing less than perfection would do. And he had seen perfection in Charlotte's work. He drew a cigarette from an antique silver cigarette case, tapped it thoughtfully on the arm of the old leather chair, then lit it. To have such amazing talent, yet be so oblivious. A quivering pang of envy darted straight to his heart. Why was life so unfair? Why did some have all the suffering, the toil, the trouble, while others glided unwittingly into fame and fortune? Indeed, why did life bestow talent on those who didn't give a damn, while denying it to those for whom it meant the world?

He took a long drag and leaned back in the deep armchair, aware there was little to be gained from such thoughts. It was too late to acquire that which God had not given him.

Still, he decided with a grim little smile, it might not be too late to redirect fate into avenues more suited to his liking. After all, there was a reason for his presence here, at this specific time.

Once more he inhaled deeply, then let the smoke curl up toward the coffered oak ceiling and shut his eyes. He was so close. So very close. And nothing would convince him otherwise.

2

Brad studied the preliminary agenda for next month's board meeting and added a few margin notes, increasing the time allotted to discuss international expansion. Harcourts may have begun as a porcelain empire almost a century ago, but over the decades, particularly since Brad had been CEO, the business had expanded to include all aspects of upscale home décor. International growth was essential and needed special attention. World markets were growing fast and he planned to be there on the crest of the wave.

Capping his pen, he tossed it on the desk, loosened the silk tie that was suffocating him and allowed himself a moment of self-congratulation. The last quarter's profits had surpassed everyone's expectations. The company was leaner and more productive than any in the industry, and the innovative publicity campaigns Sylvia had engineered for the new designer dinnerware lines had taken the public by storm; sales had doubled in several markets and Harcourts was on a roll.

And now he was obliged to carve two weeks out of the hectic and tense period before the annual directors' meeting to go to Scotland. It wasn't going to be easy,

Brad realized, drumming his foot while studying the schedule his secretary had laid on the desk this morning. He wondered briefly if there was any way of avoiding it, knowing very well he could not put off the trip to Strathaird. Based on the teleconference with the solicitors in Edinburgh, it was clear his presence was required to settle the labyrinthine legal issues related to the estate, and he owed it to Aunt Penn and Charlotte to deal with matters as quickly and cleanly as he could. He thought of what he'd discussed with Sylvia the previous evening. It was true that he wanted to go. And of course the idea of seeing the family again, spending time in a place he'd always enjoyed, had its attractions. It was just such a damn inconvenient moment.

He leaned back and swiveled the ample leather office chair, picturing the rugged fortress, battered by centuries of wind and rain, relentless waves and enemy onslaught. Lately it seemed to be beckoning him.

Learning he was a part of Strathaird's heritage had come as a shock. Discovering he had become its owner was sobering. But he'd accepted the inevitable, and now there was nothing to do but assume his duties as laird and invest what little time his busy life permitted to try and do the job right. Although he knew the place well, had climbed its rocks and walked its shores and moors since early childhood, he'd never considered himself more than a guest in his grandparents' home.

He glanced once more at the schedule, wondered if perhaps two weeks would be too little and whether it could be stretched into three. His gut told him he'd need the time. Penelope expected it of him, Charlotte probably expected it of him as well, and apparently the tenants did, too. That, he sighed, had been made abundantly clear, both in his meetings and by his aunt. Not directly, he realized, smiling at how subtle the British could be. Nothing was ever said head-on, just implied.

He rose and moved across the large office to the window and stared at the Manhattan skyline. But instead of Rockefeller Center and the Empire State Building, a riot of titian hair and violet eyes flashed before him. He pulled himself up with a jolt and glanced guiltily at his watch, remembering he was due to meet Sylvia in an hour at Julio Larraz's private art showing. Focusing on the subject of art he thought of the several Larraz paintings and two bronze sculptures he'd already acquired. He'd missed the exhibition in Monte Carlo and was damned if he'd wait for another auction at Christie's or Sotheby's to acquire another piece. Turning on his heel, he pressed a button on the chrome phone panel and punched.

"Yes, sir?" Ramon answered promptly.

"I'll be down in ten," he said, glancing again at his watch.

"Very good, sir."

A perfunctory knock was followed by the door opening. Marcia, his secretary, entered with her usual brisk step. "I've made a couple of changes to the schedule," he remarked, handing it to her while answering his cell phone. He sent her an apologetic smile while she stood patiently, with the air of one used to waiting. She gasped as she glanced at the changes.

"Right," Brad spoke into the phone. "Start buying as soon as the market opens, but not so much stock that anyone'll notice. Yeah…I learned today they've got a merger going." There was a pause as he listened. "Sure thing. Good night."

"You're not serious, Brad. Three weeks?" Marcia squeaked, her slim, blue-suited form tensing. "You simply can't stay away that long. For one thing, you have the Australian trip coming up, and the meetings in London, not to mention Chicago and Seattle. And the board meeting—''

"I don't have a choice." He picked up his briefcase, slipped in a couple of memos, then closed it. "We'll manage somehow, Marcia. I'm counting on you, as always. Sylvia's going to be around for at least the first week I'm gone." He did not notice the disapproving sniff. "Better make reservations for Friday."

She groaned. "Why couldn't they just let Charlotte and Penelope MacLeod have the darn estate? If I were them, I'd slap a lawsuit on the judge for sexual discrimination," she added, following him hurriedly out the door, into the vast, well-lit hallway where secretaries and junior executives still circulated, despite the late hour.

Downstairs the car awaited him at the curb. As he climbed in, Brad took conscious stock of the fast-paced Manhattan hub where he'd lived all his life, and wondered suddenly what it would be like to function for three weeks at the slow, lazy pace of Skye, with its grazing sheep, one-lane roads and fishing boats bobbing on a choppy gray sea.

Leaning back, he did something rare: he let his mind wander. Usually he answered e-mail or made calls, gaining time in traffic. But tonight, Scotland was uppermost in his mind. As the car crossed Houston Street and continued into SoHo, he stared at the bustling crowd on the sidewalk, remembering long summer days spent catching tadpoles with Charlotte and Colin, hours fishing together from the rocks below the castle, picnics prepared by Aunt Penn and Granny Flora, carried to the moors at sundown and set among the heather, while Dex, his grandfather, spun yarns around the campfire, and all of them laughed at the outrageous tall tales Charlotte wove with such imagination and skill. He smiled. That was something he and Charlie must do with Genny and the twins, he reflected, the thought instantly appealing.

Traffic stopped, a horn honked angrily and Ramon lowered the window to follow the loud argument going on between irate drivers over a delivery van parked smack in their lane.

"Eet's crazy, Mr. Brad," Ramon remarked, shaking his gray head disapprovingly. "Worse than Puerto Rico," he complained.

Brad murmured sympathetically, used to the city's eccentric ways and Ramon's disapproval, his mind far away in a remote part of the globe about as alien to Manhattan as you could get. Then, all at once, he realized that Sylvia was absent from his fantasy and experienced a moment's shame. Probably because they'd never been to Strathaird together, he justified. That would all change once she arrived. They'd make new memories together. Still, the more he thought about it, the more surprised he was at how appealing the trip to Scotland seemed. He couldn't help the pleasure he experienced at the thought of spending some time alone with Charlotte, catching up, roaming the estate and becoming familiar with the people and their lives. Anyway, Syl needed to stay put while he dealt with business over there, he reasoned. Of course, she'd be a wonderful help in Scotland, too—of that he had little doubt. His future wife was supportive, enthusiastic and he could not ask for a better companion. But he was relieved, nevertheless, not to be descending upon Strathaird loaded with Vuitton luggage, which might set the wrong tone with the locals, who were low-key at the best of times.

The car drew up in front of the gallery and Brad shook

off the mood. Entering the building, he was immediately engulfed by laughing chitchat, the clink of fine crystal, hot deals disguised by small talk and the feel of female eyes following him closely as he surveyed the large, streamlined space. He waved to Larraz and his lovely wife, Pilar, then caught sight of Sylvia, simple and chic in a strict black dress, hair falling blond and sleek to her shoulders, her only jewelry a pair of diamond studs and his Grandmother Ward's imposing diamond engagement ring.

Picking up a glass of scotch from a roving waiter's silver tray, he made his way among the guests to where she stood chatting animatedly to a large man in a black blazer and T-shirt. One of the L.A crowd, he figured, dropping a fleeting kiss on Sylvia's cheek before joining in the conversation. He wondered suddenly how Sylvia would react to his idea of spending three weeks in Scotland instead of two. He nursed his scotch, replying automatically to a woman in bloodred silk he vaguely remembered was a Broadway actress, and decided that the extra time on the island would do the twins good. He made a mental note to call Diego de la Fuente, the twins' maternal grandfather, in Montevideo, and convince him to join them in Skye, as Aunt Penn had suggested.

Then he observed Sylvia. She was in her element tonight, networking, enjoying the party, letting no opportunities for furthering business slip through her fingers. He wouldn't be surprised if, by the time they got back to her place, some hot new deal was cooking. The image of her sitting quietly, sipping white wine at sunset on the lawn at Strathaird, seemed painfully incompatible.

Banishing the niggling doubt, he hailed a friend and chatted for a couple of minutes. In the end, she'd be as comfortable at Strathaird as she was here. He felt certain of it.

Satisfied that everything would work out, he put all thoughts of Scotland aside and set about acquiring the painting he'd decided on.

Leaning out the window of her old Land Rover, Charlotte breathed long and deep, smiled at the pale sunbeams piercing the traveling clouds, and sighed as a strong westerly breeze carrying subtle scents of brine and heather mussed her hair. Overhead, gulls squawked and beyond the fields of grazing sheep divided by low stone walls, a soft purple haze draped the moors. Strathaird might change, she reflected with a rush of pleasure, but this would always be hers.

She headed down the bumpy single-track road, slowing when a tractor trundling in the opposite direction obliged her to veer onto the grass before coming to a grinding halt.

The driver respectfully raised a hand to his faded tweed cap. "A good day to ye, Miss Charlotte. Am nae' sure this fine weather will last, though." Old Fergus Mackay sniffed doubtfully. Eyes narrowing, he pointed to the drifting clouds hovering overhead. "There'll be rain later on," he remarked with the satisfied assurance of one who knew his weather.

Charlotte looked up and nodded in solemn agreement. He was right. When wild gusts moved inland, they brought heavy warm rain in their wake. She smiled, chatted for a few minutes and sighed inwardly. It was sweet how the locals still called her Miss Charlotte, even though she'd been married for years.

"I hear the new lordship's arriving shortly." The statement was followed by a dour sniff.

"Yes. He's meant to be here early next week," Charlotte responded enthusiastically.

"Aye. And about time too. It'll nae do fer him to stay away from the land too long."

"Brad'll be here. Don't worry. He's a good sort," Charlotte encouraged, cringing at the note of disapproval she heard in the old man's voice. Speculation in the village and among the tenants was rife.

"Aye. I remember him as a wee laddie." Fergus Mackay straightened his cap and smiled sadly, his eyes surprisingly blue and bright under thick bushy white brows. "'Tis a pity yer ain' brother Colin passed on, Miss Charlotte. A fine laird he woulda' made. We're all agreed on that."

"He would. But it wasn't to be. Brad wasn't brought up here and hasn't had the advantage of knowing you all the way Colin did, but I'm sure he intends to do his best. And the more help he gets from all of us, the easier things will be and a better job he'll do. For all of us," she added pointedly, hoping that by paving the way with old Mackay, an elder in the church who held strong influence over his peers, she'd ease Brad's transition.

They conversed for several minutes, then the tractor continued its lumbering course up the hill and Charlotte drove on down toward the sea and the village. She glanced up to her right at the castle, rising rugged and alone.

A shard of sunlight washed the weathered stones of the east turret, illuminating the faerie emblem of the MacLeod flag, fluttering proudly in the brisk breeze. Before she could stop them, another rush of tiresome tears made her jerk her head away. Stop it, she commanded herself, biting her lip. It was ridiculous to get sentimental and silly about Strathaird. The castle was moving on, as it always had and always would. It was nothing new or different from what had occurred in the past. Merely the last male MacLeod, the heir to Strathaird, was coming home, as was right and proper. But how long would he stay? she wondered, swerving into the village, past the snug harbor packed with colorful fishing boats and into the main street, thinking still of all the inevitable adjustments that were bound to take place. If Brad were to do the job properly and stake his claim as laird, he'd have to introduce his own ideas and innovations.

And what about Mummy, without whose quiet yet efficient hand everything would have run amuck? What would happen once Brad and Sylvia were installed and they didn't need her any longer? she wondered, heart aching.

Charlotte drove between the narrow row of whitewashed houses. With an effort, she sent Mrs. Bane, the newsagent, a bright smile and a wave, thinking worriedly about her mother's situation. Penelope MacLeod was an integral and fundamental piece in the smooth running of the estate. She knew everything. The tenants, their worries and needs, how to handle the drove of MacLeods who appeared every year from all over the world, anxious to trace their ancestry and who always received a warm personal welcome from Lady MacLeod herself, however inconvenient, before she sent them on their way to Dunvegan, the seat of the MacLeod clan.

As for what she herself did around the estate, Charlotte thought that was less important. Still, perhaps she valued her involvement more than she liked to admit, she realized uneasily. How would it feel, now that Sylvia, and not she, would be doing those same things?

She parked in front of the Morissons' quaint house on the edge of the village and waved to Genny and Lucy, waiting for her, heads together, on the front steps. Genny was wearing baggy pants and a T-shirt, her colorful backpack slung over her right shoulder. The friendship with Lucy had helped her become part of the group, Charlotte realized, watching as the two girls hugged before Genny came down the path toward her and circled the vehicle. As always, Charlotte had to stop herself from jumping out and helping her climb in, knowing she must allow her daughter to be independent.

"Have a lovely time?" she asked as Genny settled beside her. Gosh, how she'd grown this last year. And with her trendy clothes, really looked like a teenager. Like every mother, she smiled with pride and listened, amused, to Genny's description of the sleepover at Lucy's.

"You're not too tired?" she inquired as they drove down the village street headed for school.

"No. It was cool, Mum." Genny turned and smiled. "Can I tell you a secret, Mummy?"

"Of course."

"You sure?" Genny cocked her red head warily.

"Come on, don't leave me in suspense," Charlotte urged, suppressing a smile.

"Lucy's decided she wants to be a famous actor like Daddy."

"Really? Well, that's a change," Charlotte countered. "Three weeks ago she wanted to be a vet."

"I know, but she's changed her mind. She's going to cut her hair. Mummy, can I have a belly piercing?"

"What?" Charlotte nearly swerved into an oncoming vehicle.

"Why not, Mum? Everybody has a piercing. You have a tattoo," she added reproachfully. "If you were my age I'll bet you'd have rings all over you."

"Perhaps. But I probably would have regretted it by now," Charlotte argued, remembering the follies of her youth and feeling hypocritical all at once. "Piercing's so...I don't know. It gives me the creeps. Why don't you wait until the twins arrive and see what they think?"

"I don't need male approval to be myself," Genny replied grandly as they drew up in front of her school. Dropping a peck on her mother's cheek, she alighted slowly and Charlotte sighed. Last year it had been, "Todd thinks," and "Rick says."

She did a U-turn and drove back the few hundred yards into the main street of the village, parked askew opposite the gallery and got out, slamming the car door a tad harder than she'd intended. Frowning absently, she walked toward the gallery.

"Ah, Charlotte." The strident voice of Marjory Pearson hailed from across the street, bringing her to an abrupt halt.

"Good morning, Mrs. Pearson." There was no escape, she realized, heart sinking. Mrs. P. stood firmly entrenched on the opposite side of the street in front of the gallery, hands gripping the handlebar of her prewar bike. She was sensibly attired in her usual outfit of corduroy knickerbockers, the tweed jacket she wore rain or shine, topped by a green felt hat with a long feather acquired on one of her yearly visits to the Tyrol.

"Off to your gallery, I see," Mrs. P. remarked over the bicycle's reedy basket, plump with groceries. "I was just looking in your window," she added, shaking her head in amazement. "I'm surprised anyone would spend such ridiculous amounts of money on frivolity. It goes against the grain," she added, glancing disapprovingly toward the gallery window and sniffing. "Just shows one what the world's coming to." She peered closely at Charlotte. "I had my doubts about this venture of yours," she continued grudgingly, "but I suppose you're quite right to encourage the tourists to spend, my dear, quite right indeed. I myself thought trinkets would have been more suitable, but the Colonel was saying just the other day that he believes you have talent."

This last was said with the satisfied air of one bestowing high praise. She sent Charlotte a condescending look of approval. "I must say, Charlotte, you've come a long way," she added, her eyes narrowing, "I never would have thought after the way you behaved in your youth that you'd end up being an example of female behavior to the community. As the Colonel repeats again and again, we must not judge." She leaned over, her wrinkled face too close for comfort. "I'm very glad to see you staunch, my dear. I was saying to the Colonel only the other day that many a young woman on this island could take a leaf out of your book." She drew back, sniffed and pursed her lips. "When I think of some of the goings-on…" She ended with a meaningful glance.

Charlotte shifted uncomfortably, searching desperately for an excuse to get away.

"Your loyalty to your infirm spouse can only be applauded," Marjory Pearson continued relentlessly. "How is he, by the way?" she asked, her beady eyes glinting with unabashed curiosity.

"Pretty much the same, I'm afraid," Charlotte murmured, glancing hopefully at the gallery door.

"I'm sorry." Marjory's disappointment at the lack of gossip showed. Then she brightened once more. "I hear the new Lord MacLeod will be with us shortly. Will he be making a prolonged stay? I needn't tell you how much speculation is going on," she added, lowering her voice to a conspiratorial whisper.

"I have no idea what Brad's plans are."

"Quite a job he has ahead of him," Mrs. P. remarked, shaking her head wisely, avid to be the first to acquire any possible tidbits to pass on down the bush telegraph. "I hear he has a fiancée? One wonders what sort of female she is. Americans can be so very different, if you know what I mean."

"Sylvia's delightful." Charlotte waxed enthusiastically. "Terribly efficient, and just the right person to be the new Lady MacLeod."

"I see." Mrs. P.'s shoulders drooped. "We must hope so, indeed. We wouldn't want any changes in the village, now, would we?"

Charlotte murmured a vague assent, smiled brightly and frowned at her watch. "I'm awfully sorry, Mrs. Pearson, but I'm expecting rather an important client in ten minutes. I simply have to run. Send the Colonel my best."

"Goodness, of course. So selfish of me to be holding you back. Did that large Frenchwoman with the bun buy the necklace in the window? I saw her pass several times while I was at the butcher's the other day. She seemed quite enamored. I told the Colonel I thought it was a go. Quite amazing that you're able to command such elevated prices, Charlotte. Are you sure you shouldn't consider—"

"Must run, Mrs. Pearson," Charlotte interrupted blithely. "All's well on the home front."

"Ah. Good. Then I shall report back to the Colonel. He'll be pleased." Mrs. P. braced herself, balanced the creaking bike and readied for action, while Charlotte made good her escape.

She dashed inside the gallery, located in one of the crooked whitewashed houses bordering the main street, nestled between the bakery and the Celtic Café, run by her friend Rory MacLean. Leaning against the door, Charlotte let out a frustrated huff. "That woman," she remarked to Moira Stuart, her lifelong friend who was now a goldsmith and manager of the gallery, "is simply awful." Shaking her head, she stepped into the light, monochromatic space, dotted with glass showcases, halogen lights and burlap settings showing off her exclusive jewelry designs, then stopped short, surprised to see Armand de la Vallière, attired in tweed knickerbockers and a cap, examining her latest creation under a magnifying glass. She coughed, smothering the giggles that the sight of his costume always caused her. He looked like a fashion ad for a shooting weekend.

"Hello, Armand."

"Ah, *ma chère* Charlotte." Armand laid the delicately crafted platinum choker back in the showcase and hastened forward, raising her fingers to his lips. "Simply magnificent, *chère cousine*. You have surpassed yourself."

"You like it?" Charlotte kissed him on both cheeks, unable to squelch the twinge of pride at Armand's words. "Any sign of the Americans?" she asked Moira.

"Not yet." Her friend's eyes, shaded behind thick lenses, showed amusement. An Indian skirt and blouse and heavy leather sandals gave her the air of a tired hippie.

Charlotte turned back to Armand, grinning. "I'm glad you like the choker. I worked a long time on it. I think the jade works, don't you?"

"Exquisite. Quite unique."

"I have some other designs to show you. The ones I was telling you about the other day," she said breath-

lessly, flinging her basket on a chair behind the desk that
served as a counter.

"I would be delighted to view them. You have *un
talent exceptionel,* Charlotte."

"Do you really think so?" Charlotte asked earnestly,
clear violet eyes sparkling with pleasure at his words.
"Or are you just being terribly polite?"

"Now, now, young lady. You are fishing for compli-
ments." He wagged a finger at her. "If I were merely
polite, I would murmur a few banalities. But *non,* Charlotte. It is time you faced your own ability and gave it
wing."

"It's really just a hobby," she mumbled, fiddling behind the desk, where she felt protected. "I didn't even
mean to take it this far. The gallery and the workshop, I
mean." She waved a hand vaguely. "It just sort of happened."

"And so will the rest. It is inevitable, *ma chère.* There
is no use hiding your light under a bushel. You are who
and what you are. An artist of incredible flair. Your ability—I should say genius, rather—is *indiscutable.*"

"Oh, rubbish," Charlotte scoffed, embarrassed, dig-
ging her hands deep into the pockets of her worn jeans
and flushing, flattered despite herself. He was, after all,
a Parisian designer, a man of taste, a connoisseur who
knew the world of fashion and jewelry back to front. And
since his arrival on the island two weeks earlier, he'd
seemed genuinely enchanted with her work.

"I can assure you that I will not be alone in my opinion. Once your work is known to the world, you'll soon
see that I am right." Armand nodded wisely, smoothed
his fingers gently over her arm, and smiled. "I found it
intriguing when our Oncle Eugène mentioned that you
had taken up designing with apparent success. I now pre-

dict a brilliant and well-deserved future ahead for you, *chère* Charlotte. In fact, I would be honored if you would consider showing your jewelry with my fall collection in Paris.''

"Gosh, I don't know." Charlotte slumped, gaze shifting as she remembered all the troubles in her life. "I don't really want a brilliant future, Armand. I just want to survive the present." Success and the spotlight didn't seem important compared to getting Genny walking properly again, or finding out what would happen to John's condition.

"Give yourself a chance," Armand murmured gently.

She shook herself, aware that she'd drifted off again into one of her daydreams, and plastered on a bright smile. "How about a quick coffee before my morning appointment?"

"Why not? To be in your company is always *un plaisir.*" Armand bowed gallantly and she laughed. He reminded her of a courtly Pink Panther. The walk, the talk, the tailored tweeds—even a walking stick and moleskin waistcoat, she noticed. He should have looked ludicrous, yet somehow Armand managed to carry it off.

She took his arm affectionately and turned to Moira. "Hold the fort for a little, will you, Mo? I'll be back in under an hour. And make sure you sell something to those Yanks," she added, grinning. "I've got all the new supplies to pay for, not to mention the leaking pipe in the loo."

"Peter's coming to deal with it later." Moira looked up from the accounts and smiled.

"Thank God for that. Come on, Armand. I'll treat you to one of those sticky green cakes at Rory's."

"*Mon Dieu,* no, I beg you." He shuddered.

"All right, just coffee then."

"*Merci*. But I shall stick to tea. A much safer bet. The coffee—if that is what it really is—" he rolled his eyes "—is undrinkable, *ma chère*."

"Oh, all right, be like that," Charlotte teased, yanking the wraithlike figure by the arm and out onto the street. "If you're not careful, I'll tell Rory what you said."

Armand's lips curved and he caught her eye. "A truly gorgeous young man," he murmured wistfully.

"And married, so hands off."

"Charlotte! As though *I* would mix with the common herd!"

"Ha!" She threw back her head and let out a rich laugh. "If Rory so much as gave you the time of day, you'd be up and running, and well you know it," she teased in a loud whisper as they entered the smoky haze of the Celtic Café. She spotted Rory, tall and muscled behind the counter, his long black hair tied back in a ponytail. Charlotte waved and sent him a critical glance. His bright blue eyes were indeed a riveting sight, but being a pal, she'd never thought much about them.

"Hello, Charlie." Rory came out from behind his post and gave her a whacking kiss on both cheeks that left Armand sighing. "So, did you finally finish the move? I can help you on Saturday if you've odd jobs needing done."

"Thanks. I've got most of it sorted out."

"How was Glasgow?" He quirked a heavy eyebrow at her.

"The same." She answered shortly, making for the table. Rory sighed, shrugged and wiped the table off with a damp cloth as Armand sat down. She caught Rory's piercing gaze and swallowed. He was an old friend, one who knew her well, knew all the ups and downs in her life over the past few years. But, like Moira and her mother, he was unable to understand why she stuck staunchly by John even after the abominable way he'd treated her. None of them understood, she reasoned, seating herself. How could they possibly realize that her troubles were of her own making, that she was to blame?

"You know where to find me if you need me," Rory murmured with a resigned shrug. "Cup of tea?"

"Two, please." She smiled gratefully, glad he'd dropped the subject. "By the way, Brad'll be here in a few days."

"Great. How's he doing?"

"Engaged to be married."

"You already told me that," Rory remarked dryly, sending her a penetrating look before returning behind the counter. The three had played together as kids and the friendship went back a long way.

"Not bad," Armand remarked, lifting his glasses and peering critically at the watercolors painted by a local artist gracing the wall. "For such a backward little village, there appears to be quite a *mouvement artistique* in this place."

"Mmm," Charlotte answered, mind wandering. She still had to go up to the castle and pick up the last remaining odds and ends.

"So, Bradley is expected within the next couple of days?" Armand remarked as Sheena, the waitress, placed the tea on the table.

"Day after tomorrow, I think. Thanks." She sent Sheena a smile.

"And you're sure that you will survive in that cottage?" Armand's lips pursed in distaste. "It seems very rural, *ma chère*. And quite abhorrent that Bradley should be expulsing you from the *château*."

"Armand, you know perfectly well Brad's not expulsing anyone," she exclaimed, exasperated. "This is none of his doing, much less his fault. The judge decided Strathaird's fate, not him. In fact, he begged Mummy and me to stay on," she added more patiently.

"Then why the move?" he asked, stirring a lump of brown sugar into the strong brew.

"Because," she said with a sigh, "like it or not, things are going to change. And I know I won't be able to handle it." She flexed her fingers nervously. "It wouldn't be fair to him or me, or the others involved. It's simply time to move on, Armand, and better to get it done before he arrives."

"Je suppose." Armand shrugged doubtfully and patted her arm. "You have much courage, *cousine.*"

"It's not as if I'm moving into a cave! The cottage has every modern convenience, hot water, a washing machine. You make it sound as if we're out on the street."

"The accommodations appear needlessly common to me." Armand sniffed.

"Well, you've never been inside, so you can't tell," Charlotte retorted. "Which reminds me, why don't you come over for dinner tomorrow night? That is, if you can bear to eat in such modest surroundings." She sent him a mischievous grin, then changed the subject and set about recapturing their former lighthearted mood.

When Armand returned from his visit with Charlotte, he was pleased to see that the library was quiet. The local ladies who cleaned Strathaird had finished their ritual morning vacuuming and were having coffee in the kitchen, and Penelope had left for the village. Armand took a deep breath, trying to quell the surge of anticipation. He'd already set one part of his plan in motion this morning, and here was an ideal opportunity to take the next step.

Leaving his jacket carefully folded on the sofa, he moved to the circular wooden ladder at the far side of the room. He would begin here, searching the entire collection shelf by shelf. It would require time and concentration, but he'd already waited so long and time was no longer on his side; he'd have to force himself to go slowly, be methodical. This might be his only chance. But what if he was wrong? he wondered with a sudden pang. He swallowed, throat tight, and tried not to think about it. There were other possibilities, he reminded himself quickly. If he did not find what he was looking for here among the books, then obviously his first deduction was correct. The answer would be where he'd always believed it was.

He glanced at the door, then mounted the steps carefully. He would begin with the French novels, so that if anyone questioned his actions he'd be able to justify the choice. Once they got used to seeing him fiddling in the library, nobody would think anything of it.

Half an hour later his search had yielded little. He passed a white linen handkerchief across his forehead and nervously wiped the perspiration, leaning his right hand on top of a pile of ancient volumes on a higher shelf. As he did so, his fingers met with an object on top of the books. Steadying himself carefully on the library steps, Armand pulled it carefully toward him, amazed when he beheld a small, silver-mounted pistol. He studied it, eyes narrowed. It was definitely of another age, small and elegant, designed perhaps for a woman. The butt was delicate and exquisitely inlaid with mother-of-pearl.

The muffled sound of voices emanating from the hall made him slip the pistol into his trouser pocket and hasten back down the steps, being careful not to trip. Grabbing a book, he ensconced himself once more in one of the leather armchairs before anyone entered the room.

Charlotte turned off the Land Rover's engine and stared for several moments at the castle's ancient austere facade, softened by her mother's terra-cotta pots, spilling pink and white hydrangeas over the shallow stone steps, and thought over what she and Armand had talked about earlier. A sigh escaped her. Paris and the thought of her jewelry parading down the catwalk on Armand's models was exciting, flattering and very hard not to dream about. It was a long time since she'd dreamed about anything, she realized suddenly. John's image flashed before her, making her feel immediately guilty, but she swept it aside, determined not to allow the dark cloud to descend upon her. And for the first time in years, she dared to peek into the future.

Biting her finger abstractedly, she stared at the castle walls without really seeing them. Was Armand right? Could her designs really open up a new avenue in her life? Lately it had seemed so bleak. She sat for a minute behind the wheel, pondering, caught between past, present and future. Following the soft orange glimmer caused by the setting sun bouncing off the glistening stained-glass windows like sparks off a live wire, she let out the breath she'd been holding. Maybe, just maybe, it was time to dare. Then she jumped out of the vehicle, pulled out the planters her mother had asked her to pick up at Haldane's Nursery in the village, and carried them up the steps, torn between the budding urge to take the plunge and the overwhelming guilt that just thinking of doing so caused her.

"Ah, there you are, darling," Penelope said, looking up and smiling as Charlotte entered the hall.

"Hello, Mum. Here's everything you asked for. I told them to put it on the bill," she said, thankful for the distraction.

"Thanks." Penelope frowned doubtfully. "Do you think we should do that, now that Brad..." Her voice trailed off as she gazed down at the plants.

"Don't be ridiculous, Mum! The plants are for Strathaird. Of course you must put them on the estate account," Charlotte replied, annoyed.

"Yes, I suppose you're right. But what if Sylvia doesn't like them? Perhaps I should have waited and let her choose them herself. She sent me an e-mail this morning."

"I don't give a damn what she likes," Charlotte mumbled crossly. "I'll set these in the pantry." They walked down the steps together and along the corridor to the pantry. Charlotte dropped the plants on the counter then moved to the sink and turned on the single tap to wash away the dirt from her hands. "What did she want, anyway?"

"Something to do with Brad and computer programs. She seems terribly efficient."

"Well, bully for her." Charlotte gave the tap a sharp twist and dried her hands on an old kitchen towel. "She'll jolly well have to adapt, Mum, if she's going to do a half-decent job here. If she thinks she can waft in and turn Strathaird into her fancy Park Avenue digs, she's got another think coming."

"Don't be horrid, Charlie, it's not like you." Penelope looked at her, surprised. "By the way, I had a call from Ambassador de la Fuente. He and the twins are arriving straight from Uruguay via somewhere I can't remember, on—'' she leaned over and picked up the agenda that was never far out of reach and slipped on her glasses ''—the fifteenth. I suppose they'll arrive here by helicopter.'' She glanced up, shoulders sagging slightly. ''I don't think I can cope with picking anyone up just now. Oh, and Brad phoned to say he's arriving on his own because Sylvia has some job or other she has to finish. She'll be following in due course.''

''Good. The longer she stays away the better,'' Charlotte muttered, swinging a leg from her perch on the windowsill.

''Charlie, do stop being petty and childish. There's nothing wrong with the poor girl. In fact, the one time I met her she seemed perfectly charming. You know very well that it's our duty to make her feel at home and help her take over. Daddy would have expected no less of us.''

''Oh no, Mummy, not today, please.'' Charlotte cast her eyes heavenwards. Jumping down from the ledge, she dragged a chair forward and straddled it. ''I'm finished up at the cottage, by the way. Oh, and Armand was over at the gallery,'' she added casually.

''I know. He seems genuinely taken with your work.'' Penelope sent her daughter an encouraging smile, saw clouds hovering and sighed. Charlotte was like a barometer, up and down, that temperamental artistic nature so difficult to fathom.

''Armand wants to exhibit my stuff with his autumn collection,'' she burst in a rush.

''In Paris? That's awfully flattering.'' Penelope laid down the flowers she was holding with a surprised smile.

Charlotte fidgeted. ''Do you think it's a good idea, Mum? I mean it's not as if I have that many pieces ready and it would take time to make the others, and what with

Genny and John and one thing and another I...'' Her voice trailed off.

"Now, don't start making excuses," Penelope exclaimed, exasperated. "It's a wonderful opportunity and you must avail yourself of it. You've more than enough time and I'm sure Moira will pitch in to make whatever you need."

"I suppose so." Charlotte gave a listless shrug, then grinned despite herself. "It would be incredible if my jewelry actually took on, wouldn't it?"

"Darling, of course it would. And I don't see why it shouldn't. Look at all you've already sold. People love it. You have such wonderful taste and talent."

"You're only saying that because you're my mother."

"Rubbish," Penelope dismissed. "I say a lot of things because I'm your mother, but I wouldn't lead you to spend your time and effort on something I didn't think was worthwhile."

"I suppose not."

"Charlotte, look at yourself," Penelope exclaimed, moving into the center of the room and wiping her hands on her jeans. "You're thirty-four years old. You've spent the better part of your adult life in the clutches of a man whose treated you worse than the dirt under his feet—"

"This has nothing to do with John," Charlotte rejoined defensively.

"It has everything to do with him. With all he's stopped you from becoming, thanks to his threats and his selfish, egocentric behavior," she answered, unable to disguise her bitterness. "I don't say it's all his fault," she countered, clasping her hands. "Perhaps you should have divorced him long before this. But frankly, I don't think you stood a chance."

"That's ridiculous, Mummy," Charlotte cried, rising

so quickly she overturned the chair. "John needs me. And even if he doesn't, I can't just walk out on him in the state he's in. It wouldn't be humane."

"Was the way he treated you when he was conscious humane?" Penelope asked bitterly. "Was slapping you around when he didn't get exactly what he wanted, or flaunting his mistresses in the papers, humane? I want you to wake up and take charge of your own life, Charlotte. I find it incredible that despite all he's done to you, all you've gone through over the years, you're still determined to go on catering to him. Is that really what you want, or is it just easier than facing reality?"

"Stop it," Charlotte cried, flushing indignantly. The truth of her mother's words stung. "What has this got to do with Armand and the jewelry and Paris? I merely asked if you thought it was a good idea and look where it's got me." She threw up her hands. "I can't say anything but you throw my marriage in my face." Tears burned and she clenched her fists, determined not to give way.

Penelope sighed and dropped her hands to her sides. "I'm sorry, darling. You're right. It's not my affair and I shouldn't be telling you how to lead your life. I just pray that you won't be obliged to see your child's life being shredded to bits by some unscrupulous—" She stopped herself, let out a sigh and mustered a smile. "Forget it, darling. Coming back to Armand and the jewelry, I really think you should go ahead."

Charlotte nodded, and bent down to pick up the chair. "By the way, Armand thinks the cottage is the pits," she said in an attempt at humor.

"Armand is hardly a reference," Penelope remarked, laughing, moving the plants to the floor, relieved Charlotte hadn't flounced out in anger. "As far as he's concerned, anything short of the 16ième arrondissement is the slums. God only knows what he sees in Skye to keep him here for so long. I would have thought he'd be bored stiff by now, yet according to Mrs. McKinnon, he was ensconced in the library this morning, sifting through the French book collection. He asked if it was all right to stay until Oncle Eugène arrives,'' she added in a hollow voice. "Of course, I had to say yes, but you can imagine how thrilled I am!'' She sighed guiltily and exchanged a long-suffering look with her daughter. "The Cardinal will be here at the beginning of August. I'm quite surprised he's decided to make the trip at his age and after all these years. That means another three whole weeks of Armand,'' she added gloomily. "I must admit that my heart sank at the thought of entertaining him all that time.''

"Stop worrying, Mum, Armand's all right. I'll take him off your hands.''

"Good.'' Penelope gave her a conspiratorial wink. "I know I'm being perfectly horrid, but there are times...''

"You're not. I think you're wonderful, the way you put up with us all. Especially me,'' she said ruefully, taking her mother's hand and giving it a squeeze. "I'll be off now. As for Armand,'' she added airily, pausing at the door with a mischievous grin, "he's probably just soaking up atmosphere for a Scottish-inspired clothing collection.'' She giggled and rolled her eyes. "Just imagine, Mummy, Mrs. P. could well be next autumn's fashion icon.''

"Good Lord, what a ghastly thought!'' Penelope gasped in feigned horror. "Off with you, before you come up with any other dreadful notions. You'll be late picking up Genny unless you dash. And, darling—'' she became suddenly serious once more as her gaze met

Charlotte's "—I really would give Armand's proposal some serious thought, if I were you. It's not every day a chance like this crosses one's path. And you're very good at what you do."

Charlotte hesitated then smiled. "Okay, Mummy, I will."

"Promise?"

"Promise."

They hugged and Charlotte went on her way. Though troubled by her mother's outburst, she also welcomed her encouragement. It'd been so long since she'd thought of anything more ambitious than simply surviving each day. But the truth was she'd been longing for something to give her focus, something to help her shake the feeling that she was standing in quicksand, unable to make a move for fear she'd sink deeper.

Perhaps Mummy was right, she reflected as she climbed back into the Land Rover. Maybe she should seriously consider Armand's offer after all.

3

As the powerful Aston Martin he'd picked up in Glasgow traveled the last few miles of the winding island road, flanked by sea on the one hand and heather-bathed moors on the other, Brad allowed himself to enjoy the luxury of the solitary freedom, the purr of the engine and the ride. Yet, as the journey ended and he neared Strathaird, he felt compelled to slow down and take stock of his surroundings. The car slowed to a crawl, and he reflected not for the first time on how his grandfather's extraordinary life had shaped every step of his own existence. Well, perhaps not every step, but quite a few. He drove thoughtfully, aware that he didn't resent the fact that much of his life had been decided for him, for he'd accepted it at a very young age as part of his destiny. Sometimes though, of late especially, he had felt the sudden urge to rip off the straitjacket, cut loose and make his own choices. A childish fantasy, he acknowledged, ruefully, for this latest inheritance was Dex's final legacy, and Brad knew that, as always, he'd shoulder it and try to do a good job.

Shouldering responsibilities was something he prided himself on, he acknowledged as the car bumped over a rough patch of potted tarmac. He'd never questioned his role as the Harcourts heir and had worked tirelessly for years learning the business, guided by his grandfather and Uncle David, gradually taking on more and more responsibility. When his father and Dolores were killed in a plane crash eight years ago, he'd never hesitated in assuming the role of surrogate father to his two seven-year-old half brothers. It was only when Colin had died and his grandfather had revealed that his true identity was not Dexter Ward, but Gavin MacLeod of Strathaird, had Brad wondered if fate might possibly have made some grave mistake.

The car purred round the last bend in the narrow bumpy road, bringing him face-to-face with Strathaird Castle, standing high above the bluff. His pulse beat faster and he edged off the road, bringing the vehicle to a halt on a patch of windswept grass. His hands dropped from the wheel and he gazed up, mind and heart alive with memories, some sweet, some less so. Getting out, he stretched his legs, gaze still fixed on the castle. Now, because of ancient laws, created centuries earlier to preserve property and the homestead, Strathaird had finally fallen…to him.

Although he felt he'd inherited the property unjustly, it was a moot point as far as the courts were concerned. His solicitors had argued that the castle and its lands rightfully belonged to Charlotte and Penelope, but the law couldn't see past Dex's revelation that Brad was the true heir.

Shading his eyes, he felt a sudden shiver as he watched a flag in the east turret unfurl with noble arrogance over the ramparts, the dying sun caressing the mullioned windows. He stood a while, absorbing the majesty, sheer power and rugged sense of permanence, and for the first time accepted that he had a place here. A strange, inexplicable primal response gripped him, as if all at once the MacLeod blood coursing in his veins could somehow sense that it was nearing home.

He blinked, smiled and looked away. He must be really overtired to be imagining such things. He'd never experienced any particular connection to the place on past visits, so why now?

Shoving his hands deep into the pockets of his jeans, he turned his thoughts to his grandfather, that strange elusive figure who had given up his true identity as Gavin MacLeod after World War I, and for seventy years, assumed the identity of Dexter Ward. It was all by chance, Brad reflected, that his grandfather had found himself recruited by the New York Sixty-ninth in 1918.

But fate had finally caught up with Gavin and changed all their lives. Could it be, as Granny Flora had believed, the MacLeods claiming of their own back to the fold? He shrugged, closed his eyes and enjoyed the warm, scented summer breeze licking his face and mussing his hair. Enough of the past, he decided, peering once more at the castle. It was time now to focus on the present and all that needed to be done. Without question, Strathaird could prove his most challenging duty to date. But he wasn't daunted. Quite the opposite. He was suddenly aware that the urge to shed his shackles—a sensation he'd felt all too acutely in recent months—was absent as he approached the bluff and stared down into the violet-gray waters lapping the rocks. They reminded him of something. He frowned. The color was the same as Charlotte's eyes, gentle yet stormy. Gone was the growling swell of autumn and winter's harsh, bleak, angry hiss. Instead, expectation flowed, as though the waters were eyeing him speculatively, like the locals whose lives he was about to touch, waiting to see for themselves how the new laird, a foreigner to whom this land and sea meant little, would fare before passing judgment.

He stooped, tweaked a sprig of heather and twiddled it absently between his thumb and index finger. Just how much of his being was he willing to invest in Strathaird? he asked himself as he walked thoughtfully back to the car. Or, more likely, just how much would Strathaird extract?

He settled once more behind the wheel and resumed the climb up to the castle. As he crested the last hillock, he reflected on how little he knew about running a Scottish estate. Thank God for Charlotte and Penelope. They both played a key role in the everyday operation of the place, and would help make up for the fact that the new laird planned to be an absentee landowner.

As the Aston Martin hugged the last bend, he glanced at his watch. He should have phoned to warn Aunt Penn that he'd decided to come to Strathaird straightaway, rather than spend the night in Glasgow as he'd planned. But the temptation to hit the road, cell phone off and with no appointments to rush to, had won. He'd even lingered on the banks of Loch Lomond, and felt the eerie chill of the valley of Glencoe.

Coasting up the driveway, bordered by fields dotted with peacefully munching sheep and grazing highland cattle, oblivious to the fact that they now had a new owner, he experienced renewed relief that his initial encounter with Strathaird and its tenants was taking place on his own.

Reaching the castle, he circled the flower bed, heard the familiar scrunch of gravel under the tires and came to a standstill in front of the massive oak doors, aware that a new part of his life was about to begin.

He stood at the foot of the shallow steps, caught sight of the view and paused. The last rays of dying sun flirted languorously on the surf. In the distance, small fishing craft bobbed gently into harbor while twilight lingered in the wings. To his left, several crofters' cottages nestled at the foot of the hills. Farther up the dirt road, a single thatched cottage stood by itself among a haze of purple heather. After the rush of New York, it was disconcerting to think that year after year, season after season, little changed in this remote part of the world.

He walked up the steps, about to knock on the huge, recessed oak doors, when he realized that since the evening was so fine, the family was probably having drinks outside on the lawn.

Making his way around the west face, past the herb garden and the conservatory, he opened the gate that led to the lawn, the sudden urge to see Charlotte making him hurry. He would surprise her by giving that long titian mane a good tug. Then, after she'd squealed in surprise, he'd take her in his arms and give her a major hug.

He reached the lawn. Two figures sat in white wicker chairs next to the summerhouse. Neither was Charlotte.

"My goodness, Brad!" Penelope shrieked, jumping up and stretching out her hands in welcome. "We weren't expecting you until tomorrow." Penelope reached up and kissed him affectionately.

"Sorry, Aunt Penn. I should've called. But I lost track of time."

"You drove?" she asked, quirking a surprised eyebrow.

"Yeah. I picked up a car in Glasgow and ambled on up."

"Good. You probably needed the break," she said with her usual insight. "I hope you enjoyed the drive."

"I did. It gave me some much-needed time to think."
He smiled down at her. She was still as attractive and
lovely as ever. He took her arm. "I hope this isn't too
much trouble, Aunt Penn."

"Don't be ridiculous. This is your home now, Brad,"
she said, making him cringe. He didn't want her to think
of Strathaird as no longer hers.

She led him to the table where he immediately recognized Armand de la Vallière, rising to greet him.

"Bradley. It's been a long time. *Quel plaisir.*"

Armand shook hands warmly. Brad wished he could
feel the same enthusiasm. Armand was someone he'd
never quite figured out and whom he was ashamed to say
irritated him for no reason in particular.

"Have a drink." Penelope pointed to the tray where a
bottle of wine stood chilling in an ice bucket.

"Love one. Where's Charlie?" he asked casually,
looking around, expecting to see her walk out any minute, through the French doors and down the steps of the
castle's south face.

"Charlotte's not going to be here this evening, I'm
afraid," Penelope replied, pouring the wine.

Armand shook his head. "Charlotte is very obstinate."
He tut-tutted between sips. "This sudden necessity
to—"

"Have a life of her own," Penelope interrupted, handing Brad the glass. "Charlotte needs to get her life organized," she added, putting an end to the matter. "Now,
sit down and tell me all about New York and the twins,
I can't wait to see them. They must have grown so much
this year. Oh, and Sylvia, of course."

"The twins are doing fine," Brad responded easily,
wondering what Penelope meant about Charlotte and why
she seemed reluctant to pursue the subject. "They're hav-

ing a blast in Uruguay. Diego's hacienda is quite something.''

"So I hear. I'm so glad he's decided to come. It may do him good to get away."

"Definitely. I threatened to kidnap the twins if he didn't. He rarely leaves home now except to go to his house in Switzerland."

"I know. It's so sad. But understandable, after losing his wife and daughter one after the other," she murmured, her limpid blue eyes reflecting her own loss.

Seeing Armand pout, Brad made a conscious effort to draw him out of the doldrums that Penelope's interruption appeared to have caused.

"How are the collections coming along?" He took a sip of wine and leaned back in the chair, masking his disappointment at Charlotte's absence.

"Very well, very well indeed. In fact," Armand purred with a conspiratorial wink, "Charlotte and I are hatching plans for the autumn."

"Really?" Penelope pretended to look surprised.

"Yes, *chère* Penelope." He pronounced her name *penne-Lop,* making it sound like a pasta dish. Brad smothered a smile, knowing how much it irritated her. "I have proposed to Charlotte that she exhibit her pieces with my fall—as you Americans say—collection." Armand pronounced the words like a reporter announcing breaking news.

"That's terribly generous of you, Armand," Penelope exclaimed. "And so exciting. She must be thrilled."

He gave a modest smile. "Her talent is exceptional and should not remain hidden from the world. Charlotte is a great artist. Her work is inspired by the great master Sylvain de Rothberg—my uncle by marriage, you will recall. It has a similar feel."

"Really," Penelope murmured politely. Brad caught her quick, astonished glance. Armand was prone to name-dropping and was always underlining his relationship to the la Vallières, his late father's family, not to mention the tenuous one to the Rothbergs. Recalling the sad circumstances of Armand's tragic youth, Brad decided the impulse to embroider his family history was understandable. "I never realized she was designing jewelry seriously," he remarked.

"Neither did I until about four months ago, when she decided to open a gallery and workshop in the village. People seem to like her work, and I think it's perfectly lovely. But of course, I might be prejudiced." Penelope smiled apologetically.

"I'll bet Charlie's great at it," Brad said. "She's always had talent, but she just never bothered to tap into it or let it flourish into anything concrete."

"Believe me, she has now, *mon cher*," Armand said with a wise nod.

"I'm awfully glad you think so, Armand. Perhaps it'll keep her mind off some of her other worries." Penelope sighed and took a sip of wine, then tucked a stray lock behind her ear.

"How's John?" Brad asked in a neutral voice. He'd schooled himself to have no feelings, negative or otherwise, regarding Charlotte's comatose husband.

"Just the same, I'm afraid."

"Why do they not remove the life support?" Armand raised a disdainful brow. "To think of such a handsome man deteriorating into mediocrity. *Quelle horreur!*"

"It's not like he has much choice," Brad commented dryly.

"I would much rather pull the plug and be remembered as my true self." Armand shuddered delicately, the thought of John's movie-star looks withering away apparently too much to bear.

Brad smothered his irritation, wondering how long it would be before he got Aunt Penn to himself. Not a chance before dinner, he figured, casting her an inquiring glance all the same.

Picking up on it, Penelope smiled brightly. "Armand, will you excuse us while I show Brad to his room? I'm sure you must want to get settled and freshen up before dinner." She rose and Brad followed suit, blessing her for her quick-wittedness.

"I'm afraid poor Armand's a bit of a bore," she murmured once they were out of earshot and mounting the steps. "I don't know how I'm going to keep him entertained until the Cardinal arrives," she added as they went inside.

"Oncle Eugène's coming?" Brad asked, surprised.

"Yes, I thought you knew. I was very surprised he wanted to make the trip. After all, he's getting on."

"I hope it won't be too much for him," he agreed. "Say, what can an inveterate urbanite like Armand possibly find to keep him in Skye, I wonder?"

"I've been asking myself that same question ever since he stepped foot on the island." Penelope grimaced, climbing the last steps. "At first he said he was exhausted and needed a rest from Paris and the fashion world. Now he seems enthralled by Charlotte's work." She shrugged. "If it keeps him busy and she doesn't mind, then all the better."

"Speaking of Charlotte, when will she be back?" Brad asked, following his aunt indoors.

"You mean tonight?" Penelope's eyes moved uncomfortably and Brad frowned.

"Yes. Shouldn't she be home soon?"

"Normally, yes." She hesitated, looked away.

"Normally? What's up, Aunt Penn?" He frowned, stared at her, half serious, half amused.

"Charlie didn't tell you?" she responded, forehead creasing.

"Tell me what? We haven't talked in a while."

"I see." She sent him a quick, speculative glance then continued. "The fact is, Charlotte's left the castle and moved into Rose Cottage." She clasped her hands neatly at her waist. "I'm surprised she didn't call you to explain."

"Moved out of Strathaird?" he exclaimed, unbelieving. They were in the Great Hall, and he stopped dead at the foot of the oak staircase and stared at her. Charlie wouldn't just up and go.

"Yes. You see, she felt that it would be better—that's to say, she thought that perhaps with the changes..." Penelope's voice drifted off. Brad's expression darkened and he flexed his fingers.

"What changes? What on earth got into her head?" he asked uncomprehendingly. "It's ridiculous. This is her home. It doesn't make sense."

"Of course it does," Penelope replied briskly. "Charlotte is used to having her own space. You and Sylvia will need your own legroom, too. Plus, I think she needs the change."

"That's neither here nor there," he murmured dismissively, certain this was not the reason for Charlotte's sudden departure.

"By the way, some sort of gym apparatus arrived." Penelope pointed to two large crates at the side of the hall.

Brad followed her finger, still preoccupied with Charlotte's departure. "I didn't order any workout equipment," he said.

"Well, no. I think Sylvia did. Very sensible of her," she added quickly. "I'm sure she wants to keep up her exercise routine once she's here. She has such a lovely figure."

Brad scowled at the boxes as if they were in some way to blame. "I still fail to see what a treadmill has to do with Charlotte's decision to move."

"It wasn't the actual treadmill, Brad, but the realization of just how much is going to change. Let's face it," she added, laying a hand gently on his arm, "Strathaird is yours now and you have to be free to make it into what you want, just as every generation has in the past. I think Charlotte feels—rightly, I might add—that it would be difficult for her to see everything she's always known and taken for granted being transformed—and not just painful for her, but perhaps difficult for you and Sylvia too. After all, Brad, we can't all go on living in the past, or under the same roof."

"Why not?" He frowned, raising his hands in a gesture of incomprehension. "This is her home. I've always told you I don't want anything to change. I want you both to go on living here as you always have." He looked down at her, angry and hurt. "Charlie knows damn well I would never expect her or want her to be anywhere but here."

"I'm well aware of that, Brad dear, and so is she. But think about it," Penelope urged reasonably. "Sylvia is going to become Lady MacLeod. It's only right and natural that she should take over certain duties that up until now have been mine, and in some measure, Charlotte's. She should have the freedom to do so in her own manner. Believe me, it's much better this way."

"Like hell it is. It's an absurd decision and she must come straight back. Doesn't she ever use her brain?" he exclaimed, pacing the hall, ignoring Aunt Penn's arguments and suppressing his growing frustration. "Christ, you'd think after all these years and all she's been through, she'd have gotten some sense into that stubborn redhead of hers. And what about Genny?" he added. "Has Charlotte stopped to think of her?" He forced himself to keep his voice low and not give full vent to his feelings.

"Of course she has. And you know, Brad, that's another point. Soon you'll be married. You and Sylvia will probably be starting your own family—"

"Sylvia and I aren't planning on having kids," he interjected dismissively.

"Oh…" Penelope stopped, taken aback.

"Our lives are too busy, plus we already have the twins."

"Yes. I suppose—I didn't realize."

"Why don't you tell me where she is, Aunt Penn," he interrupted, returning to the subject at hand. "I'll talk to her and get this mess straightened out right away."

"It's not a mess, Brad, merely a fact of life," Penelope sighed, hand dropping from his arm. "She's at Rose Cottage, about half a mile up the road. But I'm warning you, her mind's made up. The cottage is all on one floor, so in a way that will be an advantage for Genny," she ended lamely.

"Advantage, my ass," he muttered under his breath.

"You can go and talk to her," Penelope murmured doubtfully, "but I don't think you'll get very far."

"We'll see," he said darkly. "Don't hold dinner for me, Aunt Penn. Please make my excuses to Armand. I'm going over there right now."

Penelope watched, concerned, as he took the front steps two at a time, jumped into a spiffy silver Aston Martin and roared down the driveway, raising dust. She was surprised that he'd taken Charlotte's departure so much to heart. After all, she'd only moved half a mile up the road.

With a resigned shrug, she turned, switched off the hall lights, and wandered back through the lurking shadows, remembering how attentive to her own children Brad had always been. With another sigh, she recalled the bantering, the tennis parties, the picnics in Dordogne and the summers Brad, Colin and Charlotte had spent clambering over the rocks and on the shore. Of course, he'd been several years their elder, which had represented a lot when he became a teenager and they were still children. Even so, he'd always had time for them and always cared.

She paused, gazing over the lawn to where Armand sat in the wicker chair sipping his wine, and wondered what would have happened all those years ago if Charlotte hadn't become pregnant and married John.

Silly to conjecture, she reflected, giving herself a little shake before proceeding down the steps. Charlotte and Brad were grown-ups now. Each had their lives to get on with and the sooner Brad realized that, the better. She herself was very well aware of what lay ahead, the responsibilities he and Sylvia would be assuming. The same ones she was relinquishing.

She stepped onto the lawn glancing sadly at the rose garden to her left. She would miss tending it, just as she'd miss the autumn mists, the churning gray waters that had become such a part of her over the years. But that was life, and part of what happened in families like theirs. She smiled as she stepped over the grass. Brad's insistence that they stay on at the castle was touching. Of course, being a man, he couldn't understand how impossible it would be for them all to coexist under the same roof.

It was getting chillier, the evening closing in fast, and she pulled the heather-colored cardigan closer. Composing her features, she approached Armand, seated with his back to her, facing the sea. The more she thought about it, the more she realized Charlotte had done the right thing by moving out. It was time that she, too, begin making plans for the future. Plastering on a neutral smile, she sat down to finish her wine. What conversational subjects could she possibly introduce to keep Armand entertained throughout dinner? she asked herself. Perhaps mentioning the Rothbergs, whom he loved to talk about, would be a good way of whiling away the evening.

4

Brad's temper rarely got the better of him, but Charlotte certainly had a knack for provoking it. She hadn't done so for several years, he acknowledged as the car swerved up the rutted, narrow earth track that led to Rose Cottage. But as he approached the pretty, whitewashed dwelling, with its bright blue shutters and quaint thatched roof, he made a mental catalog of all the other times she'd tried his patience. Like when, at age seventeen, she'd posed nude for a London fashion photographer. Or her hasty, ill-considered decision to marry John Drummond. He recalled grimly how he'd watched her walk down the aisle. He'd been furious and heartbroken in equal measure.

He brought the car to an abrupt stop, noticing her muddy Land Rover drawn up on the far side of the riotous flower beds, satisfied there would be no escape for her. Slamming the door of the Aston Martin, he stalked up the garden path, then slowed, distracted by the cheerful array of roses, perennials, hyacinths and lilacs planted with little regard to order.

All at once, he wondered if there was a deeper reason for Charlotte's sudden decision to seek a new home. His eyes narrowed as he stared at the sparkling, frog-shaped brass knocker perched arrogantly on the freshly painted blue door, and hesitated. Could he have misjudged the situation? At the sound of the wind chime he'd given her years ago tinkling merrily above the door, his lips twitched despite his irritation. He shook his head and knocked. By the time he'd reached up automatically to secure the birdhouse tottering perilously under the porch roof, a smile hovered. It was impossible to stay angry with Charlie for long, he reflected ruefully, dragging his fingers impatiently through his hair while he waited for the door to open. Strains of New Age music drifted through the open window and for a moment he was tempted to enter the cottage in a less orthodox fashion.

Even as he debated climbing in the window, the door opened. Charlotte, dressed in worn stonewashed jeans and her usual white T-shirt that displayed her slim midriff, a half-munched apple suspended in her right hand, stared at him through translucent violet eyes.

"What the hell did you think you were doing, moving out of the castle?" he asked before he could stop himself.

"Whoa!" Charlotte took a hasty step back, her flash of pleasure at seeing him dampened by the fact he was clearly in a flaming temper.

"Why, Charlie?"

As the bright blue eyes pinned hers, a slow flush flooded her cheeks. This was going to be more difficult than she'd anticipated, she realized, wishing her pulse would stop racing. But it was just Brad, after all, and she knew how to manage him. She had every right to move wherever she wanted and make a home of her own. Mustering a smile, she tossed her hair back and inspected the apple thoughtfully to buy time.

"I want an answer, Charlotte," Brad muttered, eyes narrowed. "And I want it now."

"Brad, don't get all bossy on me, I don't owe you any explanations. I can live wherever I want. And right now, that happens to be here."

"Did I make myself clear?" His tone was measured.

"Perfectly," she responded, standing her ground and trying to look a lot more composed than she felt. Then, seeing his eyes narrow dangerously, she gave in and dropped her arm, wishing her pulse would calm down. "Okay, okay, don't get all uptight. I'll tell you why I moved."

"This had better be darn good. Why?"

"Because Strathaird's yours now and I need my own place." She tried to sound reasonable and casual as she looked beyond his shoulder with a nonchalance she was far from feeling.

"That's bull," he shot back, taking a step forward. "Strathaird's your home. It always has been and will be for as long as you choose. I never intended for you to leave."

"I'm well aware of that, but I decided to go anyway." She gave him a bright, sassy smile and bit into the apple.

"Charlie, don't push me." There was an edge to his voice and his eyes remained dangerously alight. "I want you out of here and back home by tomorrow, is that clear?"

"No." Her own temper flashed at his autocratic attitude. Did he think she was still an irresponsible child who could be told what to do? "Who the hell do you think you are, barging into my home and dictating how I lead my life? I'll do what I like, when I like, and I'll thank you to mind your own business."

They measured one another in the tense silence, then he drew back, crammed his hands in his pockets and stared at her hard. "Okay, fine. Be that way. But I'll tell you something, Charlotte, you're darn selfish."

"Me? Selfish?" she spluttered.

"Selfish," he asserted, nodding slowly. "Did you stop for one moment to think of Genny when you decided to grab your stuff and come to this godforsaken hole? Or Aunt Penn? Or—"

"Oh, do shut up and stop being ridiculous, Brad," she exclaimed, irritated. "Of course I thought of Genny."

"No, you didn't. As usual, you let your pride get the better of you."

"As I already pointed out, what I do and where I live are none of your damn business. And anyway, living here will be good for Genny. The castle's just a fantasy existence," she said, annoyed she was justifying herself. Trust Brad to pinpoint her one real doubt about her decision. That was the trouble with people who'd known you all your life—they were impossible to fool.

"Coming from someone with your past lifestyle, that hardly flies," he responded witheringly. "Charlotte, grow up, for Christ's sake. Understand that you can't drag that kid from pillar to post like a gypsy. Strathaird's as much her home as yours." He eyed her in the same superior way he used to when they were adolescents, leaving her temper sizzling once more.

"I'll not have you dictating to me," she snapped, the physical and emotional exhaustion of the move coming down on her like a pile of bricks. She stamped her foot angrily on the front step. Her amethyst eyes flashed and the apple core flew over his shoulder into the flower bed. "Go boss Sylvia around, maybe she likes the macho approach. I, for one, can do without you telling me what I should or shouldn't be doing."

"Charlie, you're too old for a tantrum," he retorted, taunting her further.

"I'm not having a tantrum," she said through gritted teeth. "I'm trying to make you understand that I'm not seventeen anymore."

"Well, you've an odd way of going about it."

"Oh, stop being prissy, Brad. It doesn't suit you. I may not be picture-perfect like you, but then, we can't all be faultless examples of duty and devotion, can we?"

"You're doing a pretty good job, from all I gather," he remarked, watching her from under hooded lids as he leaned up against the cottage wall. "Still jumping to attention whenever your husband flickers an eyelid?"

"How dare you," she hissed, torn between tears and fury. "What right have you to come here and insult me? It's my life. If I want to be miserable, then it's my problem, okay?"

"No. It's not okay." He took a quick step forward. "Damn it, Charlie." He grabbed her shoulders and gave her a shake. Their eyes met and locked and she shivered involuntarily. "Why didn't you have the balls to tell me you were leaving?"

A flush crept back into her cheeks and her temper slowly abated. She knew she should have called and warned him. She had lifted the phone countless times, then thought better of it, afraid of his reaction. And apparently she'd been right.

She looked down and bit her lip, eyes softening. "I suppose I should have told you. But it really isn't a big deal," she conceded. "You can't expect everyone to comply with everything you want. Life just isn't like that." God, it was good to see him again, she realized as his arms slipped from her shoulders to around her waist. "Don't be cross, Brad, please?" she said in a more gentle tone, looking up at him through thick dark lashes. Her hand slipped to his cheek. "Come in and have a drink, there's no reason for all the fuss." In a rush of affection, she flung her arms around his neck.

He stood, unyielding, then despite his misgivings held her close, temper disappearing when she nestled her head into the crook of his neck. "It's so good to have you back," she whispered.

"It's good to be back," he murmured, breathing the familiar, tantalizing scent of her freshly washed hair, a mix of sea and wildflowers. "But it'd be a darn sight better if you hadn't taken this crazy step. Why do you always have to be so drastic, Charlie?" His fingers dipped unconsciously into her glorious hair, and automatically he began gently massaging the back of her neck.

"Do we have to keep on talking about me?" she asked, the feel of his hand making her want to sink against him, close her eyes and forget all her worries. Instead, she pulled back, hands looped around his neck, and squinted up at him. "Truce, please?" She dropped a friendly peck on his right cheek. "In time you'll understand, Brad. Believe me, it's for the best. Now let me show you the cottage." She disengaged herself and grabbed his hand, leading him through the tiny hall and into the low-ceilinged living room.

"It's pretty small," he said grudgingly, noting the skillful trompe l'oeil on the living-room wall, the tasteful flower arrangements, the hodgepodge of prints and paintings, photographs, ceramics and silver. "Not exactly your usual style."

"Small but nice, don't you think?" She gestured to the walls. "I painted the place myself. I'm terribly proud of it, so don't you dare be rude. And look—" she pointed to the mantelpiece "—I've even got you stuck up there. Now come on, let's have a drink and celebrate." She smiled mischievously. "I've got a bottle of your favorite Sancerre in the fridge."

"What are we celebrating?" he asked suspiciously, following her into the diminutive kitchen, pleasantly surprised by the aromatic scent of herbs, and the bright terracotta walls. Stopping in the doorway he cocked a curious eyebrow at the cooker. "Charlotte Drummond, don't tell me you're actually cooking food?"

"Absolutely. Stay for dinner and you'll see what a fine cook I've turned into." She twirled, sent him a roguish grin and dipped a long wooden spoon into a large copper casserole.

Brad eyed her thoughtfully, all five-foot-seven of her, slim and lovely, that heart-shaped face and huge violet eyes still as expressively haunting. Yet something indefinable had changed, something that left him feeling strangely disconcerted. It was as though she was desperately determined to master that wild tempestuous nature she'd displayed moments earlier, and rein in her natural instincts. He gave her another critical glance. If anything, she was more beautiful than he remembered, except for the deep sadness that hovered close to the surface in those huge violet pools. That she couldn't hide from him, however hard she tried.

"Open the wine, will you?" She was blabbering now, inspecting pots, adding salt and keeping up a flow of inconsequential conversation.

"Where is it?" He moved inside the kitchen, filling it with his presence.

"Fridge, top shelf," she mumbled, licking the wooden spoon. "Mmm. I hope you like it." She dipped the spoon straight back in the casserole, and Brad winced, watching amused, as she carefully added a pinch of pepper, stirred, then tasted it once more. "Ah! That's better."

He stepped over to the old fridge covered with Save-the-Whales and Greenpeace stickers, removed the bottle of Sancerre from the fridge and cast it an approving glance. Noticing a corkscrew hanging strategically on the wall, he set to work.

"I'll have a glass of wine with you," he remarked, "but that won't stop us from having a talk, Charlie."

"Of course." She smiled brightly across the newly set Mexican-tile floor that Rory had put in three days earlier, confident she was in control. "It's about time we caught up. It's been too long." She concentrated once more on the casserole as though her life depended on it. The kitchen seemed strangely confined all at once, making it hard to breathe. "Hungry?" she threw over her shoulder.

"Sure smells good." He handed her a glass, then leaned against the counter, enjoying the view, surprised to see how at home she was in the tiny kitchen, amid her herbs and her pots and pans. Not at all the way he'd imagined or seen her before.

"It's cassoulet," she stated proudly, turning down the heat. "A new recipe Armand gave me. He got it from a famous restaurant near Toulouse."

"Armand cooks?" He raised his glass then took a slow sip.

"Of course, he's French."

"Right, I forgot. By the way, what's he doing here?"

"Taking a break, having a holiday." She stirred carefully. "Pass me the herbes de Provence, will you? No, not that jar, the other one." She pointed to his left.

Brad handed her a stone jar and watched, fascinated, as she added a studied pinch. "That's about right. Here, try it." She thrust the wooden spoon at him to taste.

"Mmm. Good stuff." He gave the spoon an extra lick.

"Don't be disgusting." She grabbed it back, laughing. "Stay for dinner, please?" She tilted her head and familiar dimples peeked out at him. "Genny's at her friend Lucy's again tonight, so we'll be on our own. We can have a nice long chat."

It was a deliciously tempting offer and impossible to refuse. "I'd better call Aunt Penn. I left in somewhat of a hurry."

"You mean you stormed out." Her eyes narrowed in amusement. Oh, how well they knew one another and how impossible it was to stay distant for long. "Don't worry about Mum, she won't mind." Charlotte turned to the sink and began tossing the salad. "I'm planning to grow my own vegetables," she remarked, picking up a gratin of mixed veggies and expertly popping it into the oven. Despite the confidence in her actions, Brad got the impression of a different Charlotte than the one he'd known, a Charlotte desperately seeking solace and security.

"I'm so glad you're back, Brad," she said quietly, taking out a loaf of bread and placing it on the cutting board.

"Then why the move?" he asked gently, eyes meeting hers over the breadboard.

"Nothing personal, it's just time to move on." Her face shuttered once more as she began slicing. "Your and Sylvia's arrival merely moved it up a bit. Ouch!" she exclaimed angrily when the knife nicked her.

"Let me do that." He put down his glass, took the knife from her and gently inspected her finger.

"So stupid," she exclaimed, but he heard the wobble in her voice, and his eyes flew from her bleeding finger to the tears hovering on her lower lashes.

"Oh, baby." He drew her into his arms and soothed her, brushed a thumb over her cheek, his lips touching her temple in a gesture as tender as it was natural. Just as naturally, she reached up and their lips met softly. For an instant his blood roared, his head whirled, and he all but plundered her mouth. Then, with a supreme effort he drew back, sought her eyes and read the bewilderment there.

"Better get this taken care of," he mumbled, taking a deep breath. "Got some alcohol?"

"Of course." She turned hastily, opened a nearby cupboard and produced a bottle and some cotton swabs.

"It may sting."

"That's okay. I'll survive." Her tone was back to normal, as though the air hadn't been charged with tension and desire just moments before.

"When's Sylvia arriving?" Charlotte asked brightly, wincing as the alcohol stung.

"In a couple of weeks," he replied, feeling doubly ashamed of his inexplicable behavior. Where was his head at? He was engaged, for Christ's sake—and he'd better make damn sure he remembered it. With grim determination he slipped a bandage over the cut. "There. That should do it."

"Thanks." Charlotte turned back to the cooker and Brad began slicing the bread. "Do you think she'll like it here?"

"Who?"

"Sylvia."

"Sure. Why not? It's a great place. It would have been greater still if you'd stayed at Strathaird. You could have helped her find her feet."

Charlotte shrugged. "I don't think that would work.

Sylvia will want to make her own mark on the place and will need her own space.''

"I fail to see what that has to do with you leaving the castle. I'll say it again, Strathaird's your home. Syl and I will probably only spend a few weeks a year there. You could easily have stayed.''

"Thanks, but no thanks.'' She smiled but shook her head. "It wouldn't work. Perhaps once you've been here a while you'll understand.'' She sent him a veiled look as though about to say more, then thinking better of it, kept her thoughts to herself.

He eyed her a moment. "I was counting on your help on the estate,'' he remarked. Moving next to her, he picked up her glass, and topped it up.

"I'm not much good at the estate.''

"Why do you always belittle yourself?'' he asked, handing her back her glass. "You're good at a lot of things. You just don't give yourself enough credit.''

Charlotte shrugged and took a long sip. She didn't want to get into a deeper conversation that would involve exposing her feelings on a number of subjects. Years ago, over the phone, those conversations had seemed much easier. Now, face-to-face, she felt vulnerable. "I don't get involved with the everyday working of the estate. Plus, I've got loads of work now. Did you know I have a gallery in the village?''

"So I heard and I think that's great, but don't change the subject. We were discussing Strathaird.''

She spun round and poked at the casserole with her back to him. "Look, Brad, I don't want to get involved. Perhaps I can show you a couple of things, but Mummy'll do a much better job of getting you acquainted with everybody and everything.'' She glanced over her shoulder at him. "And Sylvia might not want me poking my nose where I don't belong."

"Why should she care?" He threw back his head and let out a rich laugh, hiding the discomfort her words had caused. "I'm sure she'd love to have you teach her how things are run."

"Yeah, right. Typical." Charlotte shook her head and gave the lamb a jab. "Only a man would say something as silly as that."

"I don't see what's silly about it," he replied.

"I don't suppose it occurred to you that Sylvia might want some independence?" She sent him an irritated glance.

"But we'll only be here a few weeks. Why would she care? We could work out something satisfactory for all of us."

"Wishful thinking, I'm afraid." She turned down the gas, left the casserole simmering and faced him. "Get one thing straight, Brad—no amount of arguing is going to get me back to the castle. It's yours and will soon be Sylvia's, too. There's no room for me there any longer and I've my own life to lead. All I'd do is make your life hell. And you've known me long enough and well enough to realize that's probably true." She jabbed his chest, looked at him through her dark lashes once more. "Deep down, you know I'm right. You just won't admit it."

"I don't agree. There's no reason for anything to change. Everything'll go on exactly as it always has."

"No, it won't and it's naive of you to believe it. Remember when you took over Harcourts? Didn't you want to implant your own management system? I remember all the ideas you had and how you were determined to see them carried out."

"Those were corporate decisions."

"This isn't very different. It's only right and proper things should change. But I don't want to be a part of it." Her eyes went misty and she bit her lip. "I've had enough ups and downs as it is. I'd resent the changes and only be a hindrance, Brad, and we'd all suffer." She swept a stray strand of hair behind an ear and turned quickly back to the cooker. "This needs a few more minutes."

As he watched her, Brad reluctantly began to understand. Her whole adult life had been a crazy insecure roller coaster. John had manipulated and undermined her constantly. Now she was slowly regaining territory, desperately cleaving to tufts of earth and rock jutting out from the crevasse into which she'd sunk, climbing out bit by bit. He wished things could remain exactly as they were, that he could keep her safe in Strathaird Castle, the one place that had always remained untouched, where she knew no harm could befall her.

"I'm sorry, Charlie." He squeezed her shoulder gently, understanding the emotional consequences of what it must feel like to have your home usurped by another. His heart clenched and his anger at fate resurfaced. Taking her face gently in his hands, he wiped another tear that had escaped onto her cheek. "God, I'd give the world to change the inheritance, Charlie, and leave Strathaird all to you," he muttered. "God knows I tried."

"Don't." She pulled away and sniffed loudly. "I know you've done all you could. It's not your fault, Brad, it's just the way the cookie crumbles." She smiled, let her hand rest on his a moment, then drew it quickly away. "It's taken me long enough to start getting my life in order, and the sooner I face these changes and get on with it, the better it'll be for all of us. Let's take the wine and sit outside until dinner and you can tell me all about the twins.''

He followed her out the French door, into the little back garden where a small bistro table covered with a checkered blue and white tablecloth stood under an open umbrella. Charlotte flopped onto one of the foldable chairs and he followed suit, listening to the soothing murmur of the sea, the relentless rise and fall of waves bathing the rocks below the bluff, the subtle scent of heather and roses wafting in on the evening breeze. Twilight still hovered, loath to surrender to the couple of stars that already shone timidly. Hermione crossed the tiny patch of lawn and curled up at Charlotte's feet, purring softly, occasionally raising a paw to the handful of bees buzzing hopefully among the bluebells and perennials. In the half-light, he could still distinguish the windswept grass beyond the picket fence and the gentle hue of heather etched on the moors soft as a Monet.

For a while they remained in congenial silence, transported back to adolescence, those long evenings spent confiding secrets, sharing dreams and cracking jokes. It felt strange to have him sitting only a few feet away after so long, Charlotte reflected, casting a quick glance at his profile. She'd gotten used to him at a distance, a phone confidant whom she trusted implicitly but with the advantage of being heard and not seen. Now Brad was very much here, his presence overwhelming. It came as a shock and she half wished for the old long-distance relationship that was far less daunting. Ridiculous, she chided herself. With Brad, there was no need for words, though God knows they could talk for hours when they wanted. She let out a long sigh, closed her eyes and tried to relax. She should be savoring the moment instead of wishing him a million miles away, particularly as this would probably be one of the last times they would share alone together. Whether Brad realized it or not, Sylvia's arrival would inevitably alter things, however determined he seemed to believe the contrary.

"Tell me about the jewelry," he remarked, breaking the spell. "What inspired you to get into designing?"

"I don't really know. It was when things were really iffy with John..." Her voice trailed off and he waited. "I saw a program about jewelry design on telly one day and it seemed a good idea. So I took a course and loved it. It really helped."

"You mean it helped you see things in a clearer light?" he murmured perceptively.

"I suppose you might say that. At the time, it seemed that way. But then John had the accident and I wondered if—oh hell, I don't know and it doesn't matter anymore," she said in a rush, gulping down the wine. The last thing she wanted was to get into a conversation that would surely end in Brad telling her she should leave her husband and get on with her life. Nobody, least of all him, could understand her reasons not to.

"I think it's great you're taking it so seriously," he responded in a neutral voice and she sighed, relieved.

"Yes. I enjoy designing and lately visitors seem to be quite taken with some of the pieces. Moira's my goldsmith, you know. She went to the Royal Academy and has been in this business for years now. Real luck, that, wasn't it?" she added, grinning. "I wasn't sure that expensive jewelry would work here on the island, but you'd be surprised at the number of tourists who've bought pieces."

"I hear you're planning something with Armand. He seems to think you're very talented."

"It's just an idea. I haven't really given it a lot of thought," she lied, taking another gulp of wine and reaching down to pet Hermione.

"You're taking this to heart, aren't you, Charlie?"

"I suppose so." She shrugged. "Keeps me busy."

"I'm glad. You needed something to fill your life."

"God, Brad! Don't be patronizing," she snapped crossly.

"Hey, sorry. I didn't mean it that way." He leaned back, laughing.

"Then how *did* you mean it?" Her eyes flashed and she plunked her glass down with a bang. "Charlotte has something to keep her busy while Genny's at school?" she mimicked. "You make me sound like one of those silly women—" She cut off, bit her lip and turned away, taking a deep breath. "I'm sorry, Brad, I don't know what's wrong with me, but I always get the impression you all think I'm a flake who can't take care of herself."

He reached across the table and placed a hand over her long, nervous fingers. "Nothing's wrong with you that can't be set right. You've been trapped in limbo in your marriage and since the accident it's been worse, because you feel so darn guilty you can't see the forest for the trees."

"I don't want to talk about it."

"We're going to have to talk about it, Charlie. It might as well be now as later," he said, determined to bring the subject out in the open. Her fingers clenched under his and he squeezed them tight before she could escape. "How is John?"

"Just the same. No change."

Brad hesitated, stroking her hand gently. "Have you thought about taking measures to end it?" he asked quietly. It was time someone made her face the fact that it might be better to let John die a natural death, rather than keep him alive, hooked up to a machine.

"No!" she burst out, snatching her hand away. "I can't and won't do it. They don't know if he'll get better or not, but while there's the remotest chance, I don't feel I have that right. And I wish you'd all stop going on at me. He's my husband, after all, and Genny's father. I have some sense of loyalty left, even if you lot don't," she spat.

"Yeah, well, maybe we were all so impressed by the loyalty he showed you over the years that it's hard to feel the same sympathy for him that you apparently do," he threw back dryly.

"It's nobody's business but mine," she muttered. "Sometimes I think his eyes flicker, but the nurse claims it's just his nerves reacting." She sighed, lifted her glass and sent him a brittle smile. "Cheers. Tell me, how are the twins?"

"They're great. Looking forward to seeing Genny." He watched as she retired once more behind that shield of self-protection. There was no point pursuing the subject, but he was glad he'd brought it up and cleared the air, for although John brought back memories best forgotten, he loomed too large to be ignored.

"She's terribly excited, too." Charlotte smiled at the thought of her daughter and the twins, who she adored. "I haven't seen them since last summer. Gosh, time flies, doesn't it? Are they huge?"

"Rick's shooting up like a beanstalk and Todd's not far behind. I'm worried about his schoolwork, though. His attention deficit disorder's a real problem and tough on his self-esteem. But we'll get there."

"Perhaps he should be in a special school."

"Yeah. We're looking into it for the fall. Sylvia thinks she may have found just the right place."

Charlotte winced at the "we." It sounded so final. A unit. One she was not part of. She was definitely right to have moved out, she realized with a twinge of determined satisfaction. Crossing her legs under her on the chair, she glanced at him. "I'm glad you've found someone to share your life with, Brad. I hope you'll be very happy. Do you think Sylvia will like being mistress of Strathaird? It's quite a job, as I'm sure Mummy will tell you. I hope she'll be up to it."

"Syl?" he gave a rich laugh and grinned. "She'll take on anything. She's so organized it's unreal. I don't know where we'd be without her at Harcourts. You should see her Filofax, and her BlackBerry pager." He laughed, shook his head and took another sip of wine. "I don't expect it'll be easy for her, but I know she'll give it her best try. And Syl's best tries are usually very successful."

"Well, that's great then, isn't it?" Charlotte jumped up, feeling suddenly antsy. "It's a bit chilly to eat out, lets go in."

"Sure. Can I help?" He followed her back inside, not certain what had prompted the sudden change in her but aware that something he'd said appeared to have displeased her. He shrugged, caught the fresh scent of her as she passed, and smiled inwardly. Charlie was mercurial as a weather vane and he was used to her ups and downs.

"You can set the table," she remarked, returning to the stove and lifting the lid off the casserole to take a sniff. "The mats and cutlery are in the drawer to the right of the sink."

Brad opened the creaking drawer, picked out two mats and frowned. "Didn't you pick these out in Sarlat one summer? I seem to remember them. It was the year you turned fifteen.''

"Good memory. I chose them for Mummy. We had fun that day, remember?''

"Very well." He placed the knives and forks and napkins on the table while Charlotte tended to the casserole, recalling amusing anecdotes that took them back many years, then placed the piping-hot gratin on the table. It felt homey, cozy and right being in her kitchen. Too cozy for his own good, he reflected grimly, Sylvia's image flashing as he picked up the cruet and placed it on the table. "We must do this when Syl arrives," he said out loud, confirming it to himself. The sooner the three of them became good pals, the better.

Charlotte swallowed a childish jab of resentment and carefully studied the table, knowing it was unfair to be jealous of his fiancée. Perhaps after a while she'd get used to having Sylvia around and even like her, who knew? But she and Brad had always been self-sufficient, never needing or wanting anyone but each other when they were together. Even Colin, her beloved brother, had sometimes been *de trop*. And even though years often went by without seeing one another, as soon as they were back together again the same natural intimacy and easy camaraderie established itself, just as it had now.

Charlotte lifted the casserole with the oven gloves and brought it to the table.

"Smells wonderful," Brad remarked, sniffing appreciatively. "I'm still trying to grasp the fact you can cook." He sat opposite her at the pine table and poured more wine.

"I recently became interested. It's creative if you don't follow recipes too closely. I let my imagination flow. The only trouble is, I never remember exactly what I did the time before, so the dish never comes out quite the same.

That can be good or bad, depending,'' she added wrinkling her nose and spooning a large helping onto his plate.

He laughed, relaxed, and tasted.

"Like it?" Charlotte waited anxiously for his verdict, annoyed that it should mean so much.

"This is haute cuisine, man. You should open a restaurant."

She flushed with pleasure, barely eating, the sight of his obvious enjoyment nourishment in itself. "Last time I made you a meal you refused to eat it."

"Yeah, well, you can hardly blame me. An outdated can of baked beans and three-day-old toast."

"It wasn't that bad."

"No, it was worse. The beans were cold."

"Yuck! That's disgusting, Brad, and a complete lie." She giggled, realizing she hadn't spent such a happy, relaxed evening in ages. "Do you remember the summer we got stuck up in the chimney at the factory in Limoges, trying to find remnants of the radio that Dex operated during the war?"

"Do I remember?" he said with feeling. "That's one of the few times he belted me, good and proper. And it was all your fault for climbing up too high."

"Dex beat you?" she asked, amused yet surprised. He'd never told her about the punishment.

"He was waiting for me when I walked in the door. I could hardly sit down for a week."

"You never said anything."

"Nope. I took it like a man." He winked at her and grinned. "You don't really think that at twelve I would have admitted to you that I got the living shit beaten out of me, do you?"

"I guess not. It's rather sweet." She grinned, struck

with insight. "You didn't tell me 'cause you didn't want me to feel bad."

"Nah, I was just being tough."

"I know you, Brad. You were always such a gentleman. You probably thought that I'd get in trouble too if you didn't take all the blame."

"Something like that," he admitted with a shrug and a smile. "What a meal, Charlie. I'll be over here every day and putting on weight if I'm not careful."

"Well, you'll be able to take it off working out on that fancy equipment sitting in the hall at Strathaird," she replied tartly. "Are you planning to transform the old conservatory into a gym?" she asked sweetly, hiding the edge in her voice.

"I guess that might not be a bad idea." He'd forgotten the offending gym equipment.

"Three large crates. Addressed to Hansen."

"I suppose Syl must have had it shipped." He gave an embarrassed laugh.

"Seems a big investment if you're only planning to spend a few weeks here a year."

"Syl's really into health and exercise. She works out for a couple of hours a day, weights and all that. It's an important part of her lifestyle. She takes great care of her diet, too."

"I see." Charlotte nodded sagely. "Then I'll have to be careful what I cook if she comes over for dinner, won't I?" she said, getting up and clearing the plates with a sassy smile that far from portrayed her mood. "Pudding? Or should I say *dessert?*" She corrected herself with an American twang.

"What've you got?" he asked, eyeing her with a suspicious grin as he carried the rest of the dishes to the sink. Their hands touched when he handed her the remains of the lamb, sending shivers up her spine.

"I have trifle," she said in a rush. What on earth was the matter with her? It was ridiculous to feel tingly just because Brad had touched her hand. Surely she wasn't so desperate for a man that now even her oldest pal turned her on? She quickly scraped the dish, then left it in the sink before extracting the bowl of trifle from the fridge.

Neither noticed the time as they chatted and reminisced over dessert, followed by coffee and brandy. Old, long-forgotten stories, fond memories and shared secrets made them laugh or seek unspoken understanding in each other's eyes, and it was past midnight by the time Brad regretfully glanced at his watch.

"Geez, it's late. I hope Aunt Penn left the door open."

"If not, the key's under the mat."

"Isn't that rather obvious?"

"So much so that nobody would ever think of looking. Plus, we've never had a break-in at the castle—or in the area, for that matter," she added proudly. "That's one positive aspect about living in a remote area like this, you can't beat the security."

Brad rose reluctantly, loath to exchange the convivial warmth of Charlotte's kitchen for his solitary bed in the master chamber, which Penelope had insisted he take now that he was the laird. He watched her, flushed and relaxed, eyes bright from wine, cooking and conversation. If anything, time had rendered her lovelier and the sudden urge to feel her close made him clamp down his self-control. But his eyes lingered on her high cheekbones and that incredibly silky white skin. Suddenly the years fell away, and he saw her lying pliant and wanting in his arms, stretched on the couch in Dex's flat as he lowered his lips to hers.

Blowing out a breath, he fiddled in his pocket for his car keys and took a step back. "I guess I won't need to lock the car here either," he remarked, dangling the keys thoughtfully and laughing to cover his embarrassment. "Good night, Charlie. Thanks for a great evening."

She opened the front door and leaned against the doorjamb watching him. "Good night, Brad."

For a moment they stood in awkward silence, then he took her into his arms and gave her a friendly hug. "You take care, kiddo. I wish you hadn't left the castle, but so be it."

She mumbled something incomprehensible into his shirtfront, then reached up and touched his cheek. "Good luck as the new laird, Brad."

"I'm still counting on your help, you know." His eyes reached deep into hers.

She hesitated, then nodded and smiled, swallowing her warring emotions. "You can count on me for whatever you need."

"I knew you wouldn't let me down." He touched her cheek lightly, then dropped a quick kiss on her forehead before walking quickly toward the car.

Charlotte stood a while, gazing at the fading taillights swerving back and forth as he avoided the ruts.

Brad was back.

And perhaps for longer than he realized. She let out a sigh. He still had no idea how much Strathaird would demand of him. Would he be prepared to give what it took? she wondered, turning back inside and switching off the porch light, trying to make sense of her mixed emotions. Perhaps she'd been too alone of late, not bothering to see friends or socialize, and this was the result. Shaking her head, she went to her bedroom. Perhaps she just needed some male company to remind her that she was young and human.

But Brad did more than just remind her of that. He

made her feel alive, something she hadn't felt in ages. Worse, he made her feel like a woman.

Entering her bedroom she undressed, then glanced at herself in the old cheval mirror. Was she still attractive? What lay hidden under Colin's old shirts and shapeless sweaters? Slowly she pulled off the T-shirt, removed her bra and stared at the woman before her. John had spent years telling her how old she was becoming, how her breasts sagged after Genny's birth, how her thighs weren't as taut as they used to be. He'd even suggested plastic surgery in a tone that left no doubt that he found her repulsive. When he'd made love to her, he'd made her feel diminished and ugly, until she'd prayed he wouldn't come near her. She shuddered, trying to see her true self and not the pitiful image he'd created. Then quickly she grabbed her nightshirt and flung it on crossly. All that part of her life was behind her now. There was no room in her new life for physical attraction. It was absurd, utterly stupid to be feeling like this, merely because she'd had a pleasant evening with an old friend, one who was very much engaged to be married.

She scrubbed her teeth and brushed her hair, then jumped into bed and cuddled under the plump goosedown duvet with her three well-worn stuffed animals. She had no business feeling anything for Brad except friendship. And you'd better not forget it, she ordered, reaching up to turn off the light, then fling herself against the pillow. There was no room for anything between them but what already existed. The fact that she suddenly wanted more just showed how much her life needed readjusting.

It was a good thing Sylvia was arriving soon, Charlotte reflected, eyelids drooping. For her own sanity, and for Brad's good, she hoped it would be soon.

5

It was already twelve-thirty and she was due at Cipriani's at one. Sylvia wondered where the morning had flown. With a precise swivel of her beige leather office chair, she turned to her computer and deftly typed in some notes. After a quick check to make sure not a hair of her sleek, shoulder-length blond coif was out of place, she straightened the jacket of her well-tailored Armani suit and rose, ready for action. The luncheon was important, the clients were major. Brad was in Scotland, so she would handle it.

A flash of irritation marred her patrician features before she picked up her voluminous black leather purse and moved across the elegant corner office toward the wide, light-wood double doors with a worried frown. Two weeks had turned into three, and now he was talking of six! Six weeks in Scotland, indeed. What on earth was Brad thinking? she wondered. Heading into the corridor, she adopted a friendly yet distant smile calculated to impart that she was in control but still accessible.

She was going to have to do something about this sudden decision of his to prolong the visit. He'd sounded so odd on the phone, barely even commenting on her news about the Australian deal. Someone who didn't know him as well as she did would have said he sounded bored. And then this bombshell about extending his visit. Spending that amount of time away from the company was simply out of the question, she decided, entering the half-empty elevator and nodding at the senior partner of a law firm that occupied one of the lower floors.

As the elevator sank fifty-two floors, she began reshuffling her own schedule. It was definitely time to get her butt over to Scotland and assess the situation first-hand. No amount of sheep could merit a six-week absence, she figured, reaching the busy marble lobby, satisfied to find her car waiting at the curb. Once she got to Skye, she'd sit Brad down and make him see how impossible it all was. Then, matter-of-factly, she switched mental gears and focused on the upcoming luncheon. Slipping into the back seat of the vehicle, she pulled out her brief on the latest market trends, and allowed herself a small smile. Aside from sex with a sensibly chosen partner, nothing gave her the same high as the prospect of clinching another deal.

It had taken Brad little more than a week to realize that, for the first time in his life, he was in over his head. Endless meetings in the study, reviewing accounts, and long sessions with Penelope discussing the histories of the different tenant families—the exact nature of their activities and problems—had been only one part of the daunting process of learning what running an estate involved. There were expeditions on horseback with Mr. Mackay—the factor, who was in charge of Strathaird's administration—to view repairs to fences in spots too remote to be reached by car, followed by lengthy afternoon visits to the homes of the tenants, where he was met by men with wary gazes and women with soft smiles who welcomed him cautiously. He was offered home-baked cake and endless cups of tea laced with Talisker, the local island whiskey. The veiled hints of what they expected from the laird did not go unnoticed. All this and more had given him a fair idea of what *was* expected of him: his mind, his body and soul, and above all, his presence.

He'd ridden the land on Colin's gelding, enjoying the windswept moors, the ever-present breeze and the strong sea air. He had stopped by the roadside to listen to complaints regarding the falling price of sheep on the mainland, and the island's lack of employment. And he was surprised to find himself being drawn into this far-flung web of concerns that until recently had been little more than another job to handle. But though it *was* a job—one that demanded far more than he'd bargained for—there was something else beckoning, something far deeper that he was unable to define. He couldn't put it into words, exactly. He just knew he was destined to do this. Doing it right, he realized somberly, riding back to the castle under a light drizzle, would require a heck of a lot more time here than he could spare.

He stared at the gray sky. It had rained all day, a tenacious drizzle interspersed with hearty wind gusts, leaving the air chilly and damp. But he didn't mind. The rain felt good, just as the long exchanges with the locals gave him a better insight into this new way of life.

He thought back to his earlier phone conversation with Sylvia, aware she was annoyed that he intended to stay longer than they'd originally planned. He'd tried to explain, but it was impossible for her to understand the need to be here, to show his face to those who depended upon him. Still, he was damn lucky he had her to stand in for him at Harcourts, he reflected as the horse clip-clopped into the courtyard at the rear of the castle. Dismounting, he led the horse back to the stables, wondering how he was going to divide himself between operating the company—a full-time job and more—and running Strathaird without stretching himself so thin he did neither job right.

He let out a long breath, handing the horse over to Andy, a redheaded teenager who mucked out the stables in the afternoons, and dragged his fingers slowly through his thick chestnut hair, searching for a solution. There was always a solution—Dex had taught him that—but what first came to mind didn't strike him as feasible. He frowned as he made his way through the back door, hanging his wet jacket on a peg among the mackintoshes in the entrance. Then, heading past the pantry, he climbed the stairs that led toward the Great Hall.

What he really needed was time, a commodity he didn't have. Time to find his feet; time to get to know these folks who'd lived on this land forever and now counted on him to understand their worries and needs; time to break down the silent wall of mistrust that he read in their unflinching looks.

He reached his study and walked over to the window, staring thoughtfully through the mullioned window at the misty scene beyond. That this could feel like home in such a short period of time was amazing. He thought of Sylvia and realized uneasily that it was almost impossible to imagine her here—in fact, to imagine her anywhere but Manhattan, in the midst of meetings, endlessly ringing cell phones, business breakfasts and working lunches.

He hoped Charlotte would be joining them for dinner. He'd spent yesterday evening and the evening before chatting with her in her cozy kitchen. He grinned, only just now thinking of a witty riposte to one of her outrageous comments, and wished she were there to hear it.

Lately he'd developed a habit of popping by her gallery most afternoons too. Somehow they always ended up sharing a pint or a dram at the Celtic Café, where he and Rory discussed politics, soccer and other burning issues. They were usually joined by Hamish, an old fisherman and pal of his grandfather's, who was only too ready to tell him long-forgotten tales, some of which were no doubt embellished but made good stories anyway.

His mind turned again to Charlotte. She'd seemed calmer the past few days, less nervous. He'd enjoyed watching her from a distance as she sat poring over her work, both her enthusiasm and talent apparent. She was obviously enthralled by the collection she and Armand were putting together. He frowned. There was nothing wrong with Armand, he supposed, but still, he couldn't stomach the guy.

He stood a while longer, peering thoughtfully across the lawn. A dreary day. One that suited his pensive mood and made Harcourts, the factories in Limoges and Taiwan, and the new stores being opened in fifteen states seem impossibly remote. How had Jamie MacTavish's sheep managed to assume the pole position on his list of priorities, he wondered. If he told Syl that, she'd definitely send him to a shrink. She'd insist he return immediately to New York, to its familiar pace, the buzz of traffic, and a healthy dose of carbon monoxide.

But, in truth, he didn't want to be there. He'd slipped into this new, peaceful existence like a hand into a smooth kid glove, and he wasn't ready to give it up yet. In fact, he realized, he could easily get used to setting his own pace without Marcia's efficient voice reminding him of his next appointment.

Not that he didn't appreciate his high-powered, highly competent secretary. Quite the contrary. It was precisely those sharp, organizational skills that had allowed him to be here without going crazy.

The only hiccup to date had occurred at three in the morning two days ago, when he'd been woken up by Mr. Chang, his director in Taiwan. He'd spent the better part of the night on the phone. Once they'd fixed the problem, he'd turned over in Aunt Penn's lavender-scented linen and gone straight back to sleep in the huge four-poster that had cradled the worries and pleasures of his ancestors for several generations.

He glanced at the carriage clock on the carved stone mantelpiece. It was almost five o'clock. Charlotte would still be at the gallery. Had she sold the silver-and-topaz earrings to the woman from Minnesota? His face relaxed into a gentle grin that almost immediately became a frown. Charlotte, with her misty smiles, scattered brain and bursts of artistic temperament, was never out of his mind. Neither was the chaste yet tender touching of lips on the evening of his arrival. He'd been careful to avoid physical contact with her since, but he found the memory of that kiss impossible to forget.

And when he thought of Sylvia, he had to concentrate to recall her face.

He shifted uneasily. His relationship with Charlie was nothing more than a close friendship. Wasn't it?

Perhaps it was just their ability to listen to each other, to unconditionally take to heart what the other said and felt, that made her so special. Not that Charlotte was talking much about herself or her life, he reflected, a crease descending between his eyebrows. He sighed, wishing that he could turn the key in the lock and open the door to the emotions he sensed lay hidden.

But he must stop wanting what he couldn't have. Charlotte was out of bounds. She always had been and always would be. And he was engaged to be married. The sooner he buried these strange resurgent feelings, the better off they'd all be.

With a grunt, he tossed his jacket over his left shoulder and headed for the drawing room for the ritual cup of tea with Aunt Penn. She was patiently wet-nursing him, guiding him through the everyday intricacies of running the estate, keeping him abreast of the latest developments, those small events of which, as laird, it behooved him to be aware. He was amazed at her memory, the ease with which she smoothed ruffled feathers, and not a little daunted by the diplomacy required. Her utter dedication to the task made him intensely aware of how unprepared he was for the role he'd been thrust into.

As he closed the study door, Brad stepped into the Great Hall, remembering that tomorrow the twins and Diego would be here and that life would take on a new pace. He looked forward to seeing the kids. Thinking of little Genny, he smiled. She was so excited that the boys were coming. Lately they'd spent an hour each day working on her math homework. He'd rarely had a moment to spare for anything but baseball practice with the twins, but he found the moments in Genny's company enchanting.

Then he sighed, wishing he felt as upbeat about Syl's imminent arrival as he did about Diego and the kids. Maybe he was wrong about how she'd react to Strathaird; perhaps she'd even find it a refreshing change from their hectic lives.

He hoped so. Still, he thought with a grin, all bets were off if she ignored his warnings and brought her beloved Prada pumps along. Marching around the moors would ruin them, and then Strathaird would forever be on her blacklist.

With a shrug he crossed the Great Hall, glancing at the huge baronial fireplace Penelope had filled with hot-house plants, in the hopes of making it seem less barren. Despite her efforts to brighten the place, it still looked gloomy and foreboding. He paused a moment, gripped by an eerie sensation, aware all at once that it was here, in this ancient fortress—in this very hall—that his ancestors had lived, planned their sieges into enemy land, held court, judged and reigned. He noted absently that the rain had increased, the gray skies outside leaving the hall dark and shadowy.

A strange current coursed up his arm as he caught sight of the portraits hanging on the weathered paneling of the ancient oak staircase leading up to the gallery. He suddenly pictured men, young and old, with heavy unkempt beards and kilts, seated at a huge table, readying for war while dogs and children played in happy oblivion in crackling dry straw at their feet. Upstairs women hovered anxiously, aware that more death and destruction was about to strike. His eyes closed and he caught the lilt of Gaelic voices, strains of a lute and the bark of hounds, a baby's wail and a mother's crooning. Then a young girl's laughter reached him and he opened his eyes, the shadowy image of a young girl he recognized standing before him, clad in rich purple, her medieval dress outlining the curve of her breast, arms outstretched in welcome, amethyst eyes alight with undisguised desire.

Coming back to earth with a bang, Brad stood silent and shaken, staring at his own outstretched hand. Embarrassed, he crammed it into his pocket and made a hasty retreat to the drawing room. It was ludicrous, but he could've sworn what he'd just seen was real. This place must be getting to him, its mysterious and romantic aura affecting his brain. Chiding himself for being an idiot, he decided to make his meeting with Aunt Penn a quick one, and then head to the village for a stiffer drink than her drawing room could provide.

The search of the library had produced nothing and after days spent planning his next move, Armand's morale sagged. The acquisition of the antique pistol that had lain discarded—possibly in wait for him—for well over a century was, of course, encouraging. But even as his instincts told him the clue had to be hidden somewhere in the castle, he realized he didn't have time to go through the books again. No, it was time to take the next step, even though, he acknowledged nervously, there was an undeniable risk that matters could go seriously wrong. Charlotte might sense that his motives weren't absolutely pure. Still, he had no choice. Of course, he reminded himself, Charlotte was likely too flighty to be aware of his subtle maneuverings. He'd always been a master at concealing his true feelings, hadn't he? Gathering his cap, he set out for the village, buoyed by the knowledge that the prize would be worth whatever he had to do.

Crossing the main street, he entered the gallery, a satisfied smile spreading over his gaunt face. Even here one could see Charlotte's artistry. The space was neither large nor pretentious, and although the light-ochre walls and sisal carpet weren't much to his taste, which tended toward rich damasks, heavy dark-hued silks and plush velvets, the decor was cleverly conceived to accentuate the jewels. Each showcase was strategically placed to attract the viewer's eye, and bright halogen lighting reflected every detail.

There was no disputing it. Charlotte had an eye for making each item stand out like a masterpiece.

And such talent.

Oh, what wonderful, glorious talent. Her ability made a man like himself, who knew his own designs rarely rose beyond the mediocre, want to rage at the unfairness of it all. He quickly smothered the ripple of anger, focusing instead on the jewelry's smooth sinuous lines, relishing its mythical symbolism, the clever use of gems so evocative of the prewar Rothberg work. And yet it wasn't derivative. Each piece bore a unique stamp that was all hers, a quality and individuality that spoke of greatness.

He glanced at Moira, seated behind the desk. With a deprecating smile he picked up a bracelet lying temptingly within reach and admired the delicate interlacing of paper-thin platinum strands. An intricate pattern, designed to set off the exquisite cabochon stones amid a cluster of diamonds. He let it rest in his palm, sighed and closed his eyes. Already he'd switched several tones in his fall collection, adapting the color scheme to better show off just such pieces as this. He could picture the hushed anticipation, the oohs and aahs, the excitement of the audience as the models strutted down the catwalk to the last movement of Beethoven's Ninth Symphony. A standing ovation would inevitably follow. In a spurt of sudden inspiration, he decided to name the show Daughters of Elysium.

Running his tongue over parched lips, Armand gazed once more at the bracelet. Instinctively he knew it would be an immediate success.

Carefully laying the bracelet back on its burlap setting, he turned toward Moira and heaved a sigh. "It is such a pleasure to bathe oneself in her work. Just viewing it is sheer delight." He heaved another gusty sigh, oblivious of Moira's curious glances.

"Charlotte's in the workshop finishing the choker," she replied, indicating the crooked door flanked by cardboard boxes at the rear of the gallery. "I can see if she's available, if you like."

"*Non, non, ma chère.* Don't bother." He waved a thin white hand. "I shall announce myself. I think we now have sufficient *intimité* to proceed to such a liberty," Armand purred, taking a determined step past a hesitant Moira.

"Perhaps I should just warn her. She doesn't like being interrupted." Moira shifted uncomfortably in her broad leather sandals while Armand, paying no attention, adjusted his well-tailored tweeds and waved her peremptorily aside.

He had never entered the hub of Charlotte's creations, the place he considered the inner sanctuary, and he paused reverently on the threshold as he might upon entering Ali Baba's cave.

Charlotte, seated on a rickety stool, her hair drawn back in a rough ponytail, was leaning over the long trestle table that dominated the middle of the low-ceilinged room. She held a small pair of tweezers in midair, cradling a tiny diamond, sparkling in the dust-speckled beam of a bright work light that cast the rest of the room in shadow. She looked like a seventeenth-century painting come to life, he thought, a study in chiaroscuro. She continued working, oblivious to his presence, and he watched in fascination, listening to her soft humming as she picked up a degree-line gauge and carefully measured the stone before placing it on tissue paper to her left.

His eyes followed the length of her arm, beyond the shirt cuff to where the heavy gold Rothberg watch dwarfed her slim wrist. Such a masterpiece. His mouth twitched nervously and he swallowed, pulse quickening, glad he'd taken the risk and entered the sacred portal. He focused now on the workshop, drinking it all in: the walls plastered with drawings, old magazine pictures and news-paper cuttings, all of it tacked up with little regard to order; the drawing table in the corner; the tools and multicolored gems distributed across the length and breadth of the wide worktable.

He peered at the pictures, realizing that some dated back to before the Second World War. He glanced at Charlotte, still immersed in her work, and eased closer to the wall. A shiver gripped him as his eyes fell upon an old 1935 cover of *Paris Match*. His fingers shook and he checked the urge to reach out and touch Sylvain de Rothberg's dark, morose eyes staring out at him from behind a film of cigarette smoke. He gazed at the eyes longingly, searching them for a clue.

"Armand?" At the sound of Charlotte's surprised voice, he spun round elegantly on his heel and moved quickly toward her with a gracious smile. He noted the scowl shadowing her features, as with an irritated gesture she shook her hair out of the rubber band.

"Who let you in here?" she asked, not pleased.

"*Ma chère* Charlotte, you must not blame the poor creature who guards this sanctum. I and I alone am to blame." He laid a palm dramatically over his heart and sent her a winning smile. "I know it is very bad manners to invade your privacy, but I could not resist another day the temptation to plunge fully into the inner world of your creations." He waved a graceful hand at his surroundings. "And now I stand here, a grateful witness to your genius. Like you, *ma chère*, your work is *superbe*. I am all the more convinced that you simply must exhibit your work with my collection. I am a supplicant before your altar, awed by your supremacy, your…" He paused, hand in midair, as he searched for the right superlative.

"Good Lord! Don't get all French and dramatic on me,

Armand,'' Charlotte replied, annoyance fading and laughter surging despite her irritation. It was impossible to stay angry with Armand for long. If truth be told, his fascination with her work had genuinely helped boost her battered self-esteem. In fact, since Armand's arrival and subsequent encouragement, she'd been working nonstop, designing with new energy. That, and their mutual admiration for Sylvain de Rothberg's legacy, had forged a tenuous bond between them.

"Here, take a look at this choker." She leaned over, picked up a narrow strip of platinum fresh from the mold, and handed it to him shyly, still afraid of the criticism that might follow. "It still needs work, of course, but I think the way it dips at the base works, don't you?" She pointed to the subtle downward curve where two teardrop diamonds already sparkled, above which she planned to place a trail of garnets. She held her breath as Armand examined it.

"It is *magnifique,*" he whispered, eyes glistening. "A reminder of the master himself, yet so distinctively yours. What a delight. It is almost as though his hand were guiding you," he murmured softly.

"Really?" She sent him a dubious glance, then shrugged and wiped her hands on her jeans. "Perhaps it's his relationship with the family that has always made him such an intriguing figure to me. I wish I could have met him. He must have been a fabulous chap. Did you ever meet him, Armand?"

He shook his head, eyes turning misty. He raised his hand and touched his chest, as though feeling for something. "I recall once, as a very small child, seeing him in the village of Ambazac," he murmured, gazing into the distance. "He was a very handsome man, dark, windswept, with a bohemian touch about him. But I don't know if that is an actual memory or a creation based on pictures I have seen since.''

"There were quite a few photos of him and Tante Geneviève at La Vallière. Granny Flora used to talk to me about them a lot. She loved them dearly. Losing them was a terrible blow, especially in such tragic circumstances.''

"Theirs was such a poignant yet profound love story, I suppose.'' He flicked an invisible speck of dust from his lapel with a slight sniff.

"I named Genny after Tante Geneviève, you know,'' she remarked, taking the choker from him and wrapping it in an old piece of silk before placing it carefully in the drawer below the worktable. "I used to dream about them as a girl. Granny Flora said she'd never seen two people so much in love.'' She tilted her head wistfully and glanced at the picture of Sylvain. "He looks like a romantic, doesn't he? I wonder where men like him hang out nowadays?'' She added wistfully, "Strong, determined men who'd face the world for a woman they loved, a cause they believed in.''

"They are a thing of the past, *ma chère*.'' Armand sighed sympathetically. "Relics of an age of elegance and good taste that exists no more. You just have to look around you to see that the plebes have taken over.'' A grimace of distaste accompanied his words and he shuddered delicately. "Everything has become so dreadfully vulgar, so excruciatingly banal. It staggers one's sensibilities.''

"Come on, Armand, it's not quite that bad.'' She grinned. He had a knack of making her laugh with his old-fashioned notions. "Look at me,'' she teased, hands straddling her slim hips and posing. "I'm not exactly what you'd call tasteful but you survive my company all the same.''

"You, dear child, are the exception to the rule," Armand replied loyally.

"Come, come, Armand." Charlotte laughed. "I know you think I look like something the cat brought in on a bad day."

"*Non,* really, Charlotte," Armand protested, shaking his head. "You have about you a certain *je ne sais quoi,* an innate elegance that defies your efforts to meld with the common herd." His voice rose and his hands flew dramatically. "Like Marie Antoinette in David's sketches as she was driven to the scaffold, jeered at by the madding crowd, yet dignified and elegant despite her rags and shorn hair."

"Good Lord." Charlotte rolled her eyes and pretended to swoon.

"Your very bearing speaks of ancient heritage and fine ancestry. Your beauty stands alone. Had you lived in the Cinquecento, you would have been the muse of all—"

"Is this Charlie you're describing?" Brad leaned against the doorjamb, catching the sudden and enchanting flush on Charlotte's cheeks. So she was enjoying all this French flattery, was she?

Armand spun round and retrieved his cane, which he'd laid against the wall. "Ah, *mon cher* Bradley. What a pleasure to see you doing something other than work." He smiled graciously. "How are you faring with your duties as seigneur?"

Brad winced. "Jesus, Armand, cut the medieval crap."

"How dreadfully American. Dear boy, it is essential you become truly aware of your station," he insisted. "You Americans have a regrettable habit of ignoring the social order." He sniffed derisively.

"No kidding! We've been working at it a while," Brad said witheringly.

"Shut up, both of you, and let's have a drink," Charlotte interrupted, knowing how irritating Brad found Armand's determination to view Strathaird as a feudal fiefdom. "Did you manage to fix the fences with old Hamish?"

"Yep, pretty much. We've ordered in new wire but the worst's been dealt with."

"Fences? You actually touch barbed wire?" Armand squeaked, horrified. "*Mon Dieu*, surely you have menials to perform such tasks." He dabbed his lips with his handkerchief.

Brad raised an eyebrow. "Actually, I enjoy going out and getting my hands dirty. Feels good. You should try it yourself, Armand. We usually leave around 6:00 a.m. You're welcome to join us."

"My dear boy, the mere thought of rising at such an hour makes one shudder," he exclaimed.

Brad watched as Armand did just that, and hid his disdain. "How about that drink, Charlie?"

"Fine. I'll let Moira lock up. Let's see if Rory's at the café. Want to join us, Armand?"

"Thank you, *ma chère*, but I shall return to the château, where the chatelaine awaits me. But before we depart, allow me to inspect the stones you were placing." Before she could respond, he moved nimbly toward the worktable and withdrew his glasses from the right breast pocket of his jacket.

Brad sent Charlotte a look. She shrugged and moved over next to Armand. He was gazing at a design for another bracelet that she'd left next to the diamonds.

"Fascinating," he murmured, peering closer. "I imagine you mean to place round diamonds in a flat-top beaded setting. Is that correct?''

"Yes. The platinum double-strap mount will center on a star ruby," she replied, immediately engrossed.

"Magnificent." His eyes glinted behind the lenses. Then, all at once he grabbed her wrist, staring intently at her watch. "You should design a bracelet along the lines of this watch. It is a Rothberg, isn't it?"

"Yes. Daddy used to wear it, and then Colin, but now it's mine."

Brad frowned. Something niggled at the back of his brain. He shoved it aside, impatient to get going.

"If you can bear to tear yourselves away, I was going to ask you both to dinner at the pub. Aunt Penn has guests tonight."

"The...pub?" Armand said haltingly as he removed his glasses.

"Yeah. Have a problem with that?" Brad growled. He was getting fed up with Armand's dramatic airs, and not quite sure he liked Charlotte's reaction to the man's flattery. Of course her work was good—incredible, in fact; he had enough experience in the art field to know exceptional work when he saw it. But it irritated him that she seemed to feed on Armand's praise, as if her self-esteem was starved.

"Bradley, *vraiment,* is there nowhere more elegant to dine in this remote land?"

"Not unless we go to the Three Chimneys, and I'm darned if I'm driving halfway across the island. Plus, I feel like pub grub. How about you, Charlotte?"

"I'm game. By the way," she commented, sending Armand a sly smile, "the pub belongs to Rory's brother, Ben. Have you ever seen him?" she asked innocently.

"I do not believe I have had that—"

"Pleasure—and it is that, believe me," she said with a wink. Brad stifled a grin. "The man is simply gorgeous," Charlotte teased. "If you think Rory's handsome, you ain't seen nothin' yet."

"Well! That changes matters somewhat," Armand said, brightening, "I am never averse to making sacrifices in the name of beauty."

6

It was Friday and the Lord of the Isles was warming up for an evening's entertainment. Several out-of-towners had arrived for the ceilidh that would take place later that evening. Brad liked the pub's informal atmosphere, the smoky haze, the dark, low-beamed taproom exuding age and malt whiskey, the faded plush velvet benches and the bar, heavy and stalwart, hewn from live oak and invitingly waxed and worn. A television droned, and occasional grunts and murmurs accompanied the rugby match, as Stewart MacDonald and Davy Murray—husband of Mrs. Murray, who worked at the castle—argued half-heartedly when their team fell behind.

Charlotte threaded a path among the tables, calling greetings as she went. Brad followed, Armand in his wake, uncomfortably aware of the sudden silence that had descended as they entered. He pretended not to notice the wary, surreptitious glances and soft murmurs that followed him and made steadily for the bar.

"Hello, Ben." Charlotte smiled brightly at the handsome Celt carefully polishing a glass behind the bar. Like his brother Rory, Ben was what Americans referred to as

Black-Irish. Here, Brad realized with amusement, if you told him he was Irish you'd be spoiling for a fight.

Ignoring the tense atmosphere, he sat at the bar and nodded a hello to Ben, who returned the greeting with a silent nod. Not exactly welcoming, he reflected. But he was getting used to the inquisitive stares, the grudging hellos and cautious smiles, discovering for the first time what it felt like to be thoroughly observed and dissected, analyzed and judged. He'd never considered political life, but now he wondered how the politicians back home survived such constant scrutiny. He perched a foot on the brass rail below the counter, showing none of his qualms, and smiled when Armand let out a deep and appreciative sigh; obviously he'd noticed Ben. The man was an impressive figure, with the sleeves of his rugby shirt rolled up above the elbow, revealing a deep tan that accentuated his bright blue eyes and thick black hair. Brad felt Charlotte's nudge and grinned, even as he wondered if she'd ever been attracted to the guy.

"I told you," Charlotte murmured, leaning toward Armand.

"You were quite right, *ma chère*. Definitely worth the sacrifice."

"Sorry to burst your bubble, but something tells me he's as far from gay as a man can get," Brad said, taking a sip of the strong island malt Ben had placed before him.

"You could have let me indulge in a few prurient fantasies before dashing my hopes," Armand lamented, clearly aggrieved.

"Sorry, just didn't want you to be disappointed, that's all."

A door leading to the kitchen burst open and a pretty redhead, balancing a tray piled high with fish and chips, swung behind the bar and sidled up to Ben, who immediately stopped pouring.

"Definitely not a player, Armand," Brad murmured laughingly as Ben's eyes softened and his hand snagged Alana by the waist, nearly upsetting her and the chips.

"Is it true about the baby?" Charlotte asked once Ben had finished kissing his wife.

"It is," Alana replied proudly. "I'm three months along."

"Congratulations."

"He'll be a fine strapping lad." Ben laid a possessive hand gently over Alana's belly and looked down at her proudly.

"What if it's a girl?" Charlotte quizzed him.

"Then she'll be as bonnie as her mum," he answered, white teeth flashing.

Brad bit back a grin as Armand sighed regretfully.

"To the baby." Charlotte raised her glass and others followed.

"To Ben's bairn," someone murmured to Brad's right.

"Aye, to the bairn."

"How's Janice doing?" Charlotte asked, once they'd toasted the future heir several times. Janice was Ben and Rory's sister, and a subject of contention just now.

"Okay." Ben's face closed and he busied himself behind the bar.

"Still with the boyfriend in Glasgow?"

"Aye, more's the pity." The Gaelic lilt in his voice made even the terse comment lyrical.

"What's wrong with him?" Charlotte cocked her head. "I mean, beside the fact you don't like the football team he plays for."

Ben let out a long huff and stared witheringly at her.

"Ye'd nae understand if I tried to explain, so I'll keep ma' peace and save us a two-hour discussion, Charlie."

"You're such a chauvinist, Ben. Poor Janice. No wonder she fled the island."

"Fled, ma' foot. Gallivanting all over the country with a good-for-nothing piece of slime is what she's doing."

"Goodness me," Armand murmured, clearly titillated by the show of masculine temper.

"Live for today and let tomorrow take care of itself," Charlotte remarked philosophically. Brad squinted at her, then decided the blithe comment couldn't go unchallenged.

"Not exactly a philosophy you live by, is it?" he remarked. Why, all she ever did was worry about the past, usually to the detriment of her future.

"What do you mean?" There was a glint in her eye that he recognized of old.

"That you're still stuck in your yesterdays. You've put your emotional life on hold, Charlie, by staying with John."

"Well, if I have, it's nobody's business but my own." She gulped her wine, fingers white and strained around the glass. Why couldn't they understand that her husband's situation was probably her fault? Just as Genny's leg was her fault, and a number of other things. She took another sip and glanced around the pub, determined to banish the looming black specter.

"One day you're going to have to face the truth."

"Look, this is hardly the time or the place," she retorted, slamming her glass down. "And you're hardly one to be doling out advice. For as long as I can remember, all you've ever done is put your own life on hold for Dex and the rest of them. You still are, since Strathaird landed in your lap because of him. And I suppose you kowtow to Sylvia's every wish and fancy.''

Where had that come from? he wondered, surprised at her acid reply. "Let's leave Syl out of this, shall we?" he responded in an even tone. "It's your life we're talking about."

"*You* were talking about." She pulled the bowl of complimentary chips toward her and began munching. "I'd rather talk about today's special, thank you very much. Ben, what's in the kitchen?" she called.

"Steak and kidney pie with mashed potatoes."

Brad watched Armand shiver dramatically behind his plastic-sheathed menu. "Perhaps," he ventured in a small voice, "you might have foie gras on toast?"

Brad rolled his eyes, and turned back to Charlotte. She seemed as taut as a bowstring, and automatically he slipped a hand over hers and squeezed. "I didn't mean to upset you."

"Then shut up and leave me alone."

"I can't," he replied simply, feeling the hand under his twitch nervously. "I care too much about you. I don't want to see your life wasted. If the circumstances were different, if he'd been a good husband and treated you right, then I'd understand. I'd even applaud what you're doing. But that wasn't the case. Maybe you have to realize that even though he's in a coma, he's still the same person you finally stood up to that last day before the accident."

"Don't go on and on," Charlotte begged, a deep flush spreading across her cheeks as she pulled her hand away. Brad looked up, suddenly aware that Ben was watching them both with a strange look.

As they placed their orders, Armand settling, with

some misgivings, on a cheese and fruit plate, the local villagers began drifting into the pub.

In the corner two old men played cards. To their left, the younger generation threw darts and drank beer, and on a low stool near the hearth, Fergus MacDowell played a merry Scottish air on his accordion while Mary MacAllister, the village nurse, sat at a nearby table, drumming her foot contentedly. An American couple with Midwestern accents were trying to convince their two small sons that the only McDonald's within a hundred miles were human, not the fast-food kind.

Soon Jamie MacPhee would arrive with his fiddle, and the place would fill up and the evening begin. Charlotte was talking to a blond girl to her left, and Armand offered a running commentary on the customs of the lower classes, to which Brad paid little attention. As he soaked in the convivial atmosphere, glad that attention seemed finally to have shifted from him, he took note of a debate heating up at the end of the bar. A very old man and a sandy-haired lad in a suit and tie were involved in an intense exchange.

"Who are they?" Brad asked Charlotte as heads began to turn and voices hushed.

"That's Rob MacKinnon and his grandson."

"Why are they fighting?" He had no doubt Charlotte knew. She seemed current with all the village gossip, the births and deaths and latest romantic entanglements.

"It's always the same old issue," she sighed. "Old Rob claims his ancestor lost his land to the MacLeods, our ancestor."

"And did he?"

"That's a moot point. Nobody knows anymore. But there are legends."

"This isn't a recent affair?"

"No, not very. I think it all took place sometime in the late 1700s."

"And they're still arguing about it?" He almost burst out laughing, then, seeing her face, thought better of it and sipped his whiskey instead.

"I wouldn't laugh, Brad, it's a serious matter that's very nearly caused significant damage over the years." She paused. "I hate to tell you this, but it's an issue you're going to end up having to deal with."

"Me?" Brad set his tumbler down with a bang and sent her an astonished glance. "What does it have to do with me?"

"Everything. He's the MacKinnon, you're the Mac-Leod. That's the way it goes." She shrugged, glancing at Ben, who had an eye trained on the scene at the end of the bar, ready to intervene if necessary. Rob Mac-Kinnon was sending fulminating glances down the counter in their direction.

Brad listened attentively, acutely aware that the entire pub appeared to be awaiting his reaction.

"Just drop it, Granddad. For goodness' sake," the young man implored, looking embarrassed.

"I'll not. It's our right. The MacLeods betrayed us and I'll nae' rest until justice is done."

"This is ridiculous." His grandson, a thin lad in his mid-twenties, cast an apologetic glance down the counter.

Armand shifted nervously on his stool. "Charlotte, if there is to be a scene I would rather depart."

"Armand, do shut up," Charlotte muttered.

"Leave now and you'll regret it," Ben commented, leaning over the counter and topping up Brad's empty glass.

Brad sent him a speculative glance. Apparently everyone present expected something of him.

A hush reigned, broken only by the monotone murmur of the television and the American family who continued to chat, oblivious of the drama taking place.

Brad weighed his options; he could pretend to be unaware and retreat, or he could confront them. Their turf, he mused, on high alert behind his calm front, and their advantage. Not by a twitch did he give anything away. There was a choice to be made. Either he showed his colors and set the tone for the future, or it might be years before the air cleared. Taking a long sip he swirled the liquid in his glass, stared at it a moment, then, taking a deep breath, got to his feet and started down the bar.

The voices at the end of the counter were rising steadily. Charlotte's hand flew out and rested on his sleeve. "Be careful—this could be tricky."

"Don't worry."

"Oh la la," Armand whispered in a soft wail, "I knew it was unwise to come."

"Buckle it, Armand. Brad can handle himself." Charlotte took a gulp of wine and watched uneasily as he made his way casually toward the end of the bar. Ben laid down the tumbler he'd been wiping, and followed Brad's progress, and the strains of the accordion waned. Heads rose and voices lowered as he made his approach.

"Excuse me." Brad addressed the young man in the suit who looked at him nervously. Smiling reassuringly, he held out a hand. "Hi. I'm Brad Ward."

The young man hesitated then shook it. "Cullum MacKinnon. This here's ma' granddad, Rob MacKinnon, head of our clan."

Brad turned to the red-faced old man and looked him straight in the eye. "A pleasure to meet you, sir. I believe we're neighbors."

The pub went silent as Old Rob glared through eyes

bleary with age. Brad held the stare, then thrust his hand out and folks held their breath, the entire audience waiting to see how MacKinnon would react. Seconds ticked by, then reluctantly Rob MacKinnon shook Brad's hand and a murmur spread throughout the room.

"Can I buy you a drink?" Brad suggested.

The old man mumbled and Brad took it as a yes. Ben moved quickly, topping up the glasses with a grin.

"So yer the new laird, are ye?" Old MacKinnon lifted his glass of Talisker in a withered white hand and sniffed suspiciously.

"That's right."

"Then ye'll've heard all about our difference."

"Of course." He wasn't about to mention that he'd found it hilarious five minutes earlier. "I believe there are issues you and I need to discuss."

Rob MacKinnon sniffed once more and Cullum moved aside to allow Brad a seat on the stool next to him.

Slowly talk resumed, the accordion warmed up, and Mary MacAllister delved into a heartfelt rendition of "Annie Laurie."

"I hear you've been fixing the fences up yon' near ma' land," Old Rob remarked.

"That's correct. They've been sorely neglected. I hope the Strathaird sheep haven't strayed off our land and inconvenienced you?"

"That land's nae' Strathaird land, lad. That land belongs to the MacKinnons."

"So I've been told," Brad responded, tone neutral. He sent Cullum a warning glance when he saw him about to interrupt. "The matter of that particular piece of land appears to have caused some problems between our families over the years."

"Aye, that it has." Rob nodded in slow agreement.

Brad indicated to Ben to top them up again, wondering if he could keep up the pace. The old man seemed to have a limitless capacity for Talisker.

"I believe it's a matter we need to settle."

Old Rob grunted, stared at the bottles stacked behind the bar and sighed. "It's nae' an easy matter," he remarked, white head swaying back and forth.

"True. But if your ancestor was indeed wronged as you believe, then you should be compensated."

"Ye can keep yer' silver talents, MacLeod, fer I've nae use for them," the old man hissed.

"I wasn't suggesting monetary compensation. I think we need to be sure of exactly what land we're talking about, then proceed from there. If it's yours, then…" He raised his hands and smiled.

"Well, I never," the old man mumbled.

"The whole thing's ridiculous," Cullum burst in. "It all happened over three hundred years ago. Nobody cares any longer, Granddad."

"Did you hear that?" Old Rob turned, wobbled precariously on the stool, and faced Brad, his white thatch shaking once more. "That's what ye get for sending the young to the mainland. No loyalty, no sense of what is due to the clan. Glasgow indeed," he muttered somberly.

"I didna' choose to leave. I went because there was no work for me here," Cullum responded belligerently. "Do you nae' think I'd be back if a' could?"

"The way yer' talking, a dinna' ken."

"My leaving Skye has nothing to do with yer' blabbering on and on about what happened before any of us were seen or heard of," Cullum responded, exasperated.

"Is that so?" Rob eyed his grandson narrowly. "Is that what ye believe, that our rights mean nothin'?"

"Don't you agree it's absurd?" Cullum turned to Brad, pleading, now caught in the crossfire.

"It's a sad day when I hear my ain' grandson speaking to me like this," Rob said loudly, while Brad desperately searched for the right approach.

"Perhaps we could discuss this privately and come to some arrangement. Believe me, Mr. MacKinnon, I take the matter very seriously," Brad assured him, looking him in the eye once more.

Rob pondered the offer. "'Tis a strange thing," he remarked, sending his grandson a withering look, "when a foreigner, a Yank no less, should have a better understanding for the question than ma' ain' flesh and blood."

"Och, ye never talk about anything else," Cullum grumbled. "It's only a wee piece of land and who knows where the truth lies anyway. Just something for ye to go on about over a dram."

"So you'd be an idiot, as well as disloyal to yer clan? 'Tis the MacKinnon honor that's at stake, lad. The MacLeods and the MacKinnons go back for as long as can be recalled," he remarked to Brad in a friendlier tone. "The MacKinnons were standard bearers to the MacLeod of Dunvegan and to yer ain' ancestors too."

"All the more reason to get this sorted out." Brad drained his glass. Better to leave while he was ahead. Signaling to Ben to top them up once more, he rose and smiled. "I'm glad we've had the chance to meet, Mr. MacKinnon. It's always good to know one's neighbors."

The old man chuckled. "You've a way about ye, have ye not, young MacLeod?" He sent him a piercing look. "You remind me of yer granddad."

"I take that as a compliment."

"And so ye should. He was straight as they come, even if at times he was confused, running off to America as he did and leaving his brother to become laird." He sighed. "He was a wee bit older than me, but I can remember when we were lads." His eyes misted and he let out a reminiscent chuckle. "Och, Gavin was a wily one, he was. And sorely missed by the lassies when they thought he was dead and buried in the Somme."

"I can believe that."

"Aye. He was brae and handsome. Ye have the look of him. Have ye a wife, I wonder?"

"No, but my fiancée will be joining me in a few days."

"Fiancée, is it?" He nodded and chuckled. "Then there's still time to find ye a good Scottish lass. I wish ye luck, young MacLeod. I like yer style and yer guts."

"Then we'll set up a meeting as soon as possible to straighten out the matter of the north field."

The old man chuckled again and gazed at him through watery eyes. "Och, ye Yanks are always in a hurry. Like young Cullum here. But ye canna' fix in days what's taken over three hundred years to create, lad."

"We can certainly try," Brad insisted, smiling.

"Aye, that we can."

"It'll be the same thing in ten year's time," Cullum muttered.

"Then it'll be up to the two of you to settle things as best ye can, as I'll nae be here meself." The old man's shoulders shook and he cackled, wiping away tears of mirth. Brad leaned forward, afraid he would keel over.

"Dinna' worry. He'll be fine, has his balance down to a fine art." Cullum grinned affectionately. Out of his grandfather's hearing, he added, "Dinna' make an arrangement of any kind or ye'll kill him. He's been feeding on this for the past ninety years. Though he'll enjoy all the argy-bargying."

Brad let out a low chuckle and nodded. "I get the picture. By the way, what do you do in Glasgow?"

"I'm an accountant. Till the end of the month, that is," Cullum answered gloomily. "The company I work for is laying off people and I'm one of them."

"I heard you mention that you hadn't left the island by choice but by necessity."

"Aye. Like most of us. There's nae' jobs here and the only way to make a living is to leave." He shrugged despondently.

Brad frowned. He'd already gotten an in-depth view of the island's economy, and knew it needed some serious stimulus. He glanced at Cullum. "Come up and see me at the castle sometime, if you have a minute. I'd like to exchange some ideas and I might just have a job for you."

"Are ye serious?" Flushed, Cullum laid his glass down on the counter, eyes narrowing.

"Never more so. I have a couple of ideas I'd like to toss around with someone who knows the local issues better than me."

Straightening his shoulders, Cullum nodded proudly and offered Brad his hand. "I'll be glad to help you out— and glad of any chance to stay here on Skye." Together they turned to look at Old Rob, who was mumbling into his glass.

"Goodbye, Mr. MacKinnon," Brad said politely.

"Aye. We'll meet agin' soon, But dinna' think it'll be easy," he warned, raising a withered shaky finger. "The MacLeod stole that land and the MacKinnon's wife along with it. It's no light matter."

"No. And as you pointed out, it will take time and research to come to a proper conclusion." The old man nodded somberly. "In fact," Brad continued, warmed by the breakthrough, "we might have to establish an investigation committee."

Cullum rolled his eyes and handed his glass to Ben, who was standing amused behind the counter. "Seems he's gettin' the drift of the job," he remarked.

"Not a bad start," Ben admitted grudgingly. "Still, only time will tell."

When Brad sat down next to Charlotte once more, she sent him a warm smile. "That was brilliant," she whispered, proud of the way he'd dealt with Old Rob. Perhaps Brad would find his feet after all. But what about when he wasn't around? How would the locals react when they realized he wasn't here to stay?

They chatted convivially as they ate, sending each other amused glances as they watched Armand pick suspiciously at his food, and when they left, Brad got the impression he'd scored a minor victory. There were several approving nods and murmurs as they made their way to the door. For some reason he found hard to explain, he was as pleased as if he'd just clinched a multimillion-dollar deal. And, strangely, this meant a lot more.

"And then," Charlotte continued between gusts of laughter, sitting in the drawing room at Strathaird later that evening, "Brad was wheedling Old Rob MacKinnon as though he'd been doing it for years," she exclaimed, giggling.

"Well done." Penelope's eyes filled with laughter. "Brad won't do badly, you'll see. Just give him time. He seems truly interested in the people and their problems and that will help him greatly."

"I suppose so." Charlotte quieted suddenly and gazed absently into the fire.

Penelope frowned. "Is something the matter, dear?"

"Nope. Just thinking." She mustered a smile. "Mum, do you think John's the same person he was before the accident? I read somewhere that some people suddenly wake up totally changed."

Penelope looked up, surprised, realizing she must tread carefully. This was the first time Charlotte had deliberately raised the subject of her husband and she wondered what had provoked the sudden question.

"I suppose that might occasionally occur," she replied warily. "I seem to remember a film to that effect. But that was fiction, of course. One would have to consult a doctor, someone who really knows."

"Mmm." Charlotte plucked the fringe of the cushion absently.

"I have heard too that sometimes people can't remember anything at all when they come out of coma—which happens rarely."

"You're just saying that to make me feel better," Charlotte responded.

"If that's how you want to take it, Charlotte, so be it," Penelope replied crisply. "You're a grown woman and it's not my place to tell you how to run your life anymore. But just think of another scenario—what if John woke up worse than he was before the accident? Do you feel that you have the right to subject you and Genny to more of that treatment?" She held Charlotte's eyes unflinchingly for a few seconds. "I'm not trying to get you to do anything you don't feel is right. All I'm saying is that people rarely change, and if they do, it's often for worse rather than better."

"Right." Charlotte ended the conversation with a bang and Penelope was wise enough not to pursue it. "I wonder if Brad is truly aware of all that's involved in running

Strathaird?'' Charlotte said as though they'd never changed the subject.

''Not yet, but I think it's beginning to dawn on him.'' Penelope shifted, curling her legs on the sofa under her. ''He hasn't mentioned it per se, but from one or two comments, I get the sense that perhaps he's more aware than he makes out.'' She sighed. ''The poor boy has such a load to deal with, doesn't he? What with Harcourts, the twins and now this.''

Charlotte shrugged, picked up her old shooting jacket and rose stretching to her feet. ''He'll manage. He always does. I just hope Sylvia understands all that's required of him.''

''So do I.'' Their eyes met and Penelope sighed. ''It's not an easy job for anyone. I was partially born and bred to it and still it was no sinecure. But then, maybe she's one of these people who adapts easily.'' She sent Charlotte an optimistic smile. ''Good night, darling. I'm getting to bed early tonight so that I'll be ready tomorrow for the arrival of the twins and Ambassador de la Fuente.''

Charlotte leaned over and dropped a kiss on her cheek. ''Night-night, Mum. I'm off to Glasgow in the morning as usual.''

''I know, darling. I'll pick up Genny. And think about what I said,'' she told her, touching her daughter's cheek. At least Charlotte was starting to question things. That was a beginning, if nothing else.

''I will, Mum. And don't worry about Genny, Brad said he'd do it.''

''That's awfully kind,'' Penelope exclaimed, though she wasn't surprised. She'd seen the two of them, heads bent over Genny's math homework, and had heaved a silent sigh of longing.

"What time are the troops descending on us?"

"Sometime before noon. I'll make sure Genny's around. She's so excited. It'll do her a world of good to be with the boys."

"Hmm. Next thing you know, Sylvia will be here." Charlotte made a face and Penelope frowned.

"I'm sure Sylvia will do her best to fit in, and we must do all we can to help her. Thank goodness the ladies are coming in every day now. Mrs. Murray's niece is home for the holidays and will give us a day or two to help with the extra washing and ironing."

"Great. Then there's nothing for me to worry about." Charlotte sent her mother a bright, brittle smile and left the room. After the door closed behind her, Penelope's shoulders sagged. She stared a moment or two at the dying embers in the grate, then rose, checked the fireguard and turned out the lights. It was useless to worry about her child, but she felt suddenly grateful for Armand and his interest in Charlotte's work. At least that part of her daughter's life appeared to be thriving. It was the first time she'd seen Charlotte throw herself so passionately into an activity that took time, effort and extreme concentration.

As she mounted the stairs, she thought of the long day Charlotte would face on the morrow. It wasn't the trip to Glasgow she worried about, though that in itself was bad enough, but the emotional strain of seeing John, lying motionless, with never any sign of change. She wondered what had provoked Charlotte's question about him tonight. It was too early to have hope that their conversation would lead to action. It was only when Charlotte herself came to terms with what she was up against that anything would change.

Reaching her room, she forced her mind onto practical

matters. There was a lot to do in the next few days, with the twins and the ambassador's arrival. She tried to conjure up an image of Diego de la Fuente, whom she'd met only once after Brad's father, Scott, and the ambassador's daughter died. The poor man had been so weighed down by grief by the loss that he'd barely functioned. She sighed, gazed at the photographs on the pretty chintz-skirted dressing table and swallowed in sympathy. At least now she was able to look at David and Colin without bursting into tears. At times, she even remembered funny incidents, happy moments spent together and smiled. She would never get over their loss, of course, but at least now she'd reached some measure of acceptance. Enough to get through each day and start planning her own future.

But first, she must see Brad properly settled at the helm. Only then could she begin thinking about herself.

7

Sylvia alighted in Glasgow from the first-class cabin of the flight from New York, tired and annoyed at having to be here, yet satisfied she'd spent her time on the plane profitably. She'd even read a book she'd ordered a couple of months back on the Internet. It wasn't going to win a Pulitzer, but *Lady of the Manor: A Firsthand Guide to Becoming a Countess* did provide sharp insight into the oddities of the British aristocracy. For example, chapter three had stipulated, "Do not refer to money. Like children, it should be seen and not heard."

Fine. She wouldn't mention money, though why it was bad manners to mention what her apartment cost when it was a matter of public record was beyond her. Still, she had read carefully and taken extensive notes, particularly on how to establish smooth relations with the natives. On this matter, she'd decided to take a studied two-prong approach: be pleasant on the one hand, but also show you meant business. She'd learned that skill the hard way, she reflected. For a moment her mind strayed to her own personal problems. But only for a minute—she'd long ago learned to separate her emotions from business. Besides, gathering from Brad's daily reports, there was a lot of work to be done at Strathaird. She knew she'd have to make it clear to the locals she wouldn't tolerate laziness or idleness simply because it was the national pastime.

Entering the crowded arrival hall filled with tired passengers, she switched on her phone and checked her e-mail.

Three from Ira, she noted, satisfied to learn the new Harcourts' ad campaign was running smoothly. There was another from her other assistant, Hamilton. Good. Brad would be pleased that both Sydney and Auckland were a go. She gave a satisfied nod and opened the last message.

Her smile faded. Instead of picking her up in Glasgow as planned, Brad had arranged for a chopper to take her straight to Skye. She squinted at the text—*Unavoidable meeting with the clan MacKinnon*—and shook her head. Swallowing her anger, she shrugged and rolled a trolley to the baggage belt. She had bigger battles to fight.

Although she had long hated helicopters, Sylvia had to admit she was excited about finally getting a look at this estate Brad had inherited. If the place was in reasonable shape, it might have real promise as a getaway. She rather liked the idea of being able to invite some of their more prestigious acquaintances to a little R&R at Brad's private Scottish castle—soon to be hers, too, she realized with a ripple of satisfaction. Of course, she pondered thoughtfully, they'd have to change the name. "Strathaird" didn't have a very glamorous ring to it.

Two hours later she gazed down uneasily from the chopper into the restless gray water below. The ride had been bumpy and rain splattered the windscreen, making it hard to see anything of the landscape beyond. This would not be a pleasant way to die, she decided with a shudder. The pilot pointed to a blob on the horizon and she followed his finger through the mist. In the distance she could make out a medieval-looking fortress, austere and unwelcoming against the bleak sky. She felt her spirits plummet. It looked grim. Then, on reflection, she decided that wasn't so bad—at least the place would look impressive to visitors. Like something right out of *Braveheart.*

The chopper circled and the castle disappeared from view. A sudden lurch made her grip the edge of the seat, her pulse all over the place as she held on to her self-control. Why couldn't Brad have landed an inheritance in a country with better weather? she wondered irritably.

When the chopper finally landed on the lawn amid strong gusts, Sylvia took a deep breath, then released it gratefully. She loathed choppers. Not that she'd ever admit to it or allow the weakness to upset her schedule. Still, it was good to feel the damp grass squelching under her black leather moccasins. Even the realization they'd probably be ruined couldn't dim her relief.

Opening her umbrella, she glanced at the castle looming somberly above her, struck by an unexpected sense of foreboding. It looked aggressively permanent, as if rather than tolerating change, it forced its occupants to bend to its will. She glanced fleetingly at the chopper, suddenly tempted to rush back across the lawn and leave. But of course, that was ridiculous. After everything she'd faced in life, there was nothing in this old pile of stone that she couldn't handle.

Bracing herself, she turned back, eyes narrowed, and faced the castle, standing powerful and ominous as though daring her to challenge it. She examined the lawn, smooth as a green velvet carpet, and began mapping out where to put the pool when she noticed a figure standing at the foot of a wide, shallow stone staircase leading up to French doors beyond. Her heart lurched. Then she recognized Penelope MacLeod and experienced a moment's relief. At least Penelope was a familiar face, though why she felt nervous when she had everything under control was beyond her. Straightening her slim shoulders, she fixed on a smile, confident that her black Calvin Klein slacks and the three-quarter-length raincoat she'd picked up at Bergdorf's struck the right note. Knowing she looked great always cheered her considerably and she gave the stark facade a scathing glance, wondering what Brad could possibly see in a remote place like this. He clearly needed to be reminded where the real world was and where his priorities lay. She would waste no time in doing just that.

Waving jauntily, Sylvia stepped across the lush green grass, wondering how quickly a competent management team could be brought in to run the place. Not fast enough, she reckoned, shivering as a gust of wind strained the spokes of the umbrella. Still, she was determined to be pleasant and not let the place get to her.

Penelope stepped forward with a welcoming smile. What an attractive girl Sylvia was, she remarked, noting the blond, beautifully highlighted hair swinging smartly, framing a face whose tanned skin looked fresh despite a whole night on the plane. She was sleek, chic and very put-together in black and white, a huge black bag draped over her shoulder and a pair of two-tone sunglasses that defied the rain. She looked more like a top model than the future chatelaine of a Scottish castle, Penelope reflected. Then, swallowing her uneasiness, she smiled brightly and held out her hand.

"Welcome to Strathaird."

"Hi, Penelope. This is some place."

Penelope caught a whiff of perfume she recognized but whose name escaped her.

"I'm so sorry Brad couldn't meet you in Glasgow," she said as they turned toward the steps. "Unfortunately, today's the big gathering of the MacKinnon clan and some issues needed to be ironed out."

"Not a problem. Doesn't he have a secretary yet to handle that kind of thing?"

"Uh, no. And even if he had, this particular matter needed to be dealt with personally. It's been in the offing for quite some time. Now, where's your luggage?" She glanced across the lawn to the helicopter about to take off.

"It's being shipped from Glasgow. It wouldn't fit in the chopper."

"Ah. Well, we must hope it won't take too long arriving," Penelope murmured, remembering the last guest whose luggage had been delivered a week later.

"I brought this for tonight." Sylvia indicated the large black leather tote she was carrying. Penelope smiled, relieved, then led the way up the ancient stone steps, pulling the pale pink cardigan of her twinset about her shoulders. "I hope you won't be cold, it's been fairly chilly even though we are in mid-summer."

"I'm fine, thanks," Sylvia responded. When they reached the French doors, she stopped on the threshold.

"Wow! This is really something. It reminds me of Henry Ford's castle," she remarked, staring at the paneling, the low coffered ceiling and the paintings on the walls.

"Really? That must be lovely and probably far more comfortable than Strathaird," Penelope remarked, laughing. "I'm sure Mr. Ford saw to it that every modern convenience was installed. Renovating can be quite a job in a place like this, what with special permits and such, due to the historical importance of the place.''

Sylvia eyed the fading chintz furniture—why hadn't they had it reupholstered?—then noticed the fine mahogany antiques stacked with ornaments and photographs. ''Is that Fabergé?'' she asked casually, impressed despite herself.

''Yes. Nicholas and Alexandra gave the Easter egg to Hamish MacLeod and his wife in the early 1900s.'' Penelope led her into the Great Hall, then turned to her with a warm smile. ''You must be exhausted. Would you like some tea or coffee, or shall I take you up right away and show you your room?''

''Thanks. It would be nice to take a nap before Brad gets back from the meeting,'' Sylvia agreed, fatigue kicking in. As she followed her hostess up the wide oak staircase, she took in the state of the castle. Frankly, the place was a mess. Not a complete disaster—in fact, she was sure some would find its shabby British chic quite charming—but the place wasn't up to what she considered a minimum comfort level. She frowned, casting a deprecating look at the threadbare carpet, knowing enough about renovating to shudder at the thought of all it would take. Was it really worth it? she wondered doubtfully. Would they use the place often enough to justify the millions it would cost to refurbish it?

As they reached the landing, she considered the corporate and social advantages. A castle in Scotland *was* a castle in Scotland, of that there was no doubt. But it was also money that could be making money. She glanced fleetingly at the forbidding faces staring down at her from the gloomy portraits hanging on the oak-paneled wall and sighed. This definitely wasn't what she'd hoped for, and with characteristic swiftness, she decided it was better to cut bait than fish. She'd insist Brad sell the place. The last thing she wanted was to cart this albatross into their new life together. The sooner she sat him down and made him see sense, the less time they'd waste, and life would return to normal.

"I'm not sure when Brad will be back," Penelope remarked as they reached the top of the stairs "I'm afraid it may take a while."

Sylvia focused her tired brain and tried to remember what they'd been talking about. Ah yes, the meeting. "Why is this meeting expected to take so long?" she inquired, curious despite herself.

"It's a long story that dates back. It all began, you see, when Duncan MacLeod supposedly kidnapped MacKinnon's wife and stole some of his land when he was away at war."

"Goodness! That would be World War II?" Sylvia asked, amazed that the natives were still so savage, even in modern times.

"Good gracious, no," Penelope exclaimed, laughing. "This dates back to the late 1700s."

Sylvia stopped in her tracks and her brows flew up. "The late seventeen—you mean they're still arguing about something that occurred back then?"

"I'm afraid so." Penelope shook her head apologetically. "Things can take a long time to get settled in these parts."

"No kidding," she muttered, horrified. It was obvious Brad was being sucked into quicksand here and needed her to save his ass.

"Why don't I show you your room? Then we'll have a bite of lunch in the breakfast room. Charlotte said she might join us."

"Great." Sylvia infused an enthusiasm into her words

she was far from feeling. She took another surreptitious peek at the eyes staring down at her. She supposed they must all be MacLeod ancestors, but they gave her the creeps. It was like walking through the portrait gallery at the Met, but far eerier. A mausoleum would be more cheerful, she decided, sidestepping a knight in armor who leaned too close for comfort. As they began the walk down the wide oak-paneled corridor lit at the far end by a large stained-glass window, she tried to evaluate what the net worth of the movable property at auction might run.

"Here's your room," Penelope said brightly, stopping before a door on her left. It opened onto a large, airy bedroom prettily decorated in blue and white chintz. Chintz, Sylvia observed, seemed very much in vogue here. Personally she preferred a cleaner, more minimalist look, but she had to admit that ruffles and floral patterns held a kind of rustic New England charm.

"It's very pretty," she remarked for something to say. "Did you decorate it yourself, Penelope?" She laid her bag and purse on the bed and moved to the window where a small sofa rested under the mullioned panes. Leaning her knee on it, she stared out across the lawn toward the sea. It looked gray, bleak and menacing. Even the dot of a red fishing boat bobbing on the surf did little to lift her spirits.

"Not really decorate, no," Penelope said in answer to her question. "Things get done when they need to around here. You know how it is, the odd sofa about to collapse, bedspreads that have deteriorated beyond rehabilitation. I agree this particular material is rather attractive," she said, caressing the bedspread with a smile. "My mother-in-law, Flora MacLeod, and I chose it together shortly before she died." Then Penelope moved toward a large mahogany armoire and opened it. "I'm afraid there's not much cupboard space, but the chest of drawers is fairly large. I can always have another one brought up from the cellar if necessary."

"Oh, thanks. That's great. I just brought what I'd need for a few days. Honestly, I don't have that much stuff. But—" she paused, looking at the cupboards "—where are Brad's things?"

Sylvia searched curiously for another cupboard or closet, or wherever it was they kept their clothes. Her business trips to London, where she stayed in a suite at Claridge's, had not prepared her for this.

Penelope gave an embarrassed laugh. "Well, I'm afraid Brad's room is on the next floor. It's the room all the lairds have occupied since the 1500s."

"Wouldn't it be easier if I just moved right in there?" She frowned as Penelope hesitated. "I mean, it certainly would be less disruptive. Brad and I—well, we'll want to be together, and I'd hate to disturb anyone." She stood expectantly, ready to pick up her things, then cocked her head. Was she missing something?

"Sylvia, I don't quite know how to put this. It's a little awkward…"

"Is there a problem, Penelope?" Sylvia stared at her, eyes questioning.

"Uh, no, of course not. But you see, things here on the island are not quite as advanced as in your world. Customs are somewhat antiquated."

"What exactly do you mean?" Sylvia failed to see her point and wished Penelope would just say what was on her mind.

"What I'm trying to say," Penelope continued in obvious discomfort, "is that people might not understand if they knew you and Brad were, um, cohabitating, so to speak, before being married.''

Sylvia plopped down on the window seat in open-mouthed amazement. "You mean, for people to—" she burst out laughing and waved her hands for lack of the right term "—you have to be married?"

"No, of course not," Penelope reassured. Their eyes met now in mutual amusement and she joined in the laughter. "It's all about keeping up appearances. Sharing the same room might not go down very well with the tenants."

"But what on earth does it have to do with them?" Sylvia asked, bewildered.

"Nothing, I suppose, and yet..." Penelope's eyebrows drew together as she tried to explain. "We try to respect their sensibilities." Her hands fluttered in an embarrassed gesture and she sighed. "It isn't always an easy task, I assure you."

Sylvia nodded slowly. She still failed to see what on earth her sex life had to do with anyone but Brad and herself, but she stayed quiet. For now, at any rate. Perhaps this was what the book had meant by *accepted code of behavior.*

"I know it's perfectly ridiculous in this day and age," Penelope continued apologizing, "but I'm afraid the ladies would definitely be upset."

"The ladies?" Sylvia said faintly, wondering how many other people she would be expected to please.

"You'll meet them tomorrow. Mrs. MacKinnon, Mrs. Murray and Mrs. Lorrie. They've been doing the cleaning here for more than forty years. They have rather old-fashioned views. I felt that perhaps—"

Sylvia nodded, jet lag catching up with her. "Not a problem, Penelope. I get the drift. Do you mind if we continue this discussion later?'' she added with a winning smile. ''Right now, I'm beat.''

''Of course, my dear. So thoughtless of me. I'm glad you understand.'' Penelope pressed her hands together at the waist and smiled. ''Is there anything else I can get you?''

''No, thanks, unless there's a map of the castle. I suspect I'll need one not to get lost.'' She grinned and decided to make the best of it. There was no use in putting people's backs up. If there was one thing she'd learned during her years of climbing the corporate ladder, it was that pissing people off didn't pay. And in her modest opinion, this wasn't so different. If she could get Penelope on her side, she might have a strong ally, she reflected speculatively. After all, Penelope had everything to gain by Brad's departure.

Penelope headed toward the door. ''Don't worry about getting lost. At first the place can be confusing, but in a week or so you'll be used to it.''

''A week?'' Sylvia's head jerked up and she frowned. By then she expected to be back in New York. She hoped to leave before the week was out. Surely seven days would be ample time to have the place up and running. Surely it wouldn't take *that* long to persuade Brad to depart. Still, she'd have to tread lightly here, and winning Penelope's cooperation struck her as a brilliant strategic move. ''Perhaps you might show me where I can freshen up?'' she asked, rising from the window seat, legs shaky from fatigue, and searching the chintz-covered walls for the door to the bathroom. She hadn't stopped all week and now it was hitting her hard.

''I'm afraid that's down the hall. As I mentioned earlier, things are a little backward here, Sylvia. It may take a little getting used to." She led the way back into the hallway.

"Are there any ghosts?" Sylvia inquired laughingly, casting a cursory glance at the watercolor prints on the wall.

"None to speak of. There was Clara MacLeod, who died in 1773 of a broken heart. She has been seen from time to time but not of late. And of course Cullum, the first laird who battled the Vikings in 900 and something, occasionally makes his presence felt. But not since Flora died. Things have been relatively quiet since then."

Sylvia was about to question what "relatively" meant, but thought better of it. Instead, she remarked lightheartedly, "How boring for you."

"We survive quite nicely, thank you. Here's the bathroom. I hope it's all right."

"Don't worry. I'll do fine." For a week, she amended silently. "Has Brad brought anyone in to begin an overhaul? I would think plumbing and wiring might be a problem in a place like this."

"Architects, you mean?"

"Yes. I'm sure you've done your very best to keep the place up, but it sure looks like it could do with some rehab." She flicked a finger over a damp stain on the wall.

"As I mentioned," Penelope said patiently, "the historical society and the National Trust have very strict rules regarding remodeling."

"Right." She could have kicked herself for not remembering. It just went to show how tired she was.

Ten minutes later, wearing a white terry robe, hair expertly wrapped in a towel, Sylvia headed briskly down the corridor. A refreshing hot shower would help her clear the cobwebs. She stepped into the bathroom, horrified to see it looked as dated as the castle. A spartan cork floor, towels hanging on metal pipes and a long white tub that predated the Jacuzzi by far stared her in the face. There was no shower.

Never mind, she decided, leaning against the doorjamb and closing her eyes. It's only for a few days. Then we'll be back to civilization and can pretend this never happened. Yawning, she moved toward the tub and absently turned on the taps before setting her makeup bag on the counter and arranging her toiletries on the small shelf above the basin. Grimacing, she placed her toothbrush in a misty glass, then turned to check the bath. A gasp escaped her and she watched in horrified wonder as dirty brown water oozed onto white enamel. "My God, what is wrong with this place?" she murmured, wearily turning off the taps. The pipes must be as old as the place itself. She took a deep breath, regrouped and tried the basin. Identical brown liquid trickled forth and she stared at it in disgust. Something must be done urgently, she reflected, shaking her head despondently. The place wouldn't even be of use to them commercially if there wasn't decent running water. She wondered if all the bathrooms were alike and if so, how Brad could stand it. You'd think after two weeks of this he'd have had enough. But either he was oblivious or blind, for there had been no mention of what she considered a major flaw.

She tramped crossly back to her room and changed into a smart pair of white pants and a silk shirt. The least he could have done was warn her. She took a critical glance in the mirror, glad she'd had the chemical peel, and done Botox around her eyes. She made a face, but her expression didn't budge. At thirty-five, it was important to keep up her looks, and the slim, green-eyed blonde staring at her from the mirror filled every expectation. She also wanted to look good for Brad.

She considered unpacking, then decided to wait till after lunch. Perhaps Brad would dismiss Penelope's ridiculous notions about having different rooms. Surly he wouldn't tolerate being pushed about by a bunch of yokels? In fact, this was as good an opportunity as any to show people how things were about to change around here.

She moved to the window and stared glumly as the waves heaved inland, endless, forceful and incessant. She shuddered involuntarily. How many lives had this angry sea swallowed? she wondered, suddenly haunted by the murky waters of her own past, those desperate times when she'd thought she, too, would drown in the ocean of misery that had once been her life. But she'd survived—even flourished, she reminded herself proudly. Only in the rarest moments—like right now—did she wonder if she'd ever really escape. She quickly banished such thoughts, knowing there was no place in her present life for self-doubt, and focused on the property.

The castle must be a prime piece of real estate, even in this remote location. Plus, for some reason she failed to comprehend, people thought of Skye as romantic. What would the estate retail in the present market? she wondered. She'd raised the issue with Brad before, but had elicited little response. She'd hinted tentatively over the phone that he should consider selling, but he hadn't picked up on it, or even seemed interested in the property's value, for that matter, which had struck her as weird at the time. Now she frowned, concerned. Back in New York, Strathaird had seemed insignificant, another obligation, certainly, but a manageable one that would be resolved, as were all the other corporate matters they dealt with daily. Now she wasn't so sure.

She turned back toward the room, glanced at the single bed with its mahogany headboard and virginal floral coverlet, and grimaced. Playing hide-and-seek on the stairs could be amusing for a couple of nights, but it would become tiring if the charade were to continue. Maybe Penelope was just being paranoid. Brad would set her straight, she reassured herself.

She picked out a black sweater from the tote bag lying half-open on the floor, and slipped it over her shoulders before heading down the corridor toward the huge oak staircase. Reaching the landing, she allowed her fingers to travel over the carved balustrade and stared down from the gallery into the Great Hall below. Impressive in its own way, she supposed, but who in their right mind would want to live in a tomb like this when they could have a perfectly nice place in town? Strathaird should be turned into a museum, for Christ's sake. Perhaps then it might even become a tax write-off?

She descended the stairs considering the matter, firmly ignoring the eyes following her everywhere. Nobody freaked her out, and a bunch of painted faces were not going to start. Then, to her delight, she heard Brad's voice echoing through the hall. With a sudden surge of relief, she hastened down the last stairs, the sight of his windblown chestnut hair and familiar smile more comforting than she cared to admit. It dawned on her that he looked different, more relaxed in an old shooting jacket, jeans and rubber boots. Then, in an uncharacteristic move, she threw herself into his arms and hugged him.

''Am I glad to see you!'' she exclaimed.

''Makes two of us.'' He dropped a kiss on her forehead

then drew back, eyebrows creased, and surveyed her. "Everything okay?"

"Well, I guess. It's somewhat archaic, sort of like being whisked back in time?"

"Yes, isn't it? Has a charm all its own," he agreed, a smile curving his lips.

"That wasn't exactly what I was referring to."

"Oh, you meant the history?" he said, nodding. "It's fascinating too. You'll have to get Aunt Penn to give you a complete tour. She knows all the tales."

"I'm referring to the present living conditions," she snapped impatiently.

"What about them?" He drew away and took off his jacket.

"Well, surely you must have noticed?" She tried to mask her rising irritation. There was no use in having a head-on confrontation, she knew that. Men reacted so much better when approached indirectly. Hadn't she always followed that sacred rule in business?

"I can't say that anything in particular comes to mind," he remarked, frowning, his expression mystified.

"Not even the tap water?" she replied sweetly, unable to keep the sarcasm from her tone. "Really, Brad, surely you must have noticed *that!*"

"Oh, yeah!" His forehead cleared and he grinned. "I forgot to warn you. The water's local. It's the same all over the island. A bit salty too, but it washes fine as any other. You'll get used to it."

"Used to it?" she spluttered angrily, forgetting her resolve. "I'll never get used to bathing in filthy water. Plus, there's not even a shower."

"We'll have one put in. By the way, your workout equipment arrived."

"Well, that's something, although I don't know if it's

worth having it unpacked,'' she muttered, taking a deep breath, determined not to lose her calm completely.

Brad moved next to her and stroked her cheek. ''Don't get upset, honey. Right now you're tired. You'll see, tomorrow it'll all be better.''

''Bradley, I am not some sweet little idiot you need to soothe— Oh my God,'' she exclaimed, pulling away and almost tripping into the huge baronial fireplace at her back.

''Careful.'' Brad grabbed her arm and steadied her.

''What,'' she asked, pointing a shaking finger, ''is that?''

Brad glanced over his shoulder. ''Oh, don't worry,'' he laughed. ''That's just Rufus.'' He summoned the dog, who moved ponderously to his side. ''He's gigantic, isn't he? A wolfhound with a bloodline almost as old as the MacLeods', but trust me, he's harmless. Unless you're a rabbit, you're completely safe.''

''Just dandy,'' she muttered, staring at the dog, still stunned that Brad would allow such a creature in the house. This laid-back attitude of his was a total surprise. It was as if she was standing before a different man from the sophisticated, driven, exacting individual she knew.

''You sure you're okay? You look kind of pale.'' He slipped a hand under her chin and searched her eyes with such affectionate concern that she melted despite her anger. ''I'm sorry I couldn't be there to pick you up, Syl. I had an important meeting with members of the MacKinnon clan that I simply couldn't miss.''

''I heard. Anyway, it was just a chopper ride.''

He smiled down at her, the familiar glint in those piercing blue eyes making her go suddenly weak. ''You hate chopper rides.''

''True. But I can stand them when necessary. What I

can't stand, though, is being relegated to a guest bedroom.'' She looked at him suggestively through her lashes and raised a questioning eyebrow. ''I mean, this is the twenty-first century, for Christ's sake,'' she lowered her voice to a whisper. ''Surely they can't be that backward?''

''What do you mean?'' He frowned.

''Penelope said it would look bad if we slept in the same room. Something about it bothering the housekeepers.''

''Geez, I hadn't thought of that.'' He frowned, then grinned apologetically and slipped an arm around her waist. ''I guess we'll have to sneak around like teenagers for a while.''

''You mean you're going to tolerate this? Brad, it's your house now—take a stand.'' She disengaged herself, thoroughly annoyed by his lack of reaction.

''I'm sorry if it bothers you, Syl, but I'm sure Penelope knows best. Surely it won't matter for a few nights?''

''Maybe to you it doesn't, but I care quite a bit, even if it is only for a few days,'' she remarked tartly. ''I didn't travel across half the world for this.''

''Of course I care,'' Brad replied patiently, slipping his arm around her shoulders, ''but we don't want to upset people unnecessarily. If Aunt Penn thinks it's better this way, then I think we should comply.''

''Jesus, Brad, you sound like a complete wuss,'' she exclaimed, disgusted. ''I think this place is affecting your sanity.''

''You know as well as I do that offending people's sensibilities unnecessarily is a stupid reaction. You're the one who's always telling me how we need to handle things with kid gloves.''

''That's in business,'' she muttered.

"This *is* business, and it's tough enough as it is," he said dryly. "I'm a fish out of water and it's taking all of my time to get these folks to trust me. We have to go the extra mile to fit in."

"I don't understand why you're so personally involved," she said with a bad-tempered shrug. She was tired, desperately wanted a shower and Brad's attitude was getting on her nerves. Added to that was her own lack of self-control. She could not allow such emotional displays to happen again. "Where's the living room?" she said at last. "I could use a drink."

Brad drew her close and turned her toward him. "Don't get uptight on me, Syl, it'll all work out, you'll see. You'll learn to love the place as much as I do."

She was about to tell him a few home truths—like the fact that the only thing she'd ever love about this place was the sight of it in her rearview mirror—but instead bit her lip and nodded. There would be time enough for negotiations when they were alone. Everything would be fine, she reassured herself, and not because she was going to pander to their ridiculous old-fashioned dictums. It would work out because she'd see to it that, by the end of the week, she and Brad were back where they belonged: New York City, thank you very much.

As they walked toward the drawing room, she speculated about how best to proceed. Okay, she'd play the game for a couple of days until she could get a handle on how best to extricate them from this situation. She glanced around her. In the meantime, she'd light a fire under the staff. For one, the place needed a good cleanup, not to mention the deplorable state of some of the furnishings.

In the drawing room Penelope sat on the sofa while Armand, the French cousin whom she remembered from a trip with Brad to Paris, sat perched on a high-backed tapestry chair next to the empty grate. He had an irritating laugh, she recalled, careful to paste a smile on her face as she entered.

"Ah, Brad, Sylvia," Penelope said. "Did you have a nice bath, dear?"

"Uh, actually, I thought I'd wait till later."

"Syl didn't expect brown water, did you, honey?"

Brad threw her a grin that left her seething in silent rage. What was the matter with him? Couldn't he see he was making a fool of her? She forced herself to keep smiling. "It was a little unexpected."

"Oh! I'm dreadfully sorry," Penelope exclaimed, rising, and tucking a strand of stray hair behind her ear as she was prone to do. "I completely forgot to warn you. It's terribly off-putting at first. Still, there's nothing really wrong with the actual water itself." Seeing that Penelope's smile was genuinely apologetic, Sylvia calmed down and turned with her toward the Frenchman. "Allow me to introduce you to Armand de la Vallière."

"We had that pleasure in Paris." Armand rose and kissed her hand elaborately, making her want to roll her eyes despite her displeasure.

"Would you like a drink?" Penelope asked. "You'll need one after such a long haul."

"Scotch and soda on the rocks, please."

"Right. Have a seat," Penelope replied.

Sylvia sank gratefully among the plump cushions of a small sofa opposite the fireplace, and felt a little more relaxed. But Brad's next words left her ragged.

"You can forget both the soda and rocks. Here they drink it neat." Brad's back was facing her, so he did not see the killer look she sent him. Where were his tact and diplomacy?

"Neat'll do fine," she replied with a bright, brittle smile as he turned to her with a tumbler.

"Is it your first visit to Skye?" Armand questioned, tilting his birdlike head curiously.

"Yes, it is. Do you live here as well as in Paris?" she asked, taking a long, welcome sip.

"Oh, *mon Dieu*, no!" he exclaimed.

Sylvia grinned. Her eyes met Brad's in a silent exchange that broke the mounting layer of ice and gave her hope. The familiar complicity left her more at ease, and she settled on the sofa, mollified, wondering how Armand might be put to good use.

After all, she'd only given herself a week.

Instinct told Penelope the rap on the door spelled trouble. "Come in," she murmured automatically, laying her fountain pen down on the desk with a sigh. It had been a long day.

"I'm sorry te' disturb ye, ma'lady." Mrs. Murray stood planted in the doorway, her striped apron straining at the waist, her steely, permed curls stiffly in place. Her expression was stony, mouth turned down in a frown. As the door opened wider, Penelope's sense of foreboding increased.

"Yes, Mrs. Murray?" she asked in a neutral tone, wondering what could possibly have happened to upset the easiest woman on her cleaning team.

"I've come to hand in ma' notice," Mrs. Murray sniffed.

Penelope rose, shocked. "What on earth are you talking about, Mrs. Murray?"

Mrs. Murray shook her head woefully with a deep sigh. "Forty-five years it's been, ma'lady, and never a complaint." Eyes turned misty with memories, she heaved another gusty sigh. "I can still remember the first day I set foot in the castle. Lady Flora received me her-sel' in this very room. Mary, she said—fer in those days I was just a young thing—ye'll start in the kitchen with Cook and I hope it'll be te' yer liking." Her red cheeks quivered as a single tear traced its course through her powder. "Never a harsh word have I heard until today—"

"Mrs. Murray, there must be some misunderstanding. Please sit down." Penelope drew her firmly but gently toward a chair. "What has happened to upset you?"

Mrs. Murray allowed herself to be seated beside the sofa and gave another long sniff. "Never did I think I'd see the day when I'd be told the house was dirty. Dirty, ma'lady!" she exclaimed, pulling out a voluminous han-kie and dabbing her eyes. "A cleaning service from Glas-gow was what *she* said. A complete overhaul." She waved her hands, growing increasingly agitated. "Need to scour the place from top to toe, were her very words. Said there must be thirty years of dreck, whatever that is."

"But *who* said that?" Penelope inquired, heart sinking.

"Miss Sylvia."

"Are you sure? Perhaps there's been some misunder-standing. I'm sure Sylvia didn't intend to hurt your feel-ings."

"I heard what I heard and I know what I know. *Filth* was the word she used and I'll nae' forget it as long as I live, Lady Penn. God knows ye've all been sae' good to me over the years and it breaks ma' heart, but I'll nae' stay working for the new laird if that's who he intends to marry." Her voice cracked, and she shook her head vigorously and dabbed her eyes yet again. Penelope racked her brains for a solution. Sylvia had obviously made some tactless comment—not the first, unfortunately, even though she'd only been here a day—that would now need major diplomacy to counter.

"Mrs. Murray, why don't you take a few days off and let me sort this whole matter out? I assure you, if I really believed Sylvia meant what she said, I'd accept your notice at once. But I'm certain there's been a mistake." She sat down next to Mrs. Murray on the sofa and tried another approach. "You see, Sylvia isn't used to our way of life. In America, things are very different. It's probably as difficult for her to adapt to us as it is for us to accept her. I know what a staunch churchgoer you are," Penelope emphasized, hoping she'd hit the right button. "And that you, of all people, would be the first to reach out and help a sister in need. So let me do a little investigating and then we'll talk about it." She squeezed Mrs. Murray's wrinkled hand reassuringly and gave her a conspiratorial grin. "Between you and me, Mrs. Murray," she added, lowering her voice to a murmur, "I think poor Brad's going to need all the help he can get. And I'm counting on you, of course. I know you have a broad vision of life and are able to understand others' limitations."

Mrs. Murray heaved another sigh but her shoulders straightened. Penelope noticed that the tears had dried and her cheeks were flushed with pride.

"Och, ma'lady, I'll try ma' best. But if that wom—Miss Sylvia," she corrected grudgingly, "produces any more newfangled products bought on some godforsaken machine, that's where I lay ma' foot down," she declared firmly. "There's a box in the pantry," she added ominously. "Take a look for yersel', ma'lady, and ye'll see," she said with a knowing glance at Penelope.

"I will. But I'm sure it was well meant."

"Hmmph."

"We should, I feel, at least give Sylvia the benefit of the doubt, don't you?" She rose with a firm smile and Mrs. Murray followed suit, sticking her hankie up the sleeve of her cardigan.

"Thank you, Lady Penn."

"Not at all. Thank you for being so broad-minded and understanding, Mrs. Murray. This modern world we live in puts taxing demands upon us, doesn't it?"

A silent look of mutual understanding was exchanged and Mrs. Murray nodded.

Penelope closed the door behind her, the smile of moments earlier transforming into a frown as she pressed worried fingers to her temples and wondered how to cope. There were days when she felt overwhelmed, and this was one of them. For the past several weeks she'd been dealing with Armand—not an easy guest at the best of times—and now Diego de la Fuente and the twins were here. All of this, while trying desperately to show a reluctant Sylvia the ropes. How was she going to iron out this latest faux pas?

She let out a long breath and stared at the blotting paper on the desk. What made it worse was that Sylvia probably meant well. She felt utterly wretched having to point out the young woman's mistakes. It was cruel and embarrassing and she knew Sylvia was suffering. What could she possibly do to smooth matters over, without humiliating Sylvia, and still keep the ladies happy?

She glanced at her watch, realizing it was getting late. Perhaps she'd better take a look at this box of products Mrs. Murray had referred to. How on earth had Sylvia gotten them here so fast? She rose and moved to the door.

"Oh, goodness," she exclaimed, stepping into the hall and nearly falling over Diego de la Fuente, who appeared to be on his way to the library with the *Financial Times* tucked under his arm. He stopped, his dark eyes alive under thick salt and pepper brows that stood out against the weather-beaten tan earned from a lifetime of sun and sailing. "I'm dreadfully sorry," she murmured as he steadied her.

"If anyone is to blame, it's me." He frowned. "Is something wrong, my dear? You seem concerned."

"Yes, no, that is…in a way, but please don't let me bore you with domestic concerns." She tucked her hair behind her ear and ignored the threatening headache, wondering all at once if talking to someone might not help. At least Diego was neutral.

"Is there anything I can do?" he inquired.

"Not really. But thanks for asking."

He kept his hand on her arm and smoothed her sleeve. "You know, one of these days you must start thinking of yourself, and stop worrying about everybody else in this household. Now, why don't you tell me what's wrong," he added, steering her persuasively back toward the sitting room.

Penelope hesitated. She needed to get to the root of the trouble with the ladies, and check the linen, but Diego's firm grasp on her arm made her realize just how tired she was, and how much she needed to confide in someone. Reluctantly, she let herself be ushered into the sitting room and together they sat on the couch.

"Now," he said, smiling winningly, "tell me all about it."

Whether she liked it or not, Charlotte reflected, she must face the fact that Sylvia had arrived and go up to the castle.

Maybe later, she decided, putting it off once again by

wielding her pencil and ferociously adding some final touches to her latest design, a brooch for her grandmother's dear friend Evelyne Franck in Gstaad. It was one of her first commissions, and she was tremendously proud that Evelyne, a true connoisseur, had ordered something from her. Tilting her head, she took a critical look at her drawing. It was imposing, she decided, a piece designed to be worn on cashmere or heavy silk, a jewel for a mature woman. There was a 1930s touch about it. But then, that could be said about much of her work. She frowned, laid the page down once more and sharpened her pencil, still searching for the final form the brooch would take. The stones were already chosen: a cabochon quartz, tourmalines and diamonds. Sylvain de Rothberg had used that same combination to great effect. Now she intended to create her own design with those same elements. She wondered if Armand would like it. Probably, since he appeared to be obsessed with anything relating to Sylvain. And he was right—there was definitely magic in Sylvain's work. Eyeing the drawing once more, she experienced a moment's doubt. Was there any in hers? She desperately hoped so, but who could say? What did it take to reach stardom? Armand seemed to think she had true talent. But what if it was just one of his crazy illusions? After all, there was no disputing Armand was a bit off-the-wall.

Setting the drawing aside, she stretched and grimaced, kicking the dilapidated stool rhythmically, wondering what Brad was doing. She hadn't seen him for five whole days. The thought made her unreasonably angry. She supposed now that Sylvia was here he didn't need her company any longer. Or perhaps they were honeymooning it up in the laird's bedroom. What irritated her most was knowing that it was none of her business, yet it bothered her anyway.

Impatiently she switched off the spotlight that illuminated her drawing table and, flinging her old basket over her shoulder, tried not to think about the couple. It was the couple bit that really got to her. She fidgeted impatiently, then picked up a few pencils, just in case inspiration hit during the night.

After procrastinating for another few minutes, she closed the door of the studio and entered the gallery where Moira was redoing the window.

"You off?" she asked, leaning back on her heels and surveying her handiwork. "Take a look at this before you go."

Charlotte moved across the gallery and glanced indifferently at the arrangement Moira had placed on the stand in the window. A bright red, white and blue silk scarf strewn next to it showed off the gold and quartz, but frankly, right now she didn't care.

"It looks great. I like the scarf," she murmured.

"It's for the Americans. But what's the matter with you? No changes, no last-minute bright ideas?" Moira rose and looked her over, surprised. She lifted her batik skirt, careful not to spoil the effect of the window display, and climbed gingerly back onto the floor.

"I have to go up to the castle to welcome Sylvia," Charlotte muttered sullenly.

"Ah…" Moira eyed her keenly from behind thick lenses that gave her an owlish expression. "And why is that such a big deal?"

Charlotte shrugged. "I don't know. I suppose it isn't, really."

"But for some reason it is," Moira pointed out gently.

"Oh, blast it," Charlotte let out a long breath and flopped onto the edge of the window display.

"Don't," Moira squealed in terror. "If you move anything so much as one iota, I shall throw a fit."

"That'd be a treat." Charlotte grinned, despite the depression hovering.

"You're not the only one who knows how to throw a tantrum, Charlotte Drummond, and just you remember it." Moira wagged a finger at her, then sat down carefully next to her. "Come on, Charlie, tell me what's up. You haven't been right since you got back from your last visit to John the other day."

"I know. It's all a bit of a muddle, really. I haven't seen Brad for five whole days. You'd think the queen had arrived, the way everyone's fussing."

"Well, she *is* his fiancée," Moira pointed out matter-of-factly.

"Don't remind me." Charlotte got up abruptly and cast her eyes heavenward. "I suppose she's already turning everything topsy-turvy up there." She jerked her head in the direction of Strathaird, aware that the change she'd so desperately feared was well and truly here.

"Well, she's not about to disappear into the mist, so I suppose you'll have to get used to her."

"You don't need to rub salt in the wound," Charlotte remarked tartly, sending her friend a dark look from under creased eyebrows. "I'm well aware that from now on I'll be a second-class citizen. It's just difficult, because Brad and I have always had such a special relationship." Charlotte stared into space. "It's never going to be the same again now that she's here," she ended, annoyed at the catch in her throat.

"Is it just the friendship that you think will change, or is there something else between you?"

"What do you mean?" Charlotte spun round, eyeing her friend defensively. "What an idiotic thing to say."

"Is it?" With the perception and liberty of old friendship, Moira plunged ahead regardless. "Maybe you don't want to admit it to yourself—which, by the way, is a habit of yours—"

"Rubbish!"

"Okay, then look me in the eye and tell me that what you feel for Brad is nothing but old friendship. From where I'm sitting, it looks very different."

"What utter rot," Charlotte exclaimed, outraged.

"And as for Sylvia," Moira plowed on, "you're just plain jealous of her."

"Of all the rotten, nasty—"

"Shut up and listen for once, I'm not done," Moira said, rising and facing her squarely. "You don't want to see Sylvia because the thought of her lying in Brad's arms is making you ill."

The two women faced one another, eyes locked in a battle of wills. Charlotte was about to protest vehemently, opening her mouth to give Moira a pithy retort, then closed it abruptly as the full force of her friend's words hit her. "No," she muttered, shaking her head, leaning her elbows on her knees and burying her face in her hands. "That's ridiculous, absurd and above all, inadmissible."

"But true," Moira insisted relentlessly.

"This can't be happening." Charlotte gave a muffled groan and Moira slipped an arm around her.

"But it is, darling, and the sooner you face up to it, the better."

Charlotte laid her head on her friend's shoulder and let out a shaky sigh. "But how could this have happened, Mo? I mean, Brad's been part of my life forever, and apart from that one little fling we had in London, years ago, I've never thought of him in *that* way.''

''Perhaps you just couldn't see the forest for the trees.''

Charlotte wiped her hand across her nose and gave a loud sniff. ''I got so used to him coming to the studio in the afternoon,'' she wailed. ''I *expected* him at the pub—plus, it was such fun whipping up dinner for him at the cottage.'' She raised her head slowly and met Moira's sympathetic gaze. ''And now it's all over. How can I suddenly miss someone so badly whose been out of my life for the past decade? It doesn't make sense.'' She stared out the window, then grabbed Moira's arm, forcing her to duck. ''For God's sake, stay down. Mrs. P.'s on the rampage.'' Moira grabbed the old dust sheet she'd used for her window decorating from the floor and they crouched under it, stifling giggles.

''When will we know that she's gone?'' Moira whispered.

Three minutes later, Charlotte peeked warily out the window, pleased to see Mrs. Pearson's large form receding into the newsagent's across the street. ''The coast's clear,'' she said, withdrawing the dust sheet from Moira's mussed hair. ''God, we look like two scarecrows. I guess I'd better get the visit over with ASAP, as Rick would say. It's amazing how the twins have grown up in a short time,'' she added, dusting off her jeans. ''Have you seen them yet? Rick looks exactly like the ambassador and Todd's a sort of mini-Brad.''

''Not yet, but your mum asked me over for supper tomorrow. That should give me the chance to get a good look at the N.Y. competition.''

''Moira!'' Charlotte declared firmly, ''we're not going to talk about this anymore, because it's silly. Nothing's going to change.'' Ignoring Moira's snort of disbelief, she grabbed her basket and threw her friend a look, determined to escape before she brought anything else up.

As she left the village she lowered the car window and breathed in the damp rainy evening. She drove slowly, in no hurry to arrive, her muddled feelings warring as she began the winding climb toward home. She had no right to expect anything from Brad but friendship. Particularly now. But Moira's words rang disturbingly true and she was obliged to ask herself exactly what it was she wanted from him. And was it want, or need?

She gripped the wheel tightly, battling the growing tightness in her throat. Ever since her last visit to Glasgow and her conversation with her mum she'd felt stifled, as though trapped in a dark, airless hole begging for oxygen. When she'd looked at her husband's lifeless figure, she'd pictured those closed eyes as they used to be, hard and hot with anger, heard his rich actor's voice berating her, telling her horrible, hurtful things like how stupid and selfish and incompetent she was. He'd systematically worn her down until she believed him.

She'd stared at the comatose body, dizzy with fear that he'd suddenly lunge from the bed and push her violently against the wall, as he'd been prone to doing. Trembling, she'd forced herself to calm down, and begun the usual process of justification: there was nothing in her life that he could find fault with now—she was living quietly, carefully trying to find her place, watching out for Genny; even if he were to recover, surely John would be content to let her go her own way if she was a good girl and didn't make a fuss; she wouldn't do anything to make him angry.

Now, thinking back to that crazy litany of rationalizations, she realized she was *still* living in paralyzing fear of John. She'd let him get away with everything he'd ever done to her. By no means had she asked for such treatment. Had she deserved it? No, she hadn't, but she'd caused much of her own misery by letting herself be brutalized. It was startling, almost frightening to realize that, as Mummy and Moira were continually reminding her, it was within her power to change all that, if only she could find the strength to forgive herself and move on. Problem was, the only time she felt truly strong was when Brad was by her side.

Charlotte gripped the steering wheel with trembling hands, tears pouring down her cheeks. She was so utterly confused and now, to crown it all, she had to face Sylvia. Evening settled on the heather-draped moors, a gentle mauve sea. The constriction in her throat grew as she headed on, past the harbor and the cluster of colorful fishing boats and up the hill. Facing Brad—and worse, Sylvia—in view of her newly discovered feelings seemed almost perverse. Knowing he was in love with Sylvia— not that it was her idea of love, when they'd discussed it over macaroni and cheese only a week ago—made her current predicament almost insurmountable.

She blew her nose hard, wiped her eyes and tried to rationalize her feelings, a hundred arguments crossing her mind. Perhaps she was imagining her emotions. Maybe the months spent wondering what would happen to John and worrying about Genny had finally caught up with her. Maybe she was just too much alone. She hadn't been touched by a man in forever, hadn't wanted to be after all John had subjected her to. Perhaps it was only because Brad was the first truly kind and charming individual who'd crossed her path that he'd grown so important again in her life.

At the foot of the castle's drive she hesitated, engine

running while she made up her mind. Then, on impulse, she drove through the fields, avoiding Strathaird, and stopped outside of Rose Cottage. She peered breathlessly into the rearview mirror, relieved, and almost laughed at the mess she'd caused by her outburst. She was probably just starved for sex, like those women she read about in magazines. A sudden, vivid image of Brad, tossed sheets and sex bolted into her brain. Catching her breath, she grabbed her basket and jumped from the car. She was in no shape to face Brad and Sylvia tonight. The meeting would simply have to wait. She'd ring up, make an excuse and join them for breakfast at the castle. Tomorrow, when hopefully her mask would be back in place.

8

Except for the odd creak in the woodwork, a shutter banging persistently somewhere downstairs and the hoot of an owl, the castle stood silent. Everyone had retired early tonight. Sylvia scowled at herself in the mirror as she brushed her hair and considered her present dilemma. It had become obvious in the past twenty-four hours that Brad was seriously entrenched here. He seemed to actually like the place. When he spoke about Strathaird, he used expressions like "family commitment" and "love of the land"—words that made her skin crawl and proved all too clearly that she had a serious problem on her hands. She frowned and pondered her options. It was definitely time to take action. Two nights spent alone in her room's narrow single bed had left her simmering with frustration. She couldn't believe Brad hadn't made an attempt to join her. Granted, the locals seemed to have prehistoric notions about sex between consenting adults, but surely Brad wasn't worried about what they thought?

She dismissed the niggling concern, opened the top drawer of the heavy mahogany chest and selected a creamy silk nightgown. The designer had been delightfully skimpy with the material, she reflected, a slow grin dawning as she slipped the tantalizing silk over her smooth naked body. Any doubts would be dispelled as soon as Brad saw her in this. Turning to the worn armchair, she picked up her robe and pulled it on. You never knew who you might meet on the way. The grin grew as she reached the door. The intrigue lent spice to the illicit nature of her plan. It might even be amusing—for a couple of nights at least—to play this ridiculous game, nipping up the flight of stairs, not knowing if she'd be caught, so that she could slip silently into Brad's bed. She dabbed a little gloss on her lips and contemplated the vision in the mirror, imagining his expression when she slipped out of the robe.

Her mouth went dry and she swallowed with anticipation. It had been too long since they'd made love. She missed him, his arms holding her, and the sense of security his lovemaking gave her. So much better than resorting to Xanax, she figured, realizing that the angry irritability she'd felt since her arrival at Strathaird was probably due to raging hormones gone unfulfilled.

She slipped from the room, peeked from left to right along the dark corridor, lit only by a dim wrought-iron sconce on the wall, then froze, cringing, when the door squeaked noisily shut behind her. Pausing once more to make sure no one was about, she quietly began the climb up the long flight of stairs. It was drafty and she moved swiftly, making her way down the wide passage to the large gothic doors of the laird's apartment. A glimmer of light shone from under it and her anticipation mounted. Was he still up reading? Or, better yet, waiting for her? A floorboard groaned. Stopping dead in her tracks, she glanced once more up and down the passage, stifling a nervous giggle. It was ridiculous to worry. Still, she felt better knowing all was quiet.

Tingling with expectation, she pinched her nipples through her gown to ensure that they'd look invitingly pert, then opened Brad's door with a flourish.

"What the—"

"Shh. It's just me," she whispered, closing it quickly behind her.

Brad switched on the other lamp and sat up. He'd almost fallen asleep. Now, as he watched Sylvia advance across the room, her silk robe falling artfully from her shoulders, displaying an expanse of soft white skin, he stifled a secret wish that she'd left him alone.

Where had *that* come from? he wondered with a guilty start. After all, this was Sylvia, the woman he planned to marry, clearly bent on seduction. "Come on in," he grinned, determined to enjoy the moment. Throwing back the covers, he patted the space beside him.

"Not so fast." She lingered a few feet from the bed, allowing the robe to slip seductively down her body to the floor, revealing long, shapely legs and firm breasts barely covered by the minuscule square of white silk she'd no doubt paid a fortune for.

"Hey!" Brad exclaimed. "Stop tempting me and get in here." He gave her his best wolfish grin and purposefully ignored the fact that her perfect body left him strangely unmoved.

Slowly she approached the bed, climbed onto the covers and sent him a sexy smile. "I've missed you."

Brad slipped his hand to her waist and drew her close, seeking her lips as she pressed her body against his. She felt warm and pliant, lean and wanting.

And he felt nothing.

What the hell was the matter with him?

He breathed in the scent he knew so well and that should have intoxicated him, wondering desperately why the feel of her fingers pressing unashamedly against him left him unaroused. He caressed her automatically, seeking the spots he knew pleased her, heard the tiny gasp when his fingers reached farther, felt her moist heat and closed his eyes. He wanted her. Of course he wanted her, he reasoned frantically as his thumb grazed her taut nipple. But his body remained disturbingly unresponsive.

"Come on, honey, now, please," she pleaded. "It's been so long. I think I'll burst if you don't come inside me right away."

"Just a bit longer," he murmured, buying himself time. "Let's enjoy it a while." He felt a moment's panic. What on earth was happening to him? He and Syl had always been great together. Why the hell wasn't his body responding to her? As his hand slid once more between her thighs, a sudden image of Charlotte, lying naked, titian hair draping the pillow, flashed before him. To his horror he felt himself harden, seized by a craving stronger than anything he'd felt in years. Before he could stop himself, he drew Sylvia on top of him and plunged into her, hard and deep. She gasped, leaned back and moved fast, hair flying, close to climax.

For a moment he rode with her, the vision of driving himself into Charlotte's willing body drowning out all sense. Then he opened his eyes and reality hit: he was making love to the wrong woman. Desire waned as abruptly as it had surged, and he pulled away, embarrassed and drowned in guilt.

"What's the matter?" Sylvia rolled off and stared at him strangely, "What happened? Something I did?"

"No, nothing. I'm sorry, Syl. I guess I'm a little tired," he murmured, flailing for an excuse.

"You—tired? You've never been tired in your life!"

"Well, I guess there's always a first," he responded

with a weak attempt at humor. Mortified, he pressed a light kiss on her forehead.

"I don't understand," she continued insistently. "It's been over a month, Brad. You must be dying for it."

"I am. Of course I am, I...I don't know what's wrong with me tonight. I guess my mind's not letting me concentrate."

"Concentrate? You shouldn't have to concentrate."

"Christ, Syl, you know what I mean."

She lay tensely next to him, her head resting on his shoulder. The note of irritation was new and she didn't like it. Something was desperately wrong. She mustn't panic. All she needed was to figure out a way of getting him away from here as soon as possible. She could feel his pounding heartbeat through the thin cotton of his T-shirt as she considered her options. Perhaps she could create a diversion, devise some strategy whereby he'd be obliged to return to New York. Once they were back in the city, she was convinced everything would return to normal.

But what if it didn't?

Sudden dread made her stiffen. Didn't he find her attractive any longer? No, that couldn't possibly be the issue. Their relationship was too time-tested for that. Could it be true, then—was he really tired? Or was it something else?

She tried to shift to an angle where she could examine his face, but he slipped an arm around her and drew her close, squeezing her tight. She lay impatiently next to him, watching roaming moonbeams cast silver threads over the counterpane.

"I'm sorry, babe," Brad murmured, kissing her ear. "Let's just forget about tonight. It's been a rough day.

We'll try this again when I can give you and your delicious body my full attention.''

Mollified by his compliment, she twisted and smiled seductively, only to open her mouth in shock when he pulled back the covers and gave her a little push. ''Better get that cute butt back down those stairs, or you might fall asleep here. We wouldn't want to get caught by the ladies in the morning.''

She glared suspiciously at his overly bright smile, and the stubborn streak in her writhed. ''I can't believe this. You sound scared.''

''Don't be ridiculous,'' he said, looking away.

''Then what are you worried about?'' she demanded.

''Nothing.''

''This is your fucking castle, Brad, and I'm the woman you sleep with, the woman you're marrying, remember? Who cares what a bunch of local yokels think about what we do or don't do? I'm staying.'' She wriggled purposefully among the sheets.

''Syl, please, just go.'' The impatience in his voice left her smarting in hurt surprise. There was something so peculiar in his manner, something so different from the man she'd last made love to in her Manhattan apartment.

''Okay,'' she replied coolly. Slipping from the bed, she gathered her negligee and the remnants of her dignity. Upset and angry, she picked up the robe from the floor, flung it over herself and gave the belt a sharp twist. ''Have a great night,'' she muttered. Then, turning on her heel, she headed for the door.

''Good night, Syl…don't be mad. This has nothing to do with you.''

She didn't bother to answer, merely allowed the door to close with a sharp bang. She made no effort to mute her footsteps and derived a small measure of satisfaction when the ancient stairs squeaked beneath her as she hurried furiously away. She'd almost reached her bedroom door when the hallway light suddenly came on, leaving her paralyzed, like a fox gazing into headlights.

"*Mon Dieu,* I thought there were intruders." Armand peered sleepily from his half-open door, then his mouth curved into a simpering smile. "You are returning from a nocturnal promenade, I gather?"

Sylvia took a deep breath. This was all she needed. Determined to save face, she sent him a sassy smile. "That's right. Good night, Armand. Cute pj's."

"Peejays?"

"Yeah. Those red pajamas suit you." She wiggled her eyebrows expressively.

Murmuring an embarrassed "Good night," Armand disappeared and she rushed for her own door, barely able to contain herself.

Reaching the bedroom, she threw herself onto the bed and indulged in an uncharacteristic bout of tears. Everything had been so right between Brad and her, and now, for some inexplicable reason that was not just this stupid pile of stone that he appeared so attached to, their relationship was floundering. She sniffed, rubbed her hand over her eyes, then sat up and tried to think. She must regroup. If *she* wasn't the problem, as he'd implied, and it wasn't the castle, then there had to be something else. And there was only one other possibility left, she realized somberly: another woman.

Fear and pain gripped her. How could he? How dare he? Her fingers balled in a tight fist and she gulped. What right did he have to come here and mess up all they had?

For a minute she sat cross-legged on the small, chaste bed, feeling sorry for herself. Then, as always, habit won, and she began formulating a plan. She would find out exactly what was going on and make darn sure she put an immediate end to it. For a while she sat, eyes narrowed, mind hard at work. Then she lay back and slipped under the covers, taking long deep breaths, determined to get some sleep. The last thing she needed were rings under her eyes. That wouldn't help her compete against whatever island milkmaid had captured Brad's fancy.

She must stay calm, she reminded herself, not get too worked up about this. Perhaps it was just a passing fancy—after all, men went through that sort of thing, or so she'd heard. But if she played her cards right, soon enough, Brad would remember what they had together and realize how much he stood to lose. Plus, she'd be willing to bet none of the single women he'd had the opportunity to meet on this waterbound rock pile could hold a candle to her.

The strain of the evening, compounded with disappointment and emotional exhaustion, finally got the better of her. Soon her lids drooped and she curled into the pillow. But just as sleep was about to catch up with her, a face flashed vividly before her. She sat up with a horrified start.

"My God," she exclaimed out loud. "Could it be Charlotte?"

Upstairs, Brad shifted uncomfortably among the sheets, unable to sleep.

He tried closing his eyes, thumped the pillow and tried to rest, praying that he was in the middle of a nightmare. Why this? Why now? He'd long ago relegated Charlotte to a convenient, determinedly compartmentalized corner of his brain, one that allowed him to treat the woman he'd once so desperately wanted to love and possess in a friendly, sexless manner. Deep down, he'd always known she could never really be that. But it had worked all these years. And tonight, inexplicably, Sylvia had released the long-suppressed genie from its bottle. What made it worse, he realized with a gusty sigh, was the sneaking suspicion the genie would prove damn hard to cork up again.

But in truth, there was more to this than just the undeniable, inescapable attraction he felt for Charlotte, he reflected, shoving his arms behind his neck as he stared at the translucent moon shining through the half-open curtains. He'd discovered a new side of himself here at Strathaird. That was something he found hard to explain to himself, let alone to Sylvia. Another woman she might understand, but not this new unexpected curve in his life. That she would never accept. Her whole being revolved around Manhattan and their life there. Skye, and all Strathaird represented for him, was about as real to her as Disney World. How could he possibly make her understand that it was fast becoming an essential part of his life?

Poor Syl. He'd treated her horribly, and she deserved better. He'd make it up to her, have his secretary select something special from Tiffany's. Or perhaps, he reflected suddenly, he'd have Charlotte design her a unique piece of jewelry. His guilty conscience began to quiet down. It might be a good way of bringing the two women together, help get things back on track in an orderly manner. As for the still-very-much-married Charlotte—he reminded himself sternly—just because his body had betrayed him didn't mean his mind would as well. What had happened tonight was nothing but a temporary aberration. He'd make damn sure of it. Charlotte would be returned to the enchanted bottle from which she'd popped out, and the stopper well secured.

Still, that didn't solve the fact that Strathaird was in his life to stay. He punched his pillow once more, realizing reluctantly that, like it or not, he'd have to make that very clear to Syl. It wasn't fair to keep her in the dark about his growing attachment for the place. After all, she had the right to know that he intended to spend large chunks of time here in the future. What, he wondered, would she say to that? He tossed, turned and flung the covers off, wishing this awful, drawn-out night was behind him. But even as he willed himself to sleep, Charlotte's image intruded ruthlessly, that same, eerie tug that had gripped him when he'd envisioned her in the Great Hall lurking persistently. He tossed again. Was Strathaird playing tricks on him? The idea was ridiculous. Yet he could almost feel her silky hair flow gently across his chest, read the longing in her eyes, picture her generous lips taking him into her mouth.

Jesus! What next? Brad asked himself, angry at his own weakness. Gripping the sheets, he bunched them in his fists and closed his eyes tight, firmly determined to eradicate any tantalizing visions that might seek to rob him of his rest.

But after several valiant tries, he realized it was futile. The thought of Charlotte echoed like a siren's song, luring him inexorably into peril. After another half hour's tossing and turning, he finally relented. With a guilty groan, he reluctantly gave in to the forbidden fantasy and allowed himself to dream.

Sylvia surveyed the breakfast table, charmingly arrayed with the fine Harcourts porcelain. A small crystal vase of wildflowers stood in the middle, a splash of bright color against the white lace cloth. But her mind was far removed from esthetic details as she eyed Brad surreptitiously over the rim of her coffee cup. He looked tired and seemed to have trouble meeting her gaze, although he'd been very solicitous and affectionate when she'd entered the dining room. Perhaps this was his way of trying to apologize for the previous evening. She watched with considerable disgust as he downed the huge Scottish breakfast of porridge, ham, eggs, kippers, oatcakes and God knows what else with ease. The mere thought of all that cholesterol gave her the shivers.

Having decided that ignoring last night's disaster was by far the wisest way to deal with a potentially embarrassing situation, she nibbled a piece of dry toast while surveying the other guests. Armand was picking at a soft-boiled egg, complaining of a bad night's rest, while Penelope listened politely. She glanced at Diego de la Fuente, who had just seated himself opposite Penelope. Mid-sixties, good-looking and in great shape, she noticed that his gaze seemed to linger on their hostess. Interesting. At least romance was in the air for someone, she thought with a twinge.

There was still no sign of Charlotte, who'd been expected to join them, though Genny and the twins had been in earlier with a bouquet of wildflowers picked for her on the moors. Sylvia was more touched than she showed and Penelope had immediately put the flowers in a vase for her room. Somehow, the children's gesture reminded her of all she might lose if she couldn't fix whatever it was that was changing Brad. Wasn't he aware of what they had together? The company, the kids, a stimulating and cosmopolitan life? She couldn't believe the man she knew would be willing to give all that up.

Still, it didn't hurt any to see that he felt guilty about last night's mess. When men knew they were in the doghouse, they were so much more malleable. The thought cheered her, and she remembered that she'd awakened this morning feeling wonderfully empowered. After all, she had a plan to mend things, and today she would put it into immediate action. As soon as breakfast was finished—and the less of this depressingly weak coffee she had to drink, the better—she'd go to the village and investigate. If Charlotte was indeed competition, then it was time to size up just what sort of danger she posed.

Brad pushed away from the table and stood up. "I'm off up to the North Farm, Aunt Penn. Anything you need to tell the Murrays?"

"No. Thank you, Brad."

"Well, I'll be up there most of the day." He glanced at Sylvia as though about to say something, then merely leaned down to kiss her. She tilted her head invitingly.

"Have a great day, kiddo. I'll see you this evening," he murmured.

"I sure plan to."

"Yes, you run along, Brad, dear. I shall be showing Sylvia the house and some of the ropes, and we're going to talk about the fête where I'm planning to introduce her to everyone. The councilor's wife should be ringing me back about tea on Thursday. Perhaps later you'd like to take a walk or drive to the village?" Penelope remarked, turning in her direction.

"I'd love to," she responded enthusiastically, glad of the cue. "I was hoping I'd get the chance to visit Charlotte's gallery," she added in a moment's inspiration. She sent Brad a sidelong glance but elicited no reaction. He merely smiled briefly, nodded and picked up the papers before leaving the dining room.

"Armand." Sylvia watched Penelope plaster on a bright smile and turn to the Frenchman. "Any plans for the day?"

"Perhaps." He sounded vague, somewhat morose. "After the consumption of this egg I shall retire to the library for a short rest. Later I shall repair to the village. Charlotte," he added in a hushed tone, "has been creating."

"Ah! Yes. Well, that's very nice." Penelope sent Sylvia an apologetic smile. Poor woman. Imagine having to deal with this all day long. Sylvia stifled a sympathetic grin.

"I would love to go to the gallery and see Charlotte's work," she remarked. "Maybe I could treat myself to a gift."

"You will not be disappointed," Armand exclaimed as though seeing her for the first time. "The originality of the pieces will exceed your expectations."

"I'm sure." Sylvia smiled tactfully. All she wanted was to get a good look at Charlotte and see if she could ferret out if anything was going on between her and Brad.

After spending the morning with Penelope, visiting the house and the garden and meeting the rest of "the ladies"—the ones who apparently would disapprove of her sleeping with Brad—Sylvia finally got directions for a shortcut down a steep, narrow path that almost killed her shoes, but that led to the road and on into the village. After removing the pebbles from her loafers, she made her way down the main street. An old man doffed his tweed cap and she felt as though she'd walked straight into a Scottish version of *Jane Eyre*. She smiled graciously at passersby. Even if she didn't know who *they* were, there was a distinct possibility they knew *she* was Brad's fiancée. It was an opportunity to make contact with the natives, she reckoned, wondering what the chances were that the newsagent she'd just passed carried the *New York Times*. Probably as slim as her chances of finding a salon that could give her a proper facial. Lord knows how her skin would react to all this distressingly fresh air.

Remembering Penelope's description of the gallery, Sylvia glanced at the quaint houses, the bursting window boxes and colored shutters. She had to concede that the village held a certain charm. Then her eye fell on the pretty, crooked whitewashed house squeezed between a café and what looked like a bakery. She crossed the road and peered in the window, then frowned, impressed. The space was sophisticated and well planned, not at all what she'd imagined. Just what *had* she imagined? she wondered, hearing a soft tinkle as she opened the door. Perhaps she was entirely wrong. The more she thought about the Charlotte-Brad thing, the more implausible it seemed. Maybe Brad really had been tired last night and nothing more.

Trying hard to feel convinced, she stepped inside. A woman with a shock of long, mouse-colored hair and thick glasses sat behind a table. She gave her best smile.

"Hi."

"Can I help you?" The woman rose. She wore leather sandals and a long Indian skirt, and looked artsy.

"I came to see Charlotte. Is she available?"

"She's in the workshop. Whom should I announce?"

"I'm Sylvia."

"Oh, hello. I'm Moira." Sylvia thought she caught a look of unease before the woman's face broke into a warm smile. "You're Brad's fiancée, aren't you? Glad to meet you. Come on in. In fact, you're in luck. Brad's in there with Charlotte right now." She led the way toward a small door in the wall behind the table. Sylvia froze. So this was what he was doing when he was supposed to be checking on some remote farm? Then, mastering herself, she regrouped and followed Moira, head high, her faltering confidence giving way to anger.

Moira opened the door with the care of one used to not disturbing the room's occupant. Then she stepped aside and allowed Sylvia to enter. Stopping on the threshold, she swallowed, throat suddenly dry. Charlotte was seated, leaning forward intently, hand moving fast. She couldn't see properly, for Brad's back was shielding her. He leaned over Charlotte, hand poised intimately on her shoulder.

Sylvia swallowed again, pulse hopping, unable to unglue her eyes. Battling anger and humiliation, she listened to their murmuring voices, her worst fears confirmed. She caught Charlotte's soft laugh, watched, horrified, as she tilted her head up to smile at Brad.

Then Moira broke the spell. "Guys, look who's here."

They turned in unison like naughty children caught in a prank. Brad stepped away, and Charlotte jumped up from her stool. "Hello, Sylvia, come on in. Sorry I haven't managed to get over to the castle. I've been dreadfully busy." She came forward. Sylvia smiled automatically, using every ounce of self-control to school her expression.

But inside, she felt as if she'd just taken a punch to the gut. She and Charlotte had met only once before, in London at the Chelsea Flower Show. She'd remembered her as a messy bohemian type, and recalled wondering how she'd managed to land a total dreamboat like John Drummond, rated sexiest actor of the year. Now, taking in the full force of her porcelain skin and violet eyes, the mass of seductive flame-colored hair, and her lithe, athletic body, Sylvia had to acknowledge that Charlotte Drummond had a rare and disturbing beauty. Even knowing she was married to a sexpot like Drummond, most men would have a hard time keeping their hands off her. Knowing the husband was in a coma might make it harder still. Sylvia smoothed moist hands against her pants, afraid she might be revealing her distress.

Extending her hand to Charlotte, she grinned brightly. "Hi. Just thought I'd pop by and visit. This place is great," she enthused, "really incredible. I'm tempted to treat myself to a gift." She sent Brad a cursory wave. "You got finished early?"

"Yeah. I…" His voice trailed off uncomfortably.

Charlotte picked up a white page from the table and glanced apologetically at Brad. "Sorry to spoil your plans, Brad, but I think Sylvia should see the drawing herself." She handed the paper to Sylvia. "Brad wants me to design you something. He wanted it to be a surprise, but frankly I think you should give your own input. That way you'll have something you'll really enjoy wearing."

For the first time in years Sylvia was caught off balance. "Wow!" she said, staring in bewilderment at the sketch, when finally she could breathe. "That's beautiful, Charlotte. Thank you, Brad." She smiled at him across the room, a knot rising in her throat. Her eyes dropped again to the sketch, face flushed, mind in a whirl. He'd been choosing something for her. She felt suddenly ashamed of her doubts. Yet, as she and Charlotte pored over the design, she couldn't quite banish the memory of the quiet intimacy that had reigned when she'd entered. Coupled with last night's episode, she was left feeling less sure of herself than she had in years.

9

Charlotte pulled up to Rose Cottage, bone tired but happy. It had been an extremely busy day at the gallery. With an unexpected busload of tourists arriving in the village that morning, the shopkeepers had been buzzing with predictions of strong sales. Even though her gallery stocked by far the most expensive items in the area, she had had more business than she could handle. One of the visitors, who'd identified herself as a fashion editor for a major New York magazine, had been especially enthusiastic, lingering over several pieces and insisting Charlotte get a publicist for her work. Up until now, Charlotte had taken Armand's extravagant praise of her talent with a grain of salt, but the woman's words had made her stop and think. Perhaps she *should* allow herself a glimmer of hope, she reflected, taking two shopping bags filled with groceries out of the Land Rover and kicking the door shut. Perhaps the woman's keen interest meant Armand's grand schemes for a Paris show had some merit after all.

Cautioning herself not to get her hopes up, she carted the bags to the front door, her imagination already brimming with ideas for new designs. She couldn't help but smile. It felt good to know that she'd have to get to work right away to refill the display cases. And if the whole Paris plan did actually take, well then, the sky was the limit.

Peering over the shopping bags, she was surprised to see that the bright blue door of the cottage stood ajar. She frowned, then shrugged. The children must have been in and out and forgotten to close it. She must tell them to pay more attention. Mercifully it hadn't rained, although storm clouds were gathering. Which reminded her, she had to pick them up later, feed them pizza and drive them to the movies in Portree. She grinned. Todd was obsessed with Harry Potter, and while Genny and Rick had enjoyed the movie once, they weren't too happy about being dragged to see it over again.

Balancing her bags, she pushed the door farther open, assailed by a sudden feeling of unease. For a moment she hesitated, then entered. All appeared as usual and she shrugged, breathing easier. Ridiculous to imagine anything ominous here on the island, she realized, pitching her car keys in the silver dish on the hall table and leaving the bags on the floor before heading to the bedroom.

But when she opened the door of her room she gasped and her hand flew to her mouth in horror. The room had been ransacked. It looked as though a hurricane had hit.

"My God," she whispered, gazing at the drawers sagging half-open, their contents strewn haphazardly on the floor. Her eyes traveled to the bed, where the sheets had been pulled back and the mattress ripped open. The duvet lay gashed like a broken toy next to it, feathers oozing from its gut. Charlotte let out a horrified cry and rushed to the dressing table. The cash she'd left there earlier in the day was gone. So was her watch. Her throat constricted as she saw the dresser's top drawer, dangling almost off its track. *All* her jewelry had disappeared.

There hadn't been much—just a couple of trinkets—and she was too upset about the watch to worry about them. The realization that the timepiece that all her life she'd associated with her father and her family was gone left her devastated. It was precious and irreplaceable. Not only because of its monetary value—it was a unique Rothberg piece—but because of all the sentimental associations that stretched back to before the war. It had been given to the family by Sylvain de Rothberg himself, and that had made her feel close to him.

She sank forlornly onto the dressing-table stool and let her head drop, desperately regretting that she'd not worn the watch today. But they'd planned to go swimming, until the imminent rain made the movies a better option, and she was scared of losing it in the sea. How had the thief known where to look? she wondered, trying desperately to think straight. Not that it would have been hard to figure out, she reminded herself grimly. The bedroom was the first place any robber would search. With her usual carelessness, she'd made it all too easy for him.

Should she tidy the room? Call the police? Do both? She sat motionless for a moment, paralyzed and overwhelmed. Something dark and ominous had ripped into the fragile new life she'd tried so hard to build for her daughter and herself, and for the first time she doubted her impulsive decision to move away from the solid security of Strathaird. Had she acted too rashly? No, she told herself sternly, this freak event wasn't going to pull her off course. Still, she realized shakily, she badly needed a strong shoulder to cry on.

All at once, she knew where she had to go. Getting up, she brushed away the tears, dashed through the hall, then out of the garden gate and ran as fast as her legs could carry her, down the rough track, hair flying, heart full. Scrambling over the low stone wall, she followed a centuries-old shortcut through the fields and raced toward the castle.

"What do you mean, you can't leave?" Sylvia stared coldly across the large partners desk, hands planted on her slim hips.

"I already told you, Syl, I need more time." Brad gestured to the pile of papers before him. "I need to be here. They need to know I'm taking charge. I have the local councilor to meet, a hundred invitations to answer."

"Get a secretary."

"These need to be answered in person," he continued patiently. "I can't roll in here like a goddamn bulldozer, Syl. They have their way of doing things."

"Maybe it's time you imposed your own style."

"Look, it's just not like that around here. Surely you've understood that by now. People expect me to be a part of the community, to participate in events. If I haven't the time, I need to communicate that in the most tactful way possible. Preferably in a hand-written letter."

"Really? And what about Harcourts?" she asked in a conversational tone. "Or have you forgotten that you have a multinational business to run?"

"I'm well aware of that," he replied tersely.

"It sure doesn't look like it. While you're playing Mary-had-a-little-lamb, writing personal, hand-written notes to the local gentry, your company is going to pot and—"

"You know perfectly well that's ridiculous." He passed a tired hand over his eyes, annoyed at her absurd comment, wishing she would leave him alone so that he could finish reviewing the estate accounts and work through the pile of invitations Penelope had handed him earlier in the day. This was the third such argument they'd had in the past five days. Sylvia certainly wasn't making things any easier.

"If anyone's being ridiculous, it's you, Bradley Ward." She leaned over the desk, blond hair swinging, jaw clenched. "I don't know what the hell has gotten into you, but you seem to have forgotten where your priorities lie."

"How many more times are we going to have to argue about this? We've been over and over it, Syl. You know as well as I do that Harcourts doesn't require my presence round the clock. Thanks in great part to you," he added wearily, attempting a smile and reaching for her hand.

She ignored it and sat down opposite him, her face set in an angry frown. "I can't believe you're planning to stay here another three weeks, Brad," she exclaimed. "It's crazy. And what am I supposed to do? Sew samplers? There's the ad campaign for the new linen line to oversee, there's—"

"Ira can handle it."

"It's not the same."

"Syl, I'm asking you to do this for me," he said quietly. "Think about it. From now on, Strathaird is going to be part of our lives. I told you I intend to spend more time here. It's a legacy I can't just sweep under the rug. I *need* to be a part of it." How could he explain how strongly he felt, or the strange feelings that drew him here?

"This wasn't in the job description when we started out," she said bitterly. "Our life is perfect. Everything is just fine. Why do you have to spoil it?" She rose nervously and stared out the window. "I hate this place. I detest the way they talk, with their hoity-toity British accents, like they're better than us. And God help me if

I so much as offer an opinion about changing how things are done," she added *sotto voce*. Then she turned away, shrugging. "I know Penelope means well, it's not her fault. But this isn't my world, Brad. I can't simply morph into the lady of the manor overnight, and I don't want to. I'm a New Yorker, through and through. Hell, a weekend in Connecticut is as rural as I ever want to get."

Her eyes pleaded with him, and guilt, never too distant when it came to this particular matter, swooped over Brad once again. He had no right to upset their lives. Yet what choice did he have? What choice had he ever been given? Was he going to comply with someone else's plans and desires yet again, setting aside his own hopes and ambitions for the sake of duty? Or was he finally going to make a conscious choice about how he wanted to spend his time? Surely a few months here couldn't be that detrimental, either to Harcourts or to their personal life?

Sylvia stood in the middle of the room, looking forlorn yet determined. Watching her, he suddenly knew something fundamental had changed in him and between them, and that even if he did go back with her to New York right now, their life would never be quite the same. This went far beyond his strange reluctance to touch her intimately, and his newfound frustration with her black-and-white approach to life. Strathaird stood between them like a rockslide blocking the road. And Strathaird wasn't going away.

"I can't force you to stay," he said quietly, rising and coming around the desk. "I can only ask."

"But you're staying anyway. Is that what you're saying?" Her tone turned belligerent. "I don't believe that this sudden need to find your ancestral roots is all that's keeping you here, Brad."

"What do you mean?" he asked, suddenly defensive.

"I don't know," she answered, eyes narrowing. "I haven't figured it out yet. I have a few ideas, though."

"After five days, if you still aren't aware of all that needs to be done here, then you've got blinders on," Brad blustered, unaccountably annoyed at her determination to pry him away. "Plus, the kids are having a great time and we need to relax."

"Relax? Here? In the land of brown bathwater? You have got to be kidding." She let out a harsh laugh and faced him.

"You made up your mind not to like this place before you even got here," he interjected. "That's not like you, Syl."

"At least I don't have rose-colored glasses on. This place is a liability. The sooner you get rid of it, the better."

"That's impossible," he said quietly.

"Why? Are you scared old Duncan MacLeod on the stairs might be upset? Hang him up in Sutton Place if he means that much to you."

"Now you're being irrational. You know that the well-being of the tenants' families hangs in the balance. I can't ignore their needs."

"Think of it as a takeover. It happens all the time. People lose their jobs and find others." She shrugged, dragging her hand across her aching, tense neck. "This is business, Brad—you're the one who made it personal. Hey, if it bothers you that much, bring in a management team, as I've suggested time and again. Maybe you could turn this place into a hotel—that would resolve your job problem. In fact, you'd be helping the island's economy."

"That's not an option," he muttered. Why couldn't she at least try to understand that Strathaird wasn't just a piece of real estate? Somehow, unexpectedly and almost overnight, it had become a part of him. He knew the defensiveness he experienced every time she criticized such feelings was totally unreasonable. He'd tried to reason with himself, but it was useless. Deep down, he knew he had no intention of following any of her sensible suggestions. Their eyes met and his conscience pricked once again when he saw tears glistening.

"I'm sorry, Syl. I never meant for this to cause you pain."

"Then stop playing lord of the manor and come home," she pleaded, taking a step closer. "You're an American businessman, Brad, not a country squire. This is just a whim," she added in a softer tone. "I know a bunch of people will be upset, but you know what? That's life." She glanced at him persuasively. "Come on home and give us a chance, honey. Please." She sidled up to him, slipped an arm around his neck and caressed his dark hair.

"I'm coming home. Just not right now."

She pulled away angrily and threw up her hands.

"Okay, be that way. But I'm darned if I'm going to spend my time compiling lists for garden fêtes and having tea with the local vicar. Jane Austen is fine at the box office, but I live in the real world. Look at these people. Penelope's a nice lady but she's totally unorganized. And as for Charlotte—" she gave a low disparaging laugh "—she's certainly not going to get far, given the way she runs her business. Her designs are pretty unique, but I give her six months at best. Did you know that she calculates what she charges for a piece based on how much she likes or dislikes the client?"

"Leave Charlotte out of this," he snapped.

"Why? It strikes me she may be very much a part of it."

"She has nothing do with my decision to spend time at Strathaird." He read the hurt suspicion in her eyes and tried to keep the edge out of his voice.

"Well, I guess we'll have to wait and see, won't we?" Sylvia cast him a sarcastic glance and moved toward the door. "I don't know what's come over you, Brad, but you're a very different man from the guy who left New York."

"Maybe I needed the change."

"Like hell you did."

Sylvia hated the fact that she sounded like a shrew, but she couldn't help herself. He was shutting her out of decisions that affected them both—and the fact that he was still avoiding her bed like the plague certainly didn't help matters. She sensed something deep inside him had changed—something she couldn't share—and the cold fear that he was slipping away made her want to fight tooth and nail to hold him by her side. She moved nervously to the window.

"Does it never stop raining in this place?" she murmured.

Just then the door burst opened. Charlotte tumbled into the room, hair wet and jacket soaking. She looked a mess. And devastatingly beautiful.

"Well, speak of the she-devil," Sylvia muttered.

Brad didn't hear her comment. He was already halfway across the room, slipping a protective arm around Charlotte while his eyes searched her face.

"What's wrong, Charlie?"

Sylvia winced. He'd never spoken in such a gentle, soothing tone to her. She listened, mesmerized, as Charlotte began speaking in an agitated manner. They might as well have been alone in the room for all the notice they gave her.

"The cottage has been burgled."

"*What?*"

"It's true. Somebody broke in sometime this afternoon. The drawers in my room have been ransacked. Several items are missing. And, Brad, my watch is gone," she wailed, "and some jewelry and cash that was on the dressing table." Charlotte stopped for breath and Sylvia watched as Brad's fingers slid through her thick mane. The gesture was so natural she caught her breath.

He cared for her.

Maybe he didn't even realize it. Perhaps Charlotte didn't either, she recognized, seeing only fear and distress in the other woman's eyes. But the way they looked at one another...there was deep intimacy there. And that, Sylvia realized with a jolt, was far more dangerous than sex. This was no sudden, physical attraction but a strong and profound bond that existed between these two, one that predated her own life with Brad. How had she missed it before?

The insight shocked her into action. Time to get out of Dodge, she decided. Trying to persuade Brad to leave was useless. He wasn't going anywhere unless some outside event forced him to go. Her only option now was to return to New York and create a sufficiently serious reason for him to come back. Once she had him on her own turf, she'd have a chance. Here, she recognized bitterly, nothing short of an exorcism was going to get this place and this woman out of his mind. Looking at them huddled together, bile rose in her throat. Time to break up their little party, she decided, moving into the room.

"Charlotte, I'm sorry your cottage was broken into," she said in a smooth voice, watching as the two figures disengaged with a start. With a superhuman effort, she maintained a polite, concerned expression. "Is there anything I can do? Have you called the police?"

"Not yet," Charlotte replied, running a shaking hand through her hair. "I'll call the sergeant at the station in a minute. Not that it'll do much good. No one's ever been broken into around here. I suppose it must have been a passing tourist. None of the bigger valuables were taken."

"Makes one wonder if it's safe to be here," Sylvia said, nodding sagely. "I think you should call in extra security, Brad. I don't like it."

"It's probably just an isolated incident," Charlotte said nervously, looking in her direction. "There have been a couple of similar break-ins near Portree. They all turned out to be petty crimes. Probably someone in need of quick cash." She passed a hand over her eyes. Sylvia noticed how her fingers still trembled. The girl was a pile of nerves and Brad seemed only too ready to soothe them. "I just wish they hadn't taken my watch," she added, her huge violet eyes filling with unshed tears. "It was Daddy's and I love it. Daddy always wore it and then Colin and then—"

"Don't worry," Brad interrupted gently, gripping her shoulder. "We'll do everything we can to get it back, Charlie, I promise. It won't be an easy piece to resell, and any effort to do so will surely bring it to the attention of the authorities. We'll find out if anyone was around the cottage this afternoon. One of the tenants or someone in the village may have seen a car."

"That's true," Charlotte murmured, and Sylvia watched in dismay as Brad reached out to envelop her in his arms.

She moved quickly across the room, unable to stomach

any more. "If you'll excuse me, I'll leave you two to sort this mess out. I have a couple of calls to make."

Charlotte smiled absently and Brad sent her a friendly, dismissive nod. She crossed the hall, fuming.

"If you think you're going to brush me aside like an old blanket, you've got another think coming, Bradley Ward," she muttered, marching up the stairs, a plan already forming in her resourceful brain. The next board meeting was coming up in just two weeks. Apparently Brad didn't intend to be there.

But she would see about that! You could bet your bottom dollar she would.

"What a terrible situation," Armand said for the umpteenth time as everyone sat in the petit salon, debating the matter of the robbery. Sergeant Ramsey had left an hour ago with the promise to investigate further, and Armand still seemed shaken by the whole event. "Worst of all is the disappearance of the watch," he remarked, face pale, the twitch in his cheeks pronounced. "It is irreplaceable, a unique Rothberg piece that—" He broke off in midsentence and shook his head. "You should have kept it more carefully," he admonished. "*Vraiment,* Charlotte, it was irresponsible of you to leave such an heirloom lying carelessly about."

"Well, I could hardly have guessed that the one day I happened not to be wearing it, someone was going to come barging into the cottage and grab my stuff," she remarked tartly. She was sick and tired of Armand, who was going on and on, repeating the same litany.

"Still, it is a dreadful shame," he muttered.

"I always wear it," Charlotte said defensively. "The only reason I didn't today was because we'd planned to go swimming. You remarked on it today, Armand, when you stopped by the shop. I told you I never wear it when we go on picnics by the sea, and you said that was wise. I'm just too scared of losing it. Then when the busload of tourists arrived, I got caught at the gallery and never had the chance to get away.''

''What's so special about the watch?'' Sylvia, perched on the arm of the sofa next to Penelope, inquired. ''I mean, apart from the fact that it belonged to her dad. Why is Armand so uptight about it?''

''It was an exceptional Rothberg piece. We never knew exactly how David came by it. Once he asked Dex about it, but he didn't seem to know either, and Flora was always so vague.''

''It is an enduring mystery,'' Armand pronounced with a sad shake of the head.

''The person we've never thought to ask is the Cardinal. After all, his sister was married to Sylvain.'' Penelope leaned toward the teapot and glanced at Diego, seated silently opposite. ''Perhaps he may be able to shed some light on the origins of the watch. Not,'' she noted sadly, ''that the information will help us now.''

''A strange business,'' Diego remarked in a low voice. ''It might be worth finding out who was about at the time. Are there any neighbors?''

''No. Brad's already set the word about, but the cottage stands on its own, as you know. The only road leads back to the castle, and frankly, very few people would have any reason to go up that way.''

''I know. Armand and I have been on walks there. It's definitely not a place a robber would simply happen upon. Too far from civilization,'' Diego agreed, a frown covering his bronzed features.

Penelope looked at him uneasily. ''Exactly. This

would all make more sense if it had been one of those cottages nearer the main road.''

"What was the watch's value?'' he asked, adding a slice of lemon to his cup of tea.

"We don't know its exact worth,'' Penelope said. "Nobody ever had it appraised. But it probably is quite valuable. It was rather bulky and sometimes I used to tease my husband about it. Then, when Colin turned twenty-one, David gave it to him. Charlotte's been wearing it ever since Colin—'' She bit her lip and Diego's hand slipped gently over hers.

"I understand. It is the sentimental value of the piece that counted.''

She nodded silently, the firm grip on her hand reassuring. Then, pulling herself together, she drew away and gave him a grateful smile.

"You know, this has created a precedent,'' Sylvia remarked in a decided manner as she crossed her legs and balanced her cup elegantly on her knee. "I think you can prepare yourselves for more break-ins. As I mentioned earlier, you should beef up security immediately.''

"Goodness! Surely that's not necessary?'' Penelope glanced anxiously at Brad. "It seems like an isolated incident.''

"Penelope, that's wishful thinking and you know it,'' Sylvia said. "Let's face it, guys, this island's going to become just as dangerous as anywhere else. I know you all want to believe you live in your own private little paradise, but I hate to burst your bubble—from now on you're going to have to lock doors, install alarm systems and take proper security measures.''

"I don't think it's that bad,'' Charlotte replied. "I think Mummy's right. It's just bad luck.''

"Or maybe you just got lucky,'' Sylvia remarked,

pointing her finger. "How do you know the guy who did this wasn't a rapist or a murderer?"

"*Mon Dieu!* Perhaps Sylvia is right." Armand paled. "Who knows what dangers may be lurking on the moors. For all we know," he added, turning to Penelope, expression grave and his voice low, "*chère*, Charlotte may very well have escaped a fate worse than death." He dabbed a dainty white handkerchief to his lips.

"Maybe Armand's right." Brad turned thoughtfully to Charlotte. "Perhaps you and Genny should stay at the castle tonight and—"

"Oh no you don't. This is perfectly ridiculous and I wish you'd all stop fussing." Charlotte jumped up, and tugged at her short T-shirt, annoyed. "Some idiot broke in and took a few things. End of story. It could have happened to anyone, anywhere. It just happens that it was me." She shrugged and pretended to make light of the matter. "There's no need to make a mountain out of a molehill." She glanced at her wrist automatically. It felt strangely bare without the weight of the watch. "I need to get over to Moira's to pick up the kids. I promised I'd take them for pizza later, and to the movies," she murmured, suddenly needing to escape.

"I'll drive you," Brad offered. "I want to take a look around the cottage myself, see if there are any clues. Do you want to join us and the kids at the movies, Syl?"

"Thanks, but I'll pass," she murmured dryly.

"Okay. I'll be back in a little. Better not wait up for me." Brad rose, moved across the room and dropped an absent kiss on her furious brow before escorting Charlotte to the door.

Sylvia almost stood up and followed, suddenly regretting her decision to stay, then thought better of it. The last thing she wanted was to appear clinging, petty or jealous. She had a plan going and that was what mattered. Let him run loose with the kids for a few more days. After all, the board meeting was in two weeks and by then she would make damn sure his mind was focused on next quarter's earnings, and not, as increasingly appeared to be the case, on Charlotte. She laid her cup carefully back on the tray, with no hint of the turbulent emotions troubling her. She must stay focused on priorities. She and Brad were engaged to be married and on a fast track to becoming one of New York City's most powerful couples. And that, she reflected grimly, was exactly how they were going to stay. She hadn't given him and Harcourts five whole years of her life just to see him walk out of it with Charlotte Drummond. Or anyone else, for that matter.

But as she watched them leave the room, she was puzzled, trying to understand what an intelligent man like Brad saw in a woman like Charlotte. Okay, she was gorgeous. But she was also flaky and vague. The woman lived in a dreamworld. Men wanted self-assured, independent women who brought something to the table and could fend for themselves, didn't they? A fey fairy creature who designed jewelry on a remote island could only be a whim, not a permanent option, she reassured herself.

All in all, she was satisfied with her own performance. For a moment she grinned. She had to admit she'd taken perverse pleasure in egging on all their fears; it was a small but surprisingly satisfying payback for all the crap she'd had to put up with this last week. She knew they were right. The robbery was probably an isolated incident. Hell, aside from a few trinkets and gewgaws, there wasn't enough in this backwater to interest any self-respecting criminal. Truth was, the only real threat to security here had just walked out the door on Brad's arm.

It was fortunate, she realized with a wry smile, that she was a resourceful woman who wasn't about to let herself be messed with. She had a few weapons of her own up her sleeve, and she wasn't afraid to use them.

"What a mess." Brad gazed around the chaotic bedroom in disgust. Clothes lay strewn in all directions, a drawer turned on its end, its contents scattered over the floor. "Whoever did this did it in a hurry," he remarked, picking up a T-shirt and laying it on the dresser. "Come on. I'll help you clean up."

"Don't bother. I'll sleep on the couch tonight and tackle all this tomorrow. Heck," she said in a bright tone that didn't ring true, "I needed an excuse to tidy up the place anyway." She stooped and picked up a photo frame. "Do you remember this?" she asked, handing it to Brad.

"The summer of '86. Sure, I remember. I beat Colin four sets to one that day. Those were good times."

"Yes, they were." Charlotte sighed and looked at the photo, then at him. Then quickly she looked away, his presence in her bedroom making her nervous. "This room is depressing," she said, turning. "Come into the living room and I'll get us a drink."

"Just give me a minute. I want to take a look around."

"Go ahead. I'll get us a snack, too, and make up a fire. It's chilly tonight."

"Fine." He squeezed her arm and their eyes met.

"Thanks for coming, Brad. I really appreciate it." She remained in the doorway, lingering, then turned and headed to the kitchen, doggedly determined not to betray her emotions. Pulling a wheel of Brie from the refrigerator, she searched the pantry for some crackers and forced herself to examine her actions. What impulse, she wondered as she carried the plate to the sitting room, had sent her rushing over the hills and into Brad's arms? Let's face it, she admonished herself as she piled wood on the fire, that's where you knew you wanted to go. Worse, you knew you had to be there.

She crouched and, picking up the matches, lit the newspaper and watched the fire take. The moment she'd felt vulnerable she'd run to him. Yet, strangely, she didn't feel mortified by her actions, but rather, emboldened, glad that for once she'd not second-guessed herself but had followed her natural instinct. Just as she had when she was young, she admitted ruefully, kindling the fire until it blazed nicely. Brad had always provided a safe haven in the far-off past. But not recently.

Still, Charlotte reminded herself, hadn't she sworn after her marriage dissolved that the future was going to be different? That she was going to depend on herself and not lean on anybody?

She rose, turned dismally to the antique painted tray that held the decanters, and automatically poured him a scotch. This was a crazy situation, one she had no idea how to handle. How to explain that she was in love with a man she'd known all her life and who, she reminded herself, was engaged to another woman? A woman who, unlike herself, was free to share his life, she recognized with a gloomy sigh. It was almost more than she could bear.

Placing the tumbler on the ottoman, she poured herself a glass of port, then curled into the deep velvet cushions on the sofa, and waited for him to return from the bedroom. How had she let this happen? How could she not have seen it coming? They'd spent a considerable amount of time together over the past few weeks, but that didn't give her the right to violate all canons of propriety.

Her heart began to beat uncomfortably fast. She was mixed up and lonely—she hadn't realized just how lonely until Brad had appeared on the scene—but that did not accord her the right to destroy his future. And there was little use in blaming her newfound feelings on loneliness and lack of male companionship, when she knew very well that it was Brad, and Brad alone, who made her feel this way. There was no use pretending. She was experiencing the same feelings as she had that long-ago night in Chester Square.

Charlotte stared into the flames, recalling her life as it had been up until John's accident: a never-ending trail of film shoots, long flights back and forth to L.A. worrying about Genny, John's giddy parties in Hollywood and her permanent feelings of guilt, even when she didn't know why. Her mother's words rang in her ears and she took a long, pensive sip. What if Mummy was right? What if behind the comatose front the same cruel, selfish nature remained intact? But even before the accident, he could transform from one moment to the next from a wonderful, charming being who overwhelmed her with jewelry, treats and attention, leaving her confused and ashamed for having thought such dreadful things about him, into a monster.

Opening her eyes, she shook off the mood and her mouth curved gently. Just Brad's presence in the cottage made her feel warm and secure, even if it was only temporary. "Your drink's ready," she called. Perhaps if she was careful not to show him how she felt, they could go on as they always had. Leaning back, she gazed again into the prancing flames and wondered if he was oblivious to her feelings or if he, too, sensed something. After all, he'd been concerned and attentive as though she were his—

She sat up with a jerk, knowing she simply must stop. Sylvia was back at the castle, she reminded herself brutally, and probably waiting for him to join her. He had nothing to gain and everything to lose: a wife who was perfect for him and a future filled with success and happiness. If she truly loved him, Charlotte realized, her heart breaking, she must be the one to take a step back. She would keep up the farce of light friendship until he was safely married and back in New York, she decided, draining her glass. Then her own feelings and desires wouldn't matter anymore.

Brad wandered about Charlotte's bedroom in mounting frustration. A gut feeling told him this was not a hit-and-run robbery. Someone had been looking for something specific. He had no suspects or evidence, so he'd have to keep his doubts to himself. There was little use in causing a panic. But at least he could search for clues to support or discredit his theory. He wished he could call in the NYPD—professionals who knew what they were doing. The robber had done a sloppy job. Surely he had left all sorts of evidence behind—if only one knew what to look for. But after several minutes of searching, he realized, discouraged, that there was little he could do except secure the windows.

He gazed at the mess and felt sorry for Charlotte. The fragile world she'd created, her first tentative step toward freedom, had been violated, and it must be tremendously upsetting. He wondered again if he could persuade her to return to the castle tonight. Probably not. He leaned over, picked up some clothes, and piled them on the chair. A crumpled negligee lay strewn in the corner and he lifted it, eyeing it with a raised eyebrow. He hadn't thought Charlie would wear anything like this. His heart beat suddenly faster and, holding the soft, pale-pink silk to his cheek, he pictured her in it.

His immediate reaction made him let go of the garment and take a hasty step back, as though it might burn him. Every sense was ignited by the thought of her clad in the sensuous silk. Dragging frustrated fingers through his hair, he swallowed, determined to control his emotions. Yet he couldn't put aside the one thought that had pre-occupied him since she'd burst into the office and told him of the robbery: in her moment of need, he was the first person she'd run to.

He glanced at the open door and hesitated. Were Charlotte's feelings for him more than merely friendly? After all, he mused, they had been once. For a moment he savored the possibility, then shoved his hands deep in the pockets of his corduroy pants, chiding himself for wishful thinking. Hell, even if she did have feelings for him, it didn't change the fact that he was committed to another woman and she was married to another man. Stark reality left no room for the adolescent fantasy that for so long had haunted his days and nights of winning her for himself. Clenching his fingers into a tight, frustrated fist, he took a last look at the room. He frowned, certain something was eluding his notice. Whatever it was, it didn't lie among the fallen clothes and overturned bottles of perfume. His eye fell on a small tray of trinkets lying on the nightstand. Moving toward it, he took a closer look, noting a strand of pearls, a couple of pairs of earrings and a sapphire signet ring. Why, he wondered, eyebrows creasing, hadn't the robber helped himself to these as well?

"Brad? Your drink's waiting." Charlotte's voice drifted through from the sitting room.

"Coming," he called back. Casting a final look about

him, he wondered if the watch had been with the other
jewelry or on its own. That might explain the discrepancy.

"What took you so long, Sherlock?" Charlotte asked
when he came in. She pointed to the tumbler on the ottoman, then settled back among the cushions holding her
glass. The soft sound of Latin jazz blended with the
crackling logs.

"Tell me, where did you keep the watch?" he asked,
sitting on the opposite side of the ottoman near the fire.
God, she was lovely, her hair shimmering, reflecting the
flames and the lamplight. Don't go there, he reminded
himself, throwing back the whiskey in one bracing gulp
as he focused on the robbery.

"I think I left it on the dressing table with the cash,
but I'm not absolutely certain," she said, frowning.

"Is that where you usually put your watch when you
take it off?"

"It depends. Sometimes I put it on the nightstand, next
to my bed."

"With the other jewelry, the pearls and the ring?"

"Yes. I slip them off before going to sleep. Oh gosh,
I hadn't thought of that." She stared at him, understanding dawning. "You mean that if the watch was by my
bed, why didn't the robber take the other jewelry as
well?"

"Exactly. Do you remember the last time you saw the
watch?"

"Yes!" she exclaimed, excited. "It was on the nightstand. I remember now because I moved it to get at my
sleeping pills."

"Sleeping pills?" He gave her a long look and she
hesitated.

"Sometimes I pop one if I can't doze off right away.

But this puts a whole new light on the robbery, doesn't it?'' she said, eyebrows creasing.

"If the watch was on the nightstand and not on the dressing table, then yes, it does. At the very least, it would mean that whoever took it knew its true value.''

"Then it would have to be someone who knows a lot about jewelry. Rothberg pieces are not common nowadays. It would have to be a connoisseur.''

"That, or someone with a vested interest in the watch.''

"Well, we can exclude that right away,'' she dismissed. "The only person interested in a watch like that would be a collector or someone who recognized it and knew they could get a lot of money for it.''

"For what it's worth, I think you should tell the sergeant tomorrow. You never know. There may have been similar robberies on the mainland. Sometimes clues can add up.''

"I will.'' She got up, refilled his glass, then kneeled next to him, placing another log on the fire. "Thanks for being so wonderful, Brad,'' she said quietly, tilting her head and looking up at him.

Their eyes met and he smiled.

"You know you can always count on me.'' He put down the tumbler.

She nodded. Her earlier tension had drained away. Next to him she felt warm, drowsy and secure. Instinctively she moved closer, she laid her head on his knee and snuggled next to him as naturally as if she'd been doing it for years. Closing her eyes, she relished the moment, the feel of his strong hand softly stroking her hair, the warmth of the fire, the peace he radiated. How she wished she could stay like this forever. Her hand played mindlessly along his thigh.

Then all at once he was lifting her, pulling her into his lap. For a moment they gazed silently at one another. Her breath caught. Then logic vanished and she let out a tiny moan and leaned forward, unable to resist any longer as at last their lips closed gently on one another.

The years fell away and tenderness turned into desperate need as their lips searched and lingered and their bodies entwined. His hands coursed to her breasts as though they belonged to him and she gasped as his thumb grazed her taut nipple through her T-shirt, sending excruciating shafts of desire to her very core. Her hand slipped below his shirt, needing to touch his firm muscled chest. Then she reached for his waistband, struggling with the button as he reached under her skirt and between her thighs. The shock when he touched her was so intense she let out a small cry of pure pleasure, as if all these years she'd been waiting for this moment. Then the button gave way and she heard him groan her name when at last she found him.

This wasn't like anything he could remember, Brad realized hazily. It was pure bliss. As his fingers reached inside her, heat and desire encased him. He caught his breath as she stroked him, forced himself to keep the rhythm of his own caresses slow, determined to lavish her with every feeling he'd been holding inside for so many years.

It was Charlotte who finally came up for air, dragging her lips from his. "Oh God, I didn't mean... We shouldn't be doing this, Brad," she whispered hoarsely. "It has to be wrong. We're—I mean me, you..." She drew back.

Brad struggled to regain his composure. "I know. I'm aware. I don't know how this happened. I—"

"Brad, if you say you're sorry, I'll—" She clenched

her fists and made a face. He laughed despite himself. "I don't know about you, but I have to confess, I've been dying for this to happen ever since you arrived. And here I thought I'd managed to grow up and put the old reckless Charlie behind me." She smiled down at him and touched his cheek. "Doesn't seem to have done much good, does it?" Then she slumped. "What are we going to do?"

"I dunno." He took a deep breath and tried desperately to focus. "Oh, to hell with it," he muttered, pulling her back against him, seeking her lips, his hands wandering once more. God, how he'd longed for her, dreamed of her. And now she was right here in his arms, pliant and giving. The fire crackled, and evening shadows grew as she shifted in his lap, making him groan once more, and her soft tongue tickled his ear. Then, all at once, the sound of an approaching car engine made them both sit up, rigid, staring at one another.

"Who can that be?" he murmured.

"I have no idea, but it sounds like the Castle's Volvo. You don't suppose—" Charlotte jumped out of his lap and moved to the window.

The headlights flashed across the panes. Then the engine went off and the lights turned out and a female form got out of the vehicle. "It's Sylvia," Charlotte hissed, guilt and embarrassment surging as she hastily straightened her hair and T-shirt and quickly glanced in the mirror. Not too bad, thank God. She turned to Brad, who was busy doing the same thing. Did they look as guilty as she felt? she wondered, moving quickly to the front door.

"Hi, Sylvia," she said brightly, opening the door before the other woman reached the end of the path. "I'm glad you came. We were about to call and see if you'd come for a drink.'' She smiled brightly, hoping she looked more convincing than she felt.

''Thanks. Is Brad still here? I thought you were taking the kids to the movies.''

''Oh my—yes! That's right. We're about to leave. He's just having a whiskey. Come on in.''

''I just got a call from the States. I need to talk to him.'' She seemed distracted and Charlotte groaned. They'd completely forgotten the children in their desire for one another.

''I'll leave you alone so you two can chat,'' she said hastily, only too glad for an excuse to escape for a few minutes and regain a semblance of composure. Besides, she had to phone Moira, with a plausible excuse for not having fetched the kids. There was no way they'd make the movie now, she realized guiltily.

''Oh, it's nothing private,'' Sylvia said with an absent smile. ''Just a problem that's come up with our ad campaign for the new linen line I was telling you about the other day.''

''I'm sorry.''

''Oh, it's not anything that can't be sorted out. It just requires my presence in New York, that's all.''

''Well, you'd better tell Brad. I'll get you a drink— Whiskey and soda on the rocks, right?''

''Yes, thanks.'' Sylvia walked into the living room. Brad was seated next to the fire, looking kind of stiff, she thought. Perhaps she'd interrupted something, she reflected acidly, all the more determined to put her plan into action. Ira had told her a couple of things over the phone that had given her the perfect excuse she needed. Production costs for the ad campaign were running double what they'd initially forecasted. Something wasn't right. Somebody was screwing up. She probably could have sorted it out with a couple of calls, but the chance to leave this backwater was too good to pass up.

"I got a call from Ira."

"Anything the matter?" Brad frowned as Sylvia poured out her concerns.

"There's only one thing to do," she concluded, after bringing him up to speed. "I have to get back home. It's just too risky to leave things in Ira's hands. I know he's good, but this may require some major decision-making. It's simply not fair to let him carry that responsibility alone."

"I don't see why we can't monitor the situation from here. Do you really think it requires your being there?" He glanced at her curiously, and she sat down next to him on the sofa.

"My gut's telling me I should go, honey. Anyway, you won't be away that much longer, will you?"

"No." His reply was noncommittal. She noticed that he seemed to be avoiding eye contact, as if he was embarrassed about something.

For the first time since entering the room she took stock of the cozy atmosphere, the soft smooth jazz and the warm embers crackling invitingly in the grate and drew her own conclusions. Yes, she decided, it was clearly past time she took things in hand.

10

God, it felt good to be back, Sylvia reflected as she alighted from the car in front of Harcourts' Park Avenue office building. Manhattan was hot and muggy, and with temperatures up in the high nineties, the city air was stagnant and still. She'd choose this over the clammy gray mists of Skye any day. Passing through the rotating doors, the artificial chill of the air-conditioning hit her full blast, and she sighed with delight.

She was home.

Back in her office, she sank into the familiar beige leather chair, swiveling to face her desk with a smile of contentment. After a long, satisfying day of hard work, the discomforts and confusion of Strathaird would be nothing more than a bad memory. She glanced at her desk, piled with memos, and turned on her computer. Eighty-five e-mails flashed on the screen and fourteen urgent phone calls required her immediate attention.

It felt good to be needed.

Slipping off her jacket, she plunged in, working intensely all morning. By lunchtime she'd returned all her calls, brainstormed with her two assistants, Ira and Hamilton, and things were beginning to look normal. At twelve she glanced at her watch, anxious not to be late for lunch. Barry Granger, the senior member of Harcourts' board, was not a man she wanted to keep waiting.

She had dressed carefully for the meeting in a conservative, light-beige suit and the exquisite string of pearls and earrings Brad had given her last Christmas. Leaning back, she twiddled her pen and carefully reviewed the strategy she'd been formulating over the last week. But the memory of Brad's rejection of her that disastrous night at Strathaird kept intruding. She swallowed an all-too-familiar surge of anger. He'd tried to make amends, but since then his embraces had felt mechanical, as if he was forcing himself to touch her. Things between them were definitely not as they had been. Nor would they be, she acknowledged, until she could break the strange spell that Skye and that woman seemed to have cast over him. Blocking out the image of Brad leaning tenderly over Charlotte, Sylvia rose impatiently, knowing what she had to do.

She caught a glimpse of herself in the small, decorative mirror she'd placed over her credenza, not pleased with the hard, angry face staring back at her. She had to compose herself; making her motives too plain would only undermine her plans. And, she reminded herself, it would take more than a quick lunch with Granger to implement this stratagem. For it to work, she would need the whole board on her side. She pulled a nail file from her purse and nervously filed an imperfection, aware that part of her was still reluctant to go this far.

But Brad had left her little choice. She had to reestablish the normal pattern of their existence before things got any worse. She gazed for a moment at his photograph sitting on top of her desk, a knot forming in her throat. That was the Brad she wanted back, the old confident, self-assured, impeccably dressed Brad, smiling up at her from the picture taken at a charity function they'd attended at the Frick last fall. With a resolute sigh, she laid down the nail file and moved toward the door.

A woman had to do what she had to do. And now was the time to do it.

"Bobby's been at it again," Moira exclaimed as Charlotte hurried into the gallery, barely escaping the sudden downpour. A flash of lightning followed by a clap of thunder made the ancient structure tremble.

"What god-awful weather." Charlotte grimaced and glanced at the window, pelted now by heavy rain.

"You're not driving the children to the crafts festival in this, are you?" Moira questioned anxiously.

"I was going to pick them up at the castle in about half an hour. Let's watch how the storm develops. It may not last."

"Don't bet on it. Hamish was at the café when I was grabbing my morning coffee. I heard him tell Old Rob there's a northwesterly squall coming in and that it'll settle in for at least the next three days. The children can live without the festival. They've already been to the movies several times."

"I know but I feel so dreadful. Brad and I promised and we let them down the other night and—"

"Rubbish. They were so involved with their video game they never noticed. Now stop feeling guilty," Moira admonished briskly.

"We'll see," Charlotte replied with a noncommittal smile. "Hamish makes his weather predictions based on how much the frogs are croaking—claims they're louder when there's lots of rain on the way. And since he's almost deaf, I suspect that's not the most reliable indicator.'' Charlotte flopped onto the chair opposite Moira and accepted a mug of coffee. ''Now, what was this about Bobby?''

''It was yesterday afternoon,'' Moira said, adjusting her thick-rimmed glasses. ''I went over to the café to get more coffee. When I came back I noticed that the door of your workshop was ajar.''

''And?''

''Well, as I went to close it I glimpsed a movement, so I switched on the light.''

''Go on.'' Charlotte frowned, a sudden chill coursing up her spine. Bobby had always followed her around like a faithful puppy, but it was a different matter altogether to invade her privacy. After she'd confronted him up at the cottage, he'd stopped trailing her for a while. But clearly, old habits died hard.

''He was fiddling at your table. I saw him slip something into his pocket. You know what he's like, almost childlike. When I said he must turn his pockets out, he did. And do you now what he had in there?''

''No.''

''A piece of casting metal.''

''What on earth would he want that for?''

''I've no idea. The poor man's half-batty. I think he just wants things of yours around him. I mean, if he'd wanted to actually steal from you, he'd have taken something of value. After all,'' Moira remarked with pursed lips, ''there's enough of what you leave lying about to satisfy any thief.''

''Oh don't start, Mo, you know I need my stuff around me to create.''

''That's all fine and dandy, but you've got to be more careful. Especially after what happened at the cottage.''

She frowned. "You don't think it could have been Bobby who broke in that day?"

"I don't know. I don't think so. He's always been perfectly harmless," Charlotte murmured, wondering if Moira could be right.

"I hope you don't mind, but I took the liberty of calling up Sergeant Ramsey. I thought he needed to know. If it was Bobby who broke in to Rose Cottage, he may be hiding your watch and the other pieces. I honestly don't believe he'd have done it to steal, but he's certainly seen you wearing the timepiece. He might have just wanted something of yours to treasure."

"But he's never done anything like that before, and I can't think what would have triggered the idea now." Charlotte frowned, then nodded. "You probably did the right thing, though."

Moira nodded, relieved. "I felt awful. I'm sure he's harmless, but you never know. Better to be safe than sorry." She looked up suddenly. "Charlotte, you don't think he might try something else, do you? One hears such awful stories about weirdos on the news. Brad was in the other day with Sylvia, before she left, and he seems genuinely worried about your safety. By the way, I gave them the piece he commissioned. I hope that's okay. Sylvia seemed thrilled. Did you see her before she left?"

"I didn't have time. I rang instead."

"Ah." Moira busied herself with some papers on the table. Charlotte got up and gazed out the window. Rain continued to slash mercilessly.

"I suppose it would be rather silly to drive to Portree in this," she muttered.

"Totally nonsensical."

"I'd better phone Mummy and tell her I'll be staying."

She moved toward the phone, dialed and listened absently to the double ring.

"Strathaird."

The sound of Brad's voice reaching down the line left her mouth dry.

"Hi. Is Mummy there?"

"She's out. You're not going to take the kids out in this, are you?"

"I'm thinking about it."

"Charlie, you can't drive in this weather, that's crazy."

"I'll see what happens in the next half hour. I—I feel terrible about not taking them the other day," she said in a rush. "Are they okay?"

"Having a blast. Diego's teaching them to play billiards. Frankly, I think we'd have a hard time getting them to leave right now. How about coming here later for lunch, if the weather clears," he added in a hopeful, persuasive voice.

Her pulse skipped a beat. To agree, Charlotte knew, was to court fate. She glanced blindly out the window. "I'm definitely taking the kids." The faster and farther away she got from Brad, the better.

There was a short silence, then he spoke in a neutral voice. "Do me a favor and wait till the rain stops, will you?"

"I've driven in this stuff all my life," she said nonchalantly

"Don't, Charlie. You're being pigheaded. For all you know, the festival may be cancelled. It's not safe and I won't have you or the kids driving in this weather. You could have another accident."

Charlotte froze at the reminder. "I'll make up my mind myself," she answered edgily, needing to escape. Hanging up, she moved toward the workshop. Should she just go, pick the kids up and to hell with it? For a moment she hesitated. But Brad was right. She could have another accident. What if something happened to her? It would kill Genny, and her daughter had already suffered enough in her young life. Besides, she admitted, it was ridiculous to be irritated with Brad because he had her well-being at heart.

She wouldn't go, she decided, heading toward the door of the workshop, but neither would she lunch with him. After all, she had nothing to offer him but heartache.

Brad hung up, his upcoming phone appointment with Sylvia forgotten, and grabbed the old Barbour shooting jacket that was never far out of reach. Charlotte wasn't going anywhere, he fumed as he headed for the door, regardless of whatever pea-brained plan she had. Feeling in his pocket for the car keys, he ran down the front steps then ducked out into the rain.

As the Aston Martin glided out of the castle and down the road toward the village, he noticed a police Range Rover stopped in front of the Hewitts' cottage. Bobby Hewitt was standing in the doorway gesticulating, while Sergeant Ramsey hovered on the front steps in a black mackintosh and police cap, trying unsuccessfully to shield himself from the downpour. He wondered absently what Bobby had done to warrant a visit from Sergeant Ramsey on a day like this.

He hesitated, then opted to drive on down to the gallery and call the station later. Charlotte was liable to go racing off in his absence and then he'd be sick with worry until she got home safely.

The street was half-empty and he parked on the curb

in front of the Celtic Café. As he entered the gallery, Moira looked up and greeted him.

"Hello. You're in early," she commented, eyebrows rising behind the thick lenses.

"Where is she?" he asked with a brief nod.

Moira pointed to the workshop, eyes following him as he made straight for the door. He entered without knocking, and closed the door behind him.

Charlotte spun on her stool then stood up abruptly, backing against the table.

They stared at one another.

"You're not going anywhere," he muttered, taking a step closer.

"I'll go wherever the hell I want," she retorted, tossing her head rebelliously, reminding him of the Charlotte of old.

"Not with the kids, you won't. Or by yourself, come to think of it." He moved quickly forward and she cringed.

"Don't." Impulsively she raised a hand, as if she thought he'd hit her. He stopped dead in his tracks, suddenly aware of the fear she'd been living with all these years. Mentally cursing John for putting such fear in her, Brad suppressed the desire to pull her into his arms. Instead, he put his hands in his pockets and looked her straight in the eye, daring her to contradict him. "You're staying right here where I can make sure you're okay," he pronounced, leaving no room for misunderstanding. He was standing over her now, watching her eyes go from violet to purple. The haunting memories of the other night at the cottage, how wonderful she'd felt, how she'd met his questing hand with eager passion, flashed. Almost without will, he stepped closer still, watching as she arched back against the table, hair fanning over onto the battered wood of the old table, mixing with the glistening gems behind her. Unable to stop himself, he leaned into her, conscious only of the need to finish what they'd started all those years ago.

"Don't," she murmured weakly as his arm slipped about her waist and he drew her, unresisting, into his arms. "We mustn't," she insisted, cursing her traitorous body. Blind panic swamped her as his lips came down on hers and she gasped. Somehow, all at once, she was back in the apartment in Chester Square, stretched out on the brocade sofa, longing for Brad to be the first to touch her, love her.

At the thought, she stopped fighting the inevitable. Her lips opened before his. Her mind went blank and she responded eagerly, arms slipping about him. The familiar feel of his muscles rippling under his shirt and sweater made her moan as she sank into him and his hands coursed up her body, seeking her breasts. Why was he the one man who could make her feel this way? she wondered despairingly. Then all vestiges of reason vanished when his thumb touched her nipple and a shaft of heat consumed her, her hunger for him leaving her melting and moist. All reason forgotten, she dragged him down with her onto the worn Turkish rug, fumbling with his shirt buttons, delighting in his tongue flicking against hers, his fingers tearing at her jeans.

The shrill ring of the phone brought her crashing back to earth with an almighty bang. It was as if the past was repeating itself, tearing him away from her yet again.

"Oh no, not this time," he murmured, as with a superhuman effort she tried to extricate herself. "Stay with me," he whispered as the phone was answered in the gallery and he lowered his lips once more to hers. In the distance she caught the lilt of Moira's voice, then consciously shut her out. This was crazy, wrong, she realized, drinking in Brad's kisses thirstily. But just this once she needed to feel him, breathe him, give life to the lost dreams of years ago. She'd need this memory to feed on in the lonely days ahead. Sighing, she succumbed to temptation, reveling in the feel of him as he nestled between her legs.

It felt so terribly good. So right it hurt.

With a shudder she realized this was like coming home.

Brad shifted, slipping one arm under her and the other under her shirt. Her breasts were as soft, and her nipples as taut and tense as he'd imagined them. Years of denying the truth had culminated in this desperate need. It was overpowering, terrifying and impossible. He caressed gently, cherishing each reaction. None of his past dreams had come anywhere close, he realized, lowering his mouth to her breast. Then he closed his eyes and drove himself deep within her, giving himself up to the glorious sensations of moist heat and passion. "Charlie?" Moira called, knocking at the door. Shocked to their senses, they pulled quickly apart, hastily grappling with their clothes.

"What is it?" Charlotte asked in a shaky voice, securing her bra haphazardly into place, swallowing her bitter frustration at having had him within her so briefly. As she zipped her jeans she glanced at Brad; he looked like a child who'd been offered pudding then had it stolen away. And despite the tension, the humor of the situation struck her full in the gut and she began to giggle uncontrollably.

"Sergeant Ramsey on the phone."

"Just coming," she spluttered, jumping up and grinning at Brad, who grinned reluctantly back as he straightened his hair. Then she rushed to her stool, picking up a pencil just as Moira popped her head around the door.

"They've taken Bobby in for questioning. He wonders if you could pop over for a few minutes."

"Of course," she replied, amazed her voice was so even. "I'll just finish this and go. Thanks."

"Coffee, anyone?"

"No thanks," they answered in unison. She looked up, saw Moira's questioning glance, the twinkle behind the lenses, and felt a dull flush spread to her cheeks. Then, withdrawing her gaze, she began drawing as though her life depended on it.

"I'll go over with you to the station," Brad said.

He did not look the least bit perturbed, she realized as Moira closed the door quietly behind her. Or as if he'd spent the past fifteen minutes with her on the rug. She drew a long breath and tried to assimilate what had happened. She wanted to rush to him, say something, feel his arms reassuringly about her. But they were like separate islands, divided by an ocean of cold reality.

"Moira told Sergeant Ramsey that she saw Bobby in here the other day," she mumbled, to mask her feelings.

"That was smart. We can't take any risks, I don't care how harmless Bobby may seem. And, uh, Charlie?"

"Mmm…" She concentrated on shading the drawing, fingers agitated.

"We need to talk."

"Not now." The pencil dropped, rolling off the table onto the floor. She jumped up. "We'd better get over there now. Sergeant Ramsey's waiting." She caught his look of frustration. For a terrified moment she thought he would insist, but he gave way and stood aside for her to pass through the door.

"My car's parked on the curb."

"I'd rather walk."

"It's still raining."

"I don't care. I need the fresh air."

"Take a brolly." Moira pointed helpfully to the colorful array in the stand near the door.

Brad pulled out a large golf umbrella, opening it as they stepped into the rainy windswept street. They fell into silent step together, shrouded by the colorful umbrella, each wrapped in thought as they trod the slippery flagged pavement toward the police station that stood alone at the far end of the street.

Brad glanced down at Charlotte. She looked tense and nervous. He knew that look and his heart sank. "Charlie, we have to talk about this," he insisted, knowing he could not allow the breach between them to widen. "We can't pretend it didn't happen."

"Not now."

"Okay, later."

She gave a quick nod but kept up the fast pace toward the dull, uninviting building now in sight.

He had to be content with that, he realized, following her up the steps into the constabulary, realizing she was still assimilating what had occurred, just as he was.

He looked past two policemen, one peering at a computer screen, the other stirring a mug of coffee, to the window of an inner office. Bobby sat slumped on a wooden chair opposite the sergeant, his thin, damp, mouse-colored hair stuck to the top of his egg-shaped head like a dummy in a store window.

Sergeant Ramsey came out of the office to greet them. "Sorry to bother ye," he said with an apologetic smile, "but I've got wee Bobby in." He jerked a thumb at the office. "I'm trying to make sense out of all his jabbering," he said, raising his eyes heavenward.

"Poor Bobby," Charlotte murmured, glancing at him through the window. "Frankly, I don't think the robbery had anything to do with him, Sergeant."

"He swears it didn't. Though he does admit he was up that way on the day. 'Course, that might not signify anything, for he goes up to mind the sheep from time to time. Come on in and see what ye can make of it. Coffee?"

"Thanks." She didn't feel like coffee but she didn't want to spurn the offer. Entering the office, she slipped a hand onto Bobby's stooped shoulder and squeezed it.

"Are you all right?" she inquired as Brad pulled two more wooden chairs from against the pale-gray wall.

"Aye," he muttered. Then his hazy eyes turned toward her, pleading. "I'd nae' do anything te' harm ye, Miss Charlotte. I'd never take anything that wasna' mine. I slipped the wee bit of metal in ma' pocket because Moira gave me a fright, that's all. I didna' mean to steal it from ye. I just wanted to take a peek at yer pretty work."

"I know you didn't mean any harm, Bobby." Charlotte smiled gently. "Sergeant Ramsey's just trying to find out as much as he can about who might have broken into Rose Cottage the other day, that's all."

"Do you have any idea?" Brad added, seating himself on Bobby's left.

"No. I've nae' clue," Bobby murmured, head swaying despondently. Then he thought for a moment. "The wee man stayin' at the castle—the one who looks like a bird and uses foreign words ye canna' understand? He was the only person I saw up there that day."

"He must mean Armand," Brad murmured, frowning. "Was he up near the cottage? At what time?"

"A' dinna' rightly know. In the early afternoon, I think. I was headed te' the fields with Shana, ma' collie.

One of the ewes got stuck in the wire up yon. I took the pliers to cut the fence. I fixed it afterward, ma'lord.''

"Sure, don't worry about it." Brad smiled reassuringly "What I'm wondering," he remarked, glancing past Bobby to Charlotte, "is what Armand was doing up there."

"He often goes that way for his afternoon walk. Sometimes Diego joins him," Charlotte said dismissively.

"I see." Brad sat back thoughtfully. Sergeant Ramsey returned with two mugs of lukewarm coffee.

"Sergeant, I don't think Bobby can help us." Charlotte sent him a beseeching smile.

"Maybe not—" he glanced sternly at Bobby "—but ye've nae' business lurking around Miss Charlotte's cottage in the dead of night, giving her frights and the like."

"A' was guarding the cottage," Bobby answered defiantly, a gleam entering his watery blue eyes. "There's strange people about."

"Well, that's very thoughtful, Bobby, but you did give me an awful scare, you know," Charlotte told him.

"I'm sorry, Miss Charlotte. I'll nae' do it again." He hung his head like a guilty child and she exchanged a look with Sergeant Ramsey.

"Surely he can go, Sergeant. I mean—" She raised her hands and gave a quick compassionate glance at the pitiful figure in the faded yellow sweatshirt and scuffed sneakers. "I really don't think there's much Bobby can do. But," she added in a bracing tone, "I'm sure he'll be the first to come forward if he remembers anything else, won't you, Bobby?"

He raised his head and looked at her adoringly. "Aye. Anything fer you, Miss Charlotte."

"Very well, Bobby. I'll drive ye home then." The sergeant put his hand under Bobby's elbow.

"Wait a minute." Brad raised a hand and turned once more to Bobby. "How close was Armand to the cottage?"

"A' couldna' say." Bobby's eyebrows creased as he tried hard to remember. "At the gate, a' think." He rubbed his head then shook it. "No. Perhaps he was nearer the field. But then, he might have been at the door, too," he added, trying desperately to please.

Brad sighed, then smiled. "That's okay, Bobby. Don't worry."

"What would it matter if Armand was near the cottage, anyway?" Charlotte asked, bristling. "He's always going for wanders up on the moors."

"Nothing. Just trying to piece all the facts together, that's all," Brad replied evenly, a new angle forming in his mind.

"Don't worry about Bobby." Charlotte smiled at Sergeant Ramsey. "I have to get back home. I can drop him off on the way. Coming, Bobby?"

He smiled at her gratefully and rose. "I'd never do anything te' hurt nae' one," he insisted, glancing sheepishly at the sergeant, who'd also risen.

"I know, Bobby." Sergeant Ramsey patted his shoulder in a friendly manner. "Now ye gae' home with Miss Charlotte and send ma' best to yer mum."

"Aye." Bobby nodded more cheerfully as they headed for the door.

"I'll buy you a bun at the bakery," Charlotte said, grinning. Bobby loved sugar buns.

"Thank ye, Miss Charlotte, I'd like that," he said eagerly.

"Charlie—" Brad's hand snaked swiftly to her arm. She glanced at him uneasily. "Will you come over to the castle later?"

"I don't know. I'll see. Bobby, you run ahead and I'll catch up with you at the bakery," she said, patting him on the shoulder. Turning to Brad as Bobby loped off hopefully down the street toward the bakery, she hesitated, glancing up at the drizzling sky. This was neither the time nor place to be announcing major life decisions. Still, she desperately needed to tell him. "There's something I—I've decided to do, Brad. I haven't told Mummy or anyone yet, so please keep it to yourself." She shifted uncomfortably, gripping the brolly firmly and staring at the wet pavement, aware of the full weight of what she was about to say. It was the most serious step she'd ever undertaken, and she hadn't taken it lightly. This was no impulsive urge like so many she'd regretted in the past; this was a conscious choice based on understanding and acceptance of facts that had taken her years to come to terms with. She'd finally understood something vital: John's accident didn't change the bigger scheme of things or the man himself. The decision she'd come to before the event was the right one.

Brad stood, crouched with her under the umbrella, lips inches from hers, eyebrows creased expectantly. There was a serious gleam in her eyes that told him that what she was about to tell him was vitally important. "Shoot," he murmured, touching her arm reassuringly.

"I—I'm going ahead with the divorce," she said in a rush. Their eyes met, locked, then she looked away. "I went to see the lawyers and it's all settled. Of course, it doesn't mean I'll abandon him," she continued. "I'll go on visiting him even after the divorce. But on my own terms."

"That's the best news I've heard in ages," he declared, grinning, and pulling her close, wanting to fold her in his arms. Then a sharp pang reminded him that though she would now be free, he was about to commit himself forever to Sylvia.

"I have to go," she muttered, anxious to leave now that she'd gotten it out. The decision had loomed for so long, a seemingly insurmountable hurdle, yet as she'd spoken the words it had sounded incredibly simple.

Movement to their left made Charlotte look up. She stepped quickly out of Brad's reach as Mrs. Pearson's bicycle rounded the corner. "Oh God, not now," she moaned.

"Hello, hello." Mrs. P. called briskly as she slowed the bike, oblivious to the downpour and the wilting feather in her hat.

"Hello, Mrs. Pearson." Charlotte mustered a smile.

"Lord MacLeod. What a pleasure to see you taking an interest in village affairs. I heard from Councilor Dumbarton that you have great plans afoot?" Her tone was conspiratorial, her eyes alive with avid curiosity.

"Absolutely," he replied blithely. "Lots of things cooking."

"Anything I can do to help?" Mrs. Pearson said, her withered face creased in a hopeful beam.

"I'm afraid it's early days. But I'm sure as soon as the councilor has his show on the road, we'll be in touch."

"Ah! I have a few suggestions of my own that might come in useful. Not that one would wish to intrude, of course," she said, with the air of one who had every intention of doing just that, "but one is fairly *au fait* with the goings-on." She leaned closer. "If at any time you feel the need for personal guidance, the Colonel and I would be only too glad. These waters can be tricky to navigate," she added with a quick glance to the right and left.

"Uh, yes—of course. Very generous of you." Brad smiled briefly, then glanced regretfully at his watch. Charlotte smothered a grin. "I'm afraid you'll have to excuse me, Mrs. Pearson, urgent business at the castle, you know."

"But of course. Far be it from me to intrude upon your duties. Perhaps you and your charming fiancée would like to pop over for a drink sometime? Does she plan to make a prolonged stay?" The eagerness in her voice was barely disguised.

"That would be very nice," he murmured blandly, skirting the last part of her question while casting Charlotte a look.

"Bye-bye, Mrs. Pearson." Charlotte nodded firmly and turned. "I'm off to get Bobby his bun. See you later." She waved and moved quickly down the pavement.

Brad watched in frustration as Mrs. Pearson cycled off lugubriously and Charlotte entered the bakery. Her words left a sudden emptiness inside. Independence was what he wanted for her. He should be thrilled, but knowing he would not be a part of her newfound freedom left him drained and listless. There were responsibilities, an engagement, the twins and the real world to contend with. None were about to disappear because of Charlotte's news. All he wished for was a magic wand that could somehow make her a part of his life.

He glanced back at the station. For a moment he considered having a one-on-one talk with Sergeant Ramsey, then thought better of it, deciding instead to head back to the castle. The talk with Charlotte would have to wait.

As he walked back to his car, he considered Armand and his often odd behavior. The man was a throwback to another era. He knew Armand had suffered a strange and tortured childhood. His mother had been shot as a collaborator during the war, and he'd been taken in by the Cardinal and educated by Jesuit priests. Clearly, the guy carried a huge chip on his shoulder as a result. His past reminded Brad of his grandfather's, all strange twists and turns and the river of revelations that had led to his own, unexpected destiny. Could there be more secrets stashed in the closet, waiting to be revealed? he wondered suddenly.

Opening the car door, he got in and for a moment gazed blindly through the wet windshield. Did the past have anything to do with Armand's unexpected presence at Strathaird?

Probably not much.

Still, he was prompted to dig further. The obvious person to ask, he realized, turning the key in the ignition, was Oncle Eugène. The Cardinal had arrived at Strathaird a few days earlier. Between his duties and Sylvia's departure, he hadn't had much opportunity to talk with his grandfather's cousin. Now he was glad to have something to take his mind off the growing guilt that hovered whenever Sylvia's image flashed. Guilt was putting it mildly, he realized uncomfortably, especially given what had happened in Charlotte's studio. He pushed the events of the morning out of his mind, knowing he'd need to address them but finding it safer, for the moment, to focus on the matter at hand. It was time, he decided as he drove back up the hill toward Strathaird, to set some feelers out and learn all he could while Eugène was still around to spill the beans about the past. *If* beans there were to spill.

Something told him there were.

11

It was Tuesday afternoon, just moments into Harcourts' board meeting. Sylvia stared at the members of the board assembled around the long polished table—all of them established businessmen in their own right, all of them eyeing her expectantly—and walked as casually as she could to Brad's deep leather chair at the head of the table.

As she lowered herself into the seat, she experienced a sudden rush. She'd never directed a board meeting before, but instantly she knew she'd want to again. Placing her papers in careful order, she looked up and smiled.

"Good afternoon, gentlemen. It's unfortunate that our chairman is unable to be with us today, but pressing matters in Scotland prevented him from attending." She stopped, looked from left to right, eyes connecting for a moment with those members she'd been talking to over the past few days. Then she continued. "As I remarked, it's unfortunate, but I hope I'll be able to stand in in an adequate manner."

"Sylvia," Barry Granger sent her an amused glance from under bushy white eyebrows, "I don't think any of us doubt that. You know more about Harcourts than the rest of us combined.'' There was an answering murmur of approval.

"Thank you.'' She smiled briefly then turned to her right and addressed a tall man, dressed in a pinstripe suit, with thick black hair and heavy glasses. "Everard, you have our agenda for today. I believe we're all ready.'' She leaned forward and studied the memo before her, careful to betray none of the nervousness she felt.

After clearing his throat, Everard launched into a preview of the items on the agenda. They were all pro forma, Sylvia realized as she allowed her mind to wander. It was eight o'clock in Scotland. What was Brad doing right now? she wondered. Was he with— Immediately she stopped herself. She mustn't let emotion cloud her mind; if there was ever a moment she needed all her faculties about her, this was it. Clearing the decks, she concentrated on Everard and the meeting, aware that now was the time to sow seeds for the future.

And plant she must, if her plan was to succeed.

The afternoon did not improve, the sky remaining cloudy. A walk, even in the close perimeters of the castle, was out of the question. Resigning himself to an afternoon of reading, Eugène de la Vallière repaired to the library with the aid of his companion and caregiver, Monsignor Kelly. There he continued to read and snooze. When the door opened quietly he shifted, wished his back weren't so stiff, his annoyance fading when he saw Brad.

"Ah! Bradley. You're home early.''

"Not much to be done outside in this weather. Thought I'd come back and dig into some of the paperwork.''

"Of which I'm sure there is much.'' The Cardinal drew the rug across his knees and, wincing, sat up straighter, better to observe him. "You have quite a job on your hands, *mon cher*. Typical of Gavin to have expected you to take it on. Though in this particular case he didn't have much choice after poor Colin passed on.'' He sighed. It seemed unjust that he himself had outlived his generation, yet young Colin had been swept away by the wrath of an avalanche in the flush of youth.

"It's manageable. At least I'm trying to make it manageable.''

"Hmm. Penelope mentioned that your fiancée did not appear pleased that you weren't returning with her to New York,'' Eugène remarked thoughtfully. ''She seemed to think your presence there was of some importance.''

"Yes, well, it's a bit of a sore subject right now.''

"I see.'' Eugène studied Brad for a moment, surprised at the agitation he read in those fine blue eyes, so hauntingly reminiscent of his grandfather's. That same agitation lurked, that same inquietude so characteristic of Gavin. But he'd never seen it in Brad's eyes before. Or only once, he amended, frowning, trying to recall the exact year of Charlotte's marriage.

"Have you seen Armand?'' Brad asked, seating himself opposite the Cardinal amidst shelves of ancient books near the fireplace, glad to have caught him alone. He had known Eugène for years; the respected priest was Charlotte's great-uncle, and had been one of Dex's oldest, most trusted friends. Brad had always valued Eugène's sharp mind and strong opinions.

The room was too warm for a fire and the grate stood empty. Brad stared at it, wondering how to broach the subject uppermost in his brain.

"I believe he went off to Charlotte's gallery.''

"No, he didn't go by the gallery.''

"Oh. You were there?''

"Yes, I was by there," he replied calmly, knowing the wily old Cardinal was fully capable of somehow reading in his eyes things he'd rather not share—like what had happened with Charlotte this morning. Still, he was curious to learn more about Armand, and Oncle Eugène was without a doubt his best source. "I was in the village and saw Charlotte. We went together to the police station to talk to Bobby Hewitt. He's a simple soul who sometimes hovers around Charlotte and the cottage. We thought perhaps he might have been responsible for the robbery."

"An odd matter, that robbery, indeed," the Cardinal agreed, a pensive frown knitting his thin white eyebrows. "Did this person, this Bobby Hewitt, strike you as guilty?"

"No. Not in the least." Brad shook his head, leaned back in the faded armchair and flung an ankle over the knee of his beige corduroy pants. "The only other person seen there that day was Armand. But of course, we excluded him immediately." He studied the Cardinal from under hooded lids, anxious to seek his reaction.

"Armand is an odd fish," Eugène remarked slowly, "but I doubt he would resort to stealing. Still..." He pondered a moment and Brad grabbed his opening.

"Am I right in recalling a story that dates back to when Uncle David was a young man? Something about Armand having tried to take his watch? The same watch," he emphasized slowly, "that was stolen from Charlotte's cottage?"

"Yes, of course, you're correct," Eugène replied, eyes brightening. "It was one summer when David was working at the factory in Limoges. He never knew if Armand was actually trying to steal the watch or merely studying it." Eugène shrugged his shoulders. "I've never been able to disabuse him of his strange obsession with Sylvain de Rothberg.''

''I gathered that. Do you think this obsession is such that he'd feel compelled to try and steal the watch from Charlotte?''

The Cardinal mused, then shook his red-capped head. ''No, I don't believe so. The thought of actually owning a Rothberg piece might have sparked something. But no,'' he dismissed his words. ''Perhaps earlier in his life, but not at this stage.''

''Why is he so fixated on the Rothbergs?'' Brad asked, curious to get a better sense of Armand.

With a sigh, the Cardinal removed his glasses and wiped them carefully with his handkerchief. ''I don't rightly know the root of the obsession, for he's never confided in me. We have never, as I'm sure you are aware, been particularly close.'' Brad murmured an assent, not wanting to break the flow. ''He was a difficult child,'' Eugène continued, ''which is hardly surprising, I suppose, when one thinks of the horror to which he was subjected. His mother was shot as a collaborator, you remember. I myself assisted her in her last moments.''

''Dex told me the story,'' he remarked, nodding. ''A rough start.''

''Yes. Already he suffered from the stigma of being the illegitimate son of my younger brother, René. His mother was the barmaid at the Café du Centre in Ambazac—you know the place?'' Brad nodded once more. ''People can be terribly resentful and mean. Those days just after the war were very different from today, you know,'' he added with a long sigh. ''Personally I never believed poor Françoise was a collaborator and told the judges so. Perhaps she even tried to help some of the Résistants, who knows? That is certainly what she claimed. You will recall, Brad, that Sylvain de Rothberg and his wife, Geneviève—my sister—were part of the underground resistance movement in the Second World War? Françoise asserted that Sylvain himself was one of the people she'd aided. I even showed the judges the Star of David she swore he'd slipped to her when he was in jail. But there was no proof of that to be found when the defense tried to establish the occurrence at her trial. If trial you can call it," he murmured acidly. "Those sitting on the benches of justice were there to condemn, not to try. It was an appalling example of petty animosity and revenge. People were too intent on getting back at one another, taking advantage of the situation to settle old scores." He shook his head sadly. "Françoise was not a bad girl. In her final hour she wrote a letter for her son that she begged me to keep until he was eighteen."

"Did you see it?"

"No. She sealed it and it remained thus in my safe at La Vallière until his eighteenth birthday, as she requested. By that time he was already on a troubled path, from which I regret he has not deviated much since."

Brad supposed he was referring to Armand's boyfriends. Otherwise, he could think of nothing that might condemn the man in the Cardinal's eyes, except that he was an annoying pedant. Still, a niggling voice urged him to pursue the subject further. It was probably absurd, but for some reason the thought of Charlotte handing over a large amount of her jewelry to Armand left him uneasy.

"What do you think of Armand's invitation to show Charlotte's collection with his own in the fall?" he asked, snapping his finger at Rufus, who'd ambled in the door.

"Frankly, I'm surprised he'd even consider it. Armand has not been known for his generosity of spirit. Certainly not in the professional sphere. From all I gather, he is a mediocre designer at best, though apparently quite well liked among his peers." He shrugged. "Perhaps he hopes that showing Charlotte's work will bring him reflected glory. He will be the 'discoverer' of new talent."

"I hadn't thought of that, but it makes sense."

"I can think of no other reason why he would so bestir himself on Charlotte's behalf. I just hope it benefits Charlotte—she has enough troubles in her personal life, poor child."

Brad looked away. "Yes, she has." And now she had the passion between them to contend with as well, he thought, overcome with guilt.

They had to talk, whether she liked it or not. Knowing Charlotte, he doubted she would come over tonight. She would flounder, try and pretend that everything could fall back into place as it had been. But it couldn't. And the sooner she realized it the better.

"You seem very silent."

The Cardinal's voice made him look up, startled. "I was thinking about Armand and all you were saying." He smiled and leaned forward to knead Rufus between the ears. "As you say, it doesn't seem likely he'd be involved in the robbery." He caught the Cardinal's skeptical glance and held it a second. Was there nothing the old gentleman didn't see? Suddenly he wondered how much he might have noticed that summer at La Vallière. If anyone had been aware of his feelings for Charlotte back then, it was probably Oncle Eugène.

He rose regretfully. "Time to get some work done, I'm afraid."

"Of course. I shall see you at dinner. And by the way—"

Brad paused, aware by the tone in the Cardinal's voice that Eugène was about to say something of note. "You should think hard about your future, *cher* Bradley. Marrying the wrong woman can result in a very unhealthy situation.''

Not knowing how to answer, he grunted an assent and slipped from the room. The Cardinal was right; he had a lot of rethinking to do.

Exactly how much remained to be seen.

Contrary to old Hamish's predictions, the weather cleared the next day, sharp sweeping gusts blowing the rain eastward. Despite her initial misgivings, Charlotte had conceded to Brad's offer and went to Glasgow by chopper. She had to admit it had made the trip a lot easier and she was back home by late afternoon. Still, as always, the depressing atmosphere of the hospital—the sterile tubes, the smell of anesthetic and the silent motionless bodies—left her anguished. How could she go on living like this, tied to a corpse? she wondered later that day, glad to be back in her gallery, surrounded by the familiar feel of her work.

Taking a sip of decaf, Charlotte watched Moira, perched on a high stool, carefully preparing a wax mold. Since yesterday morning she'd found it impossible to set her mind to anything useful. Moving impatiently across the workshop to her drawing table, she switched on the light and doodled with the new sketch of a ring—anything, she realized somberly, to avoid obsessing over what had happened yesterday morning. But it was pointless. So much was bubbling in her troubled mind. She'd gone to Glasgow today almost hoping that seeing John would convince her that she still had a husband and duties to fulfill. Instead, his expressionless figure had forced her to acknowledge that things couldn't go on as they were.

Now, as she rose restlessly and carried the empty cup of coffee to the battered sink, she pondered. Did it really matter that she and Brad had no future? What if they simply had an affair? Would that get him out of her system?

She placed the cup down, letting the water trickle in loud drops into the dilapidated metal sink, thinking of Brad's hands gliding smoothly up her body, and that brief moment of union. Could she persuade herself this was just about sex? She let out a heavy sigh. She didn't think so. There'd been so much more in Brad's touch than mere physical sensation. But only misery awaited her if she allowed matters to get any more involved, she realized, policing herself, trying desperately to banish the persistent images.

"Damn Brad," she exclaimed, bringing her palm down hard on the counter.

"Excuse me?" Moira glanced up. "Charlotte, turn that damn tap off, it's driving me nuts."

"I said, damn Brad." Charlotte gave the tap a twist and turned. "Why did this have to happen just as things were beginning to look up? Right now I need my full concentration focused on the jewelry for the show."

"Do I gather you're referring to yesterday?" Moira sent her a quizzical look.

"Yes. You know perfectly well what happened in here, so don't pretend not to."

"I'm not," Moira replied airily, returning her attention to the mold she was crafting. "You're old enough to know what you're doing."

"I wish I did," Charlotte muttered. "I feel like a whirling dervish." Her eye caught the calendar and she winced. "Do you realize that we've only three weeks left if we are going to participate in the show?"

"Of course you'll participate. And don't worry, we'll make it." Moira winked.

"I'm glad you're so calm about it," Charlotte grumbled, squinting at the bright new Swatch watch the twins had bought her. It was later than she'd realized. "I suppose I must go find Armand. After all, he's leaving in a few days and there are still so many details to settle." She gave a worried sigh. "How's the choker coming along, by the way?" She shifted nervously, then stood gazing over Moira's shoulder at the plasticene form she was creating. Suddenly, she stamped her foot, angrily as a child. "I don't know what's wrong with me," she wailed. "I can't seem to be able to settle my mind on anything."

"Maybe it's time you and Brad finally let loose," Moira murmured, shaping the gooey substance with deft hands. "You're going to be no use at all floating around in a bubble."

"But all I can think of is—" Charlotte stopped, realizing how ridiculous she must sound, and gave a short laugh.

"Brad," Moira supplied with a knowing nod.

"Yes," she whispered in a small voice, a tiny smile curving her lips. It was true. All that registered was the touch of his lips on hers, his thumb grazing her nipples in that tantalizing magic manner that had left her tossing all night and aching for more. "It's absurd to be moping like a moody teenager, Mo," she said, trying to get a grip, "and even more ridiculous for this to be happening with Brad. I've known him forever. He's engaged, for Christ's sake." She whirled around and leaned against Moira's worktable, making it impossible for her to continue her mold.

"Charlie, I'm trying to get this finished today."

"I know, but just listen for a moment. It's important," Charlotte wheedled.

With a resigned sigh Moira pushed back her stool. "Okay, but not long, I've got to finish it."

"Damn the mold. Mo, what am I going to do?" she cried, sending her friend a desperate plea for help.

"What do you want to do?"

"I haven't a clue," Charlotte lied.

"If you want my real opinion, I'd say you're both chomping at the bit. Best thing to do is jump into bed with him and take care of business, if you ask me. Now, if you moved over, I could actually get on with my work."

"It's not that simple," Charlotte remarked, shifting nervously aside, conscious of a dull ache in her heart. The truth was she wanted him, desperately. But not in bits. She wanted down to the last inch of him. And not just for robbed moments either, she reflected anxiously, aware that the only other time she'd ever felt quite like this was all those years ago when Brad had refused to make love to her. A sudden chill ran up her spine. What if she came to him, and he refused her again?

Shock that she was even considering such a thing made her stop and swallow. John had been the one and only man in her life. Sex between them had been a disappointment from the start but she had little room for comparison. John had wasted no time except on his own pleasure. But this, this was so different.

"I can't do it," she whispered, suddenly clenching her fingers. "He's engaged, I'm still married, there's Genny and the twins, a never-ending list of reasons why it simply can't happen. Plus, it would be the end of our friendship." She fidgeted, dragging nervous fingers through her hair. She paced about the workshop, then stopped in front of Moira as though expecting her corroboration.

"Don't you think it's a bit late to be coming up with all of this now?" Moira said.

"No." She shook her head violently. "I can't afford any more mistakes. Just think, Mo. It would muck everything up."

"I don't see why that should stop you, when you've been mucking your life up for so long," she remarked dryly.

"What do you mean?" Charlotte bristled.

"That you're in love with him and always have been. And have spent the past ten years in the hands of a man who, as far as I'm concerned, should be behind bars for the way he treated you."

"Rubbish," Charlotte scoffed. But in all the long years she'd been married to John, not once had she thought of his lips grazing hers the way Brad's did, or of his tongue roaming slowly, tauntingly over her temple, down her cheek to her lips, then lingering, as though he had all day.

Moira laid down the mold and looked up, voice softening. "Stop being so hard on yourself and on him, Charlie. Give yourselves a chance. Okay, it carries risks," she agreed, "but what doesn't? Surely anything's better than what you've been going through."

"I'm sure to get hurt."

"Maybe. But isn't that better than continuing in this no-man's-land you're in now?"

"Plus, there's Sylvia to consider." She sounded unconvincing to her own ears. The New Yorker's blond image seemed awfully far away. Apparently neither Sylvia nor trying to convince herself about her own obligations had acted as sufficient deterrents. Maybe Mo was right. What was the point of resisting when it was obvious she'd shot her own ground rules to hell?

"At some point you're going to have to face him," Moira added. "It's a bit much to hope Brad will let yesterday morning's incident pass without mention."

"You're right," she agreed in a hollow voice. "He'll either expect me to go to him or, more likely, he'll turn up here or at the cottage."

"Well?" A slow grin spread over Moira's broad face. "Why not take the chance? Live the moment. Stop always thinking about what you owe others, or what tomorrow will bring. If I were you, I'd go for the cottage," she added sagely.

Charlotte tilted her head, then grinned as an idea occurred to her. "Maybe you're right," she murmured. The possibility of him arriving at Rose Cottage suddenly seemed infinitely more tempting. All at once she spun around and stared at herself in the stained mirror hanging askew on the wall, next to Sylvain's photograph, and smirked at her own reflection. Mo was right. He would come, and soon. Of that she was certain. Whether she was right about what happened then remained to be seen. There would probably be one hell of a high price to pay. But what of it? She'd been paying all her adult life. At least this time the price would be worth it. Scooping her hair up with her free hand, she tilted her head and sized up the effect.

"How about that?"

"Not bad," Moira conceded. "If I were you, I'd get on home and start thinking about dinner. Brad has a healthy appetite," she added, tongue in cheek.

"How do you know?"

"Yesterday morning made it blatantly obvious. Go on," she urged, "get moving."

"All right." Charlotte made up her mind. If she went down, she might as well go down swinging. All at once she knew exactly what she would do. Rushing over to her friend, she gave her a quick hug.

"You're right, Mo, and I'm off at once. Wish me luck."

Half an hour later, Charlotte flung open her closet and began flipping through the hangers, pulling out clothes and throwing them on the bed. She held up a well-cut short white dress her mother had bought her on her last trip to London. She'd never worn it. Now she held it against herself and stared in the mirror. Not bad, she decided, tilting her head, not bad at all.

She dropped the dress on the bed with the other garments then entered the bathroom and stripped. A few minutes later she stood under the warm spray, lathering her body with scented shower gel, shampooing her hair, rinsing and conditioning. Once she felt deliciously clean, she stepped out and wrapped a large terry bath towel about her body and stood before the misted-up mirror. She wiped a portion of it, pleased with her own image. Her cheeks were flushed, teeth white and eyes bright, and she hadn't felt so good in ages.

Charlotte threw back her head and gave a delighted laugh. The last time she'd decided to seduce Brad, all those years before, she'd felt the same reckless high. Putting one foot up on the tiny tiled counter, she unscrewed the top of the scented body cream Moira had given her for her birthday and which until now she hadn't bothered to use. It smelled delicious, and felt slippery and sensual as she smoothed it over every inch of her body.

It had rained all afternoon. Then, as often occurred, the setting sun had made a last-minute appearance. Slanting through the small windowpanes, it highlighted her hair. She sighed. Glancing outside, she watched the sun disappear behind the hills. Soon it would be evening. The children would probably end up playing Ping-Pong at Lucy's, which suited her just fine, she reflected, giving the cap of the cream a smug twist as she replaced it on the shelf. In fact, she'd ring Sheila Morisson and make sure they *did* stay over.

"Let him come," she whispered at the vibrant reflection in the mirror. "But please, don't let us get too burned." Then, taking a deep breath, she went back into the bedroom and for the first time in longer than she could remember, she dressed for a man.

There was little point in letting things fester, Brad decided. He'd go up before dinner and get it out of the way. He was the one to blame, he realized morosely. If he hadn't allowed matters to get out of hand, none of this would have happened. He just hoped it hadn't damaged their friendship permanently. But it was too late to lament what had occurred yesterday—and to be honest, his only regret was that they hadn't had more time. But still, he'd been wrong, and there was only one way to make it right.

It was almost twilight as he walked up the hill. Suddenly Rufus barreled out of the undergrowth and joined him, trotting silently next to him as though aware that something important was about to occur.

It was, he realized woodenly. Tonight he would finally acknowledge that his most cherished dream couldn't come true.

The light in the window probably meant she was home.

Good. The sooner he got this behind him, the better. Then, after he'd apologized, he'd have to make a point of avoiding her, keep to himself. Perhaps even consider making the trip back stateside.

The thought of New York and Sylvia left him depressed, and as he approached the cottage, his steps lagged.

This was final. He'd spent the entire day going over his options and had come to the sad conclusion that he had none. After tonight, there would be no going back, no changing his mind. He couldn't play with Charlotte's feelings or with his own.

He opened the gate and stared blankly at the door. How could he let her go after finally tasting what they could be together?

But he had no choice. It was too late for them.

Perhaps, he thought as he knocked on the door, it always had been.

"Come in." Charlotte's voice echoed from the back of the cottage as he stepped warily into the hall. Candles burned in the small silver dish on the hall table, where usually she kept her keys, and wildflowers burst from vases everywhere. A pang of regret and a tinge of unjustified anger ripped through him, for there was something sensual and enticing in the air. He hesitated. Apparently she was expecting someone.

"I'm in the kitchen," she called. What sort of a pickle was Charlie getting herself into now? he wondered, his protective instincts surfacing. He followed Rufus's huge, furry form across the hall, drawn by the alluring scents of rosemary and thyme, and something indefinable that left him hungry as well as curious.

Reaching the kitchen doorway, he stopped in his tracks, stunned. He opened his mouth to say something, then took a long breath and searched desperately for the right words.

Charlotte was standing by the window, tantalizingly seductive in a short white dress, hair cascading about her shoulders, the swell of her breast visible at the fitted neckline. High heels made her legs seem endless, and her eyes sparkled like two rich amethysts as she leaned back against the counter, watching him, sending shivers up his spine. This was the identical woman to the one he'd seen in the vision in the hall at Strathaird.

"I hope I'm not interrupting anything," he murmured, regaining his composure as he entered the low-ceilinged kitchen that had taken on a new air, like a witches' coven filled with heady sensuous mystery. "I thought we needed to talk," he added, as though justifying his presence. But Charlotte remained where she was and simply smiled at him, looking deliciously devious and self-satisfied.

He glanced at the table, set for two. A fine jacquard tablecloth that he recognized from the Harcourts Classic line graced the table, topped with bone china, folded napkins, flowers and two silver candlesticks. Strains of a sultry Latin ballad drifted in from the living room. It was a scene set for seduction, and it was set for him.

He sent her a questioning look. "This wasn't in the program," he murmured hoarsely as slowly she moved toward him, a gloriously sensual creature who left him weak at the knees. Where on earth was the reticent, uncertain woman who'd avoided his eyes this morning when he'd tried to sit her down to talk things over reasonably? His heart lurched as he recognized the Charlotte he'd fallen in love with so long ago, the confident temptress, innocence blending with the promise of passion.

He backed away. If he succumbed, there would be no

turning back. He reached for the doorway behind him. ''Charlie,'' he said, backing off as she sidled up to him and slipped her arms around his neck, ''as much as I want to, we can't do this. Just listen to me, I've got it all figured out—'' But every good intention evaporated as she reached for his lips.

''We mustn't do this,'' he muttered, hands encircling her slim waist, the feel of her lips on his too much to resist.

''But we both know it's going to happen all the same,'' she murmured softly, flicking her tongue along his temple, leaving him shuddering.

His arms snaked down her body and he pulled her close. ''Are you absolutely sure?'' he asked urgently, control slipping as she nestled against him.

''I've never been so sure about anything,'' she assured him in a whisper, hands beginning to undo the buttons of his shirt.

''Oh, sweet Jesus, thank you,'' he sighed, eyes closing as his fingers glided along her bare arms. It was too late for logic, too late to retract. However much his mind tried to dictate, it was simply too late to look back. The die was cast and whatever came next was up to fate.

''This feels so right, doesn't it?'' he whispered, nuzzling her hair.

''Yes, it does,'' she said into the crook of his shoulder, for it did. Lifting her head, she searched his eyes, delved into those years of intense yearning, and knew with soul-deep conviction that no matter what convention said, there could never be anything wrong about what they shared.

The realization left her dizzy, overcome by a light, heady sensation like nothing she'd ever known. She wanted to drench herself in his being, bond with him so deeply, so intensely that their hearts and minds became one. Then his hand caressed the back of her neck, fisted her hair and gently tilted her head back, and the hunger in his eyes left her gasping with sharp, intense longing.

"I want you, Charlie." His voice came out husky as he searched her face, all the need in him written right there in his eyes. "I think I've wanted you all my life."

It was wondrous, frightening and exhilarating. Her mind blanked when his lips touched hers, and her body gave way. This was not the painful, impatient pawing John had forced upon her over the years, but a rough, ragged demand for mutual satisfaction. He ravaged her mouth, fired her senses, leaving her wanting and exposed. She filled her hands with his hair, felt her breasts taut and aching against his hard muscled chest, and craved the touch of his skin. When his hand slipped down her back, pressing her close, body to body, she knew just how much he wanted her.

And she him.

He came up for breath, kissed her eyelids, and she drew him back, urging his hands down the front of her thin cotton dress, delighting in his moan when he realized she wore no bra. Then he found her nipple and a rush of heat left her light, limp and wanting.

"The kitchen's not the best idea," he whispered, drawing her toward the door, but she stalled him. With something between a laugh and a groan, he slammed her against the fridge door, moving roughly against her and she clung, not caring if he took her right there. This was the most wonderful, exciting thing that had ever happened to her and she savored it, afraid that if he stopped for a moment, it might all go away.

He lifted her arms and her dress, sighed when he realized there was nothing underneath, and slid his warm hands over her buttocks. She tugged at his shirt, trying to undo the buttons, then, frustrated, ripped them free, pulling the fabric off his shoulders. Delighted, empowered, she turned her attention to the belt buckle of his jeans, surprised when she felt his hand restrain hers.

He looked down at her, eyes alive with love and longing. Then, dropping a kiss on her mouth, he lifted her in his arms.

"Brad—"

"Shh," he tenderly whispered, kissing her eyelids. With a sigh, she looped her arms around his neck and he lifted her, carrying her to the bedroom. John had never done anything remotely similar or so wonderfully romantic, she reflected.

She'd left the door conveniently ajar, and with a shove of his shoulder he pushed it open, then kicked it shut before carrying her to the bed. Eyes locked, he gently laid her down among the pillows.

A warm glow radiated from the shaded bed lamps and a scented candle flickered on the dresser, its reflection gleaming in the mirror as he lowered himself beside her.

"You can still change your mind," he muttered hoarsely, praying she wouldn't as he gazed down at her longingly.

"I've never wanted anything more, Brad," she said softly, something hungry and intense flickering over her face. "I don't care a damn about tomorrow. Whatever happens, we'll always have this."

He crushed her to him, wanting to devour, forcing himself to keep it slow. He wasn't going to hurry, wasn't going to rush or spoil this precious moment he'd dreamed of all these years. Instead, he'd give her all the love and pleasure he sensed she'd never known, everything he knew she so desperately needed.

A rush of pure satisfaction gripped him when his fingers coursed south and he felt her eager response to his probing fingers. When she opened for him, it was as if he'd been given a gift of unimaginable worth. Touching deep within her, he swallowed her gasp with a kiss, and slowly massaged her core.

She writhed, moaned, the sheen of passion making her skin glow. "Brad, darling, please," she murmured, eyes pleading.

She was all woman, unfettered scented sweetness, wet warmth waiting to be fulfilled. He would remember her forever just as she was right now, wild with longing, poised on the brink of newly discovered passion and pleasures that, he sensed with pride, only he could give her. She arched into his hand as he pressed deeper, and her sharp, shattering gasp of release almost drove him over the edge.

Then her eyes opened, spelling deep yearning as fierce and needy as his own. He gave way, thrust deep within her, mind blank as together they journeyed on a sharp rising wave, rolling inland, higher and higher.

And when at last it crested, he crashed headlong with her into the surf.

12

Armand stared, eyes narrowed, at the library shelves reaching up to the carved oak frieze and coffered ceiling. His task was not proving easy, he mused, hand fiddling nervously with the Star of David necklace that he'd been given on his eighteenth birthday, along with his mother's letter.

The Cardinal had handed it to him ever so casually, saying merely that Sylvain de Rothberg had given the piece to his mother when she saw him in prison. He remarked that Françoise was a brave girl and that he wanted Armand to have it.

Nothing more, nothing less.

But Armand knew. He had always known. And those few words had sufficed to confirm any lingering doubts. He'd never removed the Star of David since.

Pausing to better view the selection of French books, acquired mostly by Great-Aunt Hortense de la Vallière, he remembered that birthday. Everything had suddenly fallen into place, like the pieces of a bright mosaic. If his uncle had given him the Star of David, it could only be because he—Armand—was none other than Sylvain de Rothberg's child.

From then on, it had been easy for the starved, creative mind of a lonely adolescent to begin creating the myth. Unless Sylvain had been his mother's lover, he reasoned, why would she have mentioned him in her letter? He'd always known the Cardinal was ashamed of him. Eugène had told the world Armand was his illegitimate nephew, when in fact he was nothing of the sort. Sylvain and his mother had probably been lovers for years. But of course, she had been a barmaid and Sylvain was a wealthy, successful jeweler from a family of even wealthier bankers. Society would never have tolerated their union. And so, he reasoned, his would-be father must have found a solution. Perhaps it was not unreasonable to believe Sylvain had even married Geneviève de la Vallière as a decoy, an excuse to be close to the village of Ambazac where Françoise lived and worked.

It all made perfect sense.

What made less sense was why the Cardinal refused to reveal his true identity now that all that was part of the past. Only later, as Armand grew up and learned about the Lost Collection, did he come to understand his "uncle's" motives. It was crystal clear. The fabled Lost Collection was reputed to be a spectacular cache of jewels hidden by Sylvain, so as to keep his work out of Nazi hands. Obviously the Cardinal knew of the collection's existence. As Sylvain's brother-in-law and last surviving relative, perhaps Eugène hoped to find and claim it as his own.

But for what purpose? Would he give it to the Church? Of course. The Church and his own quest for personal power within it were the only things the miserable old man really cared about, Armand reflected bitterly, eyes traveling the well-worn covers. He'd spent years searching for possible clues, aware that if he, Armand, found the jewels first and was proved to be the legitimate heir, then all Eugène's dreams of glory would go up in smoke. The thought was so appealing that for a moment he stopped and stared out the window, transported on a cloud of pure euphoria.

Usually he avoided thinking about his childhood, but sometimes it pierced the carefully erected ramparts of his mind despite his determination to forget. He'd never stopped blaming Eugène for his callous disregard of a powerless and petrified boy. Armand stared again at the books before him, seeing instead the dark and terrible events of his past. He shook his head to clear it, realizing that only his sure sense of his true identity had kept him going all these long, lonely years. Knowing he was the great master's son had made it easier to ignore the snubs, the taunts, the careless insults, because what else could one expect of such ignorance? His, after all, was the bloodline of genius!

If only the Cardinal weren't spiteful and, yes, jealous, he'd have acknowledged this long ago. Instead, he'd passed him off as a poor relation, forcing his supposed nephew to seek proof of his true identity on his own. Armand recalled his futile efforts to search out other Rothbergs, but there was simply too little information, and those members of the family he could find were in America and Australia and not easily attainable. Even his youthful conversion to Judaism in the hope that members of Sylvain's synagogue would then vouch for him had been for naught. Now time was running out and he was growing old, but he refused to die as Armand de la Vallière, illegitimate son and mediocre couturier.

Not he. When he passed on, he wanted the world to mourn him, as suited the only living link to the glorious Rothberg name.

For years he'd searched all the places Sylvain had frequented but they had yielded no indication as to where the Lost Collection might be. Yet he was certain it was within reach. He'd scoured La Vallière but to no avail. Now, the only place left where Sylvain was known to have spent time, shortly before the war, was Strathaird. He'd come by the knowledge by chance, for he'd never related Sylvain to the Scottish side of the family. But a casual comment from the Cardinal several months back had set him on this track. Strathaird, he kenw, was his last chance.

All at once he came back to earth and focused again on the packed shelves, wondering if they did indeed hold the key to his fortune. He must be careful and cunning not to reveal his intentions, for until he found the necessary clues to the Lost Collection, what proof did he have? His uncle's lies would persist, and perhaps even win the day, unless he operated in maximum secrecy.

But he was so close, he reassured himself; soon the lies would end. He remembered the strange dreams that were increasingly frequent. He often spoke with Sylvain out loud, imagined long father-to-son conversations, and could sense his presence with him even now, leading him on the proper path to discovery. In a dream that had continued long after waking, he'd heard Sylvain's voice repeating that a letter would be found among the jewels, an acknowledgment to the world that Armand was his son and the jewels his legacy. The dream was so real, so clear that he never for a moment doubted its veracity. And once the Lost Collection was finally in his possession, he'd have the proof he needed to demand a DNA test. Sylvain's body had been removed from the mass grave where he was buried with those executed in the village of Ambazac. It lay now in the Rothberg Mausoleum in the Père-Lachaise Cemetery in Paris, but Armand was sure something could be arranged.

He rested his head against the cool leather bindings, lovingly fingering the small gold star at his throat, through which Sylvain's energy reached him, spurring him on toward his final goal. The same could be said for his inadvertent discovery of Charlotte's talent. It was his father who had shown him how that, too, could be used in his favor.

He sighed, eyes closed. The Germans had tried desperately to find Sylvain's collection of jewels, but had no luck. And since the war it had never come up at auction. No, he reasoned, a smile hovering on his thin, colorless lips, it was still hidden somewhere, lying in wait for its rightful owner.

It had to be.

All at once he turned, hands trembling, struck by the sudden fear that he was yet again on the wrong path, that evil forces lurked, shadowing and mocking his efforts. He thought of his psychic who'd mentioned spells and bad omens, but also that his own talent would be revealed through a new, unexpected source. How else to explain how flighty Charlotte, who had nothing to do with the Rothbergs, could possess a talent and flair so similar to Sylvain's? Was it some grand, cosmic joke?

He squashed the sudden spurt of resentment, knowing he must not let jealous feelings intrude. Instead, he must put her talent to good use. Straightening his tie, he moved toward the sofa. For over forty years he'd been searching, and now that the moment of revelation was imminent, nothing could be allowed to get in his way.

Hearing voices from the hall, he glanced furtively toward the door. It opened and his uncle walked slowly in on Monsignor Kelly's arm. Gripping the star beneath his shirt, Armand stiffened. God, how he hated Eugène de la Vallière, perhaps never so much as he did right now.

Suddenly he wanted to shout out the truth: you hid my identity from me and the world because you're jealous! You want the Lost Collection for yourself and the Church you worship like a pagan goddess!

For a moment his vision blurred, leaving him dizzy. At times the hatred was so intense that it became almost physical. How he wished he had the courage to step across the room, clasp that thin, scraggy neck between his hands and wring it like a chicken's, then watch him choke and wither.

Instead, he clenched and unclenched his fingers and mustered a smile. "Good afternoon, *mon oncle*," he said in the same mockingly subservient tone he'd used all his life.

"Ah, Armand." The Cardinal nodded briefly, not pleased to discover his nephew in the library. "I have had my rest. Now I shall read *Le Monde*," he remarked as Monsignor Kelly helped him into his favorite armchair. "Have you perhaps seen Penelope or the ambassador anywhere?"

"I believe they went on an excursion to the far side of the island." Armand snickered. "The ambassador seems very taken with Lady MacLeod."

Eugène cast him a sidelong look but made no comment. He knew Armand too well to believe the remark was innocent. He was snide, a trait the Cardinal detested in a man.

"There you go." Monsignor Kelly straightened. "Is there anything else you require, Your Eminence?"

"No, thank you, Linus. Go take your walk. You enjoy this filthy weather," he added with a spark of humor.

"Thank you, Your Eminence. A little rain never did a

body harm. Clears the spirit, too," he remarked in his rich Irish brogue, sending a wink in Armand's direction before quietly leaving the library.

Eugène leaned back, settling stiffly against the cushions, remembering his conversation earlier that day with Brad. He frowned, recalling the questions it had raised. He watched his nephew speculatively from under hooded eyelids. Armand never did anything gratuitously. There must be a compelling reason for his prolonged stay on the island and his wish for Charlotte to participate in his show. So what, the Cardinal wondered, tapping the arm of the chair rhythmically, could he be after?

"I would imagine you shall soon be returning to Paris," he commented casually as he unfolded the newspaper.

"Next week. I have much to do before the autumn collection. It will be quite something. Three hundred and fifty people in the Salon Vendôme at the Georges V," Armand remarked proudly.

"Hmm. Quite a crowd. Apparently you intend to exhibit Charlotte's work alongside your own?" He began flipping through the pages of his newspaper, not wanting to appear overly interested. "Are you pleased with her designs?"

"Very. She is a superb talent." Eugene noticed the intensity in Armand's tone and raised an eyebrow.

"You mentioned that her work reminds you of Sylvain de Rothberg's," he observed, noting how Armand stiffened. The paper rustled as he folded it in half, then allowed it to settle on his legs. Fate was indeed a strange bedfellow, he reflected, and clearly was at work.

Armand's sudden interest in Charlotte was yet another sign that the past was reaching out, demanding that its many secrets be brought to light. Again Eugène asked himself the question that for months now had been tormenting his old soul: was it best that the past be left to rest, or did the present generation have a right to know? Only he could decide the answer, for only he held the key. Of them all, only he was left, the last one alive who truly knew all the facts, the final protector of secrets buried so deep they were perhaps best forgotten.

He sighed and eyed Armand overtly. His sallow and dissipated complexion matched the drab, musty tone of his shirt. Someone should tell him to wear light colors next to the face. Perhaps, like so many other things, he should have done so himself, taken more interest in the boy.

With a twinge of guilt and sadness he recalled the brooding child Armand had been, remembered the awful day when children in the village had shorn his head and thrown stones, calling him a bastard and a whore's son. Surely no child should have to suffer so for the sins of his parents? Eugène tried, as he had for the past fifty-odd years, to feel some glimmer of affection for him, but it was near impossible. Though, as a fellow human being and a man of the cloth, he felt great pity for the hardships Armand had endured, there was nothing appealing in the man, just as there had been little to draw him to the child. He'd grown from an uneasy, maladjusted adolescent into an uneasy, maladjusted adult. Armand might flaunt airs and graces now, but Eugène knew very well that underneath them all a snake pit of insecurities festered.

"If I happen to be in Paris at that time, I might consider popping by your show," the Cardinal remarked indifferently, peering at the headlines. "Remind me to mention it to Monsignor Kelly."

Armand jolted and stared at his uncle in wide-eyed surprise. In all these years, Eugène had never once demonstrated the slightest interest in his work. He frowned. Why now? he wondered. "I should be most honored," he replied, smiling graciously. "I'm trying to persuade Charlotte and perhaps Moira to attend. Penelope is uncertain if she will be able to go since someone will have to remain with Geneviève."

The Cardinal grunted and buried himself behind the newspaper. Perhaps it was time to see just how much of the past had seeped into the present. In fact, the show might prove revealing in some way.

After that, he would judge what his next step should be.

13

Being back in New York should have been satisfying. It was, after all, Brad's town, his playground; the place where he'd lived for the better part of his existence. Yet it wasn't satisfying at all. When his secretary had called him about the unexpected, urgent board meeting, his response had been frustration and irritation. Right now, after all that had happened between Charlotte and him, the last place he wanted to be was in America, an ocean away from Skye. And when he had learned the reason for the meeting, his anger had only grown. Sylvia must be nuts to do something like this and then remain out of reach, forcing his return.

Brad hopped out of the car and stood staring at the taillights merging back into the Park Avenue traffic. For the past fifteen years he'd done just this, every day. Shaking off his somber mood, he headed across the marble lobby toward the private elevator that would ride him to the seat of his power. What the hell was Sylvia up to?

Fifteen minutes later, Brad abruptly swept open the door of the boardroom, his expression unreadable, blue eyes neutral, cool and determined. And Sylvia let out a relieved sigh. This was the Brad she knew, the businessman who gave nothing away. Her pulse raced triumphantly.

She'd done it. The ruse had worked and she'd managed to engineer his return. She rose and smiled, careful to conceal her jubilation.

"Hi, Brad. Glad you could make it. Here, take your seat." Since Terence MacGuire, the eldest board member, was away on vacation she'd been required to chair the meeting. Hastily she cleared her papers, vacated the CEO's chair and moved to the one she'd left free to her right. The other members of the board shifted uncomfortably, coughing and clearing their throats, plainly unsure what to make of Brad's surprise reappearance. But all she could register was that she'd gotten him back, away from Skye and the haunting influence of Charlotte MacLeod. Here on their home turf, their lives would finally get back to normal.

As he settled, a wave of relief swamped her. He'd come. He was bound to take issue with her tactics, of course, but that was inevitable. One day he'd thank her. Now that he was back in the boardroom of the company to which he'd devoted the greater part of his life, the company whose chairmanship he now risked losing, she was certain things would become crystal clear. Perhaps he'd already realized what a horribly foolish decision he'd been on the verge of making. Henceforth, Strathaird would be consigned to its proper place as an occasional retreat, one she'd make sure they visited only rarely. Taking a quick sip of Evian, she leaned back and waited for him to begin.

He didn't waste any time. "Since you seem to be the instigator of this meeting, Sylvia," he challenged, "perhaps you'd better tell the board why you feel I'm no longer a suitable CEO for this company?"

She caught the slight edge to his voice and experienced a moment's panic, but she wasn't surprised. She'd known he would contest her petition, and wanted him to.

Now was the time to play her ace.

With a deprecating smile, she turned and gestured to her fellow board members. "I don't believe any of us consider you to be an unsuitable candidate for the job, Brad. The question brought here before the board today is regarding your recent extended absence."

"Sylvia has a point, Bradley," Barry Granger responded, clearing his throat. "I believe I speak for all of us when I say that it is not your capacity to run the company that is being questioned, rather, whether your continued absence is in Harcourts best interests. Nobody doubts your capability."

"Nobody doubts that," Sylvia agreed, then sent the arrow. "We just need to know whether you'll be here for it to continue."

"That's right." Granger raised a bushy white eyebrow and his slate eyes rested questioningly on Brad. "According to Sylvia, you're thinking of allocating much of your time to this place you've inherited in Scotland." He cleared his throat once more. "You implied the same thing to me over the phone a couple of weeks ago."

Sylvia heard the murmurs and watched anxiously as Brad leaned back, twiddling his Mont Blanc pen pensively, as though debating the matter. Her foot began to twitch as seconds stretched agonizingly, the expectant silence broken only by the shuffle of papers and the odd cough. As if there was anything to think about! She clenched her fingers nervously in her lap. Come on, she urged—tell them it was all a misunderstanding, that you're back to stay. But he seemed oblivious, lost in thought.

Brad sat silently, remembering the first time he'd been in this very room. He must have been twelve or thirteen when Dex had brought him to his first board meeting, making sure that he understood from an early age all that would be expected of him up ahead. How many such meetings had he been in since then? Probably more than he could count. The future of Harcourts had been mapped in this room, and for years he'd been an active part of every decision. He glanced at the wall where the portraits of both his grandfather and great-grandfather, John Ward, hung. The board members sat expectantly. Some like Barry Granger, who'd known him since childhood, frowned in genuine concern. Others were merely curious. But all awaited his decision. Obviously they expected him to retract, to reassure them he wouldn't be an absentee CEO. He hadn't immediately done so, and they were left waiting uncomfortably, idle curiosity turning into general unease.

Then his eye rested on Sylvia, and all at once he understood what she had done. This wasn't about how much time he spent at Harcourts, or whether his divided focus had affected his business decisions; it was about them, about their relationship. It was her way of making sure he returned to New York and gave up Strathaird. She'd dragged the board into the matter to force him to make a choice.

He experienced a moment's irritation. But as the minutes ticked by, he realized that perhaps she'd done right. By forcing him to come here against his will, she'd made him face the truth: that this was not his place any longer. Here was everything he'd worked for, everything he'd built, the sum of his accomplishments. He could say the word and everything would continue as it always had. There would be a general sigh of relief and everyone would leave for lunch, or the Hamptons, or wherever they were going, comfortable in the knowledge that nothing had altered.

But to his perplexed surprise, he felt strangely removed from this room and all that, up until now, had seemed so familiar. To his amazement, he realized that it was he who'd changed. He was suddenly viewing everything that had gone on here in past years—including Sylvia— as part of another existence. He glanced sideways, read the anxiety she was desperately trying to hide and felt a surge of pity. It wasn't her fault his priorities had changed, and she had every right to fight. But life for them could never return to what it had been.

Finally he leaned forward and took a deep breath, aware of the enormity of what he was about to do. There would be no going back once the words were spoken. But the choice was clear to him. He'd outgrown Harcourts and the need to be part of the fast-paced bustle of the business world. Now a new life beckoned, a life he truly wanted. And for the first time in memory the decision was his. He'd always be a part of Harcourts, but he didn't need to shape its future any longer.

"Ladies and gentlemen. Reluctant though I am to admit it, I have to agree with Sylvia. This company needs an active CEO. We've built ourselves an unequalled place in the market, and only constant vigilance will keep us there. But I'm afraid I won't be able to fulfill that role any longer."

There was a shocked murmur. Sylvia blanched.

"It is true that from now on I plan to spend much of my time on the Strathaird estate in Scotland. Therefore, it wouldn't be fair for me to continue in any capacity beyond that of nonexecutive chairman."

"But that's absurd," Sylvia burst out, horrified, as the

full impact of his words hit home. "You can't just give up Harcourts! It's yours!" He wasn't just leaving the company, he was leaving the life they'd planned to build together. Staring at him aghast, she knew, heart plummeting, he'd already made his choice. All her efforts, all her stratagems and maneuvering, were for nothing, she realized bitterly. The battle was over and Strathaird had won.

Aware that every eye in the room was upon her, she swallowed her bile and rising wrath and made a superhuman effort to regain control. If this was how he wanted it, then so be it. But if he thought she was going to be party to this new future he envisioned, he was wrong. No way was she going to spend her days in that miserable godforsaken hole. She wasn't about to lose everything she'd worked and fought for all these years because of a whim. If this was the end, then she'd go out fighting.

"In that case, I move to have you replaced right away," she threw out harshly.

"And I second it," Brad declared, turning toward the board members. "Moreover, I propose that Sylvia Hansen be elevated to the position of CEO, and that the measure be put to Harcourts' shareholders with the full backing of the board."

Sylvia gasped, barely able to absorb his next words. "I have no doubt she'll do a magnificent job and lead Harcourts into the future with all the drive and capacity she's always exhibited. I can't think of a person better suited to the position." He turned and smiled at her, then glanced around the table for approval.

Sylvia stared speechless into her lap and saw that her hands were trembling. Then she gazed wide-eyed at Brad, unable to believe what she'd just heard. He was making her CEO?

All at once the hopes and dreams of years battled with the woman within. He'd betrayed her emotionally. And, apparently, he was leaving her for another woman. Yet he was also making her most precious dream come true.

It was almost too easy.

For as long as she could recall, she'd envisioned herself fighting tooth and nail for a toehold on the corporate ladder. She'd advanced quickly at Harcourts, to be sure, but knew she was years away from the top executive position. As a woman, she expected she'd have to work harder and wait longer to reach the top. Yet here Brad was offering her a chance to leapfrog the learning curve. It was what she wanted more than anything in the world.

She swallowed, trying to school her features into a picture of cool confidence. Losing Brad would be hard, but losing Harcourts would be worse. It would mean giving up everything she'd striven and fought for so desperately. In her darkest hours she'd dreamed of this moment; the unwavering belief that one day she'd reach the top had saved her from self-destruction.

Slowly she raised her eyes and took a fresh look at him. He really had changed, she realized suddenly. Or maybe this was who he'd truly been all along. There was no uncertainty in his eyes, no impulsiveness in his attitude, rather the sure confidence of a man who knows he's made the right decision.

She sighed an inner sigh and braced herself. She would not become Mrs. Bradley Ward. They would not share a life together. Instead, when she walked from this room, she would do so as one of the most powerful women in the city. She swallowed hard, surprised to find herself near tears, and watched him for a long moment, knowing she would never forget what it felt like to be held in his arms, to feel his lips on hers, to feel him moving inside her, the well-orchestrated existence she'd become so accustomed to. But that was the price she had to pay, she reminded herself sternly, the sacrifices a businesswoman of her caliber had to make to reach the top.

When she was sure she'd successfully fought back the tears of pain, gratitude and regret, she allowed her eyes to meet his and met with mutual, unspoken understanding.

It was time for her to move in and him to move on. But not together.

He reached out his hand. Concealing her bewilderment she took it, fingers trembling uncontrollably. She'd walked in here minutes before with the sole objective of getting him back in her life. Now, he'd given her hers.

"Ladies and gentlemen, I would like to put Sylvia's candidacy as future CEO of this company to a vote. Will all in favor please raise their hands?"

Every hand at the table rose and the motion passed unanimously.

Her fingers still shook and he squeezed them hard. "Congratulations. You'll do a great job, Syl. This is where you truly belong."

She could only nod, the knot in her throat preventing her from speaking. Then, in a courtly gesture so typical of Brad, he rose, smiling, and offered her his chair. She hesitated, knowing that this was not technically correct. But it was a rite of passage, and taking a deep breath, Sylvia mustered all her strength and stood at his side.

"You go, girl," Brad whispered, hand firmly gripping her shoulder as she sat carefully down in the CEO's place. "I'm counting on you, and you've never failed me yet."

Paris was sweltering, hot damp air and fumes mingling as Armand walked down the Rue St.-Honoré. He sniffed, sending a disparaging glance at the tourists—window-shoppers who wandered along, holding up the flow of pedestrian traffic. He had a lunch appointment with a friend at Costes, after which they would repair together to the Georges V, the hotel where the show would take place. He shook his head with a worried frown. All morning he'd attended to business, while stylists flurried in and out, making calls to the florist who'd mistaken the arrangements, causing him an hour's panic. Not to mention Charlotte. She was driving him mad. One minute it was the tiara, the next the delivery. At times he wished he'd never gotten her involved. Time was getting short, he reasoned nervously as he hurried down the pavement, reviewing his conversation with her. He really didn't have time for all this nonsense. And now she'd decided not to come. He raised long-suffering eyebrows. He hadn't intended to discourage her from coming to Paris, but when she'd told him of her plan to file divorce papers, he'd stated the obvious. Word of her decision to divorce John Drummond was sure to find its way into the tabloids, and media speculation would be rife once news of Charlotte's participation in his show got out. In fact, there was a real danger it might overshadow the show itself. And, as Charlotte herself had pointed out, he justified reasonably, the last thing she wanted was for the press to believe she'd timed the action as a publicity stunt to coincide with the launch of her jewelry line. She wanted her work to stand on its own.

As he crossed the road, narrowly escaping a swerving motorcyclist and passing yet another herd of bovine tourists, a delicious thought struck. He stopped dead in his tracks and gazed blindly at a bright silk scarf in the window of Hermès. Perhaps the idea had been hovering on the edge of his consciousness for some time.

He'd just never voiced it, not even to himself.

Now, as he eyed three suspicious-looking individuals loitering on the corner, Armand shivered. His fingers gripped the mother-of-pearl butt of the antique pistol he'd discovered at Strathaird, now safely hidden in his pocket. It reassured him to know it was loaded. He approached the restaurant in rising excitement. What had at first struck him as outrageous now seemed increasingly feasible. It was a daring move, one that could all too easily backfire. Still, as he entered Costes and smiled at the maître d', he felt certain the risk was worth taking.

"*Bonjour,* Monsieur de la Vallière." Armand nodded graciously. "Monsieur Arnaud *vous attend.*" The maître d' lead the way through the crowded restaurant.

Armand followed, exchanging absent hellos with acquaintances and nodding to others. By the time he reached the winter garden where Hugues Arnaud awaited him, he'd made his decision. It might prove disastrous, he acknowledged, approaching the table with a fixed smile. But as the waiter pulled back his chair and he kissed Hugues on both cheeks, all he could envisage was that single triumphant moment of glory he'd longed for forever.

"So, it is because you've finally taken a wise decision in your personal life that you have decided to back out of the show, Charlotte?" the Cardinal questioned, sending her a speculative glance from the deck chair where he sat, propped against faded floral cushions and wrapped in a tartan cashmere rug. The weather had improved, allowing for brief interludes in the warm afternoon sun. Charlotte lounged in one of the wicker chairs around the garden table and sipped Ribena despondently. She had just poured out her doubts about attending the show to her great-uncle and was already regretting it.

"It seemed wiser to cancel my plans to go," she insisted. "Armand's right. One of the tabloids is sure to get a hold of the fact that I'm going through with the divorce. Can you imagine what a treat that would be for them? They'd think I was seeking publicity for my jewelry line. I had a conversation with John's former agent and he thought it wise, too."

"A divorce is a serious matter. In your case, however, it is utterly justifiable. No one has the right to treat his partner in the manner to which you were subjected."

Charlotte's head shot up in surprise. "You don't disapprove?"

"No." The Cardinal shook his white head. "I am glad that you have finally come to the decision to free yourself from what can only be considered a curse. I believe the Church would pardon you. I shall seek a dispensation."

Charlotte nearly gasped. Could her great-uncle, an advocate of marriage and fidelity, truly be encouraging her? Relief swept over her and she let out a pent-up sigh, one she'd been holding for longer than she could recall.

"Don't you think you're giving the divorce too much importance?" the Cardinal continued, unaware of Charlotte's conflicting emotions. "After all, John Drummond has not been in the media for a while. I do not imagine he is what you young people refer to as a 'hot item,'" he remarked dryly.

"No, I suppose not," she agreed. "Still, you have to admit, Oncle Eugène, it would make for a good story. I shiver to think of the headlines."

He looked at her sternly. "Perhaps it is time you stopped quaking and fleeing from headlines or what others may say or think, my dear. Perhaps it is time you took your life into your own hands instead of living in your husband's shadow.''

She returned his gaze, eyes wide with surprise. ''But I'm doing my own thing with my jewelry, Oncle Eugène, even though half the projects I undertake usually end up being a dismal failure.''

''Rubbish. Ridiculous. You haven't given yourself a decent chance, *mon enfant*. You must be in Paris for the show.''

Her shoulders slumped. ''Let's face it, whether I'm there or not won't make much difference. I'm just too preoccupied with other matters.'' She stared across at the sea, bright blue today and surprisingly calm, determined not to be hurt that Brad had left without even saying goodbye. To be fair, she'd been in Edinburgh the day he'd left, but still, she'd had no word from him since, not a sign, a phone call. Nothing. It was as though he'd disappeared into thin air. She sighed, dejected. Back in New York, he would likely see sense. By now, he and Sylvia were probably huddled over plans for the famous St. Regis winter wedding Sylvia was so keen on. She thought of her interlude with Brad and swallowed. Not an hour went by when she didn't burn for him. She'd picked up the phone a dozen times and dialed, only to lay down the receiver, determined not to run after him. If he wanted her, he'd come.

But oh, how she missed him, longed for his touch, his hands fleeting over her body, making her remember what it felt like to be a woman. She sighed and stared at her lap. At least the interlude with Brad—and it seemed that was all it was destined to be—had helped her take the necessary steps to move ahead in her life. Whatever happened, she was grateful to him for that.

She drained her glass and prepared to take leave. There was still so much to do for Armand's show, so many last-minute details to see to. She never would have believed the huge effort that went into preparing a show like this. It was both exciting and exhausting, and a bit anticlimactic not to be there after all the work. But the divorce would be finalized by the end of the month and Genny would need her at home. It was impossible to even think of leaving the island right now.

"I leave for Paris next Tuesday," Eugène remarked, interrupting her reverie. "I am staying there expressly so that I can attend Armand's show. I haven't informed him, though—I couldn't bear all that twittering about. He makes me nervous enough as it is. Monsignor Kelly tells me the show will take place at the Georges V." He sniffed. "Not my favorite place, but so be it. I hear it has undergone a serious and much-needed overhaul. Do you know, Charlotte, why I am not immediately traveling to Rome?" He pursed his lips and watched her expectantly.

"So that you can see Armand's collection, I imagine. It should be magnificent. Armand certainly has flair," she remarked, trying to keep the disappointment from her voice. It seemed suddenly cruel that she wouldn't get to see her designs exhibited, or hear the crowds respond. Waiting to see whether they loved or hated them would be agonizing, she realized, but oh, how she longed to be there.

"I haven't the slightest interest in Armand's clothes," Eugène muttered dismissively. "The only reason I wish to be there is to see your creations welcomed by the world." He watched her as she stared at him, astonished. His eyes narrowed. He could see the stark resemblance now, wondered how it had escaped him all these years, and sighed. Perhaps he'd been a coward. But did he have the right to go to his grave in silence? He plucked the fringe of the rug, pondering the proper course of action. "I think you want to go to the show," he observed casually, "even though you hesitate to make a public spectacle of yourself."

"Well, of course I do," she replied tartly. "But I can't very well march in there and parade myself before the press, can I?" She gave a humorless laugh. "Perhaps I should wear a djellaba and pretend I'm a client."

"I think I have a better solution," the Cardinal responded with a thoughtful smile. "It occurs to me that there may be a simpler way, should you wish to go incognito, so to speak."

Hope flickered and her eyes turned a darker shade of amethyst. Memories of an identical pair of eyes made him wince. His chest tightened.

"How?" she asked urgently.

"You can come with me. We shall arrive in a limousine, and you can pull your hair back or wear a hat and a pair of dark glasses. No one will believe the designer would deign to appear with an old cleric, believe me. Those who know me will think I'm there because of Armand, everyone else will expect you to be behind the scenes with him."

"I don't know…I suppose it might work." She bit her lip, but he could read the excitement in her smile.

"Has he sent you a program yet?"

"Apparently they still haven't come back from the printers. Armand was worried when we last spoke. He's all atwitter. Apparently one of the models dyed her hair the wrong color." She giggled despite her tension. "You know, I can't believe my name's going to share billing with Armand! I told him to list me as Charlotte MacLeod, not Drummond. Part of the moving-on process," she remarked with a rueful grin.

"Excellent," he said approvingly. Though there was another name that might suit her even better, he reflected. But enough. For now he needed to persuade her to face herself and her own future. The past would have to wait its turn. He had his own reasons for wanting her in Paris, but those too could be addressed later.

"Then why don't we do the following," he remarked, pressing his advantage. "You return with me to Paris on Tuesday and we shall go to the show on Wednesday night together."

"It's awfully tempting, but I don't know if I can manage it," she murmured, finding excuses. "Genny's vacation is almost over, and she'll be starting school again…"

Eugène looked her straight in the eye. "Charlotte, you know very well your mother will be only too glad to help you. You must stop creating pretexts. This trip will teach you who you are and all that you can achieve," he added, thinking of the many changes that lay ahead for her.

She hesitated, then let out a huff. Could the Cardinal be right? "All right," she exclaimed, taking the plunge. Jumping out of her chair, she came over to his side and knelt next to him. "Thank you, Oncle Eugène. I know I've tried you dearly over the years, but you've always been so patient and—and wonderful. Thanks for doing this for me."

Her voice, shaking with emotion, and her trembling smile left him weak, the light in her violet eyes so like his beloved Geneviève's. The years rolled back and his sister's image flickered before him, sending a sudden shaft of pain searing through his heart. It was as though *she* were kneeling here at his side. Charlotte slipped her slim hand in his, and for a moment he closed his eyes, seeing Geneviève and Sylvain plainly before him, their gaze falling on Charlotte, filled with love and hope. He shivered, unable to control the sudden tremor in his fingers.

"Oncle Eugène, are you all right?" Charlotte squeezed his frail fingers, her worried voice reaching him through the haze.

The vision faded and he opened his eyes. "I'm fine, *ma chère*," he murmured, returning the pressure. Reclining his head back against the cushion, he rested his eyes upon her. She was so young, so beautiful, so full of life and hope. Just as his dear Genny had been before they massacred her. She had been almost the same age as Charlotte. His grip on her hand tightened and for a moment he stared fixedly at her. "You must not turn your back on the future, Charlotte," he said suddenly. "You have a destiny to fulfill. You, and Bradley too, must face the future and not seek excuses to flee it."

Charlotte frowned. "I—I'm trying my best," she murmured, not understanding his sudden outburst.

"*Oui, bien sûre,* of course you are." He smiled reassuringly and patted her hand gently. "But there is so much—" He stopped himself and shook his gaunt head. "Not now, my love, another time. Go and fetch Linus, please. I find myself somewhat fatigued."

Charlotte rose, confused and concerned. He looked so frail, as though a sharp gust of wind might blow him away. "Are you sure you'll be all right by yourself?" she asked, worried, glancing toward the castle, wishing someone would come out. She didn't like the idea of leaving him alone, even for a few minutes.

"Don't worry about me, *ma petite,* I haven't survived this long only to die in a deck chair without completing my mission. But that is another matter. Now run along and get Linus before I catch cold.''

Charlotte ran hastily back across the lawn and up the worn steps to the drawing room, wondering what he could possibly mean with his talk of missions and destiny. He'd looked at her with a penetrating gaze that seemed to see into her soul. She frowned as she reached the library door and knocked. It was almost as though his so-called mission had something to do with her personally.

But as she opened the door and Monsignor Kelly put down his glasses, already rising expectantly, she forgot about her strange conversation with Eugène. Instead, the possibility of seeing her work at the show filled her with an excited rush, and she knew then, without a doubt, that she'd be there.

14

After several fruitless attempts, Brad gave up trying to reach her. He should have known Charlotte wouldn't own a damn answering machine. Or know how to pick up messages on her mobile phone. God knows, he'd left a few.

But Charlotte never remembered a damn thing, never adhered to convention. And he wouldn't want her any other way, he realized with a half smile. Still, he was annoyed that she was making herself unreachable. It worried him. He didn't want her thinking he hadn't bothered to call. His sudden departure hadn't allowed any time for explanations. Was she upset, or hurt, or had just decided in good-old-Charlotte fashion to ignore what had happened between them? God, he hoped not. He was determined not to allow her to hide once more behind a barrier of pride and guilt. The only thing that kept him from going insane with worry was Penelope's news that Charlotte had gone to Paris with Eugène for Armand's show. She'd also revealed that Charlotte had visited a lawyer in Edinburgh and was seeking a divorce. Of course, he was already aware of that, but telling the others was an important step. It meant she was truly committed to the decision.

That, more than anything, gave him hope.

Perhaps, just maybe, dreams really could come true. He'd always wanted a life with Charlotte. But the want had grown so much deeper now that he knew it might be possible. He was eager to tell her about the extraordinary board meeting and how dramatically things had changed. He'd barely had a minute to himself, between running around town, making sure the twins were okay, settling Todd at his new school and sorting matters out at the office, but he'd never felt less stressed or more excited about the future.

Leaning back, he glanced out the plane's window. The Gulfstream V had been acquired by the company only three months ago, replacing the Learjet Dex had bought some years back. As he watched New York recede on the clear blue horizon, a pang of nostalgia hit. But he wasn't leaving forever, he reminded himself. He'd be back. The twins were busy with school, and under the watchful eye of Mrs. Browning, their longtime housekeeper. Right now, Strathaird needed him and it was where he wanted to be. He glanced at the papers before him. Daring to hope that Charlotte would want to make a life with him was a risk, he acknowledged. He'd indulged the hope once before and when it had died, it had taken him years to get over the disappointment. But this time was different. He thought back to their time together, to their lovemaking in the cottage. God, what wouldn't he do to hold her once more in his arms, feel her body melding into his like no one else's ever had or ever would. He closed his eyes. Surely this had to be as unique for her as it was for him?

Everything seemed to rest on whether Charlotte, after

suffering so many disappointments, estrangements, inner and outer battles, could finally let go of the past and give herself the chance to look toward the future.

His eyebrows knit. At least all the other hurdles that stood between them had been cleared. He had no regrets about relinquishing power at Harcourts, certain it was the right decision. He got up, stretched, then sat down again, remembering the talk he'd had with Sylvia immediately after the board meeting. Surprisingly, ending their engagement hadn't been as awful as he'd expected. Sylvia had calmly agreed it was for the best; indeed, she'd been far more interested in discussing her ideas for Harcourts. Amazingly, he'd felt no anger at her machinations. It was her way of defending her turf, he realized.

Still, he worried that he'd left her little choice but to accept the terms he'd presented to the board. Had he subconsciously maneuvered the whole thing? Somehow he'd sensed that she wanted power even more than she wanted him, and he'd made her an offer that she couldn't refuse. And once the offer had been accepted, they'd gone from being lovers back to being friends and business colleagues with ease. It was almost troubling.

He wondered if she had any regrets, but doubted it. Deep down, wielding power was what Syl had always wanted—and now that it was within her reach, he had no doubt she'd exercise it with skill, flair and fairness. He hoped she would find someone who shared the same ambitions and who would make her a heck of a lot happier than he ever could.

"Your whiskey, Mr. Ward." Amy, the attractive blond flight attendant who'd been with the crew for several years, extended the small silver tray.

"Thanks, Amy. How are the kids doing?" he asked, picking up the tumbler.

"Growing faster than weeds. But now that Bill's home most evenings, life's getting a lot easier." She smiled. Brad watched her neat, uniformed figure returning to the galley, and realized he'd miss all the people at Harcourts; he'd come to know most of them over the years, and had always been sure to show them he valued their service. Still, there was a whole new world of people to meet in Skye—ones who wouldn't give him the benefit of the doubt simply because of his name. Somehow, the challenge excited him.

He sipped his whiskey slowly. Skye could be tackled later. Right now, all that mattered was getting to Charlotte. He could picture her, nervous and uptight, awaiting the show and projecting every possible disaster. He needed to be near her, let her know just how much he cared. What could possibly come between them now that they were both free? he wondered. False pride? Misunderstandings?

Surely those could be ironed out. Still, he'd have to tread carefully. He knew she was terrified of unbalancing the fragile foundation of stability she'd worked so hard to build for herself and Genny. And here he was, determined to turn that world upside down.

Picking up the *Wall Street Journal,* he glanced briefly at the headlines, wishing he could have flown directly to Paris. Instead, he was required to attend a meeting at Harcourts' offices in London. It was only fair, since he'd promised the board that he would carry out his duties as CEO until the end of the year; then Sylvia would officially take over. But he'd see to it the meeting was brief and that the plane crew was on standby. With luck, he would make it to the show just in time.

He leaned back in the wide, white leather seat and imagined Charlotte cruising with him at twenty thousand feet. Perhaps they'd be making love? The thought made him shift in his seat. Think of what she's doing now, he ordered himself, picturing her wired and anxious on her big day. He had to get there. She might need him. He didn't want to smother her, of course, but he couldn't help feeling protective. He wasn't about to let anything get in the way of the success and recognition she so deserved.

He thought suddenly of Armand and frowned. Charlie was so trusting and forthright, always believing the best of people. He couldn't shake the feeling that Armand's motives in sponsoring her work weren't entirely pure. Deciding he was being paranoid, he picked up the remote and flipped through the movie channels, wondering if CNN would cover Armand's show.

"Shall I close the blinds, sir?" Amy asked.

"Yeah, thanks. Might as well get some shut-eye," he agreed, yawning. He'd slept little the past few nights. Accepting a cashmere blanket, he leaned back, put his feet up, and closed his eyes. He fell asleep almost immediately, but his dreams were troubled.

The limo weaved its way amid Paris's notorious afternoon traffic, battling deft motorcyclists swerving dangerously between vehicles and hot, frustrated motorists who weren't shy about using their horns. As Oncle Eugène muttered about modern contraptions breeding contempt, Charlotte followed the perilous trajectory of two teenagers maneuvering their skateboards adroitly among the bustling pedestrians on the sidewalk.

"Such confusion," the Cardinal tutted, drumming his thin fingers on the plush ebony armrest.

"Well, now, that's Paris for you, isn't it?" Monsignor

Kelly replied soothingly in his soft Irish lilt. "But we'll soon be at the Georges V."

Eugène sniffed witheringly. "So many poseurs and parvenus there. Trust Armand to choose it. *Mon Dieu*," he exclaimed, shocked as a croppedheaded young skateboarder scraped past a pretty brunette in a very short skirt and high heels. There was no need to understand French to follow the ensuing curses and exclamations. "At this speed we shall never arrive," he remarked, before addressing the chauffeur. "What is happening, Jean? Why are there all these delays?"

"It's another *grève,* Your Eminence. The S.N.C.F. are on strike. That means no trains are running today."

Eugène shook his head somberly. "I don't know what the world is coming to. No one seems content with their lot in life anymore. Strikes, indeed. It becomes impossible to travel."

Charlotte smiled, accustomed to Oncle Eugène's oldfashioned prejudices. She stared up at the colored awnings on the chairs of the giant Ferris wheel in the Place de l'Etoile. It hovered weightlessly, a colossal sphere linking heaven and the Champs Elysées. As the traffic moved forward once again, she made an effort to curb her increasing anxiety about the evening ahead.

Thirty minutes later, they stepped into the glistening marble lobby of the Georges V. Even the amusing spectacle of Oncle Eugène sweeping regally toward the reception desk, murmuring disparaging remarks despite the attentive bellboys and the concierge's determined efforts to please, failed to dispel the jitters in her stomach.

They were here at last. She gazed through the glass doors to the inner courtyard, where guests sat on attractive white-cushioned wrought-iron seats under *ombrelones,* sipping tea and discussing business, or glued to their cell phones. The effect was charming, the opulence of the past melded with modern flair. She smiled, watched the decorators changing the gigantic purple and magenta flower arrangements that reached toward the high, illuminated ceiling in massive minimalist designer vases. The effect was stunning and unique. Whatever Oncle Eugène might say, the Georges V was impressive.

And it was here in this fabled palace that it was all about to happen. Her work would be viewed by the public for the first time in this magical environment, where the whims and fancies of the rich and famous had been catered for so long. Here Hollywood had rubbed shoulders with such legends as Mrs. Roosevelt and the Maharaja of Kapurthala. She knew for a fact that both Sylvain de Rothberg and Dexter Ward had been frequent visitors to the hotel.

And now it was her turn. As she followed the immaculately dressed hotel director to one of the massive presidential suites that overlooked the Avenue Georges V, her mouth went dry.

The door of the apartment was solicitously opened. After voicing several complaints, Oncle Eugène finally settled in his cream-and-gold-colored room for his afternoon rest, somewhat mollified by the impeccable attention the hotel provided.

Charlotte retired thankfully to her own spacious suite a few doors down the corridor, glad to be alone. She decided to unpack, then take a nap. Outside, the weather was hot and muggy and the thought of lying between cool, pressed sheets struck her as extraordinarily appealing. She pulled the thick brocade curtains closed and crossed the shaded room, realizing she hadn't had a decent night's rest since Brad had left. She sank onto the plush canopied bed, vaguely aware of the humming traffic in the avenue below, and thought of him, of how they'd made love, of the way he seemed to know just where to touch her and the extraordinary way she'd reacted. Stop! she ordered, turning on the down pillow, knowing it was foolish to yearn for the impossible. After all, he hadn't communicated with her since his departure and was probably regretting what had occurred between them, now that he and Sylvia had obviously resumed their old life together.

To her surprise, she woke to a room that was nearly dark. Realizing it must already be late, she jumped up, slipped on the thick terry bathrobe provided by the hotel and hastened through to the glistening marble bathroom. It wouldn't do to be late, she reflected, gazing at herself in the wide mirror. It was almost time for drinks, she realized with a groan, wishing now that she hadn't allowed herself to be persuaded into coming. What was the point, when she was just going to huddle in a corner, pretending not to be there? Perhaps she should have told Armand about this trip after all. Or better yet, stayed home.

Stomach lurching, she entered the shower, determined not to think about the show getting closer by the minute. She stood under the full blast of the powerful spray and concentrated on the soothing rivulets running down her back. Relax, she told herself over and over, ignoring the growing nausea in the pit of her stomach, and tried to think of a souvenir she could bring Genny from Paris. Mummy was right, she realized, to have made her stop off in London and make the hop to Armani. At least she'd be properly dressed. The beautifully cut shantung cream pantsuit was stunning.

Stepping out of the glass shower, Charlotte wrapped herself in one of the huge, white, monogrammed terry towels, then hoisted a foot onto the beige marble counter and smoothed body cream up her leg. If this was to be her night, she decided with a toss of her head, then she was damn well going to look good, incognito or not. After spreading the lotion lavishly, she dried her hair strand by strand until it fell shining and glossy over her shoulders. She applied make-up with a light hand, finishing with a light touch of violet mascara that enhanced the color of her eyes and some lip gloss. The image staring back at her from the large gilt-framed mirror was satisfying. At least she looked her best. She clasped the fine platinum necklace with a drop diamond she'd designed for the occasion around her neck with a pleased smile. It was the only jewel she would be wearing tonight.

The idea of a drink was beginning to have some appeal, she realized, letting out a long breath as growing doubts assailed her once more. Oh God, what if everyone hated her designs? What if instead of praise, tomorrow's press was filled with disparaging articles? Or worse, that the jewelry would be deemed too inconsequential to merit any comment at all!

Perching nervously on the edge of the gold-tapped marble tub, Charlotte dropped her head into her hands. If only Mummy or Moira or someone she could confide in were here with her. But none of them could get away. Oncle Eugène was all very well, but hardly the ideal candidate to burden with her worries. Worst-case scenario, there was always Monsignor Kelly, she reflected with a moue, the thought of the rotund Irish priest making her smile. Then her features tensed and sudden sadness engulfed her; the only person she really wanted here was thousands of miles away in New York and probably not even thinking of her.

Torn between longing and hurt pride, she determinedly blotted his image out. Obviously, he was history. That much had become plain over the past few days. Not one phone call, not one word of encouragement. What had transpired between them had obviously not touched him as it had her, and this was his way of letting her know. But how could she ever forget those magical moments spent in his arms?

Charlotte chided herself: she was doing what she always did—jumping to conclusions like a temperamental adolescent. Surely she'd come further than that? Perhaps it was wrong to write him off without at least giving him a chance. For all she knew, there could be a number of reasons for his continued silence. But if it *was* only a brief affair, she had only herself to blame. He was, after all, engaged to another woman and she didn't even have the excuse of not knowing. She'd gone straight in, eyes wide open, and this was the result.

A sudden flush of shame suffused her cheeks. Perhaps it was disappointment at her performance in bed that had driven him back to Sylvia. After all, John had spent the better part of their marriage reminding her what a hopeless lover she was. *Frigid* was an adjective he'd used all too frequently, she recalled.

She turned away from the mirror, not wanting to see the old, insecure Charlotte reflected there. Where was the confident woman who'd smiled back at her after she and Brad had made love? She closed her eyes, bracing her hands on each side of the basin, overwhelmed by just how much she missed him.

Tears welled but she forced them back and breathed deeply.

This was no time to be indulging in self-pity and regret. After all, she was on the verge of what might be the most important night of her life. She had no business blubbering in the bathroom just because the man she happened to love had dumped her for his own fiancée.

And hadn't even called to wish her luck.

That hurt, she realized, moving away with an angry start. But at least the interlude had served its purpose, she justified, tossing her hair back. Now she was ready to move on and make a life for herself and her daughter, to let go of the fears that had shadowed her all these years. Giving her lips a final dab of gloss, she braced herself, determined to live the moment to the full.

Straightening her shoulders, she headed back through to the bedroom. She'd get dressed, then join Oncle Eugène for drinks in the salon. And after that…well, she'd see what the night would bring.

Eugène watched Charlotte enter the room, pleased at the transformation. Her hair was beautifully coiffed, the wild curls trained into thick flowing waves that glistened in the warm glow of the crystal chandelier. Her suit, he noted, satisfied, was exquisite and discreet. Tonight, she reflected her true heritage.

"You look very lovely, my dear," he remarked. Rising stiffly, he reached beneath the wide watered-silk band at his waist, and produced a faded jewelry box from a pocket deep within his scarlet-trimmed black soutane. Charlotte recognized the blue velvet of Rothberg's and held her breath, peering with excited anticipation when Oncle Eugène carefully raised the lid. Inside lay a pair of exquisite heart-shaped clustered-diamond earrings.

"These were Sylvain's first gift to Geneviève," he remarked, his voice betraying a slight tremor. "I remember how excited she was. Like you. It is amazing how you resemble her so much." A nostalgic smile hovered on his thin lips, eyes alight with memories. "I would like you to have these and wear them tonight. You seem to feel such a strong connection to Sylvain. He would have… It is appropriate that you should be wearing one of his creations," he ended, sending her a strange look. Then he cleared his throat. "Perhaps the earrings will make up somewhat for the loss of the watch."

Charlotte gazed at he sparkling gems, awestruck, eyes swimming with unshed tears. She could picture Sylvain in his workshop, pouring every ounce of his love into these exquisite pieces, carefully placing each stone into its setting. She lifted one of the heart-shaped earrings reverently, fingers fumbling nervously as she fixed it into place. The other followed. Then she turned and faced the gilt-framed mirror above the fireplace.

Eugène stood behind her, mesmerized. It was as though his dearest sister Genny were before him once again. He closed his eyes, overcome by the same sensation he'd felt that day on the lawn at Strathaird, the feeling that Sylvain was here with them.

"Thank you, Oncle Eugène," Charlotte whispered hoarsely, throwing herself in his arms. "You've no idea what this means to me."

"Don't cry, *mon enfant*," he murmured softly. "There is no cause for tears. Quite the contrary. Tonight will be your night of triumph."

"I don't know," she wailed, taking the handkerchief he handed her. "I'm scared, Oncle Eugène. What if no one likes my jewelry? The whole thing may be a complete flop, and then Armand will regret having taken a chance on me."

"Come, come, Charlotte," he responded, patting her arm. "You must not be negative. I am very proud of the

courage you have shown. It is not easy to open oneself
to public criticism."

"Armand said the same thing. I hope at least he'll
succeed," she remarked gloomily.

"Armand will always find the spotlight—he seeks it.
But you, *mon enfant,* something tells me you will shine
despite your efforts to stay hidden." His eyes softened
as he tilted her chin and stared intensely at her. "You
have his talent, Charlotte, and your own uniqueness.
They must be so proud of you tonight," he murmured,
gazing past her into long ago.

She frowned, mystified at his mutterings, wondering
whom he was referring to. Who would be proud of her?
Then suddenly he swayed and she rushed to help him.

"Are you all right, Your Eminence?" Monsignor
Kelly entered the room and hurried to his side. Together
they sat Eugène down in the nearest chair.

"Just a slight dizzy spell," he murmured, waving off
their assistance. "Turn around again, Charlotte, and let
us see you properly. And Linus, pour the champagne, *s'il
vous plaît.* This is going to be Charlotte's big night. We
must drink to her success."

"And Armand's," she insisted. "If there's any success
at all, it will be thanks to him."

"*Je suppose.*" The Cardinal pursed his thin lips then
smiled at her once more, eyes kind and bright in his withered face. "Now stop worrying, *mon enfant,* and have
your champagne. I have no doubt that all will go well."
Then abruptly he changed the subject. "Why is Bradley
not here tonight?"

"I have no idea," she muttered, following his example
and raising her glass, as though the matter meant little to
her either way. "But I'm sure he has far more important
things to do than worry about all of this."

There was little time left to think of Brad as she excused herself to run quickly back into the bathroom and correct her smudged makeup.

Five minutes later they were mingling with guests, making their way down the monumental staircase that led to the marble-columned elegance of the foyer Auteuil, where already a crowd of socialites and paparazzi was assembled. Charlotte glanced toward the doors of the renowned Salon Vendôme where the show was to take place and wondered how Armand was feeling. He was probably a pile of nerves by this stage. Should she have told him she was here? She had a moment's hesitation as they descended the last steps of the stylish staircase, then thought better of it. He might suddenly decide to get her involved.

She absorbed the atmosphere, the extravagantly attired guests sipping champagne expectantly. Soon they would begin making their way into the white-columned gold and gray Salon Vendôme, the perfect backdrop for the show, entitled the Daughters of Elysium. She liked the idea of a theme name—it had been Armand's idea—and as she glanced at the usherettes, sylphlike models draped in long pearl-gray Grecian chiffon robes now guiding the guests to their seats, she admired Armand's sense of detail.

There was no sign of any programs, she realized, relieved. The thought of seeing her name in print was scary; it called forth too many memories of seeing it in the tabloids as they salaciously detailed yet another rumor about John's latest conquest. Maybe she'd gotten lucky and the printers hadn't come through on time. That way, if the show was a flop, at least it wouldn't be quite as shaming a defeat.

Taking a deep breath, she followed Oncle Eugène and Monsignor Kelly into the sparkling Salon Vendôme. An exclamation of wonder slipped from her lips. Never could she have imagined her work being shown in such a perfect setting. Everything—from the huge, multitiered chandelier to the gold-trellised chairs set along the sides of the catwalk, the exquisite pillars of white roses intermingled with candles perched on wrought-iron stands—was breathtaking.

They proceeded toward the catwalk, halted several times by clamoring guests anxious to engage the Cardinal in conversation. But he was brief and distant in his responses and did not introduce her. No one seemed concerned, most of them more interested in making contact with the various celebrities in the room than in talking with the nobodies like herself. Gradually she began to relax, amused by the extravagant outfits, the multilingual conversations, chitchat that reminded her of the premieres she and John used to attend. A familiar face crossed her path and she spun hastily in the opposite direction. She hadn't counted on so many movie personalities being present. At this rate it would be hard to remain anonymous.

Sticking close to Eugène, she ducked her head, following him and one of the lovely usherettes to their seats in the front row facing the catwalk. She touched her right ear and smiled, a warm rush coursing through her. Sylvain must have experienced similar jitters, she reminded herself, trying to forget her fears by imagining what was happening behind the scenes.

Time dragged.

She looked about her, desperate to know what was going on backstage. Now that she was actually here, it was impossible not to speculate about the preparations taking place only feet away in the next room. Was everything under control? Were the final effects Armand had envisioned working out as they'd hoped? Would the tiara perch adequately on the model's head? Had she modified the shape sufficiently to provide a better grip?

Then the first strains of Beethoven's Ninth Symphony sounded, and a hush fell. The room's lights dimmed to a flickering glow. Pulse quickening, she caught her breath and lowered her agitated hands to her lap, only to have Oncle Eugène slide a program into them. She glanced at it in trepidation just as the spotlights focused on the cat-walk, making it impossible to read.

Let the show begin, she reflected, holding her breath as the curtain parted.

Then all else was forgotten as the first model strutted onto the stage. With a thrilled gasp, she recognized the cabochon ruby bracelet sparkling on the girl's alabaster skin. The redheaded model extended her long white arm and flicked her wrist for the crowd to get a better look. There was an immediate murmur among the audience, followed by spontaneous clapping.

Her heart lurched. Could she, Charlotte MacLeod, who'd done nothing but mess up most of her life, really be the creator of something so exquisite?

"I told you," Oncle Eugène hissed. "And that, *ma chère*, is only the beginning."

Bulbs flashed and exclamations buzzed as the models streamed down the catwalk, angular hips thrust out and shoulders swinging. Armand's designs were beautifully calculated to show off each piece of jewelry to perfection. The perfect marriage, she realized with a surge of emotion. A lovely black model came marching out, dressed in cream silk, sporting the platinum choker she'd spent so many hours designing and which Moira's loving hands had crafted with such care. Shivers ran through her. She'd poured so much of herself into the piece, so much effort, so much hope. The crowd's murmurs had turned from warm murmurs to an excited clamor, their applause enthusiastic as the music rose in a bold crescendo. Charlotte clasped her hands tight, biting her lip, holding back the rush of tears, both happy and sad.

If only Brad had been here to share this with her.

And suddenly, the joy of moments earlier was drained from the evening. She sat numb, staring blindly at the stage as one by one the models trooped out. It was as though someone else, not she, had designed the pieces. She tried to push Brad from her mind and recapture the magic, determined to revel in it and allow nothing to spoil her pleasure.

Then at last Armand's bride floated toward her, a vision of white taffeta and tulle, and the elation returned. Clasped around the model's throat was the pearl and diamond necklace she'd finished only days before. Perched high on her head, the simple diamond tiara that had caused them so much agony glistened. Charlotte held her breath as the stunning young woman twirled, veil flying as in a waltz. The tiara sparkled over the girl's golden mane that cascaded to her tiny waist. She was exquisite, a fairy princess in an enchanted setting. And she, Charlotte, was partly responsible for the spell.

For seconds, the crowd stayed hushed, then suddenly it erupted. All around her, exclamations of delight and murmurs of surprised appreciation burst forth. Charlotte watched in dazed pleasure as Armand, dressed entirely in black, appeared onstage. It was all thanks to him, she reflected gratefully, a smile lighting her face as he took the bride's fingers lightly in his and together they walked down the catwalk before a delighted crowd. He was transformed. Never had she seen him so handsome, so alive and fulfilled, and unshed tears shimmered as she watched him. At last he'd realized his dream of success. The clothes were an exquisite backdrop that deserved the praise. She clapped till her hands hurt, thrilled to see Armand smiling and bowing to an admiring public.

"It's perfectly wonderful, Oncle Eugène, I'm so proud of him." She leaned over to speak directly in the Cardinal's ear. But before Eugène could answer, Armand reached the end of the catwalk and raised his left hand, waving triumphantly. His cuff receded and Charlotte let out a horrified cry.

It couldn't be. But there, only feet away, was her beloved watch, clasped to Armand's wrist.

"Oh my God," she whispered, stunned.

"What is it, *mon enfant?*" Oncle Eugène followed her gaze to Armand's wrist and he froze.

"Mon Dieu," he whispered, blanching. *"Ce n'est pas possible!"*

As Armand's confident figure retired, bowing, behind the scenes, the Cardinal grabbed Charlotte's hand and rose.

"We must go at once," he declared, beckoning Monsignor Kelly to follow. "There can be no delay."

With a mystified frown, Monsignor Kelly followed close on their heels as they hastened through the applauding crowd toward the side entrance that opened onto the improvised dressing rooms.

A sturdy young man with a shaved head and black T-shirt stood firmly before the door, his arms crossed. "I'm afraid no one's allowed past this point without a pass," he declared.

"Rubbish," Eugène snapped. "Move aside immediately. I have no time for this nonsense."

"But—"

"Move." The Cardinal's voice remained low but his eyes spoke with such authority that the young man hesitated. Thugs and the curious he could deal with, but he hadn't been trained for this kind of opposition. Mumbling and lifting his hands in a Gallic gesture of defeat, he moved aside.

Inside, the place was in an uproar. Half-dressed models chatted excitedly, retrieving clothing, giggling and exclaiming. Makeup artists and stylists carried on animated high-pitched conversations and assistants rushed hither and thither.

Eugène eyed the scene with disgust. It did not take him long to locate Armand on the opposite side of the room, surrounded by journalists and photographers.

"Look at him," he exclaimed, revolted. A thought suddenly occurred to him and he turned, frowning, to Charlotte. "Have you looked at the program?" he asked, eyes narrowing. He opened the pages of his own program, scanning them rapidly.

"No," she whispered hoarsely. "It was too dark. Oncle Eugène, I can't believe Armand stole the watch, I—" Her voice broke.

"Your name isn't anywhere on the program," he interrupted, his fingers flexing angrily.

Charlotte flipped anxiously through the pages. Her designs were there, but not her name. Each piece was described as an original Armand de la Vallière.

She swallowed in shock and gazed across at Armand, unbelieving. The man responding to the journalists' questions, smiling broadly for the cameras, didn't even resemble the old Armand she knew.

He was transformed.

"How could he?" she whispered, pain searing through her. "How could he?"

The Cardinal stared grimly at his nephew. "Why don't we ask him," he murmured bitterly. With a swish of his robes, he advanced.

15

Brad sent an irritated glance around the table of the London boardroom, desperate for an excuse to close the meeting and head straight for Paris. It was past 4:00 p.m. and the meeting showed no sign of being over anytime soon. The items on the agenda were irrelevant and the discussion increasingly trivial. As Brad's impatience increased, he wished he could wring Major Godfrey Whitehead's scraggy throat. But Whitehead was a long-standing member of the board and as such had to be respected.

He let out an impatient sigh, aware that his chances of making Charlotte's show were getting slimmer by the minute. Brad glanced at the Major, his booming voice echoing through the room, and exchanged a look with Jeremy Warmouth, the president of Harcourts Europe and his old Yale friend. Warmouth raised a long-suffering eyebrow. The occasional board meetings were obviously a highlight of the Major's retired existence. A reason to get away from rural Sussex, and a chance to hear the beloved sound of his own voice.

Brad sorted the papers on the table before him, then made a production of slipping his pen into the inner breast pocket of his gray suit. He was about to bring the meeting to a close, when the Major cleared his throat dramatically, as if to signal an important announcement. "After tea I believe we should discuss the dress code issue."

"I'm sorry, gentlemen," Brad interrupted, finally fed up. "But I'm going to have to leave you shortly."

"But you can't leave now," Whitehead exclaimed, distressed, his trim mustache quivering. "The skirt matter must be settled here and now."

"Major, as far as I'm concerned, the PR department should be the one to decide whether or not our female sales staff should wear longer or shorter skirts," he responded wearily.

"But Harcourts' traditions should be upheld," the old gentleman blustered, his face growing red.

"Have we had any complaints?" Brad asked, trying to keep a straight face, amused despite his anxiety to be on his way and reach Charlotte. His eyes met Jeremy Warmouth's once more.

"Nothing like a good pair of legs to boost sales," Jeremy murmured.

Major Whitehead sent a withering glance down the long mahogany table and Jeremy retreated behind his glasses, tongue in cheek.

"I don't mean to belittle the matter," Brad said, hoping to assuage the Major's ruffled feathers, "but I'm afraid I have a plane to catch."

"I'm sure your aircraft can wait for you, Bradley. The extra few minutes won't make you too late for whatever rendezvous you have awaiting you in Paris."

Was it that obvious? he wondered, digesting Whitehead's withering comment. Brad let out a resigned sigh. It was wishful thinking to believe the meeting would end without the sacred break for tea. "Okay, let's have a quick break then finish off," he said, rising.

"Sorry, old chap, not much to be done," Jeremy muttered, straightening his Harrovian tie with an apologetic grin. "Old Whitehead has a bee in his bonnet about the skirt business. Just have to sit it out, I'm afraid."

"But I need to be in Paris, for Christ's sake." Brad dragged his fingers through his hair then grasped at an idea. "Say, do you have CNN here?" he asked suddenly. Perhaps there would be some coverage of the Paris shows.

"There's a telly in the partners' room," Jeremy responded doubtfully.

"Great. Let's switch it on right away." Brad hurried to the door.

They crossed the hall. Harcourts' London offices had always reminded him of a well-lived-in English country house, the walls painted dull green and hung with nondescript oil paintings. He saw Finch, the company's longtime butler, pushing the tea trolley reverently toward the partners' room and stopped him.

"Hey, Finch," he said, grinning. "How's it going?"

"Very well, thank you, sir. Is there anything I can do for you?" Finch drew himself up to a full five foot four and waited.

"As a matter of fact, there is. Find me the remote control of the television, would you? I need to see if I can catch a fashion show in Paris on CNN."

"Fashion show…?" Finch's voice trailed to a whisper. "I fear the Major wouldn't approve, sir."

"I'm aware that I'm breaking a scared rule, Finch, but it can't be helped. This is an emergency. Did you know that Miss Charlotte is presenting her first jewelry collection in Paris at the Georges V hotel? I believe there may be some mention of the show on television."

Finch's face softened. He'd had a soft spot for Charlotte, whom he'd known since she was a little girl. "Well, in that case, sir, I shall see what can be done."

"Thank you." Brad smiled gratefully.

"Didn't know Charlotte was designing jewelry," Jeremy remarked as they followed close on Finch's heels.

"She is. The show is with Armand de la Vallière's fall collection."

"Ah. Sylvia not joining you on this trip?" Jeremy asked casually while Brad drummed his foot, curbing his impatience.

"Syl?" Brad hesitated then glanced at his friend. "That's actually something I need to talk to you about, Jeremy. There are going to be a couple of changes at Harcourts in the future."

Jeremy stiffened. "Such as?"

"Well, I've decided to step down as CEO."

"You've what?" Jeremy collapsed into the nearest chair and stared at him. "Did I hear you right?"

"Yes. It's a long story but it's the right thing to do. I'll explain in detail when I have time."

"Who, may I ask, is succeeding you as CEO?"

Brad glanced at Jeremy. "Syl's taking over."

"Sylvia?" Jeremy jumped up, horrified. "What the hell made you do that?"

"It's a long story," he responded. "I can't explain now. Just trust me on this one."

Jeremy sat, silent, flabbergasted by Brad's news, and Finch reappeared with the remote control.

Brad turned on the television. In a few minutes, the story he was hoping for appeared on the screen.

"This is Mark Clancy at the CNN center in Atlanta.

Now, joining us live in Paris is fashion correspondent Marian de Soto, who's covering the hottest items of this season's shows. Good evening, Marian.''

Brad watched anxiously as the camera focused on the reporter. ''Good evening, Mark. As you can see, I'm standing outside the Georges V hotel in central Paris, where I've just attended one of the most amazing fashion shows in recent memory, that of the Parisian designer Armand de la Vallière. As you'll see from the clips, the show caused a sensation.''

''Too damn late!'' Brad exclaimed, his shoulders sagging. But as the screen flipped to models strutting down the catwalk, he leaned forward in anticipation.

''Any luck?'' Jeremy asked casually, following his gaze.

''Maybe.'' Brad's eyes narrowed, a smile dawning as he recognized the flash of Charlotte's ruby bracelet. ''There, that's Charlotte's,'' he said, pointing to the model.

''As you can see,'' Marian continued, ''there's a tremendous emphasis on jewelry in this collection, and it was stunning pieces such as this one that have the fashion world cheering. This is de la Vallière's debut effort in this medium, but it's clear he's already a master.''

''What the hell—'' Brad stood up and stared at the screen.

''Something wrong, old chap?'' Jeremy raised a questioning eyebrow.

''It is absolutely remarkable,'' the commentator continued enthusiastically. ''No one's even bothering to talk about the designer's clothing line—it's his spectacular jewelry that's on everyone's lips.''

''The bastard,'' Brad swore, staring at the screen.

''Are you sure that's Charlotte's design? The reporter

mentioned La Vallière,'' Jeremy remarked, eyebrows creased in a frown.

"Of course it is. That son of a bitch has had the nerve to pass Charlotte's designs off as his. I knew in my gut right from the start that something wasn't kosher.''

"Good Lord, poor Charlotte,'' Jeremy said. "She must be feeling awful. Wait, it looks as if they're about to show more.'' The two men's eyes stayed glued to the screen and cold anger gripped Brad as he watched.

"Now, if I can squeeze my way behind the scenes,'' Marian was saying, "I may get a chance to talk to the man of the hour. Well, as you can see, that's impossible right now, so I'll leave you with the final moments of what I can only describe as the most significant jewelry showing of the past decade.''

The camera zoomed in on Armand saluting the crowd and Brad let out an oath. "That's Charlie's watch on that bastard's damn wrist. It was stolen recently,'' he hissed through clenched teeth.

"Good God. You mean he stole Charlotte's watch? What sort of a character is this fellow?''

"One you'd rather not know,'' he retorted angrily as Mark Clancy's image flashed back on the screen.

Brad turned off the television. "All along, I've had reservations about Armand's sudden desire to promote Charlotte. Obviously, I should have paid them more heed.'' He slammed the remote down on the table.

"May one inquire what on earth is going on?'' Major Whitehead appeared in the room, followed by the other partners.

"I'm sorry, Major. An emergency. I have to leave at once.''

"Good God, you look positively peaked, dear boy,''

Sir Lawrence remarked, peering at him through his monocle.

"Jeremy, can you give me a ride to St. Thomas hospital? I have a chopper waiting there."

"Of course."

Brad turned and addressed the room at large. "You'll have to excuse me, gentlemen. I have an important appointment I can't miss."

They hurried out of the partners' room to the boardroom, where they grabbed their jackets, then headed for the elevator.

"I don't suppose you'd like to put me in the picture, as far as your fiancée and the CEOship of Harcourts is concerned? This has come as rather a shock," Jeremy remarked in measured tones.

"She's not my fiancée anymore," Brad replied, glancing at the buttons of the elevator. The car was taking ages. "I can't believe that little shit Armand had the guts to pass off Charlotte's designs as his."

"A bloody nerve, I agree. But what's this about you and Sylvia?"

"I really can't explain now. I shouldn't have broken the news to you as I did. Totally unprofessional, I know. I guess old friendship breeds familiarity." He gave his friend an apologetic grin. "Suffice it to say that I believe Syl will do a great job. I know you find her too American, too direct and to the point, but she does a hell of a job."

"As you said, we'll discuss it at another moment," he murmured dryly. "By the way, I don't suppose Charlotte has anything to do with the breakup?" he asked as they reached the garage.

"Uh, as a matter of fact, she does."

"Why am I not surprised?" Jeremy murmured, casting his eyes heavenward. Those two had been playing cat and mouse for as long as he could remember. "And what, may I ask, do you plan to do with your time, now that you'll no longer be with us?" he asked as they reached the car. "Seek early retirement?"

"I'm off to Scotland to become Lord of the Manor." Brad threw him a mischievous grin.

"Well. That's certainly come as a surprise. Anything else you'd like to tell me while we're at it?" He pressed the remote and the Jaguar's doors opened.

"I think that's it for today."

"Good. I hope you've made the right choices."

Their eyes met over the car roof and Brad said quietly, "For once, they're my choices."

Reporters were still spilling out of the Salon Vendôme into the splendid foyer and up the majestic stairway to the hotel lobby, Armand realized, delighted. He could barely see past the flashes bursting in his face, or answer the bevy of excited questions thrown at him from right, left and center. He, Armand, was the epicenter of this deliciously mad chaos. For a moment he thought he might expire from delirious happiness.

His most cherished dream had finally come true.

He blinked back tears of joy and wonder. He'd always been a second-tier player during Fashion Week, forced to watch the press fawn over the work of others, hoping vainly that he'd have a question or two shot his way. Now he was the center of attention, all of Paris at his feet, raving with excited delight, hands waving in expressive gestures of admiration. At long last, his genius was being recognized.

With each new question came a newfound surge of power. With great drama, he explained to a hushed audience that his jewelry had been inspired by Sylvain de

Rothberg's work, all the while whetting their appetites with hints that there might be more to the Rothberg connection than met the eye. He could almost see his father's face, beaming with pride as his son took his rightful place. As the moments elapsed, he relished each precious instant of adulation, lapping up the glorious sensations with the appreciation of a connoisseur tasting the finest vintage wine.

Of course, Charlotte had some small role in his success. He'd almost forgotten her in the ruckus. But he minimized the fact, relegating it to a nether region of his brain. After all, it was obvious she would never have achieved this on her own. It was all thanks to his ingenuity and Sylvain's guiding hand.

Now, as he answered more questions, an inner warmth hitherto unknown swept over him. The moment gave credence, he realized excitedly, to everything his psychic—whom he'd paid a fortune to over the years—had constantly predicted. It was only right, he justified, that he, and he alone, receive all the kudos.

"Armand." An unmistakable voice penetrated the hubbub and pierced his reverie. He froze for an instant, and then realized he was being foolish. It could only be his memory playing tricks on him, some nightmarish vision coming to deprive him of his joy. He smiled once more at the cameras and graciously answered another question.

"Armand, you will put an end to this charade at once." The Cardinal's voice rang loud and clear, its icy timbre sending shivers through him. Armand stopped and stared, aware that the left corner of his mouth had begun to twitch uncontrollably. His hands shook, growing clammy as he suddenly recalled that his uncle had mentioned he might be present.

They were turning away, he realized, gazing horrified as the press fell aside to allow the imposing, scarlet-caped figure to pass through the crowd.

Armand stayed rooted to the spot, unable to budge. This could not be happening, he told himself over and over. This was not how things were meant to play out. Desperate, he reached for the arm of the closest reporter. He needed to tell them, to explain. Surely they would understand. He would reveal his true parentage and keep them agog at his side.

But no one was paying attention to him any longer. Armand watched as every eye in the room focused on his uncle. His guts ached and a slow sweat broke out on his forehead. He opened his mouth to beg Oncle Eugène not to smash his dreams.

But no sound came.

The figure surged forward relentlessly, a tidal wave ready to engulf and annihilate, leaving him no room for escape. Like a trapped animal, he stared helplessly as the Cardinal brushed his adoring press aside like bothersome flies. He felt weak and his legs shook, just as they had when as a child he'd committed some misdemeanor and awaited punishment.

"Have you gone mad?" Eugène declared when he finally reached him. "Have you lost all notion of right and wrong?"

A hush descended upon the room. Half-dressed models stopped to listen, stylists and hairdressers held their breaths, and the press waited in throbbing anticipation as the scene unraveled. A scandal! What more could they ask for, to round off the evening's surprises?

"*Mon oncle,* I beg of you, not now, not here," Armand whispered hoarsely.

"You shall come with us immediately," Eugène

forced through clenched teeth. The words stung like the lash of a whip. Armand wished to protest, to stop the torrent of disaster he sensed rolling implacably toward him, but the scathing contempt his uncle wielded stole his words. "Come," the Cardinal ordered. "We will not make a public spectacle of ourselves for the rabble."

Taking a fearful step in his uncle's direction, Armand willed his hands to reach out and strangle the man. But they remained glued to his sides. Nothing could diminish his intimidation, not his seething unleashed anger, nor the knowledge that he was the victim of a lifetime's persecution.

Then he saw Charlotte.

His vision cleared and he focused again with a bang, heard the babbling voices, the curious looks greedy for gossip, his uncle's relentless gaze. His eyes flitted nervously back and forth. He hadn't counted on her presence. *Mon Dieu.* But here she stood, only a step away, staring at him silently. For a moment, regret and shame mingled. But only a moment. He racked his brain for a feasible justification for his actions, but could come up with nothing.

Slowly his eyes met hers. He read horror and pity. His breath caught and the full impact of what he'd done struck home. He'd deceived her, stolen from her. She could expose him as a fake. Yet something in her expression gave him hope and he clung to it like a drowning man to a sinking liferaft. Perhaps she would help him. Maybe she, an artist, would realize how vital this was to him, and understand why he'd had to do what he did. Maybe she could save him from his uncle's wrath.

No. Even if she were willing, the Cardinal wouldn't permit it, he realized bitterly. His mouth went suddenly dry and his vision narrowed, the room closing in on him like a pitch-black tunnel. He fought for control, willing himself to make a graceful exit. Licking his lips and straightening his spine, he murmured excuses to the swarming reporters and followed in the Cardinal's wake.

"No more questions," Eugène ordered, motioning to Monsignor Kelly to deal with the press. The kindly Irishman placed a large hand on the lens of an obstructing camera.

"That'll do for now," he said, firmly following the others out.

Charlotte stood near the marble fireplace in the presidential suite's salon. The Cardinal sat opposite, robes falling about him on a straight-backed, Louis XV armchair. Her feelings careened between fury and pity. The atmosphere was tense and silent. Armand cowered in the middle of the room, features gray and haggard under the shimmering crystal chandelier. He was a liar and a cheat, yet her bewildered gut told her his actions were rooted in something much deeper than the mere desire for fame, and she sought desperately to understand the reason for his shameless behavior.

At first she'd been too stunned to speak, too shocked to react. Now, with an effort, she pulled herself together. Armand would have to explain why he'd stolen her watch and her designs. Yet he appeared so pathetic, eyes fleeting back and forth like a trapped rabbit, a shadow of the vibrant man who'd preened before the press only moments earlier. It was as if he'd aged a decade in the space of an hour.

"Hand me the watch," Eugène ordered.

Armand fumbled with the heavy gold band, then, fingers shaking, handed it to Monsignor Kelly, who took it to the Cardinal. Eugène studied the piece silently and frowned. There was something hauntingly familiar in the bulky octagonal shape of the face. After a long moment, he raised his eyes to Armand. "It pains me to see that you are a thief *and* a liar. But I am not surprised. You are a blight to the name I misguidedly allowed you to use. Once we are finished here, you will call a press conference and tell the world that the designs you passed off as your own are Charlotte's," he continued coldly.

"Please, *non,* I beg of you, not that." Armand shook his head vigorously, wringing his hands. "You do not understand, *mon oncle.* You never have."

"What? That you are *un bon à rien?* A good-for-nothing wastrel, capable of such a despicable act as this?" The Cardinal's voice cut like a sharp knife. He gave a short, harsh laugh. "You underestimate me, Armand. I knew that from the moment I first laid eyes on you. Your father, my own brother, I'm sad to say, was a shame to our family. It was a blessing he died in the war. Your mother, God rest her soul, was a poor misguided wench."

"Don't speak about my father in that way," Armand hissed. His face contorting, his shoulders straightened as he rounded on his uncle. "My father was a brilliant man, a brave man who died for this country and for his beliefs. How dare you insult him?"

"Whatever you wish to believe is a matter of indifference to me. I can only tell you, though it pains me to do so, that René de la Vallière was never known either for his valor or his good habits."

"I'm not speaking of René de la Vallière," Armand cried, eyes shooting venom. "I'm speaking of my real father, Sylvain de Rothberg."

Eugène stared at him blankly. "Sylvain, your father?

What on earth are you talking about? Have you gone mad?''

"Stop pretending, *mon oncle*. You know very well what I mean. You have known all these years," Armand spat. "But I know the truth—that you've lied and masqueraded for your own benefit."

"You must be truly mad," Eugène said, shaking his head, genuinely confused. "There's no link between you and Sylvain."

"Of course there is. Stop denying it. Face the truth and that famous God of yours, *mon oncle*. It is you who should be ashamed, you who preach honesty, integrity and truth from that trumped-up pulpit, wielding unjust power in the name of the Lord from your precious Cardinal's perch. You," he cried, pointing a trembling finger, "are the one who has perjured yourself, stolen my identity and lied. All these years, you have hidden the truth from the world, afraid that should someone discover Sylvain's Lost Collection of jewels, *I* would be acknowledged as its rightful heir."

"What are you talking about—?" The Cardinal blanched.

"Don't pretend to misunderstand me," Armand interrupted with a harsh, hysterical laugh. "I know very well what you had in mind." His eyes simmered with years of hate, narrowed to tiny slits as he approached the armchair menacingly. "You thought that as Geneviève's brother, and the last living survivor, you could claim the fortune."

"But how can you possibly have arrived at such idiotic conclusions?" Eugène exclaimed, horrified.

"I knew the moment you gave me the letter all those years ago."

Eugène frowned. "Are you referring to your poor mother's letter? What has that to do with it?"

"Everything," Armand whispered hoarsely, eyes aglow with a new fervor. "She spoke to me of the Lost Collection. It was her last gift to me. But my confirmation was this." He wrenched the Star of David from under his shirt and stuck it in the Cardinal's face. "This," he said, shaking it, "is how I knew. Why would you give me this unless Sylvain de Rothberg was my father? You would never have given me anything so personal of his had there not been a specific reason. And, poor Maman, she was too terrified to tell me that Sylvain, not René, had been her lover. His marriage to your sister Geneviève was nothing but a dupe and a decoy," he continued, trembling. "An excuse for my father to be close to my mother in Ambazac."

"Armand, this is madness. You must stop this ridiculous fantasizing immediately." The Cardinal attempted to rise but the effort was too much and he leaned back, overwhelmed by the enormity of what was occurring. Could some misguided action of his have led this tormented boy to believe this ridiculous tale? "I have no clue where the Lost Collection may be," he murmured shakily, "none at all. But let me assure you that you have no connection to the Rothbergs whatsoever. The chain and star were there in the safe with the letter. I couldn't give them to Sylvain's real son. Sylvain had met your mother in prison, managed to slip the star and a note to her and asked her to give it to me shortly before his demise. I gave them to you out of sentiment—to commemorate your mother's courage in smuggling them to me. As for Sylvain's son—" All of a sudden he stopped and stared at Charlotte, still standing rigid next to the fireplace.

"I am his son, his only son," Armand yelled hysterically. "I know it. I've always sensed it. You are telling lies to protect yourself."

"No," Eugène insisted, genuinely distraught, "you are not."

"Then who was his son?" Armand demanded, eyes mad with tormented desperation.

After a moment's hesitation, the Cardinal turned toward Charlotte. "David MacLeod was Sylvain's son."

Charlotte's head shot up. "What?" she murmured, aghast. This just couldn't be. Her whole world was spinning. "That's not possible."

"But it is, *mon enfant*. I cannot explain it to you right now, but rest assured—if anyone in this room is Sylvain's heir, it is you, Charlotte."

"There must be some mistake. I can't be Sylvain's granddaughter. Angus MacLeod was—oh my God, this is too confused." She leaned her head on the cold marble mantel, trying desperately to assimilate the news. But in her heart of hearts, she knew it to be true. It all made sense.

"You're right not to believe him. It's not true." Armand plunged his hand into his pocket and in two strides reached the fireplace, pressing the muzzle of a small pistol at Charlotte's temple. "Once again you lie," he spat at the Cardinal. "But this time I will not be the victim of your sophistry."

Eugène rose, horrified. "Armand, I beg of you, put down that gun at once—"

"She is not Sylvain's heir, I am," he replied in high-pitched hysteria. "Just as the jewels she designed are his legacy to me, not to her. He came through her in spirit and guided her, used her as a vehicle to convey his talent to me, so that finally I could come into my own."

"Armand, put that gun away at once and stop acting in this hysterical manner," Eugène commanded. But his words sounded more confident than he felt and he leaned heavily on Monsignor Kelly's arm.

"No." Armand pressed the gun closer into Charlotte's temple, making her wince. "She can't be Sylvain's granddaughter—not this...this bohemian."

"Yes, Armand, she is."

"Then I shall kill her and there will be no one left but me."

Eugène swayed. How could things have come to this? How could he not have seen that the man was crazy? Charlotte's head was pressed against the marble mantel, the titian mass of hair dripping like blood. His breath came short. He must avoid bloodshed at all cost. "Armand, put down the gun and allow me to explain. Charlotte is in no way to blame for the past. No one is," he added in a bitter voice, "except me, perhaps, for not having revealed the truth earlier."

"Ah!" Armand exclaimed triumphantly. "So you admit you are to blame, then."

"*Au nom de Dieu,* Armand, put down that gun and I shall tell you the truth."

Charlotte's legs quivered as she tried desperately to keep her balance. What would happen to Genny if Armand killed her? The pistol pressed hard against her temple, and Armand's viselike grip hurt her arm. But beyond the terror lay despair. How could she die now, when she was finally on the verge of living? Every instinct rebelled. She would not let him steal her life as he had her watch and her creations. She would fight. She had no idea how, but somehow she would find a way.

Somehow, she would come out of this alive.

* * *

Brad forged a path through the lobby of the Georges V, swarming with paparazzi and guests, making his way quickly to the reception desk.

Three minutes later he was riding the elevator heading for the third floor, certain Charlotte was there. He could only imagine her horror at Armand's actions, and wondered again what on earth must have occurred after the show. Had she confronted the man? Had there been a showdown? Had the Cardinal gotten involved? Brad raced down the corridor, desperate to reach her. And when he found Armand, he vowed, he'd beat the living shit out of the conniving bastard.

Reaching the door of the suite, he halted. He could hear raised voices and recognized Armand's high-pitched accent, but was unable to make out the words. Then Eugène's sober tones answered haltingly and the urgency in his querulous voice made Brad shiver. All senses came alive. Something wasn't right. When the voices rose again, he turned the handle and eased open the door.

What he saw left him frozen.

16

Brad peered through the half-open door, heart in mouth, and forced himself to quell the rising panic as he took in the scene. Under the sparkling crystals of the three-tiered chandelier, Armand held Charlotte in his grip. Her head was pressed against the marble mantel of the fireplace. Armand brandished a small pistol and seemed out of control. Oncle Eugène leaned on Monsignor Kelly's arm, face colorless and horrified. Brad watched motionless as the scene played out, like a slow-motion movie, reflected in the huge period mirror behind Charlotte's head.

"You must listen to me," the Cardinal was saying, "you must understand."

"The only thing I understand is that you are a liar. Tell me the truth or I'll shoot," Armand hissed.

Brad fought the urge to rush forward. Even as his heart called for action, he knew that one wrong move could be deadly. As the seconds dragged by, he fought to control his breathing and assessed the scene. Armand had his back to him. Charlotte's face remained hidden from view, so he couldn't signal to her.

He fought desperation.

What if Armand lost control and shot her? He closed

his eyes a moment, pulse racing as frantically he sought a solution. But he had nothing to attack with, no gun, no way to intercede unless he threw himself on top of Armand, and that was a risk that might prove to have fatal consequences.

"Let the gun go and I swear I will tell you the truth." He heard Eugène's reedy voice and watched as Monsignor Kelly helped him cross the room.

"Don't." Armand swung round and pointed the gun at them. "Stay where you are. I have no need for your confessions, *mon oncle*. I know the truth."

Brad frowned, wondering what it was that Armand thought he knew.

"You must listen to me, Armand. I am telling you the only real truth. David MacLeod was Sylvain and Geneviève's son. You must accept that."

"No," Armand shook his head in denial. "I won't."

"You must." The Cardinal took another step forward, only to stop as Armand pressed the gun to Charlotte's head once more. "Listen. I beg of you to listen," he continued urgently. "After my sister Geneviève died at the hands of the Germans in the massacre at Ouradour, we were in despair. Sylvain was on the Gestapo's most-wanted list. Dex and Sylvain knew they must get the baby out of the country, or the Germans would use the child to force Sylvain out of hiding. David was only days old."

"All inventions," Armand yelled. "Lies to hide my heritage from me."

Brad had never been so terrified. The man was clearly insane. He felt utterly helpless. Should he rush inside or go downstairs and seek help? He glanced down the empty corridor. If someone appeared, he could tell them to call the police. He clenched his fist and turned back. There was no telling when Armand would go over the edge.

Brad inched his way inside the door. Whatever had triggered this madness, it had something to do with Sylvain de Rothberg. In fact, if Eugène's astonishing words were true, it meant that Charlotte was Sylvain's granddaughter. He'd been right to believe Strathaird held yet more secrets. In the midst of the tension, he realized it all made sense. She had inherited her grandfather's passion and talent. But at what cost? he wondered.

Armand shifted and Brad finally caught sight of Charlotte's rigid white face, squashed against the marble. He went cold with dread. She looked paralyzed with fear. He wanted to burst in, finish it off right now. But again he restrained himself. Instead, he tried to focus on Eugène's words, hoping they would give him a clue to Armand's behavior.

"Just listen," Eugène begged, "and you'll understand. Dex used his contacts in London, and organized the operation to take the baby out of France." The Cardinal moved closer to the fireplace. "When it was time to put David on the plane, Sylvain took off his watch and put it around the baby's ankle. Dex told me of this later, how Sylvain blessed the child in Hebrew. That is how the watch came into the MacLeods' possession."

"Lies, all lies," Armand repeated, but his voice was fainter now, as if he was growing confused.

"No, not lies," the Cardinal insisted gently, "but the truth. Why can you not accept who you are, Armand? I realize now that I've made mistakes. Perhaps I should have told you this earlier. I should have helped you more during your youth. But my blunders don't change what is basic fact—you are my brother René's son."

Armand let out an anguished cry, and Brad gazed at

him, horror-struck. The man was about to crack. He felt sick with dread—and utterly powerless.

It was obvious the Cardinal was trying to distract Armand while he and Monsignor Kelly edged their way closer to where Charlotte was pinned. All that was needed was a small diversion, Brad realized, something to take Armand's focus off Charlotte.

He searched desperately. Then the glistening crystals of the chandelier sparked an idea. Recalling a trick he'd seen in a movie, he fished out his wallet and removed a platinum credit card with a holographic logo. It was a crazy plan, but all he had. Carefully he held the credit card toward the chandelier, catching the light reflected off the gleaming crystals, playing with the reflection in the mirror, frantic for Monsignor Kelly or the Cardinal to pick up the signal. For Christ's sake look at the mirror, he begged. As though in answer to his prayer, Monsignor Kelly frowned. Look this way, Brad coaxed, just look this way. Armand's back was to the reflection. If his plan was going to work, this was the moment. Then, to his utter relief, Monsignor Kelly's eyes blinked. He glanced up then veered toward him. They acknowledged one another with a discreet nod, then the priest indicated that Brad should wait for a sign. Brad wiped the sweat from his forehead, tension rife, and plunged the credit card back into his pocket, still following the bizarre exchange between the Cardinal and Armand.

Charlotte tried to shift, sure her head would burst. She could hear her own heartbeat thudding in her ears. The Cardinal's bewildering words reached her and she tried to move beyond the gripping fear and understand. Oncle Eugène was saying that her father was Sylvain's son. So she was…Sylvain's granddaughter? How could that be?

It was impossible to assimilate, and hardly significant before the terror she was experiencing, yet instinctively she knew the Cardinal was speaking the truth.

She wished Brad were here, longed for his arms around her. Instead, she felt only a ruthless pulling on her scalp as Armand yanked her head around. He stared into her face, his eyes wild and full of hate. With crystal clarity, she realized that he didn't really see her. Instead, he was a private witness to some profound inner torment. Then she saw that he was cocking the gun, preparing to shoot at the demons he somehow saw in her face.

She let out a scream and tried to move. With superhuman effort she turned and faced the mirror. As Armand's finger touched the trigger, she caught sight of Brad's reflection and her heart leaped. Then all became chaos as Brad took advantage of Armand's distraction and threw himself at them. The force of the impact sent her stumbling onto a Louis-Seize stool, which in turn hit the coffee table. Crystal glasses shattered, ice cubes showering the floor as the champagne bucket tumbled. A vase of deep red roses scattered about her like splashes of blood as she crouched trembling next to the sofa. Charlotte gripped the cover, trying to hoist herself up, her heart pounding as Brad attempted to wrench the gun free from Armand's frantic fingers. She was too overwhelmed to even wonder how he'd suddenly appeared out of nowhere. All she could do was stare fixedly at the horrific silent scene unfolding before her. She let out a scream as Armand hit Brad with the pistol butt, then watched him rush frantically toward the French window leading to the balcony.

"Drop the gun," Brad shouted, still reeling from the blow. "Let it go, Armand. Nothing will happen to you. We'll get you help."

"Non!" he screamed, voice hysterical, eyes gleaming and insane. "No one can help me," he moaned in a clear voice that rang across the room. "No one at all."

Then all at once he seemed to crumple. Tears poured down his tired gray cheeks and he sagged, trembling against the cream satin curtains. His hands fell limply to his sides and for a few never-ending seconds, the air ran thick with tension. Would it end now? Would Armand break down completely? She held her breath, too terrified to run to Brad. Then suddenly, Armand raised the gun to his temple.

"Don't," she screamed, scrambling to get up.

"It's too late," he said, *"C'est la fin."*

The chandelier shuddered as the shot reverberated through the room and they gazed in silent horror at Armand, lying in a heap on the floor.

"Oh my God!" Charlotte stumbled to the body lying in a heap before the French window. Dropping to her knees, she cradled Armand in her arms. She barely noticed the warm blood pooling in her lap, seeping through the silk of her pantsuit. Then Brad's arms encircled her and her tears were finally released.

"We never helped him," she whispered. "None of us ever bothered to see he was suffering."

The Cardinal sank onto the sofa, burying his face in his hands while Monsignor Kelly took out his rosary and began murmuring prayers.

"It's too late to do anything," Brad said, gently pulling her away from the body. "There's nothing you can do for him any longer, Charlie."

"We should have realized something was wrong," she wailed, head sinking onto his shoulder. "We should have tried to help him."

"Look, no one knew this would happen. It's obvious

he was living in some private hell... I doubt he'd have wanted our help, if it meant giving up his fantasy." Brad scrambled to find the right words, but frankly, all he cared about was that Charlotte was safe and in his arms. Armand's death was tragic—but he'd never forgive the man for trying to take Charlotte with him.

"When did you get here?" she asked dazedly as he led her to the opposite side of the room, aware the hotel staff needed to be made aware of the incident.

"I came as soon as I could. I wanted to be with you for the show, but the meeting in London took so long. I've tried to call you, but I could never reach you." He stared into her eyes, hoping he was breaking through the lingering panic he read there. "I saw what happened on CNN, Charlie," he said, smiling. "You're a success."

"I suppose so," she said distractedly. Then she twisted her head and gazed again at Armand. "I can't believe he's dead," she said in a distant voice. "He stole the watch and my designs, yet I feel so sorry for him. What a miserable life he must have led, trying to believe he was someone he wasn't. It's awful."

"You are right." The Cardinal's words echoed through the high-ceilinged salon, making them both turn. He raised a weary face and nodded sadly. "I should have paid more attention to him when he was a child. I am to blame for what has happened here," he said grimly. "I should have tried to understand him. Instead, it was easier to ignore him—and this is the result."

"All of us should have been more attentive and less judgmental," Charlotte replied between sobs. "We thought of him as a joke, when all the time he was a fragile individual in desperate need of help. I feel awful when I think of all those hours we spent working together, planning the show. He was so excited. It was all he cared about. And I don't understand, about Daddy and Sylvain or anything. It's crazy,'' she added as Brad wiped her tears. "Why did he imagine he was Sylvain de Rothberg's son? It doesn't make sense.''

"Yes, it does,'' the Cardinal murmured sadly. "*Pauvre* Armand. He was desperately seeking an identity and he ended up creating one in his tortured mind. I never saw the letter his mother wrote, but it must have contained something that led him to believe he was Sylvain's son. My misguided action in giving him Sylvain's Star of David must have confirmed his imaginings.'' He shook his head sadly.

Charlotte leaned on Brad's arm, seeking his strength, and faced Oncle Eugène. "But what about Daddy. You said he was Sylvain's son. Surely that's not possible. I mean, it sounds awfully far-fetched, the baby smuggled out and—gosh, if it's true, that means Nathalie and Daddy weren't really twins! And what about Granny Flora and Grandpa Angus?'' Her voice rose. "They must have been privy to all this,'' she exclaimed, slowly assimilating the enormity of the drama.

"I know, *mon enfant,* and I shall explain.'' He gestured, exhausted. "But first, Bradley, it may be necessary to contact my old friend, the *préfet de police,* to deal with this situation. Total discretion must be upheld.''

"Surely that can't be the most important item on the agenda here?'' she said angrily. "Armand's dead, I've just learned that I'm not who I am and you're worried about discretion?''

"You have every right to know the truth, *mon enfant,* and know it you shall. But I will tell you that story later,'' he said. He stood beside Monsignor Kelly. "Now we must administer the last rites to poor Armand and then deal with this whole episode as quietly as possible.''

"He's right," Brad muttered, feeling her tense. "There's no point in letting the press get hold of a scandal like this. You'd be the hardest hit by it," he added, squeezing her shoulders. "Let me take care of business, Charlie. It'll be okay."

Eugène turned and stared fixedly at the mirror above the fireplace. "It is entirely possible others have heard the gunshot. We may need to pull some strings to avoid publicity."

Monsignor Kelly held the Cardinal's hands as he painfully lowered himself to his knees. Despite her confusion, Charlotte's sense of outrage faded as she observed the deeply troubled face and watery, haunted eyes. All at once, she understood the price Oncle Eugène had paid for carrying so many ancient secrets.

She and Brad stood solemnly, hand in hand, tears pouring down her cheeks as the Cardinal made the sign of the cross over Armand's forehead. In a halting voice he began the litany: "Through this holy unction and his own most tender mercy may the Lord pardon thee whatever sins or faults thou hast committed…"

Two hours later, the corpse had been discreetly removed from the premises and the authorities dealt with, thanks to the former *préfet de police,* who had immediately taken charge. Tomorrow's papers would still be full of scandal, but at least the details would be omitted. Armand's death would be described as a heart attack and all rumors of the suicide hushed up.

As she stumbled, exhausted, into the white marble bathroom, Charlotte caught sight of her reflection in the huge mirror. The white Armani suit was splattered with drying bloodstains that formed a strange pattern down her right leg. She stared at it, mesmerized.

That was Armand's blood she was wearing.

Suddenly she ripped her clothes off. Putting on the terry robe, she stuffed the pantsuit, her bra and panties and tights into a laundry bag with a shudder. No amount of washing would ever cleanse the memories associated with them. Even though it was now well-past midnight, she picked up the phone and dialed housekeeping. Grabbing the plastic laundry bag, she hastened back through the room and opened the door, depositing the bag outside with a sigh of relief.

Minutes later, she was under the shower, desperately trying to cleanse herself of the tragic event.

It had been the most ambiguous night of her life, she reflected as the warm water slid over her. Her fears of failure had been followed by recognition and the public's applause, only to suffer the shock of seeing her watch flaunted on Armand's wrist.

She tried to forget what had followed as she lathered herself thoroughly, determined to eradicate every trace of horror.

And finally Brad had come.

She stopped scrubbing and her hands moved in softer movements over her soft skin. All this time she'd thought he didn't care, yet as always, he'd turned up just when she needed him. In a few stolen moments, he'd explained why he'd left so suddenly, and told her that he'd ended his engagement to Sylvia. She smiled for the first time in several hours. It was comforting to know he was only a few doors down the hall, where he'd taken a room, probably in the shower, too. He'd tried to insist that she leave the hotel and go with him to the Plaza Athénée instead. But Charlotte was loath to abandon the Cardinal. They'd been through this together and she was not about to jump ship.

Reluctantly Brad had agreed. He would come and see her later, once they were showered and dressed. Knowing him, he would insist she eat. Charlotte wrapped herself in the terry robe again, grimacing at the thought of food. After wrapping her hair in a turban, she returned to the bedroom and sank onto the bed, exhausted. What a night this had been, she reflected, yawning, eyes drooping as she curled on top of the bed to wait for Brad. She lay down, pulled a pillow under her cheek and, despite her certainty that she wouldn't close an eyelid, drifted into a light slumber.

Brad stood next to the bed and gazed down at her in relief. When he'd knocked and there was no answer, he'd experienced a sudden rush of fear. Charlotte was an emotional time bomb and he hastily called the concierge and had the room unlocked. Watching her lying there asleep in the center of the huge bed, wrapped like an Eskimo in her robe, she reminded him of the little girl he remembered. After covering her, he switched off the bedside lamp. Pulling off his shirt and pants, he did what seemed natural and slipped in beside her under the covers.

She sighed, mumbled and snuggled close under the covers. Brad put his arms around her protectively. Nothing could tear them apart now, he reassured himself, basking in the soft warmth of her body. He'd been able to have a few words with her before they'd each gone to shower. He hoped he'd assuaged all her awful imaginings about the reasons for his trip to New York. They were nothing more than fantasies born of insecurity.

The towel on her head had come loose and he drew it off, letting her hair cascade over the pillow. Gently he stroked the long damp strands. He loved her unconditionally, he realized, feeling her turn.

The robe slipped off her shoulder, revealing firm white breasts outlined by a shard of moonlight that snaked through the half-closed curtains. He swallowed, watched as, half-asleep, she threw the robe off onto the floor then turned over, rubbing her cheek gently against his bare shoulder. His arm closed tighter around her. She murmured his name and her arms came around his back. For a long moment they clung, each sensing that together they could wipe away the evening's horror.

Gently their lips met.

Charlotte kept her eyes closed. She needed to feel him, know he was next to her, that he would never let her go. A rush of tenderness made her press closer. She felt his hardness and instinctively cleaved to him, basking in the sheer power of his body and the overwhelming need for him to plunge deep inside her, obliterating the disturbing shadows that still lingered in their midst. His fingers sought her inner core, and she gasped, impatient to know him deep within her, the yearning more powerful than anything she had ever known. It was an elemental need for survival, for procreation, for union of body and spirit, as though nature's forces, once merged, would finally vanquish death.

Soft words and tender caresses gave way to pent-up emotions, bursting forth now in a frantic rush. Another time he would caress her for hours on end, but right now his need to be inside her was too great. Through the darkness he sought her eyes, read the same insatiable hunger coupled with a feral need. He thrust, hard and fast, reckless and demanding, heart throbbing wildly as she arched, legs curling around him, as they reached for the depths of each other's soul.

This was how he'd wanted her, dreamed of her, yearned for her all these years. With a final thrust he took her, then felt her body give as together they crashed, racked by the violence of a climax that shattered the boundaries of sanity.

There was no need for words.

Brad pulled her head gently onto his shoulder and stroked her back tenderly. She was his as never before. Armand's death and the revelations of the previous evening had sealed a new bond between them. As he went to sleep, he prayed that they would still be like this in forty years.

By the time Eugène finally entered the bedroom of the presidential suite, he was exhausted. But this awful evening's events would allow him no rest. He sighed. He was too old to carry such burdens. He wondered, as he had so often these last few months, when the *Bon Dieu* would see fit to let him set down his load. It was long past time for him to leave this wearying life. His friends and closest family, so many faces from his past, were gone now, and he yearned to see them again.

Not that he expected an unquestioning welcome when the Lord finally called him to his side. No, he knew his own sins too well to assume that his stature within Christ's earthly church would earn him an automatic place in his heavenly kingdom. But surely, once he was before the Lord and could explain himself, he'd be granted absolution for the many mistakes he'd made. He sighed heavily and moved to the mahogany dresser by his bed.

Sadly he removed his pectoral cross, carefully folding its scarlet and gold cord, and laid it next to the square gold box where he'd kept it for over fifty years. He stared at it thoughtfully, the night's occurrences still fresh in his mind. The box had been Sylvain's last gift before he disappeared into hiding, he remembered sadly. For a moment he studied the enamel inlays, the heavy lid with the unique octagonal recess in the middle, set with a strange pattern of precious stones.

Then, with another sigh, he looked away. Tonight had been a long, traumatic evening, with a tragic outcome he could never have imagined. How had he not sensed, not known Armand was living in such hell? Even more troubling, he wondered if it was one to which he'd unwittingly contributed. Clearly he'd played some role in Armand's unhappiness, and for that he could not forgive himself. His nascent sense of guilt weighed heavily on him, and he longed for repentance and absolution. He must seek out his confessor when he returned to Rome. Perhaps then he might be granted a little peace of mind.

He sat unsteadily on the edge of the bed, still in his robes. He would say prayers for Armand's soul, and request that the priests in the dioceses under his control do the same. Perhaps with so many voices interceding on his nephew's behalf, the poor boy might find in death the peace that had eluded him in life. But it troubled him still that Armand could have constructed such an elaborate fantasy. Of course, he would have found it exciting and romantic to be associated with Sylvain de Rothberg, rather than René, particularly after the untimely death of his mother under such shameful circumstances. Still, the madness must have been in him from an early age.

He moved his frail limbs and tried unsuccessfully to rise. He'd give himself another few minutes, he decided, wondering where Linus had gotten to. He needed his help to undress. Most likely he was still negotiating some final detail with the authorities, though the *préfet de police* had seen to matters most efficiently. Neither could he find fault with the hotel staff. Perhaps, he decided grudgingly, the Georges V was not as bad as he'd believed. Tomorrow he would thank the director personally for all the attention bestowed.

Making a huge effort, he rose stiffly, felt a strange bulge in his pocket, and removed the heavy gold watch he'd forgotten to return to Charlotte.

Sylvain's presence was certainly everywhere tonight, he realized. Tomorrow he would sit down with Brad and Charlotte and tell them about the past. The time had come. But tonight he simply hadn't the strength.

He handled the watch gently then stared at it for a long moment. There was something familiar about it. Frowning, he glanced at the enamel box on the dressing table. *"Bon sang,"* he exclaimed, taking a trembling step forward. Desperately, he tried to remember Sylvain's exact words when he'd given him the box. Something about holding secrets?

His breath came faster. Unsteadily he picked up the box in his right hand, still holding the watch in his left. A sudden chill ran down his spine as he looked from one to the other. "Carry the secrets," Sylvain had whispered when he handed him the box, almost as a benediction. At the time, he'd wondered what Sylvain had meant— *"Mon Dieu,"* he whispered, gazing from one piece to the other.

Then, with trembling fingers, he brought the two together.

There was a tiny click as the face of the watch snapped into place on the box's lid. Eugène gasped. How could he have lived with the box under his nose all these years and never thought of it as anything but a gift from his beloved brother-in-law, in which he'd kept his assorted accessories? Hesitating only an instant, he turned the face of the watch as he would the lock on a safe.

A spring gave way and the heavy lid split in two. As the upper tier popped up, he let out a long amazed breath and removed the top half of the lid, now divided into two separate parts, and looked inside. Gently he pried a thin envelope from its niche. It was addressed to him in Sylvain's copperplate writing. Shaking, he took out a flat bronze key and gazed at it, lying in his palm. It was the key to a safe, or some safe-deposit box, he realized, pulse racing. He swallowed, mouth dry, and laid the box and watch reverently on the dresser, overcome by emotion. Then he reached for his letter opener. Sitting down shakily on the bed, he gazed blindly at the envelope. Slitting the top precisely, he drew out two leaves of neatly creased paper that crackled as he unfolded them. The sight of Sylvain's writing, his elaborately drawn letters unmistakable, brought tears to his eyes. Could this be—literally—the key to the Lost Collection? He skimmed the text and his vision blurred. It was all here: the name of a bank he knew well in Switzerland, the number of the account, the safe, the codes and a notarized power of attorney delivered in his name, all signed for and sealed by Sylvain himself.

Eugène's hands shook again as he laid the letter on the dresser. Destiny had caught up with them at last. His thoughts turned to Charlotte, to the resounding applause of the crowd earlier that evening, then to Armand's untimely death, which perhaps was a blessing in disguise. Silently he fell to his knees. "Seigneur," he murmured, his withered hands clasped on the brocade eiderdown, "show me the way and bless me with the right words to tell her." He prayed, thinking of the immense responsibility that was about to fall upon Charlotte. "May she be wise enough now to handle this legacy that you have seen fit to send us.'' Then quietly, he thanked God for allowing him to fulfill his mission.

Exhausted, he laid his head on the eiderdown pillow and stretched his fragile body along the pressed linen sheets, too tired to go on. Disregarding the clothes he still wore, he closed his eyes, surprised to feel a new-found sense of peace. For a few moments he reveled in it. So this was what it was like to know true serenity.

For the first time in memory, Eugène cast aside his pain and worries and fell quickly into a deep, dreamless sleep.

17

It was 11:00 a.m. and still the Cardinal had not appeared. Breakfast had come and gone. Charlotte shifted nervously on the sofa in Eugène's sitting room, flipping again through the papers. Somehow the news had leaked out that she, not Armand, had designed the la Vallière jewelry collection, and the phones had been ringing nonstop since early morning. Brad had finally ordered the hotel switchboard not to pass on the calls. He'd also efficiently dispatched two reporters who'd made their way up to the suite.

There was just too much going on, Charlotte decided, knowing her stress level must be off the charts. Restlessly, she rose and crossed the room to stand beside the French window of the new presidential suite the Cardinal had been transferred to after last night's horrible incident. Trying to forget that Armand had shot himself in front of a similar window just down the hall, she stared out across Paris. She felt as if she'd woken up this morning in some alternate universe. Her work was being celebrated in the world's most famous fashion capital and she had learned she was the granddaughter of her idol. And, of course, Armand was dead.

It was hard to assimilate.

So much was still unclear. And there was only one person who could provide the answers. Impatiently she glanced at Oncle Eugène's door, willing him to put in an appearance. She must learn the truth about the past. Only then could she move on and deal with the present, and the future. She needed to know.

She'd talked to Mummy earlier this morning and told her the amazing news. Both had suffered the same reaction; anger and sadness that David, her father, had lived his life under a false pretense. She'd asked her mother to tell Genny only the necessary facts, so that she wouldn't learn of Armand's death through the media. Charlotte would tell her daughter the rest when she returned home. But now all they could do was wait for the Cardinal to reveal the story behind his secrets, a story he'd apparently carried for a lifetime.

"He's taking so long," she exclaimed, turning to Brad at the desk answering e-mails on his laptop.

"Calm down, Charlie, he'll come out when he's ready. Yesterday was incredibly traumatic. He was very tired last night. Give him a chance to recuperate." He smiled at her from across the room.

Whenever he smiled like that, Charlotte felt the tension within her loosen. There was something about being in his presence that calmed her. Even the sound of his voice over the phone did wonders when she was wired. She smiled back at him. How handsome he was in his dark suit and tie, how tender, how strong and wonderful.

And at last he was hers.

Just as she was indisputedly his.

The thought sent shivers down her spine and she crossed over to where he sat. He set his laptop computer on an adjoining table, patted his knee invitingly and she dropped into his lap.

"I love you," she murmured, slipping her arms around his neck and fastening her lips to his.

"I love you too," he mumbled between kisses. "More than I ever thought it possible to love." His voice was hoarse and he held her close.

For a moment they simply held each other tight, needing to feel the other's warmth. It was blissful to know that nothing could keep them apart ever again. She nuzzled his neck, breathing in the delicious scent of his aftershave. "I like that," she said, sniffing. "It smells like Dex."

"Not surprising. Roget & Gallet, the cologne Dex always wore. It's old-fashioned but I like it. He introduced me to it when I was fifteen." He nibbled her ear, sending delicious shivers through her.

"That scent has stayed with me all these years, ever since Chester Square."

"And will do so for the rest of our lives, I hope," he murmured, hand slipping to her breast, fondling tenderly through the thin white cotton shirt.

"Don't," she moaned, "or I won't be in a fit state to concentrate on all Oncle Eugène has to say. I can't believe Sylvain really is my grandfather, can you? It's so incredible. I've practically worshiped the man. No wonder Granny Flora said I looked so much like Geneviève, and I don't resemble any of the other MacLeods. I suppose I'm a throwback," she added. "It's like a fairy tale."

"You're right. It is. But since you're a fairy princess, I guess it's only appropriate." He massaged the back of her neck and drew her mouth to his once more.

It was a long, tender kiss, a gentle communing, each

seeking the other's core. When Charlotte raised her head, her vision swam. She dropped her forehead to his and sighed. "Guess that makes you my knight in shining armor. Lord knows you've come to my rescue often enough."

"No, Charlotte, it's you who's rescued me," he said solemnly. Then, teasingly, he pinched her cheek, breaking the intensity that had suddenly sprung between them. If things continued in this vein, Brad realized, Eugène was going to get a rather shocking eyeful when he opened his door.

"Up you get," he ordered, lifting her off his lap. "We need to focus on your new career. You need a publicist, young lady, someone to deal with PR and set up a press conference."

"But I can't do a press conference," she exclaimed, horrified.

"You don't have a choice, Charlie. Your collection has generated tremendous excitement, and the bizarre circumstances surrounding its debut have made this more than just a fashion story. You're going to be hounded until you set the record straight—and what you do now will establish the tone for the rest of your career. Everyone is expecting something of you."

"Oh God!" She grimaced and flopped into the nearest chair. "Why can't I just design my jewelry back on Skye and be done with it?"

He took her hand patiently. "I know you don't like the limelight." He looked her straight in the eye. "You, of all people, should know what stardom implies, you've lived with it long enough."

"Don't remind me of that." She whisked her hand away and jumped up, returning with a brooding frown to the window.

"I'm not trying to remind you of anything. I simply want to make you aware of reality." He pointed to the door. "The minute you step out there the place will be swarming with reporters, TV cameras, the works. So you'd better be prepared. That's not just the fashion press down there, Charlie. Hell, half those reporters couldn't tell a cluster setting from a cluster bomb. They're here because they smell something big—a fat juicy scandal. Only you can ensure that the coverage goes in the right direction, that something positive comes from it—otherwise this might degenerate into some gruesome reflection on Armand."

"Couldn't we just disappear?" She shifted uncomfortably, remembering John's premieres, the scrutiny she'd shied away from all these years. But now she was the one in the crosshairs, and Brad was right, she'd have to deal with it. Another thought occurred to her. "What do you think will happen when people find out that I'm Sylvain's granddaughter? Don't you think they'll imagine this is all just some tasteless PR stunt?"

He eyed her a moment, then shook his head. "No. You've made your mark on your own. No one knows about Sylvain yet. And unless the Lost Collection happens to turn up one day, I don't really see why it would be that important. People will remember his talent and say you've inherited it, that's all." He shrugged, sat down again at the desk and started jotting some notes.

At that moment the door opened. Charlotte spun around anxiously and watched Oncle Eugène walk into the room on Monsignor Kelly's arm. He looked pale and fragile, as though a sharp gust of wind could simply blow him away. She held her breath as he made his way across the room. She couldn't deny she'd felt some hard feelings toward him over the past few hours. She was genuinely angry that he'd kept so much from them all these years, but as she watched his slow, arthritic movements, her resentment lessened. As Mummy had pointed out when they'd talked, Dex and Granny Flora were equally culpable. They, too, had known the truth but had chosen not to reveal it. And, clearly, they'd have had powerful reasons for withholding that truth. Who was she to judge them?

She moved toward the Cardinal and in a sudden rush of affection sat down beside him, slipping her hand in his withered one.

"Are you all right, Oncle Eugène?" she asked anxiously. "This has all been a terrible strain on you."

"It has, *mon enfant*," he agreed, patting her hand kindly, "but I confess it is also a tremendous relief to unburden myself. I have prayed so often over the years, sought guidance as to what I should do. You know, to carry the secrets of others can become wearisome, even to a priest," he said with a wry smile. "While there were others alive to share them, the responsibility was not wholly mine. But when I became the last living witness, everything changed. I thought that when I died, so would the past. Perhaps it is a blessing that now the truth will finally be revealed, *mon enfant*. God's way of righting matters," he sighed, "for he works in a mysterious way that we mortals are unable to comprehend."

"You said Daddy was Sylvain's son. But he never knew that, did he?" Charlotte tried to keep the bewilderment and bitterness from her voice. It seemed dreadfully unfair that her father should have lived and died without any awareness of his true identity. It was odd enough for her to suddenly discover a whole new facet to her being. "Why did none of you tell us? What made you and Dex and Granny think you had the right to hide this from us all these years?'' She stared hard at the Cardinal, trying to master her anger.

"I know, *mon enfant*. Times were strange. Afterward, once the war was over and life went back to normal, it seemed better to preserve the status quo.'' He shook his head sadly. ''Genny and Sylvain had been killed in the war, and David was settled at Strathaird. He was only a baby. It is true that David never knew the truth about himself, but did it change much in his life? Was he any less content not knowing that he was Sylvain's offspring? He lived happily, believing he was Angus and Flora's child, and they loved him as a son. It is too late to look back, to wish things had been different. We must accept that now and make peace with ourselves and with God.''

His face creased with weariness and his thin lips quivered. ''Of course, it is hard to see how Armand's death could have been part of the Lord's plan. I suspect much of the responsibility for Armand's actions rests with me, and that, I'm afraid, is a burden I shall carry with me to the grave,'' he murmured, passing a hand quickly over his eyes.

Charlotte wrapped an arm around his shockingly bony shoulders, aware now just how deeply he'd been affected by Armand's death. It was impossible not to feel for him. She frowned and sent Brad a quick glance. He moved around the table to join them.

''But enough.'' The Cardinal became suddenly brisk. ''Linus, bring me what I asked for.'' He straightened against the sofa cushions as Monsignor Kelly came forward, carrying Charlotte's watch in one hand and a small enamel-inlaid jewel box in the other.

Charlotte's pulse quickened as he laid them carefully on the smooth tabletop. She leaned forward, eyebrows knit. The box was clearly Sylvain's work. Its top had an octagonal indent set with precious stones. She glanced at her watch, then back at the box, gripped by a sudden ripple of excitement: both pieces were the same odd shape, each one a mirror image of the other.

"I want you to place the face of the watch into the slot on the lid of the box," the Cardinal said, turning to Charlotte and gesturing toward the table.

Brad leaned forward, and Monsignor Kelly smiled encouragingly.

Fingers trembling with excitement, sensing that something of great moment was about to take place, Charlotte picked up the watch. Carefully she placed it facedown into the recessed octagon on the box's lid, letting out a gasp when it fell precisely into place.

"My God," she exclaimed, hands shaking. "These were made for one another."

"Now twist the watch to your right," the Cardinal continued, ignoring her.

Holding her breath, Charlotte twisted the timepiece. She heard a tiny click, and watched in openmouthed amazement as part of the box lid sprang open, revealing the secret compartment within. "I don't believe it," she whispered, clutching the two pieces. "This is incredible."

"The box has been in my possession since the spring of 1940," the Cardinal murmured, his voice vibrating with new emotion. "It was Sylvain's last gift to me before he and Genny disappeared into hiding. I have used it over the years to hold my cross, never suspecting what it contained. To think I have looked at it, day after day, for over sixty years, but never suspected the truth until now."

"That's astonishing," Brad remarked, fascinated. "But what prompted Sylvain to create such a box?"

"This." With a dramatic gesture, the Cardinal held up a folded piece of paper and a bronze key.

Charlotte jumped up and stared at them in wonder. "You mean...?" She could not go on.

"The key is to a safe at the Union de Banque Suisse on the Bahnhofstrasse in Zurich. The secret codes for the numbered account and the safe references are all recorded here in Sylvain's own handwriting."

Charlotte let out the breath she'd been holding. "It might be...?" She couldn't end the sentence.

"Yes." The Cardinal nodded, face serious. "I believe we may have discovered the whereabouts of the Lost Collection."

"Oh my God." Charlotte dropped into the nearest chair. Brad moved next to her and placed a firm hand on her shoulder.

"It's unbelievable," she whispered, reaching for his hand, hers trembling. "But if it's there, who will claim it?"

"You will, *ma chère*. You are, after all, his rightful heir."

"Me?" Charlotte sat up ramrod straight in the chair. "But I can't claim Sylvain's collection. That's ridiculous."

"Not at all. The information described in this letter is very clear. Take a look for yourself." He handed the letter to Brad, who unfolded it and skimmed the contents.

"The UBS on the Bahnhofstrasse in Zurich. If I'm not mistaken, the bank has been in the same location since the twenties, which means the safes have probably remained intact. And this," he remarked, raising a second piece of paper, "is a notarized power of attorney in Eugène's name. They can hardly refuse that."

"Precisely. I also happen to be well acquainted with

the directors of the bank. Not only do we have la Vallière family accounts there, but I oversee certain Church investments that are managed by that particular establishment.''

"I see," said Brad.

"In fact," the Cardinal continued, glancing at Charlotte, who was still sitting in dazed silence, "I have already made arrangements for Sylvain's descendant to visit the bank and verify the contents of the safe."

"You mean me?" Charlotte put her hand to her mouth and swallowed.

"Yes, *mon enfant*. Now that your father and brother are gone, you are Sylvain's one and only legitimate heir."

"Surely they won't just take your word for it. They'll want proof, DNA tests, something," she cried desperately, the responsibility of such a legacy so great she could barely think straight.

"That will be dealt with in due course. There will be one or two bits of paperwork required, but I think I've managed to cut through most of the red tape. I assure you, with my sponsorship, no one will challenge your claim," he added with a sniff and a dismissive wave of the hand.

"But what would I do with it?" Charlotte asked in a small voice.

"I have no idea. That is a problem we shall deal with later. For all we know, he may not have been able to smuggle his jewelry out of France. The safe may well hold nothing more than gold coins and perhaps some precious stones. At this point we cannot conjecture or elevate our expectations too high."

"No, of course," she murmured automatically, trying

to pull herself together, grateful for the warm support of Brad's hand on her shoulder.

"Still," the Cardinal went on, eyes misting as he re-membered, "when he gave me the box he said certain things that, in hindsight, may have been intended as a signal. Ah, who knows..." He hesitated, staring into space.

Charlotte wanted desperately to ask what Sylvain's parting words had been, but something stopped her. There were some secrets that were Oncle Eugène's alone, and she didn't have the right to pry.

"Time has a funny way of catching up with us," the Cardinal said, focusing once more. "Maybe the collection has been waiting for you, Charlotte."

"What do you mean?" she asked, frowning.

"Waiting for you to find yourself, *mon enfant*. You might not have been ready for the responsibility before. Linus tells me this morning's papers are full of your success." He watched her carefully. "They seem to have found out the collection was yours and not Armand's. One wonders how, *n'est-ce pas?* None of us here has said anything. Perhaps other forces were at work, pre-paring for this moment." He sent her a mischievous smile and patted her cheek before turning to the others. "Now," he said in a matter-of-fact tone, "this is how we shall proceed. You, Bradley, will accompany us to Zurich." Brad nodded. "Linus will deal with the press and the paparazzi here. We shall have to leave the hotel via the lower floors. I suspect we shall discover how Vic-tor Hugo's characters in *Les Misérables* must have felt," he added with a touch of humor. "But never mind. We must head for Zurich at once and clarify this matter im-mediately."

Charlotte glanced up at Brad. This was all so unexpected, so overwhelming. Could it be that after all these years the Lost Collection was finally going to be found?

"What will we do with it if it's there?" she murmured to the room at large.

"That, *ma chère,* would be entirely up to you."

"But what if I don't want that responsibility?" she challenged.

"Then I would say you underestimate yourself. But I have the feeling that now you are ready to shoulder what, even a few months ago, might have seemed impossible. You have changed, Charlotte. It is time you recognized your own strength."

She looked at him, surprised. Yet what he said was true. Little by little, her self-confidence was growing. Even the tremendously difficult decision to go ahead with the divorce had finally been faced. She nodded, feeling a sudden sense of surety. "Let's go then, Oncle Eugène. You're right. We must settle this matter as promptly as possible and then get on with our lives."

"Good. Bradley, will you see to the reservations? Linus, you call the Baur Au Lac hotel and tell them which suites to reserve. As for you two," he remarked with a weathered smile, "I'm glad that before I pass on to a better world I will have had the pleasure of seeing you two reunited. It was meant to be."

Brad and Charlotte exchanged a look of surprise, then realized one should never underestimate the Cardinal's powers of observation. The man had the eyes and ears of a hawk.

"Very well. I'll see to the reservations. Will you be ready to depart this afternoon?" Brad asked Eugène.

"Of course. We can be at the bank before lunch tomorrow. After so many years, Sylvain's mystery will be solved."

* * *

At ten o'clock sharp the next morning, Charlotte, Brad and the Cardinal sat in the office of the bank's president. The gray-haired, gray-suited man carefully reviewed all the information Eugène had provided, including Sylvain's letter, which had been examined by an expert and declared authentic. Charlotte waited, studying the paneled walls hung with nineteenth-century watercolors of Lake Zurich, trying to remain calm. Her eyes traveled to the window. It seemed strange that only steps away in the fine shops of the Bahnhofstrasse, people were shopping, or sipping coffee and reading their newspapers on the terrace at Sprüngle, the famous Swiss chocolatier, unaware of the drama unfolding in their midst. She returned her gaze to the desk, only to discover the bank president was smiling discreetly at her.

"Everything seems to be in perfect order, Your Eminence. If *madame* and you—" he indicated Brad and the Cardinal "—would like to follow me, we shall take the necessary steps to proceed further."

Now nothing remained but to descend several floors into the bank's subbasements, where the safes were housed. How many of the world's important treasures remained stashed here? she wondered, awestruck. Brad gave her hand a quick squeeze and she glanced back at him with an anxious smile. If the Lost Collection were indeed here, she had no idea what it might consist of. There were rumors, of course, of fabulous pieces and breathtaking artistry. Presumably he would have wanted to keep the exceptional ones out of the Nazis' hands. Perhaps she would have to open a museum. A panoply of possibilities fanned out before her as they entered an elevator and descended in silence, touched by the magnitude of the moment.

Reaching the lowest level, they stepped into a marble-floored hallway. The president stood aside, allowing them to pass through into an antechamber where two supremely serious bank officers, clad in similar gray suits, immediately rose to greet them. The president turned and shook hands with a small middle-aged man standing a few steps away, holding a briefcase.

"This is Mr. Bauer from the Zurichoise Insurance Company," the president said, making the introductions. Then he presented the bank officers with the number of the safe. Eugène was asked to sign the registry. His signature was checked. With a murmur and nod to his colleagues, one of the bank officers disappeared through a door at the back of the room. He returned several moments later with a key similar to the one Charlotte clutched in her damp palm.

This was it.

The moment had arrived.

A button was pressed and massive metal doors opened. The group followed the bank officials through the doors, passing rows of safes before they stopped before a large one, set at eye level, marked 1939.

The year it was last opened.

There was utter quiet as the bank officer placed the first key in the lock. Then he turned toward her. With shaking hands, she placed her key into the lock next to it. The two keys were turned simultaneously and with a creak the door gave way.

Specks of dust floated to the floor as the bank officer opened the door wider and all eyes stared within. Charlotte blinked. At the front of the safe sat a pile of gold ingots.

"Would you like us to remove them, *madame?*" the president asked.

"Please," she agreed, her voice faint.

One by one the ingots were placed in piles on a nearby table. As they were removed, she began to distinguish new shapes in the depths of the safe. When the last bar of gold was gone, she could see more clearly. There, neatly stacked, were a number of blue velvet jewel boxes.

She drew in her breath. Heart pounding, she glanced at Oncle Eugène. He nodded encouragingly. In an agony of anticipation she took a trepid step forward and, hands shaking, carefully pulled the front pile toward her. The boxes were flat and thin. As she removed the first one and pressed its tiny snib, she closed her eyes. The last hands to touch these had been Sylvain's. Composing herself, she raised the lid and gasped.

The necklace that lay on the white satin bed was more beautiful than any she'd ever beheld. Seconds ticked by as she stood rooted to the spot, dazzled by the piece's exquisite perfection. Flawless diamonds of remarkable shape and color completely dominated the almost invisible platinum setting that supported them. Exquisite baguette diamonds were channel-set, surrounded by smaller ones placed in pavé settings. The larger round ones, of extraordinary quality and clarity, were set in open-shoulder frustum-cone bezels. She swallowed in silent wonder, knowing what patience and experience were required to even contemplate the execution of such a piece.

The bank officer stood waiting beside her and she handed him the box, which he handed to the insurance appraiser. The small man immediately placed it on the table, and began examining the necklace with a jeweler's loop.

Tentatively Charlotte looked toward the other boxes. Could anything be lovelier than what she had just seen?

Silently she opened the next one. In it lay three bracelets. With a sharp intake of breath, she stumbled back.

''Look,'' she exclaimed.

Brad and the Cardinal moved closer. The first bracelet was almost an exact replica of the ruby cabochon piece she'd designed for the show. She stared at it, disbelieving. It had the same double strap mount, the same central stone. But this piece centered on what must be a hundred-carat star sapphire of such beauty and perfection that she wanted to weep.

Somewhere behind her, she heard Eugène murmuring. Her eyes traveled to the other two bracelets, a platinum mount centering on four square-pronged corner-held emerald-cut diamonds that had to weigh at least two carats each. God only knew what the extravaganza of perfect, round, prong-held diamonds surrounding them must weigh, but she judged there were at least twenty carats set in rows.

''Perhaps, after the lot has been appraised and the insurance rate established, you would prefer to have the collection delivered to the Baur Au Lac,'' the president noted, clearing his throat. ''We shall have to arrange for an armed guard, of course. I...I must confess, I've never seen anything like it. It is, of course, imperative that everything be fully protected. These are rare treasures.''

''Oh, yes,'' Charlotte replied, horrified at the thought of the collection leaving the bank. ''That is why all this must stay here until we decide what to do. It would be too much of a risk to remove it.''

''A good decision,'' Oncle Eugène approved. ''We shall leave Mr. Bauer to appraise the contents of the safe.''

''Very well.'' The president bowed his head in acquiescence.

"Excuse me." The bank officer next to her handed Charlotte an envelope. "This fell out of the safe as you were removing the box."

"Thank you." She stared at the elegant writing, then at Eugène. It was addressed to him. "This is for you," she said, handing him the missive reverently.

Eugène took the letter and gazed at it thoughtfully. Then he slipped it into a breast pocket under his soutane.

Regretfully, Charlotte laid the box with the bracelets onto the table. Part of her wanted to stay here all day and revel in the magnitude and beauty of the discovery, but she knew that wasn't possible—or even wise. It would be easier to work through her turbulent emotions in the peace of the suite at the Baur Au Lac.

Taking Brad's hand, she followed the others out of the vault. Had Sylvain expected to return, or had he known, deep down, that he was leaving his legacy for another generation to discover? All at once she stopped, turned and took a last look at Mr. Bauer stooped over the necklace with his equipment, a bank guard by his side.

For an instant she closed her eyes, and a strange and pulsing warmth coursed through her. "I'll do the right thing by all this, Grandfather," she whispered. Then, hand clasped in Brad's, she walked, head high, to the elevator.

Suite 529 was enchanting. Recently redecorated by the hotel director's charming wife, it reflected her exquisite taste and clever decorator's eye. Muted red, sage and gold-striped drapes hung from a central pelmet, looped onto bronze holders on each side of the vast bed. Reflected in the mirrored closet doors opposite, the whole effect was light and luminous. The suite was on the top floor under the eaves. The curtains, set against eggshell walls under a classic white ceiling and frieze, hung on brass rails at a slight angle, imbuing the room with singular charm. The effect was delightful and airy, elegant, yet cozy and comfortable. A small balcony set with cushioned chairs and a table looked out over the gray-tiled roof to the Baur Au Lac Club on the right and Lake Zurich beyond.

Charlotte had never visited the city before and found herself gazing, enchanted, at the mountains rising majestically at the far end of the lake, snow-capped peaks like frosted candy glistening in the September sun. A steamer puttered across the still waters linking Bürkli Platz Pier with Küsnacht, while to her left the dome of the opera house framed the picture-postcard scene.

"Wasn't it amazing seeing Sylvain's signature in the hotel guest book?" Brad remarked, joining her on the balcony and slipping an arm round her waist.

A soft breeze blew in from the lake as together they gazed at the pier a few hundred yards away, decked with jaunty red parasols, children playing and mothers pushing strollers, enjoying the last days of summer.

"Everything about this day is amazing," Charlotte answered, leaning her head back against his chest. "To think he stayed here with Chagall. Do you realize this is where Paulette Goddard met Erich Maria Remarque, the author of *All Quiet on the Western Front?* They met again in 1958 and got married. The concierge told me the whole story."

"Not to mention all the presidential visitors and conferences that have taken place within these walls. This place has history crawling out of the woodwork."

"I know. Frankly, I'm finding it difficult to absorb so much at once," she murmured, turning and slipping her arms around his neck. "Forty-eight hours ago, I was quaking in my shoes, terrified that my designs would be a flop. Now, suddenly I'm speaking with reporters and discovering that I've just inherited one of the world's great jewelry collections. Certainly the one with the most mystique.'' She shook her head and raised her eyes to his. ''What do you suppose we should do with it? We can't leave it sitting in the safe. But it's too sacred and too valuable to display without a great deal of planning.''

''I agree. Take your time. It's been sitting there all these years. A few more months won't hurt.'' He touched her cheek, then dropped a kiss on her mouth. ''You could open a museum.''

''True. But I have the feeling Sylvain's wishes may be expressed in the letter he left in the safe for Oncle Eugène.''

Brad planted a kiss on her forehead. ''You may be right. I think that now you need to relax. Sylvain, wherever he is, must be very proud of you. He couldn't wish for a lovelier or more talented granddaughter. But you've also got your own life to think about. By the way,'' he added, grinning, ''the Christmas-tree comment you made to that reporter in the phone interview hit the headlines.''

''What do you mean, my Christmas-tree comment?'' she asked blankly.

''Here. Take a look.'' He handed her the paper.

''Oh, Lord.'' She giggled, despite the emotions of the past few hours, and read aloud.

'' 'Newly discovered talent Charlotte MacLeod says she herself rarely wears much jewelry'—that's not much good for promoting my line, is it?'' she remarked, grimacing, then continued reading. '' 'According to Ms. MacLeod, quality and not quantity are the stamp of a truly elegant woman.'—God, I'm hardly a reference,'' she groaned, reading on, amused. '' 'I'd hate to look like a Christmas tree, Ms. MacLeod declared in a hastily arranged phone conference that took place at the Georges V hotel in Paris after the untimely demise of her cousin, designer Armand de la Vallière, whose show took Paris by storm. The absence of Ms. MacLeod's name on the program, which led to a misunderstanding as to the authorship of the designs, was apparently due to a printing mistake. Ms. MacLeod professed great sadness at her cousin's sudden heart attack shortly after the show, and declared that the la Vallière clothing line will be continued, in memory of the designer who came into his own so shortly before his death.' Well!'' She handed the paper back to Brad. ''At least Armand's reputation is preserved. I think Eugène handled that rather adroitly, don't you?''

''I never expect any less from him,'' Brad remarked with a dry laugh. He pulled her toward him and back into the room, taking a good look at her. She'd blossomed over the past few weeks, confronting her doubts and taking her destiny into her own hands. And it showed. He drew her toward the bed.

''Isn't it rather early in the day?'' she asked weakly, allowing herself to be led.

When he stopped next to the bed and slowly began undressing her, she let out a sigh, smiled and unbuttoned his shirt, quickening the pace as a shaft of heat raced through her when his fingers brushed her breasts. His hands fluttered down her ribs then slipped her skirt and panties to the floor. She stepped out of them and her blouse and bra followed.

''God, you're beautiful,'' he murmured huskily, hands coursing over her milky skin then gliding between her thighs. She let out a gasp of delight. Wherever Brad touched, no matter how briefly, his fingers left a volcano of feeling in their wake. Her body went fluid, her muscles melting. She made short work of his clothing, then pushed him onto the bed, where they lay feeling, caressing, enjoying one another. Then Charlotte drew away and Brad looked up, surprised. With a conspiratorial grin, she moved down his body, and with her hair falling around her, shielding her face, she took him gently into her mouth.

Brad let out a grateful groan. Her artist's creativity wasn't restricted to her designs, he realized. He'd never felt such pleasure. Charlotte's caresses were laced with emotion, as though her soul was being poured into every intimate kiss. When he could bear it no more he pulled her head away and, turning her over on the coverlet, thrust deep within her, feeling her moist heat sheathing him body and soul. Eyes locked, they reveled in one another, the worries and excitement of the past days forgotten as they writhed in each other's arms. Then Brad felt her urgency as she arched beneath him, drawing him deep inside until he touched her core, reaching the summit of their climb before slipping over the edge into blissful oblivion.

They'd dosed off, when the sharp ring of the telephone brought Charlotte groggily back to earth. She shifted onto her elbow, reached over Brad's naked shoulder and felt blindly for the phone on the nightstand.

"Hello."

"Darling, it's Mummy." Penelope's strained voice came clearly down the line.

"Oh, hello, Mum." She yawned, rubbed her eyes and frowned. "Is everything all right at home?"

"Yes. Genny's fine." Penelope hesitated, and Charlotte quickly sat up. "There's something you need to know, darling."

''What?'' A deep sense of foreboding came over her. She glanced fearfully at Brad, half-asleep next to her on the bed, and swallowed. ''What is it, Mummy? Tell me.''

''I think you'd better prepare yourself for a shock,'' Penelope murmured, falling silent once again.

''What is it? Don't keep me in suspense,'' Charlotte said impatiently. ''Just tell me.''

''It's John.''

''What about him?'' Her eyebrows knit and she tensed.

''He...he's awake.''

A chill ran through her as she stared at the receiver, unable to register. ''What do you mean, awake?''

''Darling, he's come out of the coma. The hospital just called. It's quite extraordinary. The doctors can barely believe it but he sat up this morning, talking and smiling as though nothing had happened.''

Charlotte shook her head, wondering if she'd heard right. Was she in the middle of some bizarre nightmare?

''Are you all right, darling? I know this is the most awful shock to you...'' Penelope's voice trailed off.

''Yes. Oh, Mummy, what am I going to do? Oh God.''

''Charlotte, are you all right, darling? You must come home, but don't worry...we'll find a way—''

''Of course. I'll...'' She passed a hand over her eyes as the news sank in. ''Mummy, I'd better call you back. I—I'll call you back.'' With a dazed movement she hung up the receiver, then stared through the window at the sparkling lake.

Never, even in her darkest hours, had she imagined something as awful as this. She glanced at Brad, heart aching. The only obstacle that could come between them and shatter their happiness had reared its ugly head.

Burying her head in her hands Charlotte collapsed among the rumpled sheets and wept. It had all been too good to be true, but now reality had caught up with her.

18

The Park Hotel normally remained closed in the autumn, but John's agents and producers made arrangements for him to recover there in the total privacy of the half-empty Swiss mountain resort of Gstaad. No one, his representatives agreed, must be allowed to see the star before he returned to his former self. After a thorough round of background checks, a small cadre of assistants—masseur, private trainer, esthetician and speech therapist, all sworn to secrecy—were placed at his personal beck and call, and a carefully prepared regimen of exercise, diet and fitness was established.

John Drummond's dramatic comeback was the hottest item in the movie world and everyone knew it.

Charlotte sat in the large, empty bar while John lounged in a chair to her left, a script open on his knee. She tried not to yawn. Ron Berkowitz, his pugnacious agent, sat opposite, his sharp eyes not missing a thing. Gina Slater, the new publicist they'd hired after John had dismissed the last one, perched on the opposite chair, neat, blond and attentive.

Charlotte felt trapped in a time warp. It was all so eerily reminiscent of the past. The ego-building conversations, the fawning laughter every time John made some mediocre joke, the relentless toadying. She leaned back on the leather couch, watching the scene before her play out as though it were a movie on a huge screen.

In some ways he'd changed, she reflected, eyeing him, recalling her first impression of the gaunt figure propped up in the hospital bed. A shudder of fear had coursed through her at the time, but had gradually diminished. It was remarkable that he had made so much progress in such a short time. Even the doctors shook their heads, amazed at the fast track John's rehabilitation was taking. He'd put on a fair amount of flesh and muscle, and gradually the traces of illness had faded. Watching him now it was hard to assimilate that the dynamic, very much alive creature seated next to her could be the same wax-like mannequin she'd visited only weeks ago. At times he could be disconcertingly tender toward her, rather like some of the roles he'd played in past movies. That in itself was proof he hadn't fully recovered, she thought cynically.

Her eyes narrowed and her mind wandered. It had been more than a month since she'd left Brad and the Baur Au Lac in a horrified daze, yet still she hadn't told her husband she was leaving him for good. She swallowed, remembering the deep sadness in Brad's eyes as they'd kissed goodbye. He'd been so understanding and gentle, she remembered, swallowing the sob that clutched her throat. He'd been the one to tell her to go, to muster up her courage and get on with it.

And now he'd returned to New York. It was not clear why, now that he'd given up the CEOship of Harcourts, and she frowned. Of course, the twins required his presence, and all the changes that he was implementing in his life needed to be administered. She'd barely talked to him since that last day in Zurich, she'd been so consumed with John's recovery, and then the aftermath of her success in Paris. There were brief phone calls, of course, a quick meeting, a kiss and a hug at Strathaird before she'd left for Switzerland, but no time to share thoughts, to tell him how much she truly loved him, how much she missed not having him in her life. He'd seemed distant at that last encounter, she recalled, a niggling sense of impending doom descending over her. It was almost as though he'd taken a step back. She fidgeted and bit her nail, wishing she could just hop on a plane, go to New York and topple straight into his arms. She felt lonely and in limbo, on edge with the knowledge that she still had to extricate herself from what was becoming an increasingly complicated situation.

Berkowitz had planted various teary stories in the press about how John's desire to see his wife and daughter again were the only things he'd been conscious of during his lengthy coma. Much to her dismay, Charlotte had been portrayed as his long-suffering but ever-faithful bedside companion—nurses at the hospital having vouched for her regular visits—and now John's career comeback was being billed as a testament to the restorative powers of their rediscovered love. If she hadn't been consumed with managing her own sudden fame, trying to pull together all the details of the jewelry line, she would have insisted Berkowitz issue a retraction.

But it was too late for regrets. The damage was done. Plus, orders for her work were flowing in every day from around the world. Incredibly, she was producing inspired drawings despite the problems surrounding her, scanning the final results into her laptop before sending them with a detailed description to Moira back in Skye. In fact, drawing was her only means of escape. It allowed her to flee into her imagination, avoid the phone calls from magazines and ignore her new publicist's insistence they put together a line for some fancy department store in New York.

She wanted none of that. Right now, all she wanted was to sort out her private life once and for all. She worried about Genny, back on the island with her mother. Instead of being thrilled at the news of John's recovery, as Charlotte had anticipated, the child had instead retreated into her shell. It was puzzling. When she'd brought Genny to see her father, John had lavished her with attention, showered her with extravagant gifts and taken her on his knee, something he'd never done previously. Surely Genny must have longed for such an affectionate reunion.

She focused for a brief moment on what Berkowitz was saying, but her mind was still on Genny. The child's limp had become more pronounced and her dreams more fearful since her father's recovery. They'd even had a bed-wetting incident, something that had not occurred for years. Perhaps she should tell Mummy to get her an appointment with a top psychologist.

She listened once more to Berkowitz and the others, noticing how their voices echoed through the large vacant space. In winter, the room buzzed with visitors assembled around the huge open fireplace, but now was stark and empty. She glanced at the bored uniformed waiter idly polishing glasses behind the bar and felt suddenly trapped in the same old celluloid cage of jaded glitz and glamour, where nothing but John's career mattered.

This wasn't what she wanted! She'd be damned if she was going to relive a life she'd loathed the first time round. She had new dreams to strive for, dreams of her own where John had no place: a lifetime with Brad, a family with Genny and the twins. That and deciding the destiny of Sylvain's Lost Collection were what really counted.

A smile hovered as she thought of the long phone calls with Oncle Eugène these past few weeks, the cherished conversations that had taught her so much about the past that was unexpectedly shaping her future. The letter Sylvain had left for Oncle Eugène in the safe had clearly outlined her grandfather's hopes for the future, some of which had subsequently become real. He'd written eloquently of his wish that there would one day be a recognized State of Israel. His dream had come true only a few years after his death, she reflected, pondering the idea of donating several pieces of the collection to the Israel Museum in Jerusalem. It seemed appropriate that Sylvain's memory be honored there.

As Gina subserviently handed John a preview of an article about to run in *Vanity Fair*, Charlotte's disgust returned. *If his comeback is a flop, they'll all run, like rats from a sinking ship*, she thought.

"What do you think, Charlotte?" Ron turned his head toward her, looking like a missile ready to launch.

"Uh, I think it's a little too long," she commented, presuming they were referring to the article.

Ron and Gina exchanged a quick, irritated glance, then Ron frowned. "You think we should cut it?"

"She hasn't been listening to a word you've been saying," John interrupted. He sounded affectionate but she caught the familiar tone that spelled trouble.

She shuddered.

Downing a sip of white wine, she forced herself to concentrate on the upcoming schedule, the wave of articles and publicity events, the rerelease of John's last movie. She knew she had no intention of being a part of it.

The question eating her gut was when to drop the bombshell.

The more she delayed, the more involved she would inevitably become. But was it fair to announce her departure before John was fully recovered?

She glanced at him and frowned. He'd always been strikingly handsome, of course, but his well-defined features had taken on a new maturity and charm. If anything, he was better-looking than before. And his personality had altered somewhat. But how much of that change was put on for her benefit? The fact that she refused to sleep with him must immediately have set him on alert, but he'd been almost gracious about it. The old John wouldn't have hesitated to force himself on her. Just, she reminded herself, as he wouldn't think twice about feigning weakness if he thought it would keep her by his side.

Did she owe him the benefit of the doubt? After all, he was the father of her daughter. Yet her life was on hold while she catered to this man who'd brought her so much unhappiness. Of course, now that Brad was back in New York, she reflected glumly, wouldn't he think twice about becoming permanently involved with a woman like her, whose life was jam-packed with complications? In her most agonizing moments, she worried that he might be reconsidering a relationship with Sylvia. It certainly promised him a saner existence than any he could ever hope for with her.

Unconsciously she began biting her nail again. Should she give this marriage another chance for Genny's sake? Did she have the right to subject her daughter to a drama that would inevitably be splattered on the front page of every tabloid? It was not that she didn't want to face the divorce proceedings, she rationalized, it was just simply the deep-rooted fear of making any more mistakes.

She should have told John the whole truth yesterday, when he'd found out that she'd filed for divorce. But he'd turned so pale, and she'd wanted to avoid a row. When he'd insisted she put an immediate stop to the divorce proceedings, she'd been noncommittal.

But for the first time, he'd reminded her of the John of old.

He'd moved so swiftly, taking her in his arms and holding her alarmingly close, leaving her stifled and anxious. She'd quickly found an excuse to leave the room.

She wasn't surprised this morning when Berkowitz sought her out—John must have run to him in a panic— and patiently explained to her, as though to a small child, all the disadvantages of a divorce at this time.

She'd lied and told him she'd think about it. And hated herself for being a coward. It was only postponing the inevitable.

She'd moved on in every sense. Even the physical terror that John's presence sometimes raised was nothing but past conditioning. It had been an exhilarating surprise to discover that the guilt, fear and anxiety that had clouded so much of her life had disappeared. She could now view John critically, as though confronted by a complete stranger. Yet until she took the final step, she would remain inextricably tied to her old life. And only she could break the links and force the chain to give.

Unable to sit still, she got up and stretched. "I'm going down for my massage," she said.

"Okay, darling. I'll see you later." John blew her a kiss and flashed the smile he'd been studying in his old photographs before turning his attention back to Gina. Charlotte wondered fleetingly if they were already sleeping together. She stifled a hysterical giggle, trying to imagine what Gina would think if she told her to go for it. What was it that had attracted her to someone as superficial and empty and cruel as her husband? she wondered. Her steps echoing dully through the vacant hall, she was cynically amused by the way John never asked for her opinion or permission, but merely expected her to comply as she had in the past. It just went to show what a wet rag she'd been.

Well, she reflected as she stepped down the stairs to the spa, those days were over. John might be making an effort to be nice. Perhaps he'd even changed.

But so had she.

Collecting a couple of towels at the reception desk, she entered the empty locker room and sank onto the wooden bench. The truth was, she wasn't the same person, and however hard they tried to ignore that, their marriage would never work. She must screw up her courage and tell him that she was leaving him, for all their sakes.

She got up and undressed, feeling lighter for the first time since that last happy day with Brad in Zurich. Wrapping her hair in a towel, she headed for the steam room. At the first opportunity she had to catch John alone, she would go ahead and impart her decision.

And deal with the consequences once the deed was done.

Sylvia glanced across the massive desk that would soon be hers and frowned. Brad didn't look great. He seemed tired and edgy and not at all himself. She'd never seen him like this before and she didn't like it. She took a final glance at the memo from marketing before laying it down, wondering if his mood had anything to do with the sudden reappearance of Charlotte's hunky husband. Damn inconvenient, she mused, feeling sorry for him.

Brad was a good guy. Unfailingly kind. Both a player and a gentleman. And even though he'd betrayed her emotionally, she'd gotten over that. She understood that they weren't suited and that what was happening between him and Charlotte dated back a long time. Now that she was able to think of him as a friend and colleague, not a lover, she truly hoped the romance between him and Charlotte would flourish. Though with John Drummond as competition, she had her doubts.

The guy was the hottest thing going right now. All the entertainment shows, and even some of the networks, had run pieces on his miraculous resurrection and pending return to the big screen. The fact the movie star was holed up somewhere secret, recuperating, while rumors swirled around him, only fanned the public's interest. From a strictly practical sense, Charlotte would be an idiot to drop him now that she had her own fame and fortune in the offing. Luckily for Brad, Charlotte had never struck her as the pragmatic type.

Sylvia jotted a note to remind herself to call Charlotte. She'd mentioned her jewelry line to the director of Bergdorf's, who was dying to get her hands on an exclusive deal. Maybe she could engineer an agreement, and somehow get Charlotte to New York in the process.

She peered at Brad, eyebrows knit over the document he was perusing. He'd changed from the man she'd thought herself in love with; he was softer now around the edges. Personally she preferred the harder, tougher Brad. Charlotte was probably right for him, though. She took a sip of Evian from her ever-present bottle, wondering what the outcome of all this would be, now able to view it from a distant shore since her own future was settled.

At first she'd been scared that once the news got out that she was single again, the invitations would stop pouring in. Surprisingly, they hadn't. Or at least not significantly. She still wasn't *exactly* where she wanted to be—that would take a bit of time and maneuvering. But once she was officially named CEO of Harcourts, she'd wield more than a little clout. Still, she yearned to make some sort of statement on her own, something that had nothing to do with Harcourts and yet elevated her in the eyes of New York society.

She wanted to make her own mark.

Brad shifted in his chair, and she looked up, concerned by the brooding fatigue she saw there. "This seems in order," he said dully, tossing the paper on the desk. "Still, better pass it through the legal department just in case."

"Fine. You look as though you could use a pick-me-up." There were lines around his eyes that hadn't been there a couple of months back. "How about we chow down at my new place? You'll like it. After seeing Jeffrey Bilhuber's fantastic work at the Soho Grand, I paid him a fortune to do my interiors. We can pick up some Thai on the way home."

"Good idea. The twins are hanging out with friends tonight." He loosened his tie. "I could use a drink."

"Coming right up. Let's get out of here." She picked up her purse, trying to decide how to get Brad to tell her what was on his mind. He obviously needed someone to talk to. And why not to her? After all, she'd been with the man for over five years. That still counted for something.

* * *

An hour later, Brad sat sipping scotch and water at the bar in Sylvia's sleekly contemporary penthouse on Central Park West. The Manhattan skyline, ringing the vast expanse of the park like a glittering necklace, almost took his breath away. He loved this view, but right now he wished he were back in Skye. Strathaird needed him and he needed Strathaird. But after his last brief meeting with Charlotte, he'd decided to stay away. She'd acted vague, almost aloof. They didn't need to talk for him to realize she wanted to be on her own to sort things through.

That was a month ago.

Now he wondered if the decision he feared so much had already been made. Maybe she'd gone back to John and didn't have the guts to tell him.

How presumptuous they'd been to believe nothing could come between them, even as the one improbable event able to destroy their happiness had been barreling in on them like a tidal wave. He could still picture the emotions on her face as she'd told him the news—shock, dismay and, most ominously, duty.

He'd returned here, to the city he knew and loved, to the house he shared with the twins, and to hard work, the only antidote he knew. It had rescued him once, and he hoped would do so again. At least transferring his duties to Sylvia required enough time and attention to keep his mind off the problem, if only for a few hours.

He took a long sip of his drink. If the truth be told, *he* was the one who'd kept the conversations with Charlotte short and to the point. He'd stopped phoning, waiting for her to take the initiative, still clinging to the possibility that she might have enough courage to make the break.

But as the weeks trailed by and no news came, he'd realized he was being stupid. Charlotte was Charlotte, and she would never change. She'd allow her guilt—over depriving Genny of a father, over leaving the man to whom she'd given so many years—to dictate the way she lived. Her own needs and desires wouldn't even be part of the equation.

And he was damned if he was going to stand around, watching her crawl back into her self-designated hell.

Better never to see her again.

Perhaps she was right, he sighed. Now that Genny had her father back, the trauma of losing him again through divorce might simply be too great. He just hoped Charlotte wouldn't allow her own newfound talent to be over-shadowed by John's recovery. Being able to bury herself in work might be the only way to make that marriage bearable.

But if John so much as raised a finger to her, he would personally tear him limb from limb. He gripped his glass, knuckles strained and white; what was truly killing him was the thought of her in another man's arms.

He placed the glass on the granite counter with a thud. He was a fool to think he could banish her from his being, he realized, pouring another stiff whiskey while Sylvia puttered around the glistening chrome kitchen, un-packing the take-out they'd picked up. He could pretend to be reasonable and gentlemanly, but when it came to Charlotte, the code of conduct he'd followed all his life collapsed. And that, he decided, fists clenching, was why he had to stay away.

"Here you are." Sylvia placed two elegantly prepared Japanese porcelain plates onto the sisal-and-leather place mats. A single white orchid was reflected in the gleaming counter.

"This looks yummy," she said, perching on a bar stool opposite and sending him a quick glance. "Boy, am I hungry. Try it, it's good," she remarked, nibbling some steamed vegetable dumplings and seeing him glance indifferently at the food.

"I guess I'm not that hungry."

"You gotta eat. Sitting round moping about Charlotte isn't going to do you any good," she remarked, pursing her lips. "You look like shit, by the way."

"Gee, thanks." He let out a short, humorless laugh. "And I'm not moping about Charlotte," he added, irritated.

"Yeah, right. Who exactly are you trying to fool, Bradley Ward?" she asked sweetly, tilting her head.

Their eyes met and held, then he took a long sip of his drink. "Guess you know me too well, huh?"

"I should hope so, after all this time. Heck, we lived together long enough."

"Ouch!"

"Sorry." She waved a manicured hand. "I didn't mean that the wrong way. You know very well that I think things have turned out for the best. I just want you to be happy too," she added, dipping her fork into the pad thai.

"Yeah, well...you know how it is."

"Nope. I don't. Perhaps you'd like to tell me?"

"Give a guy a break, Syl," he muttered, beginning to eat.

"Okay, so you're mad because Charlotte's still sorting things out with her husband. What's the big deal? Give her a chance."

"She's not sorting out zip. She's gone back to him."

"Did she tell you that?" Sylvia asked, fork frozen midair, watching his reactions.

"No, not exactly. But it's clear enough. John Drummond is back on the scene. Whenever I've phoned the number she gave me, some officious prick named Berkowitz answers and tells me *Mrs. Drummond* is out walking the fucking dog with her husband, or that *the Drummonds* are indisposed.'' He pushed his plate away and leaned back in his chair, disgusted.

''Look, Brad, it's only normal that she's at the guy's side at a time like this. What about later?''

He ran his fingers through his hair. ''I think she's decided to stay,'' he sighed. ''For Genny's sake, above all else.''

''Boy, you sure don't give her much credit, do you?'' she said, flashing him a curious look. ''I thought you guys were *Love Story* with a happy ending.''

''I guess I did too. Just goes to show.''

Sylvia pushed back her stool and crossed the kitchen to the refrigerator, pulling out a bottle of his favorite Pouilly-Fuissé. ''Come on, let's go sit over there and you can tell me your troubles.'' She gestured to a massive beige Ultrasuede sectional that dominated one corner of the apartment.

''Good Lord,'' Brad remarked, ''you sure we won't get lost in that thing?''

''Jeffrey wanted it even bigger. He thinks there's nothing more horrifying than three people wedged together on a sofa. Says it's like waiting at a luxurious bus stop.''

''Hell, this is more like an airplane runway.''

''Well, one doesn't argue with New York's hottest designer.'' She laughed, placing two glasses on an equally enormous rock-slab coffee table and settling back on the sectional's plump cushions. ''So let me get this straight. You're just going to back off and let the best man win, is that it?'' She took a sip, glancing critically at her glass. ''Not bad,'' she murmured, watching him bristle. Good. She was finally getting a reaction.

''It's not that simple, Syl. Charlie has a hell of a lot

more on her plate than just John Drummond to deal with. She has a whole new life in front of her now that her designs have been such a success. Plus, she has the Lost Collection to deal with,'' he muttered, lifting his glass.

"Lost Collection?" Sylvia pushed a strand of glossy blond hair behind her ear, suddenly attentive. "What collection are you referring to?"

"Shit," Brad exclaimed, annoyed at himself. "I shouldn't have mentioned it. I guess I must be more tired than I thought."

"Well, the cat's out of the bag, babe, so you might as well tell me about it. You know very well it won't go any further."

He hesitated, then set his glass down. "I know I can trust you, Syl. If I didn't, you wouldn't be taking over Harcourts. But this isn't my secret to tell."

"It's weighing you down all the same. Why not get it off your chest?"

He sat motionless for a few seconds, then nodded his head imperceptibly. "Okay, but this is for your ears only, got it?"

"Scout's honor." She raised her hand and smiled.

A wave of relief swept over him. Syl was right. He needed to bounce this off someone, and she was certainly the best person around. He pondered a moment, wondering where exactly to begin. "You remember Armand and how obsessed he was with Sylvain de Rothberg?"

"Yeah." She nodded. "His dying of a heart attack right after his show sure was weird," she remarked, frowning. "Hey, wasn't Rothberg the guy whose fabulous jewelry collection was lost during the war?" she exclaimed, suddenly excited.

"Not lost. Hidden. That is, until now."

"Wow!" Sylvia's eyes widened in understanding. "But how? When?"

"Remember when Charlie's watch was stolen?"

"Of course."

"Armand was the one who took it."

"You're kidding!" Her fork clattered to her plate. "What a jerk. Why?"

"Well, it's rather a long story," he began, explaining how Armand had come to believe he was Sylvain de Rothberg's legitimate son, and had thought—rightly, as it turned out—that the watch held some clue as to the Lost Collection's whereabouts.

"But how did the MacLeod family end up with the watch?" Sylvia asked, eyebrows knit in a puzzled frown, trying to keep the facts straight.

"Sylvain's wife, Geneviève, was massacred at Oura-dour, days after her baby's birth. Dex and the Cardinal knew they had to get the kid out of France, because if Sylvain was caught by the Gestapo, they wouldn't hesi-tate to use the baby as leverage to make him surrender. It could have compromised the whole Resistance opera-tion in that area. Sylvain put his watch around his son's ankle, and then the baby was smuggled to Skye."

"Wow! You have to be kidding. It sounds like the movies!"

"I kid you not."

"So who was the baby?"

"David MacLeod."

"You mean Charlotte's dad?" she squeaked, hands clasping the stem of her glass, excited.

"Yes. Angus MacLeod and Flora pretended the baby was a twin of Nathalie, their daughter born days later."

"Wow!" she repeated, shaking her head. "This is bet-ter than a movie. Are you *sure* it's real, Brad? You're not just making this story up? Here, have some more wine,'' she added, pouring another generous glass. ''It's simply amazing. And—oh my God, now I'm getting it,'' she gasped, setting the bottle on the table with a bang. ''Somehow the watch led you guys to the missing jewelry, and Charlotte's inherited the lot!''

''Yep.'' He nodded, detailing the events that had brought them to the safe in Zurich. ''It was all there,'' he concluded, ''exactly where Sylvain had deposited it in 1939.''

''Unbelievable,'' she murmured. ''Charlotte must have been totally amazed.''

''Put it this way, she's had a lot to absorb in the past few weeks,'' he said dryly.

''What on earth is she going to do with it? Heck, even little ol' me from Arkansas knows Rothberg's Lost Collection would be like, the Holy Grail of the jewelry world.'' She giggled as Brad stared pointedly at the sumptuous surroundings and serious artwork on the cream-colored walls. ''Okay, so I'll admit I'm a little more sophisticated than I used to be. Still,'' she said, suddenly serious, ''that's an immense responsibility. She'll need to choose her venue very carefully. A museum would be ideal, someplace of irreproachable repute.''

''Yes. Well, maybe now you can understand why I'm leaving her alone to make her own decisions. You can imagine the uproar once the press gets a hold of this.''

''I certainly can,'' she added soberly. ''What a story. And on top of that, her husband wakes up and screws you guys. Poor kid. This sure has been her year for surprises.''

''That's the understatement of the decade.''

Lifting her glass, Sylvia moved over to the wide windows overlooking the park. This was so different to her own life, to all she'd had to contend with, and she couldn't help imagining what it must feel like to suddenly discover you owned one of the world's legendary art collections.

Daunting but wonderful, to say the least.

She wondered what she would do in similar circumstances. Probably sell part of it and invest the proceeds in real estate, she reflected, eyes resting on a building she coveted several blocks down. But knowing Charlotte, she'd be horrified to break up the collection.

And who knew, she mused, gazing out over the city, maybe she was right. She turned. Brad was still seated at the sectional, morosely sipping his wine. She had to figure out a way to help these two. From what Brad had hinted about Charlotte's marriage, she'd never find happiness with John Drummond, even if he was the world's hottest Adonis. He was a bastard and an abuser and she had her own reasons for hating men like that. And she didn't care what anyone said. Coma or no coma, people did not change, *ever*. Too bad the actor was such a lout, though. Now she'd never be able to see his gorgeous face without wanting to give him a good kick in the balls.

"I'd better get on home," Brad said, glancing at his wrist. "The twins'll be waiting up for me. Hey, do you want to go to Newport this weekend? There's some sailing event the kids want to watch."

"Sure, why not?" She smiled, knowing from his tone that he'd have issued the same invitation to a buddy.

"And, Syl, thanks for dinner and for listening. You were right. I needed to get some of that off my chest." He smiled, dropped a kiss on her cheek and picked up his blazer, throwing it casually over his shoulder.

"Anytime." She gave him a friendly hug.

For a moment they stood locked in each other's arms. Incredible, she reflected as they broke apart with easy grins, how a few weeks ago that same hug would have stirred so many feelings. But this newly platonic relationship felt right.

She couldn't have him as a husband, but it felt good to know he would remain her friend.

Three days later, Mr. Mackay, Strathaird's administrator, called with the news that a severe storm had hit Skye. Many of the tenant cottages had suffered serious damage.

It meant having to return at once.

Leaving Sylvia in charge at Harcourts, he made the journey back across the Atlantic with mixed feelings. Part of him craved Strathaird. The other part wanted to stay as far away as possible from anything that reminded him of Charlotte. But he had little choice. Arriving in Glasgow, he once more decided to drive up north and went straight to the car rental desk. The drive gave him time to make the break between the two worlds he now occupied.

Several hours later, he drove over the bridge from the mainland, gusts of westerly wind shaking the car as he finally reached the island. Seeing the sun setting languorously over Skye, creating a postcard-perfect picture, it was hard to believe, only days before, ravaging winds and rain had left substantial damage in their wake.

Realizing he was hungry, Brad turned off the road at Armadale, deciding to stop and have a sandwich. It would save Aunt Penn from having to bother about dinner, he figured, drawing up in front of a pub he vaguely recalled. When he finally placed it, he frowned. Penelope had pointed it out to him as the last stop Charlie and

John Drummond had made before the fateful accident several years ago that had injured Genny's leg.

He parked in the small gravel parking lot that looked out over the swells and, fighting blustering gusts, made his way toward the low white building. The sign above the door creaked in the wind as he entered.

Inside, the atmosphere was cozy, noisy and welcoming. A substantial Friday-night crowd was already assembled in the low-beamed taproom, its paneled walls scarred with age and memories, covered with hundreds of photographs plastered on every square inch of free space. The pub boasted a four-hundred-year reputation, he recalled, moving toward the bar. It was said that Bonnie Prince Charlie himself had stopped here for a drink. But then, quite a few places on Skye boasted the same.

He sat at the bar and smiled at the burly individual in a bright tartan waistcoat and jaunty bow tie polishing glasses behind the counter.

''Now, what canna' I do fer ye', ma'lord?''

''Talisker, please.'' It was apparently impossible to travel incognito on the island.

''Here ye go. I'm Frankie Calhoun, by the way,'' he added, extending a friendly hand and a broad smile.

''Brad Ward,'' he replied automatically.

''In America, maybe—'' the man let out a loud guffaw ''—but here on the island yer' known as the MacLeod.''

Brad grinned. Frankie picked up a glass that was never out of reach and raised it. ''Te' yer very gud' health, ma'lord.'' Brad raised his and together they drank. ''How's Miss Charlotte doing these days?'' Frankie asked, taking a pint glass off the shelf behind him and turning to the taps on his left, carefully setting about the intricate task of building a head of Guinness for the middle-aged man two stools down.

"She's doing okay. You heard about her success in Paris, of course?"

"Aye, that we did. 'Tis a wondrous thing indeed, and we're all mighty proud of the wee lass. She's a credit te' us all. Te' think of all that lovely jewelry being made right here on Skye warms the cockles of ma' heart." He let out a gusty sigh. "But I dinna' ken if I like that actor husband of hers coming out of his coma, though," he added with a shake of his curly gray head and a doubtful sniff. "If ye ask me," he went on, leaning closer and lowering his voice, "he was better off where he was."

Brad could not have agreed more, but he wasn't about to voice an opinion. He saw the man for whom Frankie had built the pint nod in silent agreement.

"A' remember the day they were in here," he suddenly remarked, turning sideways. The man wore a well-worn Arran sweater and a faded tweed cap. "A' never understood how that accident came about," he added, frowning.

"Why not?" Brad sipped, attentive now, watching closely as the man exchanged a glance with Frankie before continuing.

"Well, a' suppose it's none of my affair and a' shouldna' be poking ma' nose in others' business," he murmured with the look of one who has every intention of doing just that, "but if a' recall rightly, John Drummond was the one holding the car keys when they left here that night."

"Aye, that's true," another voice joined in and Brad turned toward a small wiry man in his late thirties nodding vigorously from the far, dusky corner of the pub. "They were quarreling about who should drive. She said she was too tired."

"Aye, and he marched out in a huff with the keys.

Didn't even bother to hold the door for his wife and the wee girl,'' Frankie added disapprovingly. ''No manners at all, these acting types.''

''A' always found it strange the driver's seat was set so far back,'' the man in the corner continued, taking a long ponderous puff on his pipe.

''Jimmy's the mechanic who saw to the car afterward,'' Frankie explained, jerking his thumb at the man in the corner, who had risen from the worn leather bench and was making his way, glass in hand, toward the bar. ''Miss Charlotte's a tall lass,'' Jimmy said, reaching Brad's side, ''but nae' sae' tall as that.'' He placed his empty glass on the counter.

''Give us another round, Frankie,'' Brad ordered, determined to find out all he could. Was it possible that John and not Charlotte had been driving the car that awful night? But if so, how had Drummond kept the matter hushed up all this time? It seemed far-fetched, but if Charlotte had been knocked unconscious, he might have had just enough time to switch places with her. His pulse quickened as he listened for a few more minutes to the opinions being bandied about. No one flat out accused Drummond of concealing his role in the accident, but it was clear to him the locals believed the man guilty all the same.

If so, what could he do about it? he asked himself angrily. Go running to Charlotte and try to win her away from Drummond with this new piece of damning evidence? Not bloody likely.

He finished his drink in one go, ordered another round for the house, and after an extended bout of warm handshaking, left the pub.

It would not surprise him to learn John Drummond might have gone to such extremes, he reflected, gripped by icy fury as the rental car wound up the coast of the island. He'd never known anyone so preoccupied with his own image. It was just possible that the threat of bad press had made him do the unthinkable.

Then, all of a sudden, he stepped on the brake and took the next bend very slowly, struck by a chilling thought.

Charlotte had been found unconscious at the scene, but Genny, despite her injury, had been found awake and quietly whimpering.

Good God, he speculated numbly, what had she possibly witnessed?

19

Gstaad was dead during the month of October and Charlotte wandered aimlessly down the middle of the empty cobblestone promenade, passing darkened shop windows that during the holiday season abounded with enticing trinkets and gorgeous woolens.

But she didn't care. Anything to escape from the endless hype, the never-ending ego-boosting taking place up the road in the echoing salons of the Park Hotel. She stopped and listened to the soft sound of water pouring from the spout into the stone fountain, and the murmur of lilting Swiss German as she passed two elderly ladies in green loden coats, chatting opposite the pharmacy. It felt normal and comforting, and worlds away from Berkowitz, Gina and the rest of John's entourage. She couldn't bear listening to them discuss their complicated strategies any longer. Tonight, she'd tell John the truth: she was leaving him and the marriage was over. She glanced into the window of Cartier, staring at the vacant stands where diamonds usually glittered. Perhaps she should open a store here, she reflected absently. The past few weeks had been filled with endless phone calls, magazine interviews and press releases. The flow of orders had been unending.

Her cell phone rang. She answered it quickly, glad of the distraction.

"Hello." She turned and wandered down the street, waving to the waiter at the Rialto, one of the few restaurants still open at this time of year.

"Charlotte?"

"Speaking." She didn't recognize the voice.

"This is Sylvia Hansen."

"Hello, Sylvia," she murmured, face flushing. She hadn't spoken to the woman after her departure from Skye. Since then, the engagement had been broken and she herself was the cause. She swallowed, suddenly tongue-tied.

"Brad mentioned you were in Gstaad. That must suck at this time of year. How's the weather?"

"Lousy. It's starting to rain."

"Here it's okay. But that's not why I'm calling."

"Oh?" Charlotte waited anxiously.

"No. I…look, Charlotte, you mustn't be mad at Brad, but he told me about your grandfather and the Lost Collection."

Charlotte jolted and stared, stony-faced, at the varied array of chocolate truffles in the window of the Early Beck bakery. "He had no business mentioning it to you or anyone," she said stiffly.

"I know. I'm aware of that. But he's been pretty down the past few days. I think he needed to let some things out."

"Is he all right?" she asked anxiously, anger at Brad's indiscretion replaced instantly by concern.

"He's gone back to Skye. You heard about the storm, right?"

"Yes. It was awful. But everyone's fine, thank goodness. Perhaps you'd better tell me what he told you about the collection."

"Basically that you don't know what to do with it."

"That's true," she admitted reluctantly.

"I can understand *that*," Sylvia's voice sounded sympathetic. "To be landed so unexpectedly with a responsibility of that nature and worth must be pretty staggering."

"Yes, it was—is." Charlotte hesitated. "Is Brad okay?"

"I guess." Sylvia sounded doubtful and Charlotte frowned. "I see him quite a bit at the office. He came over to my new place for take-out Thai the other night. That's when he told me about the collection. He's in one of those don't-touch-me-I'm-in-my-cave type modes. I've seen him better."

Charlotte let out a deep sigh and held back tears. She could hardly expect things to be otherwise, given how poorly she'd treated him. All the more reason for her to take the bull by the horns and get on with telling John the marriage couldn't be salvaged. Then she could go to Brad with a clear conscience in the hopes that he might still want to make a life together.

"You there?"

"Of course, sorry, just thinking," she murmured. It was beginning to drizzle. Charlotte concentrated, aware that if Sylvia had mentioned the Lost Collection, it was for a reason.

As though reading her thoughts, Sylvia continued. "You must be wondering why I'm calling you."

"Well, yes, as a matter of fact, I am. I mean—"

"Don't worry. No hard feelings, Charlotte," Sylvia interrupted quickly. "Everything's worked out just fine for me. I won't say I wasn't pissed when I realized you and Brad had a thing for one another, but that's all past history. I'll be CEO of Harcourts before the end of the year, and to tell you the truth, honey, at this point I think I'm getting the better deal. Brad's been a bear to be around. You've got him with my blessing.''

"I see." She let out a relieved sigh. "Thank you for…for being honest. It's more than I deserve."

"Hey, stop beating yourself up over it. The point is, Charlotte, I have an idea for your collection."

"What sort of an idea?" she asked warily. Brad should not have given away her secret. Sylvia probably had found some buyer and that was the last thing she wanted. She would never consider selling any of her grandfather's pieces. They were a collection and would remain as such.

"Listen. There's an exhibition next month at the Met. A retrospective on pre-World War II art, fashion and lifestyle. It occurred to me that this could be the ideal venue to present the collection to the public. I'm sure they'd do a fantastic job. They might even do a special Sylvain de Rothberg exhibit in a room of its own."

Despite the protests that flew to her lips, Charlotte hesitated. The Met was the Met, and Sylvain had loved New York. And the rest of the Rothberg family was still there. Sylvia was right. What better place than the Metropolitan Museum of Art to display a collection of such important historical and artistic value?

"But surely there wouldn't be time to arrange it," she said finally, walking down the street, past Wittwer's flower shop and into Charlie's Tearoom.

"Not a problem."

"How do you know?" she asked suspiciously, seating herself on one of the aqua benches, following the movement of kids jumping the ramps in the skate park through the window to her left.

"Well, I can't be absolutely certain, as I haven't contacted anyone yet—and wouldn't dream of doing so without your consent, of course. But I'm sure that if you agreed—within, let's say in the next forty-eight hours?— I could get it organized."

"Must I decide so soon?"

"It'll be on a countdown as it is."

"True," she acknowledged, the idea growing on her by the minute.

"I'll do everything I can to help put this together, Charlotte."

It was incredibly decent of Sylvia to want to do this for her, she realized. "Let me think it over. In principle I like the idea. I think you're right. The Met is probably the ideal venue for sharing the collection with the public."

"Look, I know you're going through a tough time right now," Sylvia said, sounding suddenly sensitive to the doubt in Charlotte's voice. "Is there anything I can do?"

"Thanks. But the only person who can clean up the mess I've managed to create for myself is me."

"I understand."

"I'll get back to you tomorrow or the day after, then." She hesitated. "Are you *sure* there would be enough time to organize this properly? Goodness, they must have been planning their prewar exhibition for months."

"Years, but believe me, honey, if they could get their hands on something like this, they won't let it pass, even if they have to work double teams twenty-four seven."

Charlotte laughed. "You're an amazing woman, Sylvia. I'll talk to Oncle Eugène tonight. He's been so closely involved in all this that I couldn't really make a decision without asking his opinion.''

''Of course.''

''And Sylvia?'' Charlotte watched the waitress approach. ''I'm sorry about everything that happened.''

''Forget it. Believe me, you send this collection my way and it'll more than make up for any damage. We'll have the society biddies gnashing their teeth with envy.'' Her contagious laugh rippled down the line and Charlotte grinned before laying down the phone. Turning to Heidi, the smiling blond waitress whom she'd come to know from the time she spent sitting here in the past couple of weeks, she ordered a cup of thick hot chocolate. Sylvia's idea might just prove to be the answer. As for Brad, knowing she'd decided to face the situation with John tonight left her feeling better than she had in days.

Would the old Cardinal agree? Sylvia almost pulled a nail ragged with worry, but then remembered she was due at Dolores Rawlinson's penthouse for dinner and stopped herself. Laying down the receiver, she prowled her office excitedly. If Charlotte agreed to the exhibition, it was a major piece of good fortune and the unique opportunity she'd been seeking.

Amazing that it had taken Brad's abandonment for everything to suddenly fall into place for her. And to think that Charlotte, of all people, might help engineer her social triumph. She walked to the window, flexed her fingers and bit her lip impatiently.

It was so close it hurt.

Anyone who was anyone would know that she, Sylvia Hansen, future CEO of Harcourts, was the one who had pulled this together and brought the legendary Lost Collection to the people of New York. Eat your heart out, Blaine Trump! She felt like dancing with glee.

Returning to her desk, she sat down again and forced herself to relax. A few weeks ago she'd been in the depths of despair because of losing Brad. And now look at her! She was on the fast track to a damn fine future.

Life sure had a funny way of fixing itself.

Outside, the wind howled, but here in the sitting room a fire crackled, casting a warm glow on two gilt mirrors that reflected the muted pattern of the new silk drapes. On the rug before the grate, Genny sat curled, playing Pick Up Sticks. Brad lounged thoughtfully next to her in the armchair, ankle thrown over one leg and Rufus's massive head snoring lazily atop the other.

Penelope glimpsed at her watch. "Time for bed, pumpkin," she announced.

"Oh, Granny," Genny moaned.

Brad and Penelope shared an understanding grin. Penelope had blossomed over the past months, he reflected, admiring the way her blue eyes matched the soft hue of her cashmere twinset.

"You need to be up early for the expedition tomorrow," Penelope insisted. But Genny tossed her head in a huff and her shoulders slumped.

He frowned. There was something different about the child, a sort of melancholy. "Don't you want to go tomorrow?" he asked.

"I don't care." Genny gave an indifferent shrug before picking the sticks up one by one and slipping them into their box.

"Why not, darling? I thought you were looking forward to it. You love going to Inverness." Penelope stroked the child's hair, concerned. When Genny pulled crossly away, she exchanged a worried look with Brad. "Perhaps you should stay at home if you don't want to go."

"I never said I didn't want to go," Genny answered impatiently, heaving her leg up and placing the game in the middle drawer of the mahogany Queen Anne highboy.

She was limping more than she had during the summer, he realized, frowning, and seemed paler than usual. In fact, her whole being spelled unhappiness.

"Why don't we see how you feel in the morning?" Penelope said, slipping soothing arms around her granddaughter. For a moment the child stood stiffly, then gave way and leaned against her grandmother, eyes tightly closed.

Something was obviously very wrong.

The misgivings prompted by his meeting at the pub loomed once more. Could the child have been carrying a load of pain and guilt all these years? As soon as Genny was tucked up in bed, he decided to confront Penelope.

"Good night, Uncle Brad." She came limping over to him and he held her close.

"Take care, baby." *Tell me if something's torturing you,* he wanted to add. But instead he gave her a warm hug and a pat on the cheek. "Sweet dreams, princess."

Her eyes flickered and she blinked nervously before giving him a quick smile and leaving the room.

"What's wrong with Genny?" Brad asked, accepting Penelope's offer of brandy. "She wasn't nervous like this when I left."

"I don't know." Penelope shook her head and let out a long, worried sigh before handing him the snifter. "I've tried to pry it out of her but she's as closed as a clam.

Frankly, this has been going on ever since John regained consciousness.''

Brad swirled the snifter pensively, wondering how much he should interfere. ''Do you think something might have occurred?'' he said at last. ''Something she remembers from the past that could have sparked this change in her?''

''Perhaps. It's difficult to say. She's never mentioned anything specific, never complained, but God only knows what she may or may not have witnessed.'' Penelope stared into the fire, a bitter edge to her voice.

''Right.'' Brad cleared his throat. The mere thought of Charlotte suffering physical harm at the hands of the man she'd married made him see red. Curbing his frustration, he took a sip of brandy. ''You know, something happened as I was driving up here.''

''Oh?''

''It's rather unlikely, but you never know.''

''What do you mean?'' Penelope's eyebrows knit.

He hesitated. ''I stopped at the Highland Arms when I got off the bridge.''

''Yes?'' She looked at him expectantly, hands folded in her lap, face anxious. ''And?''

''Well, the owner, Frankie, and a couple of other guys began chatting.''

''Of course.'' Penelope's eyes rolled and she smiled despite her tension.

''They started talking about the night of Charlotte's accident.''

''Oh?'' She frowned. ''Why was that? I mean, apart from the fact that they stopped there just before it happened, I really don't see what...'' Her voice trailed off.

''The mechanic who checked the vehicle afterward said he was surprised the driver's seat was pushed so far back. 'Too far back even for a tall lass like Charlotte,'" he paraphrased in a fair imitation of the man's Gaelic brogue. "Another guy commented that John was the one carrying the car keys when they left the pub and that Charlotte had been heard telling him she was too tired to drive."

Penelope sat up like a bolt. "Oh God! You don't think he might have—"

"Switched places with her?" He shrugged and gazed at the pattern of the ancient Uzbekistan rug at his feet. "I can't confirm anything."

"Knowing his vanity and how obsessed he was about his image, I should think it more than likely," she cried, clasping her hands together nervously. "Why didn't any of us think of this ourselves?"

"Because it's so goddamn outrageous."

"But possible."

"Very possible. Say, wasn't Genny conscious after the crash?"

"Yes. We were so grateful she hadn't—" She frowned, then stared at him in horror, clapping a hand over her mouth. "Oh, Brad. You don't think…?"

"If Genny wasn't unconscious, she may have seen something."

"Oh, goodness, how simply dreadful. But if she had, why wouldn't she have mentioned it in all this time?"

"Maybe because there wasn't anything to see and I'm wrong. Who knows?" He took another sip of the smooth brandy. "But it strikes me as damn odd that Genny should be acting so strangely, when you'd think she'd be thrilled to have her dad back. Remember how she used to constantly watch that movie where John plays a loving father, rewinding it over and over?"

"Yes, she did." Penelope nodded. "For a while it was

almost obsessive. Unfortunately, that role couldn't have been further from the truth,'' she said thoughtfully. ''He was not a...caring father. I'll have to talk to her, Brad, and see what I can find out.'' She stopped, then looked at him in dismay. ''You don't think he could have black-mailed her?''

''I've no idea, but I think it's time to find out,'' he responded grimly, finishing the rest of the brandy in one gulp. He needed to be alone. Being back at Strathaird had brought up too many memories and he had his own hurdles to face.

''Thanks so much for telling me.'' Penelope rose and they kissed one another good-night. ''And, Brad—'' she reached up and touched his cheek gently ''—I do hope everything will work out in the end for you and Charlotte.'' She looked up into his eyes, her blue ones swimming with unshed tears. He gave her a grateful hug.

''Don't worry, Aunt Penn. Give it some time. Charlie needs to make up her own mind. And if she's decided to stay with him, that may be right too.''

She heaved a deep sigh. ''I honestly don't see how it could be. I just hope and pray that this time she doesn't make another mistake. I don't know if I could bear it.''

''I must know this menu by heart,'' Charlotte remarked lightly as she and John dallied over a last glass of Barolo. ''But I love the agnollotti. I don't think I'll ever get tired of them.''

Vincenzo, the efficient Italian waiter whom they now knew well, stood attentively nearby.

''Anything else, Mr. Drummond?''

''Just the bill, thanks.'' John smiled and slipped a hand across the crisp tablecloth.

Charlotte stiffened, forcing herself to stay calm and not

pull away. She should be grateful. For once they weren't surrounded by the usual entourage of Berkowitz and Co.

This was her chance.

Taking a deep breath, she glanced up at the equestrian paintings on the wall, marshaling her courage. Only two other tables in the inner section of the restaurant were occupied. An older couple munched in somber silence, while the other table held a merry group of young people chattering in a language she didn't recognize.

John leaned closer and began reviewing the afternoon's activities. "I read this new script today, but I'm not sure," he said, frowning. "My comeback role needs to be something very special that the whole world will identify with, that they'll relate to my personality and aura. Something totally out of the ordinary."

"I thought you liked *Wonder's Work*," she remarked, forcing herself not to twitch. She noticed how much better he looked, eyes matching the new aqua sweater he'd bought for a small fortune at Hermès. His skin had lost the grayish cast of weeks earlier and he was slowly acquiring a rugged look, thanks to the mountain hikes up the Santesch, bicycle rides and regular workouts prescribed by his trainer.

He was well enough to handle the truth, she reflected, withdrawing her hand.

Folding her napkin carefully, she laid it next to her half-empty glass and took a deep breath. "John, you and I need to talk."

"I thought that's what we were doing." He grinned, teeth flashing.

It occurred to her that he was lucky he'd had them capped shortly before the accident, or his teeth might have deteriorated during his illness. *Stop thinking about nonsense,* she ordered, *and get on with it.* Screwing up her nerve, she looked across at him. "I mean really talk," she said in a firm voice.

"What about? We talk all the time. Don't you care about my career? We need to go over this stuff."

"This is about us, John."

"Well, that's all settled, isn't it? You called that lawyer chap and canceled the divorce proceedings, right?" he asked casually.

"No. I haven't."

"Why not?" His voice turned suddenly icy.

"Because we're going ahead with it," she blurted out.

"Pardon me," he drawled, "but I don't think I understand."

"I think you do." She watched his eyes turn hard and flinched despite her newfound courage.

"Berkowitz has made it clear to you that a divorce is out of the question right now. My whole comeback has been structured around our, quote, wonderful marriage. God knows how much is being spent on the campaign." He took a long sip of wine, then, irritated, signaled the waiter for more.

"That's all you think about, isn't it?" she replied, hotly. "Your whole universe consists of your damn career and your bloody ego. Well, guess what, I've had it." Her voice rose and he took an anxious look at the other tables.

"Let's get out of here. I can't afford a scene. I probably shouldn't be dining in such a well-known place anyway." He waved to the waiter and handed him his credit card.

"Stop worrying about what you look like, and listen," she hissed, goaded by his attitude. "If you think for one minute that you can stop this discussion from taking place, you're wrong. I refuse to go on like this."

"Rubbish. You did it for long enough, you'll get used to it again." All the seeming affection that had infused his voice over the past few weeks was gone. In its place was the harsh arrogance she knew all too well.

"This is not rubbish. It's the truth. I want to do this in the quietest, most civilized manner possible. Don't make it more difficult than it need be."

"It's out of the question. I won't discuss it."

She held back her answer while the waiter returned with the bill and John signed.

Smiling perfunctorily, she rose.

They walked in stiff silence past polished wooden tables and windows facing the terrace and the promenade. The waiter took out their jackets from a large antique Bauern cupboard near the entrance. As they slipped them on and said good-night, Charlotte braced herself for the next round. The familiar nausea that for years had accompanied her day in, day out, rose once again in the pit of her stomach.

Once they were out in the promenade and they'd begun the ten-minute walk back to the hotel, she let out a long breath, determined to get it over with.

"John, please be reasonable," she insisted, trying desperately to regain control. "We have Genny to think about as well as ourselves. If you and I are unhappy, then she will be too. If we're sensible about this and work something out, then she won't suffer." It was silly to get angry and only served to make matters worse.

He stopped abruptly in front of Grima, the renowned jeweler's. "You don't think I'd give Genny up, do you?"

"What do you mean?" she asked, swallowing a rush of fear. "You could see her whenever it was convenient for you—we can arrange that with no problem."

A slow, cruel smile curved his lips. "You think I'll

simply let you walk out on me, as cool as you please,'' he said, his mocking tone as brutal as a slap. ''That I'll let you muck up my career because of some half-assed *accessory line* that you've convinced yourself is a success.'' He let out a low, harsh laugh and took a step closer.

It took all her willpower not to raise her arm to shield herself from the blow she was sure would follow.

He stared at her scornfully. ''Just look at you. You think you're a hotshot because a few Parisian critics said your stuff's okay. Well, I've got news for you, baby. Your jewelry sucks. The only reason you got any notice at all is because of *my* name. Without me, you're a seven-day wonder, and the sooner you realize it, the better.'' The refined accent he'd cultivated over the years gave way to a guttural East-End twang. ''Stop thinking you're anything but what you are—a society bimbo who was lucky somebody looked at her when there was still something worth seeing. You should be damn glad I'm willing to put up with you. I mean, look at you, for Christ's sake. You're in your mid-thirties, you dress like shit and you can't carry on a normal conversation without looking bored. What man would want what you're selling?''

''This is not about me, or what I look like,'' she returned icily, ''and frankly, your opinions are of no interest to me. We have an issue to settle. The sooner we do it, the better for both of us.''

''Oh my, aren't we being hoity-toity?'' His face took on an ugly twist and he loomed over her menacingly. ''Don't you play Lady of the Manor with me, Charlotte MacLeod,'' he snarled, grabbing her hair and yanking her head back. ''Maybe you need to be reminded of just who and *what* you are.''

Pain seared and her eyes stung. She clenched her fists

so tight her fingers ached. But she would not give him the pleasure of seeing her cry. *Stay calm,* she repeated, forcing her eyes to meet his blazing ones. He was a bully, she reminded herself, and therefore a coward.

"I'll give you one last chance to get your fucking act together," he muttered, letting go of her hair when he saw someone approaching, "but I won't take any more shit from you, understood?"

She stood trembling in front of the store window and stared at him woodenly. Then, all at once, what he did to her didn't matter any longer. He could slap her, throw her against the wall, give her a black eye—goodness knows it had happened before—but nothing would break her resolve.

"I don't care what you do," she said calmly, holding her head up high. "I'm still going ahead with the divorce."

His face turned a dull red. "You'll do no such thing, bitch, do you hear? If you so much as think about going to the lawyers, I'll fight you for custody of Genny."

"You'd never get it," she scoffed. But even as she tossed her hair defiantly, the fear that gripped her insides was worse than anything she'd ever felt. She stared him down. "No judge in his or her right mind would consider you an able parent."

"Oh, really?" he leered. "How about trying this on for size—I've just spent a year in a coma, my child's been deprived of her dad, and now you want to divorce me? How's that going to look in front of a judge? Plus, I'll file in a venue where the likes of you won't stand a chance," he added with a glint of satisfaction. "Just try me."

"You can threaten all you want, John, but it's over," she said stonily. "And the sooner you get that message, the better. You can tell Berkowitz and Gina and all the other flunkies who run around you day and night, to count me out of their megapublicity schemes. I'm not playing.''

She recognized the rush of uncontrollable rage in the split second before he lunged. Fighting the paralysis of old, she stepped deftly aside at the last instant, leaving him flailing, face squashed against the store window, staring straight at a Jubilee picture of Andrew Grima's prized customer: the queen of England. ''I don't care how hard you try to get Genny,'' she spat furiously, ''I'll fight you every inch of the way.'' She watched him straighten and braced her shoulders. ''The choice is yours,'' she said in a voice that was ten times more confident than she felt. ''Either you do this quietly and avoid a lot of bad publicity for yourself, or it can hit the front pages of every damn tabloid from here to Timor. I really don't care. You see, unlike you,'' she added sweetly, ''I don't have to worry about what people think of me. My work is what interests my clients, not my private life.''

Pulse racing, she turned on her heel and hurried down the promenade, back toward the station.

She'd done it.

Exhilaration exploded. She wanted to leap in the air, dance a jig, shout with joy.

Finally she was free.

But he had threatened to take Genny, she reminded herself, a rush of cold fear dampening her excitement. With an effort she brushed it aside. She'd gotten this far and nothing was going to stop her now. She would fight him, dig up the past, find witnesses to the physical abuse she'd suffered—hell, she'd drown him, if need be.

But she would win.

She walked smartly past the Bernerhof Hotel to the

taxis parked in front of the station. She must get back to the hotel before he did, grab her bags and her passport and leave. She jumped into a taxi and gave the driver directions.

There was no sign of John as they pulled up in front of the Park and she breathed easier. "Can you take me to Geneva?" she asked the driver. If she was lucky, she might still get a flight out tonight; if not, she'd be on the first one out in the morning.

"Of course, *madame*," the taxi driver, a middle-aged man with glasses and a curled mustache, responded amiably.

"I won't be long. I just have to get my things. And, please, don't leave."

He nodded politely and she skipped out of the car and into the lobby. Thank God it was empty, except for one individual manning the reception desk. She grabbed her key and rushed up to the suite. Inside, she dragged her suitcase from the cupboard and began throwing clothes into it. Then, racing through to the bathroom she swept her toiletries into a bag and hurried back into the room, stopping short at the sound of voices in the corridor.

She stood paralyzed, listening, then hastily pulled the zipper of the case shut. Not waiting for a bellboy, she grabbed her jacket and purse and, carrying her case, stood behind the door.

The voices were getting closer.

Closing her eyes, she prayed anxiously. Seconds dragged by like hours while she waited, certain they would stop at the door. When they passed on and she heard German spoken, she went limp with relief.

Letting out the breath she'd been holding, she opened the door cautiously, glanced up and down the corridor, then made a quick dash for the elevator. She stepped inside, staring fixedly at the faux book bindings covering its walls, until at last the car descended.

The doors opened onto the lobby. She hesitated, then peeked out. John was heading angrily in her direction, with Berkowitz and Gina trailing in tow.

"Now calm down, John," Berkowitz was saying as he hurried after him. "We'll reason with her."

John shook off his arm. "If that dumb bitch thinks she can mess with me, she has another think coming," he spat. "I'll teach her to think for herself. Screw her and her fucking—"

"Shut up," Berkowitz ordered. "If anyone were to hear you, there'd be hell to pay."

"John, please," Gina whined in her nasal Brooklyn drawl, "you have to think of your image, honey, you just can't say things like that." She tottered up to him on impossibly high heels and kissed him on the cheek.

"Fuck it," he snarled. "Leave me the bloody hell alone, the lot of you."

He was almost at the elevator.

In a moment he would see her.

God only knew what might happen then.

Trembling, Charlotte pressed the button to the spa level. A cold sweat enveloped her as the elevator descended. She could hear his curses fading as the door opened and she ran through the wide dark passage, passing the beauty salon and the gym, out into the underground garage. She stepped on the automatic opening device then rushed through the gaping garage door, welcoming the sudden rush of cold night air as she ran up the incline toward the front entrance. As she approached, the taxi caught sight of her, turning on his headlights and gliding out from under the covered porch to where she stood.

The driver scrambled out and took her case. "Are you all right, *madame?*" he asked, frowning.

"Fine." She swallowed hard. She'd gotten this far and nothing would stop her. Holding on to the last remnants of her self-control, she climbed into the vehicle. "Just get me out of here as fast as you can."

As the taxi turned into the street and wound its way down the hill, past the dairy and on down to the round-about that entered onto the main road, she let out a long pent-up sigh, then realized that her hands were trembling.

It had taken a big chunk of her life to get this far, but she'd made it.

She brushed away tears of relief. She should have fought this battle years ago. That she'd waited so long perhaps wasn't to her credit. But she would win, whatever the cost.

As the taxi drove past the hamlet of Gsteig and began the steep ascent up the Col du Pillon, she leaned back against the soft leather seat and stared out at the inky sky. Gradually the tension dissipated and her limbs went limp.

It wasn't completely over, but at last she was free. She fingered her cell phone in her pocket, tempted to call Brad, and then thought better of it. He wouldn't want to hear from her until everything was signed, sealed and settled. And, unfortunately, she wasn't even close.

Closing her eyes, she settled into the corner of the cab and tried to ignore John's threat to take custody of Genny. Surely she was right and no judge would consent.

Maybe not. Still, she'd only sleep soundly when the issue was resolved once and for all.

20

Wasn't anyone going to pick up the damn phone? Brad wondered, reaching across the desk for the receiver.

"Strathaird Castle," he muttered, jotting a question mark next to an item on the account sheet he was checking.

"I'm looking for Charlotte Drummond," a confident male voice demanded. "Is she there?"

He frowned. "Who would like to speak to her?"

"This is her husband."

"Hello, John," he responded, after a bit of hesitation. "This is Brad Ward."

"Oh, hello, old chap. Is Charlie there? She said she would reach the island not later than nine. I hope she's all right."

"I thought she was with you." He frowned, controlling the rush of anger that the sound of the other man's voice caused.

"She was. In fact, we were having rather a wonderful time together here in Switzerland. After all, we needed to make up for lost time." The low, insidious laugh that followed made him clench his fingers till they hurt. "But she was worried about Genny. Thought she should make a quick hop over and just make sure our baby's safe and well.''

''I see. Well, there's no sign of her yet.''

''I suppose she'll be arriving shortly. Her cell phone's off, as usual. Could you give her a message for me, old chap?''

''Sure.'' Brad swallowed, a new ache gripping his heart, determined to keep his temper under wraps. What he truly wanted was to tell the bastard exactly what he thought of him.

''If you could tell her I got the specs for the house she wants in Mauritius? I have to say, it is magnificent. I wasn't mad about the idea myself, but you know what women are like, have to keep 'em happy. Oh, and another thing…''

''Yes?'' He all but smashed the phone.

''Thank her for last night, will you? Tell her it was a glorious surprise, one I won't forget anytime soon,'' he purred, oozing innuendoes. ''And tell her I hope that I'll be able to repay her in kind.'' John's laugh came low and insinuating down the line. With an effort, Brad stopped himself from slamming the phone down. It would only cause unnecessary aggravation, he reminded himself—not that he cared much anymore. Charlotte had made her choice, that was now obvious.

''I'll tell her,'' he replied shortly.

''Great. Then that about sums it up. Good luck over there on the island. Charlie tells me you're doing a super job. Keep up the good work.''

Brad dropped the receiver back in place, not bothering to reply, and sank deeper in the chair. It was his own fucking fault and he had only himself to blame. Hadn't he known all along something like this would happen?

Rising abruptly, he left the papers he'd been working

on strewn across the desk and stalked from the study, slamming the door hard. He was damned if he was sticking around to see Charlotte. Let her pick up her messages in person. They sure seemed personal enough.

Taking the stairs two at a time, he reached his bedroom and flung open the closet bathed in icy fury. She couldn't see beyond that man. She never had, and never would. Despite all John had done to her and all he suspected still remained to be discovered, she still went back for more. But that was no longer his problem. She'd made her choices. And as usual, what hurt the most was that she hadn't had the guts to tell him.

Throwing a couple of shirts and pants in a tote bag, he headed back downstairs blinded by anger, seething jealousy and a searing pain that slashed right through his heart. Throwing the bag down hard in the trunk of the Aston Martin, he jumped in the car and didn't hesitate.

The farther he got from Charlotte, the better, he reflected, changing gears angrily. Once again, he'd fallen under her spell, and once again he'd been a damn fool. But not anymore, he vowed, streaking out of the castle gates, not any fucking more.

Her flight from London was delayed and the chopper had taken longer than usual to make the trip to the island, but at last she was here. Charlotte smiled up at the ancient turrets and sighed with relief as she halted the Land Rover in front of the castle. Jumping out, she ran up the castle steps, anxious to see Genny, clasp her in her arms and allay the fears that John's parting threats had sparked.

However hard she tried, she couldn't get them out of her head.

Even though a quick call to her lawyers had made it clear a judge would most likely dismiss his claims, her fears were not entirely alleviated. For despite their confidence, the lawyers had admitted there was always an outside chance that the judge might accord him custody. Particularly in Scotland. Perhaps she should have gone to London and filed there instead of in Edinburgh. But now proceedings had begun and it would be nigh impossible to change the venue.

She hastened inside the castle and crossed the hall. "Mummy! Genny! Brad!" she called, voice echoing.

"We're in the sitting room."

Her mother's voice and the sudden appearance of Genny at the sitting-room door filled her with relief. Hurrying forward, she folded her child tightly in her arms and held her close. "It's so good to see you, darling," she whispered, eyes shut tight. Silently she made a vow: nothing was going to take this child away from her.

"It's good to see you too, Mummy." Genny hugged her back and for a long moment they clung quietly to one another, no need for words. "How's Daddy?" Genny asked finally, eyes shifting as they disengaged.

"Doing much better. He's really quite well now."

Genny fiddled with her hair band. "Does that mean he'll be coming to live with us?"

Charlotte hesitated. "Not necessarily, darling," she said carefully, her eyes meeting her mother's over the child's unruly red curls. She was going to have to tell Genny the truth, however hard it might be for her to accept.

"Why not?" Genny tilted her head. She looked almost hopeful, Charlotte noted with confusion.

"It's something we'll have to discuss later. Hello, Mum," she said with a warm smile, profoundly grateful that she was finally home.

"Did you have a good trip, darling?" Penelope studied

her daughter carefully. The dark rings under her eyes and the nervous smile she knew so well did not escape her. But despite Charlotte's obvious exhaustion, there was a reassuring light in her eyes.

"Where's Brad?" Charlotte asked, settling next to Genny on the couch and taking her daughter's science project from her with a smile. Penelope bustled about getting drinks while Genny began turning the pages, explaining the ins and outs of fungus, babbling on about the twins and the e-mails they'd exchanged.

"He's not here."

"What do you mean?" Charlotte sat up straighter, clutched by sudden dread.

"He left suddenly for New York, shortly after you phoned. I wasn't here, but he phoned from the road. Something about an emergency, but it wasn't clear what." Penelope cast Charlotte a quick, perceptive glance then handed her a stiff gin and tonic. She had her own suspicions about Brad's sudden departure. But for now her mind was taken up with her granddaughter. She just prayed Genny would muster the courage to tell her mother what she herself had learned only days earlier.

She watched Charlotte sink back silently among the cushions, relieved that John Drummond had shown his true colors. Personally, she wanted to strangle him for what he'd subjected his child to. But she was proud that Charlotte had finally found the courage to stand up to him. When she'd called this morning from Geneva airport to explain that she was proceeding with the divorce, despite John's protest, Penelope had nearly wept with relief.

She sat down on the opposite sofa and chatted inconsequentially, even as her mind buzzed with all she needed to tell her daughter. It was terribly tempting to just barrel in, to pull her aside and pour out everything she knew. But Genny had begged her not to, saying she needed to tell her mummy herself. Anxious as she was to get the conversation over with, Penelope respected the child's wish, knowing how essential it was to establish a trust that would remain with them for the rest of their lives. The news would only confirm what Charlotte had already decided, but it would also relieve any hovering doubts and resolve the custody issue that was hanging over her head like the Sword of Damocles.

Oblivious to her mother's inner turmoil, Charlotte curled up with her daughter on her favorite sofa, next to the fire and Rufus, and soaked in the soothing calm of Strathaird. Whatever her problems, she could always count on this bastion of peace. Even though it technically didn't belong to her any longer, she realized that didn't matter anymore either. She had her own road to travel, her own home to make and her own worlds to conquer.

Her mother had kept her apprised of all the changes Brad had implemented. Two months ago, she would have taken them as a personal affront. Now she saw the sense in them, and even approved. Somehow, it seemed appropriate that she and Strathaird would undergo their respective transformations together. It was Strathaird that affirmed that the past and the future could peacefully co-exist, that even a battered and bruised foundation was still strong enough to support all their hopes and dreams.

She gazed at the fire, watching a crackling log shift and another flame spark. Like their lives, she reflected, one moment burning low, on the point of being extinguished, the next shooting up with bright new hope.

But Brad's departure left her thoughtful and uneasy. He'd sensed her desire to build a new foundation and had given her the tools—hope, trust, support, and above all, love—to make it happen. But something had come between them in the past few weeks, and this latest disappearing act of his left her deeply worried that he was pulling away from her. If only she could sit down with him, face-to-face, and explain all that was happening, she was sure they could get beyond this impasse.

She'd hoped to talk to him tonight, but now that was impossible. He was determined to avoid her. That much had become obvious. She wished now that she hadn't phoned from the Geneva airport, but rather had simply arrived, denying him the chance to escape. Instead, like it or not, she was going to have to wait.

"What's happening on the exhibition front? Have you arranged anything with Sylvia?" Penelope asked, handing Genny her knitting needles now that she'd caught her granddaughter's fallen stitches. "By the way, have you finished your homework, Genny?"

Genny nodded, folding up the science project with a sigh. "All except my math. I wish Uncle Brad was here to help me. I'm hopeless."

"Me too," Charlotte grimaced. "I'm a confirmed mathematical misfit." She ruffled her daughter's hair and gave her an affectionate hug. "We'll go up in a little while. Perhaps we'll have time to catch a movie before bed." She noticed the quick exchange of looks between Genny and her mother, sensing a sudden discomfort in Genny's eyes and in the nervous way she began fiddling with the knitting.

Telling herself she was imagining things, Charlotte began telling her mother about Sylvia's plans, as well as her enthusiastic talks with the Cardinal and the director of exhibitions at the Met. "Sylvia seems to have it all under control," she said, smiling despite her exhaustion.

"Her energy and capacity for details are incredible. She's managed to put this all together in record time."

"Yes, well, we all know she's a dreadfully efficient young woman." Penelope sighed, wondering how long it would be until Genny would talk to Charlotte.

"And actually rather nice, once you get to know her better," Charlotte admitted, picking at the fringe of the cushion.

Penelope raised surprised eyes. "I must say it's good to hear you two are getting along so well. Now, what about the divorce?" she asked tentatively. "Genny knows," Penelope added, seeing her hesitate.

Charlotte cast her daughter an anxious look. She was busy with her knitting, and didn't seem to be listening. "It's nearly over. I told you about John and the falling-out."

Penelope nodded. "I'm sure it'll sort itself out."

"I hope so. Although I'm still afraid of the custody issue, whatever the lawyers say. That's why I came home in such a rush."

"I won't go with Daddy," Genny interrupted doggedly, red curls bouncing about her freckled face.

"Of course you won't, darling." Charlotte reached out and pulled her close. "I'd never let them."

"You promise, Mum?" There was a new element of concern in the child's voice that went beyond mere doubt. Charlotte frowned and sipped her drink, then ruffled the child's head again. "Of course not, pet." She could not explain to Genny or her mother how everything had fallen into place, like the last piece in a puzzle. Watching the freak show of John and his entourage at the Park Hotel, had made it all crystal clear to her. John was the poison in their relationship, not her. She had no idea why it had taken her so long to realize what everyone must have seen from the start, but at least she had. Stroking the child's rebellious curls, she experienced a rush of heartfelt relief, as though a horrible cloud had been lifted.

"I can hardly believe I've done it," she murmured to her mother across Genny, who was cuddled in her lap.

"Well, you have. And make sure you stick to it." Penelope sent her a meaningful glance across the coffee table, piled high with magazines and swatches of material she'd had sent from London to choose new bedcovers for the guest rooms. "You and Genny have your own lives to think about now."

"You're right, Mum. I know I've been awfully difficult in the past," she added with a penitent smile, "and I should have listened to you more often. You're such a brick, Mummy, you really are."

"No, darling, not a brick, just a mum," Penelope replied affectionately, leaning over and taking her daughter's hand in hers. "That's what being a mother's all about. You'll do the same for Genny." She smiled softly, eyes falling on the child in Charlotte's arms, remembering the bright-eyed, rebellious teenager that still lurked below the surface in the beautiful woman Charlotte had grown into. Thank goodness those youthful energies were finally channeled now into new, constructive avenues.

"I'd better get you up to bed," Charlotte said, dropping a kiss on her child's forehead. "Thanks for holding down the fort and looking after Genny, Mummy."

"Wait. Before you both go upstairs, there's something Genny needs to tell you."

The child's head shot up. To Charlotte's amazement, her daughter huddled among the cushions. She watched anxiously as Genny stiffened and her eyes met her grandmother's in pleading supplication.

"You must tell Mummy, darling," Penelope insisted.

But Genny shook her head vigorously, her red hair fanning out rebelliously over the cushions, and hugged her knees, staring blindly into the glowing fire.

"Is something the matter, darling?" Charlotte asked, worried, sending her mother a questioning glance across the room.

"There's something Genny needs to talk to you about, Charlotte."

It sounded terribly daunting. Charlotte stopped herself from grabbing Genny's hand, aware that this was one of those special mother-daughter moments. Had Genny gotten her period while she was away? She hoped not. She wanted to be with her daughter when those benchmarks in her life took place.

"Go ahead, darling. Whatever it is, you know you can tell me."

Genny hesitated again, fiddling nervously with her old pink bunny whose ear had long since dropped off. It was a sure sign she was deeply troubled about something, and Charlotte sought her mother's eyes once more for guidance. But Penelope's gaze was fixed on her granddaughter.

"You must tell her, Genny." Penelope's voice was firm. Charlotte flexed her fingers. She'd rarely seen her mother look so determined, as though what was about to be revealed was essential to their lives.

"Whatever it is, you know you can tell me, Genny," Charlotte repeated. "I'll always listen to anything you have to say and if there's a problem, I'll try to help you solve it."

Slowly Genny raised anguished eyes to her mother's. Charlotte's heart jolted at the fear and distress she read there.

"It's—it's about Daddy." The words tumbled forth as she began to rock side to side.

Charlotte's heart froze. "What about Daddy?"

"It's difficult to tell you," she mumbled, and Charlotte tried not to panic. What on earth had happened?

"Go on," Penelope urged softly. "You can do it." There was strength in her voice and Charlotte watched as her mother slipped from her chair and came to perch on the arm of the sofa next to Genny.

"You can tell me anything," she said hoarsely, eyeing them both fearfully. What could have occurred to make the child react in this manner?

"I know... It's just—" Genny swallowed, eyes swimming, and plucked the pink rabbit's dangling paw "—I feel so terrible that I never told you before," she whispered in a rush.

"All that matters is that you're telling me now," Charlotte responded in a soothing tone.

"You promise you won't be cross?"

"Darling, of course not. I promise." She smiled reassuringly, trying to defuse her daughter's fears.

But Genny merely clutched the rabbit closer as Penelope gripped her shoulder, encouraging her to go ahead.

"Mummy, I—I saw everything," she whispered at last.

"Saw what, dear?" Charlotte asked, mystified. Was she referring to the time John had slapped her, and Genny was discovered hiding behind the door?

"In the car." Her voice was barely audible.

"What car, darling?"

"When we had the accident."

A sudden chill ran down her spine. "What exactly did you see?"

"Well, you were lying in the front seat, as if you were

asleep,'' Genny continued nervously. ''Now I know you were unconscious.''

''Yes, and what happened?'' She waited tensely for Genny to go on.

''Daddy had been driving, but after we hit the tree, he pulled you over into his seat.''

''He what?'' Charlotte sat numbly on the edge of the couch in disbelief. ''Are you sure, darling? You didn't just imagine it?''

''No.'' She shook her head vigorously. ''He said it was to make you more comfy. My leg was sore and I didn't really know what was happening. I didn't think about it. But when I came home from the hospital, Daddy talked to me about it.''

''What did he say?'' Charlotte's tone became low and measured as an anger such as she'd never experienced coursed cold and feral through her.

''He made me promise I would never tell you that he'd done that. So I asked him if it was bad.''

''And what did he reply?''

''He said it wasn't bad, but that it would make you dreadfully unhappy.'' Her eyes filled with tears. ''Oh, Mummy, I'm so scared of him. When I saw him this time, he said it again. He asked me if I'd told you and he looked at me in such a funny way. I'm so frightened. You promise you won't tell him, will you?'' she said, eyes wild, hands tugging desperately at the rabbit's good ear. ''If he knows I've broken my promise, he might do something terrible.''

''Oh, darling.'' Charlotte pulled her daughter into her arms, her eyes meeting her mother's in silent horror. How had she not seen the signs? How had she not guessed what he was capable of?

You bastard. You bloody bastard, she cried inwardly,

wishing she could see him hanged, drawn and quartered. Nothing would ever sufficiently punish him for what he'd done. Not only had he traumatized her child, but he'd put the blame for the accident and Genny's limp on her, absolving himself.

"Darling, it's all right." She hugged Genny close and allowed the sobs to subside. "I promise he can't do anything to you. There's something *I* need to tell *you*." She drew back, placed her hands on Genny's shoulders and smiled. "What Granny said earlier is true. I'm getting divorced from Daddy."

"You are?" Genny, who seemed not to have taken it in, gulped and sniffed and her eyes widened in surprise.

"Yes. And after what you've just told me, I can assure that you'll never have to see him again unless you want to."

"Are you sure?" Genny peeked at her uncertainly through wet lashes.

"I'm absolutely one hundred percent certain. What he did was very wrong, Genny. He had no right to make you frightened, or blame me for something I didn't do."

"You're not angry with me?" she whispered, as though needing to make sure.

"Angry? I'm devastated that you've been through all this by yourself, darling. I'm the one who should have seen something was wrong." She shook her head and let out a long sigh.

"Now, don't start taking the blame, Mum," Genny said in a voice that sounded very grown up. "She mustn't, must she, Granny?" she urged with a watery smile. Charlotte brushed away her own tears and she and Penelope laughed despite the tension.

"You're absolutely right, darling," Penelope agreed. "Mummy must stop doing that."

"I've promised myself I will." Charlotte gulped, smiling down into her daughter's tear-stained freckled face.

Genny moved over so that Penelope could squeeze onto the sofa next to them and they held hands. "I'm glad he won't be back, Mummy. Aren't you, Granny?"

"Very," Penelope replied emphatically.

"I've been so scared."

"Well, you've no need to be anymore," Charlotte responded firmly. "I'll never let him hurt you again, darling, I swear."

"Over my dead body," Penelope confirmed as the three of them clung together in a long, loving hug. Then, disengaging herself, Penelope tenderly tidied her daughter's and granddaughter's hair. Charlotte folded her legs beneath her. One question still bothered her.

"Genny," she asked. "What prompted you to tell me this now?"

"It was Granny."

"Oh?"

"She thought I should tell you."

"But Granny can't have known about this." She glanced at her mother questioningly.

"No, but one night before going to bed, she asked me if something had happened the night of the accident. All at once I knew I couldn't hide it any longer."

"Thank God for that," Charlotte whispered to herself, sending her mother a long look of gratitude, wondering what had prompted her to ask.

An hour later, after much talking, she finally tucked Genny into the small four-poster bed in her old room, which Brad had insisted remain intact. She placed the pink bunny next to her and allowed Hermione to stay curled in a cozy huddle on her daughter's toes. There would be no more nightmares, she vowed, switching on the small night-light before dropping a last kiss on the child's forehead and quietly leaving the darkened room.

As she descended the wide staircase, her wrath gave way to cold, hard calculation. She now had a weapon that would smash all her husband's empty threats in one sharp blow. She almost wished he would file for custody so that she could fell his ambitions once and for all. She smiled grimly, suddenly glad John had emerged from his coma; he'd come back just in time for his comeuppance.

"It's incredible!" Sylvia laid down another heavy vellum invitation and sighed with delight. "Since word got out that I'm the one bringing the Lost Collection to town, I'm on everybody's A-list."

"So you should be." Brad grinned. "You've done a fabulous job in record time."

"Have you talked to Charlotte lately?" Sylvia asked, peering at him closely as he opened another file and loosened his tie.

"Just briefly," he answered curtly.

Okay. So he didn't want to talk about it. Fine.

What was it about these two? she wondered. They knew each other so well and almost seemed able to read one another's thoughts, yet they were capable of the most ludicrous misunderstandings, too. Maybe it was a British thing, she concluded, blithely ignoring Brad's American heritage. Maybe they never stated the obvious, but instead simply allowed it to simmer below the surface while maintaining a stiff upper lip. She shrugged. Just how Brad thought he was going to finesse it through the art opening without bumping into Charlotte was a mystery. But he'd made it plain he didn't want any part of the show. Brad was a sweetheart, but he could be as stubborn as a damn mule, she reflected.

She rose, knowing she had a meeting with the museum director. She would have to return to the matter of Brad and Charlotte at some later date, when she could do something concrete about it.

"I'm off," she announced.

"Bye," he replied.

Seeing him firmly entrenched in the financial report for this quarter's earnings, she shrugged, sighed and picked up her ever-present purse, then headed for the door. She looked back, about to say something, then thought better of it and nodded sagely. Her gut, which never failed her, told her that the only thing standing between those two was pride and misunderstanding.

She smiled. Clearly what was required here was some good ol' American meddling.

21

He hadn't bothered to come.

Flopping dejectedly onto the deep, striped couch in her suite at the Lowell Hotel, Charlotte kicked off her high heels and grimaced at the amethyst silk suit Sylvia had made her buy for the opening.

"It makes your eyes look so incredible," she'd insisted during their shopping expedition to Bergdorf's. "Brad'll go nuts when he sees you in it." And as she'd dressed this evening, she'd felt truly beautiful, and grateful for the chance to finally clear things up with him.

But that was all over now.

She huddled in the muted lamplight among the cushions, not giving a damn if her outfit got crushed. She'd been foolish to assume he'd be at the Met, and more foolish still to believe that their lives would simply pick up where they'd left off in Zurich and continue on to a happy-ever-after ending.

Life just wasn't like that. She rolled her stiff shoulders then massaged her toes, aching after hours of standing chatting with a champagne glass poised in her hand, face sore from smiling.

There was no doubt that the presentation of the Lost

Collection had been a smashing success, just as Sylvia had predicted. Accorded top billing within the Met's prewar art exhibition, the Rothberg jewels had been the undisputed hit of the evening. Sylvain would have been so proud, she consoled herself. But nothing could make up for the fact that the one person she'd longed to see had not appeared.

What had she expected? That he'd at least put in an appearance, she thought angrily. After all, she reasoned, he'd been part of the collection's discovery from the beginning. He couldn't suddenly disappear and pretend it hadn't happened.

Even Sylvia had said the same. Funny how she and Brad's ex-fiancée had become close over the past weeks. She'd learned to appreciate some of the other woman's finer qualities. Several major disasters had been avoided thanks to her organizational skills and determination. Tonight she'd watched Sylvia work the glittering room, superbly elegant in a sleeveless black sheath, the Rothberg diamond bow that Charlotte had insisted she wear for the event pinned to her left shoulder, smiling, introducing bejeweled guests to one another amid clinking crystal, low laughter and high-powered chitchat. And, Charlotte thought admiringly, doing it all to perfection.

Some of the brilliant outfits and jewels nearly competed with the Lost Collection in magnificence. Everyone had opened their safes, and, despite the extra insurance premiums, brought out their prized pieces, filing past her in sparkling splendor. Charlotte had forced herself not to gape at superlative Tiffany brooches, a gaudy diamond tiara owned by the wife of a Texas oil tycoon, and a couple of unspeakably ugly necklaces that Sylvain, she was certain, would have despised.

She should have been thrilled and delighted by the

excitement that the collection had created. But as the guests from around the globe marveled at the beauty and rarity of Sylvain's pieces, agog with curiosity generated by the extraordinary circumstances surrounding their discovery, Charlotte could think of one thing and one thing only: Brad's notable absence.

By midevening she'd known he wouldn't come, but she'd carried on with a brave smile anyway, posing next to each glass case and beside the photographs of Sylvain, expounding on his life and career, describing in enthusiastic detail the drawings discovered in the safe. In other words, she'd done her job.

Displayed at the far end of the room, under the focused beam of a single spotlight, was Geneviève's portrait, shipped from La Vallière. It presided over a glass-encased, white satin stand that housed the three-tiered emerald and diamond choker Sylvain had presented to her on their wedding day. The photographer had insisted that Charlotte stand beside her grandmother's picture, enchanted by the staggering resemblance.

She'd done that and more, determined to sparkle despite her disappointment. She owed that to Sylvain and the past. But now, as she stared blindly through the French window at the twinkling lights of Manhattan, she realized it was all over. Brad was finished with her. Perhaps it wasn't surprising that, after all the ups and downs of their relationship throughout the years, he wasn't prepared to risk another disappointment. But that didn't make it hurt any less.

When her plane had first landed in New York a week ago, Charlotte had wanted to see him right away, only to learn he was in California. By the time she'd discovered he was back, he'd hightailed it off somewhere else.

At first, knowing how busy he was, she'd tried to make

excuses for him. And of course, she was frantically on the go herself, between meeting with the people at the Met and finalizing her divorce. In the end, she'd decided John wasn't worth the drama that leaking his story to the press would cause, so she'd settled for the simple pleasures of blackmail, letting him know she wouldn't hesitate to spill the beans if he ever came near her or Genny again.

But once everything had been settled and it became clear Brad was still avoiding her, she ran out of excuses and had to face the truth: Brad just didn't want her anymore.

For whatever reason—and there were many, she conceded sadly—he'd decided she wasn't worth the trouble. She heaved a long, crestfallen sigh and fought back tears. How naive she'd been to think that she'd get a second chance.

She rose, walked across the elegantly decorated sitting room in her stocking feet, and took an Evian out of the refrigerator. Uncapping the bottle, she chugged down the cool, crisp water.

And as she drank, her brain cleared.

Stop feeling sorry for yourself, she commanded, plunking the bottle down with a bang. *Stop letting yourself be knocked out at the first round.* There was a choice to be made. Either she could get on the plane back to London and admit that she'd lost everything she'd ever wanted, or she could go locate her missing spine and face the man she desired.

She wandered to the window, heart quickening, and gazed out into the night, barely aware of the wailing sirens, angry horns and constant cacophony of sounds that made up the song of the city. It was a hell of a risk.

And it just might become the most humiliating experience of her life.

But she had to try.

All at once she stood taller. Brad was the man she loved, the one she'd wanted all her life. Surely he was worth taking a chance on?

A grin lit up her face as she thought suddenly of what Sylvia would say in that wonderful down-to-earth way of hers: *The worst you can hear is a no, honey.* Pulse racing, she walked back to the bedroom. The bed seemed huge and empty. What was she willing to sacrifice to have him there, by her side, sharing each moment of her existence? Her pride? Of course. Her heart? No problem. *So go do something about it!*

It was all in her hands. She could get out there and fight, or she could slink away, licking her wounds, and be miserable for the rest of her life. Of course, there was no guarantee she'd win. Still, if she didn't scrape up her courage, she would never know. And she wouldn't be able to live with herself.

Her eyes closed and she bit her lip. She would do it.

A wave of relief swamped her now that she'd made the decision.

After all, she had nothing to lose.

He'd walked away from the woman he loved and the decision was final. By not going to the Met, he knew he was sending the message that he was finally putting an end to the masochistic game they'd played for over ten years. It was the hardest thing he'd ever done.

And today Brad was drained.

He'd spent yesterday evening alone, sipping brandy in the darkened library of his home on Sutton Place. It was appropriate, he'd figured glumly, that he should live out this moment in a setting that had witnessed so many of his ancestors' joys and disappointments.

He came out of the shower, toweling off the excess water, and entered his walk-in closet. Rows of immaculate suits, shirts, ties, blazers, shoes and pants swam before him. For most of his life, he'd lived in this fast-paced but meticulously ordered existence, knowing precisely what he would wear, what he would do, whom he would talk to, what deal would get cut. Now all he thought of was Skye and Charlotte and the twins and Genny and everything that he'd lost.

Picking a gray cashmere suit from a cedar hanger, he started to dress. Traditionally, this was the time when he planned his day, strategizing and coming up with solutions. Instead, today he stared in the mirror at the man in the gray suit, impeccable white shirt and designer tie, and wondered who he was.

He turned away. What had truly kept him from facing her last night was anger. At her. Penelope had told him that Genny had finally revealed to her mother the terrible truth. How could Charlotte, knowing what the man was capable of, still want to stay with her husband? Surely now she must see him for who he really was?

But apparently not. He hadn't had a chance to have a word with Penelope, who'd flown over for the exhibition and was staying at Sutton Place. In fact, he hadn't seen her or Diego or the twins since getting back from his business trip yesterday afternoon. He'd been so busy he'd barely allowed himself time to think. But after that awful conversation with Drummond at Strathaird, he didn't need to ask Penelope for an update. And he certainly hadn't wanted to go to the Met just so he could gaze longingly at Charlotte from the shadows. No. He'd come back in plenty of time to make the event and had given himself the choice to go or not. And he'd chosen not to.

He walked down the wide marble staircase. At the top of the wrought-iron balustrade were his great-grand-father's initials, entwined in gold leaf. At the bottom, two scruffy backpacks—one with Go Knicks scrawled on it—sat ready for school. All his life he'd taken care of the legacies of other men: John Harcourt Sr., the founder of Harcourts; his grandfather, Dexter Ward, who had left him Strathaird; even indirectly his father, by inheriting the twins.

But what about his own legacy?

He crossed the black-and-white marble hall toward the breakfast room, glanced at the glorious flower arrange-ment gracing the drum table, and knew it was time to do what the kids in skateboarding lingo called a five sixty. He smiled, despite the gloominess weighing on his heart. Maybe he'd take the twins out of school, buy a yacht and sail around the world for a year.

Whatever.

All he was certain of was that he was out of here. Today, if he could swing it.

He'd finally had enough.

"Perhaps this wasn't such a good idea, Miss Riley," Charlotte murmured, shifting uncomfortably and watch-ing the slim, impeccably attired middle-aged receptionist seated behind her battery of chrome telephones on the top floor of Harcourts. "I think I'll just pop back in later when he's less busy," she said, fixing a smile on and slipping her purse back on her shoulder.

"But I already told him you were on your way up. He's expecting you, Mrs. MacLeod." Miss Riley quirked a questioning eyebrow from behind her rimless designer glasses.

"No, please—" Sudden panic gripped. She couldn't do it. There was no point and she shouldn't have tried, she realized, watching in paralyzed horror as Miss Riley pressed the intercom button.

"Really, you mustn't bother."

"But he pays me to bother. Mrs. MacLeod to see you, sir," she announced, leaning toward the intercom triumphantly.

Charlotte's pulse raced. Her heart did a double somersault and landed in her mouth.

This was it.

She couldn't back out now. She was probably about to make an even bigger fool of herself than she already was, but at least she would have tried.

Bracing herself, she straightened her shoulders, tossed her head back and followed Miss Riley to the huge double doors. "Mrs. MacLeod," the secretary announced, holding the door wide, leaving her no choice but to enter.

She watched him rise and come out from behind the long teak desk, heart pounding as he stepped forward, lips set in a smile that didn't reach his eyes. He barely brushed her cheek when they kissed hello.

"Come on in and sit down. Can I get you something? Coffee, tea, champagne? Though I imagine you must be saturated after last night. I'm sorry I couldn't make it—plane landed late." He gestured to the black leather sofa.

Charlotte sat down in a daze. She'd never seen this side of Brad. It was as if she was standing before a complete stranger. She swallowed, murmuring a polite refusal to the offers of refreshment while trying not to show her utter astonishment. This was just Brad, she reminded herself. The man who'd held her in his arms and made love to her and whom she'd loved back with more passion than she'd ever dreamed she possessed.

The man to whom she'd given her heart.

"Sylvia told me the Lost Collection's a howling success," he remarked, sitting opposite her, casually flinging his ankle over the other knee. "Apparently they showed some of your designs as well?"

"Yes, just a couple of pieces," she said blankly, wondering how to begin. This superficial chitchat was getting her nowhere. She glanced around the spacious, airy office, taking in the vast panoramic windows, light-gray marble floor, designer leather furniture, halogen lighting, a couple of abstract paintings on the wall and an orchid in a chrome pot. All part of his life. All of it armor for the man she was facing.

She sat nervously on the edge of the sofa and clasped her hands in her lap, palms damp. She rubbed them surreptitiously on the skirt of her pale Armani suit and reminded herself just why she'd come.

"Brad, I need to talk to you," she said, taking the plunge.

She saw his face close and her heart sank. "I don't think there's much to talk about, Charlotte," he replied in a measured tone, making her long to stretch out her hand and clasp his.

"Will you at least hear me out?" She rose, unable to sit still.

"Sure." He sounded dauntingly indifferent.

Taking a deep breath, she launched into her speech.

"I know we've had our ups and downs," she began, wishing the words sounded more appropriate, "but I think it's time we put them behind us."

"Fine. That just about puts it in a nutshell. Frankly, I see little point in belaboring the matter. An unexpected impediment made our relationship redundant. I've accepted that. I suppose you're here to tell me you want to go back to being friends. But I'm afraid it's too late for that.'' He rose, his expression hard, and turned his back on her abruptly.

Charlotte trembled. They'd lost each other once; she couldn't let it happen again. Okay, she'd been a fool and maybe she'd blundered. But as she stared at the tense set of his shoulders, a sudden rush of love surged through her. All she wanted was to feel his warmth, to kiss away all the misunderstandings and grievances, and pledge herself to a new beginning.

''You might at least look at me when I'm speaking to you,'' she remarked tartly, taking the bull by the horns.

He turned reluctantly.

Was she at all aware of how much he was hurting? Just seeing her standing here before him, so vibrant and lovely, having her within his reach and yet being unable to touch? ''Okay. Say whatever it is you have to say and then let's both get on with our lives. I have a busy day.''

His callousness sparked new courage in her and her eyes flashed. If he thought he could scare her off with a little *boo!* he had a lot to learn.

''I didn't come here to spar with you, Brad.''

''Then why did you come?'' It was out before he could stop himself. ''Just what exactly are you doing here, Charlotte?''

''Telling you the truth.''

''Oh. *That*.'' He gave a harsh, hollow laugh.

''I came to tell you that I love you.'' She took a step toward him.

''You sure have a weird way of showing it.'' He backed away, desperate to put distance between them.

''I—I've come to ask you to make love with me again.''

His head shot up.

He stared at her, unbelieving, opened his mouth, then closed it again. Before him stood the same medieval

Charlotte he'd seen that day in the hall at Strathaird, all passion and invitation. He closed his eyes and gave his head a shake. "That's not amusing," he said at last.

"It wasn't meant to be," she responded, barreling ahead before he could reply, "but I don't know how else to say it."

"Uh, won't Drummond have a problem with the sudden reversal? You're a married woman and hardly in a position to be propositioning anyone."

"Not anymore."

"What do you mean?" Eyes narrowed, he moved toward her.

"You knew I'd filed for divorce."

"That was before your husband resuscitated," he replied witheringly.

"You think you're awfully well informed, don't you?" she said, matching his sarcastic tone. "Pretty presumptuous, given that you've never bothered to ask me directly what's going on."

He hesitated then shook his head. "Don't play games with me, Charlie. We've known each other too long and too well. Let's just accept that it wasn't meant to be and move on. I understand."

"No, you don't," she retorted. "I'm trying to explain but you're not listening. Perhaps you didn't hear your secretary announce Mrs. MacLeod?" They were almost touching now and a rush of heat swept over her. Taking a deep breath, she stepped back and slipped off the jacket of her suit, the camisole beneath enticingly bare. "It's quite hot in here, isn't it?" she remarked casually. "Don't you ever open any windows?"

"No. The air-conditioning system doesn't allow for— what the hell are you talking about, Charlotte?" He took a step toward her, hardly daring to trust the implication of her words.

"I'm divorced, Brad. It finally came through." She dropped the jacket casually on the couch and faced him.

"I don't believe it." He swore, shook his head and shoved his hands in his pockets.

"That's precisely your trouble," she said, stabbing his chest with her finger. "You never believe anything I say, because you already think you know exactly what's in my head. You never thought I was capable of taking my life into my own hands, did you?" She stepped closer, glaring up at him, hand planted on her slim hip. "You still think of me as the spoiled brat who vomited champagne all over you at a wedding a quarter century ago," she fumed. "Well, I've got news for you, Bradley Ward—I grew up."

"That's not true," he said weakly, still reeling from the onslaught.

"Oh, yes it is. And let me tell you something else— *poor Charlotte* is history."

"I never thought of you as *poor Charlotte.*"

"Yes, you did, and well you know it."

"What am I supposed to do?" he retorted, rallying. "Wallow in a mire of guilt because over the years I tried to protect you from some of the messes you managed to create for yourself?"

"No. Of course not. I'm asking you to stop hiding behind this chrome-and-teak shield you've created." She gestured disparagingly at the office. "Maybe this is what you want," she challenged. "Maybe it's all you really need. Maybe you're afraid *poor Charlotte,* with all her problems and eccentricities, will mess up your perfect little life, inject a little more disorder than you can handle, or—worst of all—force you to admit you've been wrong!" She crossed her arms across her chest and stared at him defiantly.

"Hey, wait a minute!" he exclaimed, eyes blazing.

"I've loved you all my life. God knows how I burned for you. You've haunted my dreams and broken my heart. And all these years, I've watched you suffering, trying desperately to climb out of the rut you got yourself into, knowing that maybe somehow I was to blame by not having made love to you that night in Chester Square. And now you accuse me of being incapable of loving the woman you've become? Well, fuck it!" Before she could react, he pulled her into his arms, mouth ravaging, slamming her body to his.

He cared. All she could register as his mouth wreaked havoc was that he cared.

"And let me make one other thing clear," he growled, coming up for breath. "I've had enough. You drive me crazy, and I'm not about to let you disappear on me again."

"Then marry me?" she whispered, heart beating faster as his grip tightened. "Marry me, Brad darling, and never let me go."

"What?" He drew back like a scalded cat and her heart plunged.

It was now or never.

"If you married me," she murmured, toying with his loosened tie and peeking up at him through her lashes, "you wouldn't have to worry about losing me anymore, would you?"

His arm circled her waist and he stared down at her, suddenly serious. "Are you absolutely certain this is what you really want?"

"Oh, but I am." Slowly she reached her hand into her pocket, pulled out a box and opened it.

"What's this?"

"Well, I wanted to design something for you myself— I thought maybe a ball-and-chain motif would be appropriate—but this'll have to do for now." Taking his hand in hers, she slipped Sylvain's gold signet ring on his finger, then glanced at the marble floor. "Do you mind if I don't do the knee thing? It might tear my stockings." She took a deep breath. "I'm asking for your hand in marriage, Bradley Ward."

"You are?" He stared at the ring, at her, head reeling. "Why?"

"Because I'm desperate for a title. Lady MacLeod," she gushed, twirling in his arms and grinning. "I think it rather suits me, don't you?"

"I need a drink." He dragged his hand through his hair and let out a laugh.

"Well, personally, what I think you really need is to say yes, but if you tell me where the bar is in this maze of opaque glass and paneling, I'll get you one."

"Charlie, are you aware of what all this implies?" he asked, gripping her shoulders and staring deep into her eyes.

"Absolutely. Are you?"

"Of course I—hey!" he exclaimed, laughing and drawing her back into his arms. "I'm supposed to be the responsible one around here, not you."

"To love and cherish, till death do us part?" Her eyes filled with unshed tears and a lump formed in her throat.

Squeezing her close, he lifted her face to his and grinned down at her lovingly. "Actually, that doesn't sound quite long enough to me," he whispered softly. "I think I'll opt for eternity."

* * * * *

*Fiona Hood-Stewart welcomes you
to Sylvia's story,
in the following excerpt
from her upcoming novel
SILENT WISHES
Available from MIRA Books
September 2003*

1

Jeremy Warmouth chewed angrily on the end of his Cuban cigar, then glanced at his thin gold Patek Philippe watch, a present from his late uncle, the earl. Sylvia Hansen would be here in less than an hour, and he was no closer to having an explanation for the Marchand fiasco than when she'd called him three days ago. Damn. It infuriated him that she'd decided to descend on the London office—*his* territory—to look into matters personally. Worse, he knew she had every right.

How the hell could a blunder of such magnitude have occurred in his organization? He'd been over the list of suspects again and again, had grilled Reggie Rathbone, the head of design, and the team over and over, but nothing tallied. He couldn't even come up with a motive— why would any of the designers, all of whom were highly paid, want to sandbag their own work? It just didn't make sense. Yet the truth must be faced: there was a traitor among them and, ultimately, he was responsible, as head of the division where the conspiracy had evidently been born. Raised to revere trust and fair play, he'd given the team members an unprecedented amount of autonomy, and up till now, they'd rewarded his loyalty with designs that were the talk of the industry. Now, one or more of them had used that freedom to pass proprietary information to Harcourts toughest competitor. He'd barely slept the past few nights, tossing and turning in his flat in Lennox Gardens, trying desperately to answer the question: Why?

And now, to top it all off, he had Sylvia Hansen to contend with.

The prospect was more unsettling than he cared to admit. Knowing her, she'd probably spent the whole of her transatlantic flight sharpening the knives she planned to plant in his back.

Glancing gloomily at the rain trickling relentlessly down the high ancient windowpanes, he gave a humorless laugh. The nasty weather afforded him a certain degree of satisfaction. Sylvia hated rain, and England, and tea. He smiled grimly, toying with the idea of inviting her to tea at Fortnum & Mason's, just across St. James's in Jermyn Street, and making her walk there in the rain, being sure that she got properly sodden. Serve her right for interfering. She could have at least given him a chance to investigate things on his own. But no. As usual, she'd barged in, shoving her bloody oar in where it was least wanted, as though only *she* knew how to take care of business. He ground his teeth and ended up with bits of tobacco sticking to his tongue.

Twenty minutes later, he was still at the window of his spacious wood-paneled office when a large black Mercedes drew up. Ah! Quickly he turned and glanced in the large gilt-framed mirror hung above the fireplace. He straightened his old school tie and made sure his hair wasn't out of place, wishing it didn't have that damn wave in it, though why anything so inconsequential should come to mind at a time like this was beyond him.

Standing to his full six feet two, he adopted a calm expression that was far from how he was feeling. He never quite knew how to deal with Sylvia.

Not that he underestimated her professional ability. Far from it. Her business skills were unquestionably impressive. Sometimes he even wondered why he'd been so against her becoming CEO when he knew perfectly well Brad had made an excellent choice. It was just... He shook his head, perplexed. Perhaps it was her manner, her brash, forthright way of dealing with things, that bothered him so.

All too soon he heard feminine voices exchanging greetings in the hall, the office manager, Harriet Hunter's, raspy Benson & Hedges monotone a sharp contrast to Sylvia's lilting American twang. He sat down quickly behind the huge mahogany partners desk and pretended to be busy. Why did the woman make him nervous, for Christ's sake? It was absurd, and must immediately be controlled.

When the knock finally came, he uttered a bored "Come in," and continued writing for fifteen seconds before looking up. When he knew she'd been standing just long enough to begin feeling ill at ease, he rose and smiled graciously. As usual, she looked stunning, vibrant blue eyes clear and sparkling, her glowing creamy skin supremely soft. Annoyed with himself for even noticing, he marshaled his thoughts and spoke in a welcoming tone. "Hello, Sylvia, do come in."

"Hi, Jeremy." She moved across the room and accepted the seat he offered on the well-worn leather couch. She smiled and crossed her legs and deposited a large Hermès handbag next to her while taking in the man. The fifteen seconds had not been lost on her. So this was how he wanted to play it. Very well. Despite the fact that he aggravated her—from that upper-crust British superciliousness to his rejection of her candidacy as CEO— she could not help but recognize that he was an exceptionally handsome man. Tall and well-built, he probably worked out three times a week, she reckoned. His hair was brown and slightly wavy, and he had an attractive golf tan. She glanced out the windows draped in heavy, dull-green brocade and wondered how on earth you picked up a tan in a climate like this. But of course, you didn't. You went to the Algarve, or Deauville or some other place with a fancy name.

She wondered, watching him, if he was going to marry that skinny stick of a woman he'd once introduced her to—Lady Clarissa something-or-other. Not only had the woman been too pale and too thin, she was clearly the type who broke out in a rash whenever circumstances forced her to mingle with the hoi polloi. For a moment Sylvia forgot the serious nature of the meeting, overcome by a sudden desire to giggle. But she kept a straight face and answered Jeremy's innocuous questions. He sat nonchalantly, one pinstripe-suited leg flung carelessly over the other.

The trouble with Jeremy was she could never tell what the man was thinking. Did he resent her sudden arrival? Not by a twitch had he shown anything but bland politeness. His vague half smile looked as if it had been surgically set in place. Much as she'd love to unsettle the man, she was determined to stick to the decision she'd made back in New York: she would seek cooperation. This was no time for cat-and-mouse games, much as she enjoyed crossing swords with him. Right now she needed everyone bright-eyed and bushy-tailed, rowing in the same boat and in the same direction.

But would he want that?

For a chilling moment, she wondered if Jeremy was in league with Thackeray. After all, it had always been obvious he resented her role at Harcourts. Perhaps he and Thackeray had together decided to take her down. She leaned back into the ancient chesterfield, aware of the cold sweat that had broken under her pale silk blouse. No, she decided after a brief moment of profound panic, she was being paranoid; he might act like a stuffed shirt, but he was also as straight as they come. His next words confirmed her thoughts.

"I don't know who's responsible for this mess, but I assure you, we'll get to the bottom of it and root out the culprits. I'm very sorry it's happened here," he added grudgingly, "and I hold myself ultimately responsible. Still, I can't think who it can possibly be. Reggie and I have talked with everyone on the design team, and have reviewed anyone from outside who might have had access, but frankly, we still haven't come up with a damn thing. The only other option is the factories in Colombia. Still, there was no need for you to go to the trouble of coming across. I could have handled it perfectly well on my own."

The sharp edge in his voice was not lost on her but Sylvia pretended not to notice. Instead, she merely nodded, surprised at his candor. "It's not going to be easy. This is Aimmon Thackeray's way of telling us he's trying to take over."

"Bastard," he muttered between his teeth.

It was the first time Sylvia had seen him show any emotion and she found his muttered oath and dark expression reassuring. At least that was one positive among the many negatives she'd been dealing with over the past few days. Not that she could let her guard down. He might still try to use this to turn the board against her.

But then, she could do the same to him. In fact, she was in the stronger position. Sylvia shifted and straightened her back. She raised her head and met Jeremy's eyes, and an uneasy silence fell between them.

Minutes later, a brief knock announced Reggie Rathbone and they both sighed with relief. She liked the short, rotund, balding Reggie. There was something open and pleasant about him. Too bad his agreeable nature hadn't rubbed off on Jeremy, she reflected, eyeing the two men.

"The whole thing's a bloody cock-up," Reggie exclaimed, accepting a glass of sherry from Jeremy and plunking himself on a faded ottoman, elbows leaning heavily on his thighs, his sandy, bushy eyebrows knit.

"Any ideas who might be involved?" Sylvia asked, feeling more at ease now that he'd joined them.

"Not a clue. We've interviewed all the design team—I felt like scum doing it, since I know them so well—and dragged in a detective from a private agency. We didn't want to call in the Yard," he explained, turning to Sylvia. "Too much risk of this leaking out."

"Bad enough as it is," Jeremy agreed. "Too many people are aware of what's going on already. We need to take some fast action to counter this whole thing or our stock'll start falling. Market's already in a rotten state. Bloody awful timing." He cast a dark glance her way and Sylvia got the impression she was being accused.

"This would have been a disaster at any time," she retorted crisply. "As for countermeasures, I've gone ahead with all the deliveries, as you know, and given orders to cut the initial prices by thirty percent. We'll take a hit, but at least we'll be priced lower than Marchands. I'm working on an aggressive marketing campaign to draw customers into our stores. Worst-case scenario, we have a worldwide blow-out sale.''

Jeremy sipped and looked doubtful but Reggie nodded enthusiastically. ''Quite right. It's the only way. Even though it will mean a sustained loss, we'll save face and ride the worst of it.''

''I already have some figures drawn up.'' Sylvia opened the briefcase she'd deposited next to her on the floor and handed them each a document. ''Not good, I'm afraid, but better than the alternative.''

''Phew!'' Reggie whistled, reviewing the documents.

''This is absurd,'' Jeremy commented, flipping the page. ''We can't sustain such decreased earnings. Our whole market position will be badly affected.''

''Any other ideas?'' she asked sweetly.

''I'm working on them.''

''Great. Once you come up with them, send me an e-mail!'' The sarcastic words were out before she could stop herself and she immediately regretted them. Hadn't she sworn she wouldn't let him get to her?

Reggie's eyes flitted from one to the other. He was used to the tension that reigned whenever these two were in a room together. It permeated the place. But this was even more intense than usual. He cleared his throat, thinking fast about how to redirect the discussion. ''I think this is the right idea. At least we stave off immediate damage. What really concerns me is the future and what's going on inside our own offices. It damn well can't happen again. We simply must find out who did this.''

''Do you think Thackeray has other moves up his sleeve?'' Jeremy addressed Sylvia suddenly, eyes narrowed. ''This seems like a very well planned strategy to me, rather like the first significant move in a game of chess.''

"Could be," Sylvia agreed, sensing the return of the nerves that had been her constant companion over the past week. Jeremy's words exactly described her own fears.

"What do you think of Thackeray? After all, you know him personally, don't you?'' He sent her a piercing glance, as though she was hiding something.

Despite her anger, Sylvia felt a dull blush rising to her cheeks. "He's a tough guy who came out of nowhere and made it too big, too fast."

"Yes, but you know the man," Jeremy insisted, never taking his eyes off her.

"Yes, I know the man," she answered, unduly annoyed. "I've met him on occasion. I consider him a low-life, a reprobate and a criminal, and I don't want anything to do with him."

"Well, that's putting it bluntly!" Reggie looked at her, surprised.

"Sounds about right," Jeremy muttered dryly. "But if that's how you feel, one wonders what the hell you were doing dining with him three weeks ago."

The wrath in his voice left Sylvia taken aback. "I— what damn business is it of yours whom I dine with?" she said furiously, wondering how he'd found out about the last-minute meeting.

"It becomes my business when events such as these occur, don't you think?'' His tone was smooth and calculated, his eyes cold and unforgiving. For a moment, Sylvia fought the desire to dump responsibility for their current crisis at his door. Grudgingly she pulled herself together.

"I dined with Aimmon Thackeray because I was networking,'' she said deliberately, swallowing her anger. ''Believe it or not, it's considered good policy to be on talking terms with one's competition.''

''Oh? Then why did you flounce out of Cipriani's in a towering rage?'' Jeremy leaned back, twiddled his pen between his fingertips and eyed her questioningly, as he might an erring adolescent.

''I did not flounce—and how do you know what I did and didn't do? Do you keep spies in Manhattan?'' She slammed her sherry glass down, furious at his domineering manner. How dare he accuse her?

''I have friends who happened to be dining there on the same evening and found the scene intriguing.'' He shrugged, slipped the pen into his breast pocket and leaned forward. ''But it does seem somewhat coincidental.''

''I don't owe you any explanations.''

''Of course not. Merely curious.''

Stay calm, she ordered herself, suppressing her fury, don't let him get to you. Finally, she spoke in a low, measured voice. ''Thackeray had the gall to suggest I get into bed with him in more ways than one. He made a none-too-veiled suggestion that together we could control Harcourts. That's why I *flounced* out. Satisfied?'' She sent a smoldering look at him.

Jeremy merely raised a satirical brow.

Reggie cleared his throat, embarrassed.

''I have this gut feeling,'' Sylvia continued, ignoring his sardonic expression and wishing she didn't feel the sudden need to justify actions that were nobody's affair but hers, ''that he's throwing up smoke screens to conceal a bigger agenda. Honestly, I think he wants to take over Harcourts at whatever cost. He's finally shaken his reputation as a corporate raider and won't want to mess with his new image, but—''

"We can't base business strategies on gut feelings," Jeremy interrupted witheringly.

"Why not? Some of the best strategies are built on just that," she retorted swiftly, sitting up straighter on the couch and meeting his hooded eyes dead on. "I know you're a CPA—"

"Chartered accountant," he murmured, leaning back.

"Whatever. They're one and the same thing. A bean counter. No imagination."

"Really? Perhaps you feel this particular situation needs artistic flair? I hear you're remarkably proficient at…interior decorating." He raised the cynical eyebrow once more, set his elbows on the arms of his chair and steepled the tips of his fingers. Sylvia breathed deeply, determined to contain her anger, but she would have given a lot to wipe that amused smirk from his mouth.

"Look, I didn't come here to argue," she said, restraining her temper. "I came to cooperate." Then, turning a dismissive shoulder on him, she addressed Reggie. "I think I'll go to the hotel now and get my stuff sorted out. We can meet again later. By the way, I'll need an office." With a swing of her silky blond hair she faced her nemesis once more. "I thought about borrowing yours, Jeremy, but I've decided I need something a little less gloomy."

She couldn't resist peeking out of the corner of her eye to see his reaction, but he didn't so much as blink. "Of course," he replied stiffly. "Miss Hunter will arrange it."

"Absolutely," Reggie concurred in a voice that was just a little too hearty. He jumped up solicitously and smiled. Jeremy followed suit at a more sober pace. "You must be tired. I'll pop over with you to the Stafford, Sylvia." Reggie bustled about, helping her with her briefcase. "Has your stuff been dropped off? We can walk. It's literally around the corner."

Sylvia glanced ruefully at the pouring rain, then down at her Dolce & Gabbana pumps. "Sure thing. Thanks. Got an umbrella?" she added gamely.

She shook hands formally with Jeremy, not missing his obvious truculence. She was tempted to pull rank and show him just who was boss around here, but knew it would serve no purpose. Like it or not, they had to work on this together for the common good of Harcourts and its future. Their personal feelings about each other were neither here nor there.

Determined to make one last attempt at civility, she racked her brain for something to say to break the ice. She refused to start on the wrong foot this time around. But he made things so damn difficult. Taking a breath, she looked at him directly and, smiling brightly, went with the truth. "I know you feel bad about what happened, but please don't think that I'm laying all this at your door. It could just as easily have happened in New York under my watch. I'm sure that, working together, we'll come up with solutions. I know I need your help, and I hope that you'll accept mine." She turned before he could answer and left the room, followed by a grinning Reggie.

Jeremy, knowing he'd just been bested, stood stunned in the middle of the room, staring at the closed door.

The woman was a bloody menace. How dare she come hurtling into his domain, implying that what had happened here wasn't his direct responsibility? As if he wasn't man enough to shoulder it. Who the hell did she think she was, interfering, telling him how to run his business? And letting him know in that high-handed, insufferable manner that henceforth *she* planned to run things. It was humiliating, unthinkable, intolerable! And must be dealt with immediately.

Damn, damn, damn.

Picking up his glasses, annoyed, he flopped down at his desk. Networking, indeed. Hobnobbing with the enemy was more like it. But he had no doubt that what she'd said was the truth. However annoying the woman might be, she didn't take shit from anyone. As Thackeray had apparently found out to his cost, he observed with a reluctant smile.

He stared at the papers before him. He'd meant to walk over to Boodle's for lunch but had lost his appetite. Returning his mind to the business at hand, he pressed the button of the intercom. "Miss Hunter, could you come in here a minute, please?"

Just because Sylvia was technically his boss didn't mean he'd let her get the upper hand. He didn't care how many schmoozy little speeches she made about cooperating and working together. He had his ducks neatly in a row, didn't he? Or nearly. And very fast he'd let her know precisely how superfluous her presence here was.

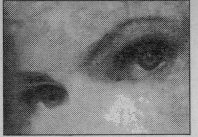

Grace Notes

New York Times Bestselling Author
CHARLOTTE VALE ALLEN

Grace Loring is a successful author with many devoted fans who find comfort in her honest writing. Accustomed to abused women contacting her via her Web site to ask for advice, Grace is sympathetic when a troubled young woman e-mails her. In the course of their correspondence, Stephanie Baine reveals details of a nightmarish life: her terrifying abduction as a teenager; the complete lack of support from her parents; the abuse at the hands of her husband. But after several weeks of an intensive exchange, the e-mails abruptly stop and Grace begins to fear the worst. Then the e-mails resume. What Grace comes to learn casts doubt on everything she believed about the person she thought she knew. Who is Stephanie Baine? Has *anything* she's told Grace been true? Is she really a woman in danger, or is something else—something sinister, even deadly—going on?

"A moving portrayal of the power of love to heal."
—*Publishers Weekly* on *Parting Gifts*

MIRA®

Available the first week of March 2003
wherever paperbacks are sold!

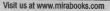

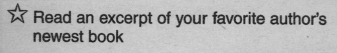

FIONA HOOD-STEWART

66833	THE STOLEN YEARS	___ $5.99 U.S.	___ $6.99 CAN.
66606	THE JOURNEY HOME	___ $5.99 U.S.	___ $6.99 CAN.

(limited quantities available)

TOTAL AMOUNT	$_____
POSTAGE & HANDLING	$_____
($1.00 for one book; 50¢ for each additional)	
APPLICABLE TAXES*	$_____
<u>TOTAL PAYABLE</u>	$_____

(check or money order—please do not send cash)

To order, complete this form and send it, along with a check or money order for the total above, payable to MIRA Books®, to: **In the U.S.:** 3010 Walden Avenue, P.O. Box 9077, Buffalo, NY 14269-9077; **In Canada:** P.O. Box 636, Fort Erie, Ontario L2A 5X3.

Name:_____
Address:_____ City:_____
State/Prov.:_____ Zip/Postal Code:_____
Account Number (if applicable):_____
075 CSAS

*New York residents remit applicable sales taxes.
 Canadian residents remit applicable GST and provincial taxes.

MIRA®